# MONSTER

*Arca Book 4*

## KAREN DIEM

# Copyright

Cover art by Deranged Doctor Design.

★★★

eBook version 1.0, published May 5, 2019.

First Paperback Printing: May 30, 2019.

ISBN: 978-0-9975740-7-4

To contact Karen Diem or subscribe to her newsletter, go to http://www.karendiem.com.

# Dedication

Dedicated to the heartless punster who suggested Vic's name and the awesome readers who helped shape Dmitri. Also dedicated to my wonderful family who totally doesn't mind all the sandwiches they get for dinner because I was on a roll and forgot the time. Not a literal roll, a figurative one, though bread *is* delicious.

# Table of Contents

# Chapter One

**It's stupid to wake a dragon.** It's suicidal to wake one by repeatedly poking it with a pointy stick.

From the looks of the scene on the television, someone had not only found Dragon, a murderous metahuman from the Seventies, but they had also found a stick long and pointy enough to wake him. The town of Al Jawf now burned as a consequence.

Zita Garcia—extreme sports enthusiast, tax preparer, and secret vigilante—blinked sleep out of her eyes as she watched her best friend's television. "I hope they missed hitting him with those tactical nukes all those years ago because it'll be pretty hard to take down a creature that survived direct hits." As she spoke, she yanked on the purple Spandex-like sportswear she had to wear when using her powers. The special fabric disappeared when she shapeshifted to an animal form but reappeared when she claimed a human one. Any other clothing shredded, and people took her even less seriously when she was naked, much to her annoyance. Plus, sometimes she got cold or needed to carry snacks.

Wyn cinched the belt on her silky teal bathrobe, hazel eyes troubled. Despite the early hour, her hair still cascaded in perfect chestnut ringlets over her slim shoulders, and she appeared to have escaped a high-end pajama party photo shoot for a magazine. A minuscule cup of tea and an e-reader sat abandoned on a table nearby, next to a tidy pile of lavender fabric. Almost identical lilac-point Siamese cats sat on either side of her crimson sofa, like malevolent, glaring bookends. "They're going to need our help there, regardless of what happened with the missiles in the Seventies. You didn't get dressed before you came here? Or at least comb your hair?"

"You woke me from a sound sleep and said it was an emergency. I thought you were in trouble, so I grabbed my basic Arca gear and came. Snuck in and everything in case you were being held hostage and didn't even stop to grab the new sweatshirt part of the costume. Was I supposed to hesitate?" In a concession to her friend, Zita paused to smooth down her short black hair, every strand of which seemed to be going in a different direction, save for the side she'd been sleeping on, which was flattened by her pillow. Her night clothes, a well-worn sleeveless white undershirt and fuzzy rainbow leopard print pants, lay in a heap at her bare brown feet.

Wyn sighed. "No, I suppose not. At least Andy's not here to blush. Do you want your phone or shoes?"

Zita shook her head. "Phone wouldn't work overseas anyway, and I have to go in flying, so might as well leave the shoes here... so they're not wrecked when I shift. We'll have to just use party line," she replied, referencing the telepathic communication that Wyn could create between herself, Zita, and their friend Andy.

After sighing, Wyn inclined her head. Her eyes unfocused as she stared into the distance.

Warmth ran through Zita as Wyn connected to her mind. *Thanks.*

Distantly, Andy's presence joined the connection, his thoughts groggy. *Hi, guys. Z, you couldn't have Wyn wake me with a phone call? Do you seriously believe the government has tapped our phones?*

*Órale, you never know. I don't think any of us want to chance it, though, and the disposable phones definitely won't work in Libya.* Zita focused on the town, preparing to teleport.

*Where? I'm guessing it's time to watch the news.* Andy's mental voice sharpened.

Wyn sent, *You got it. Top story right now.*

Based on the television coverage, Al Jawf had begun as an obscure Saharan Desert oasis. Now, it was an odd mix of sleepy desert agriculture, an oil refinery, and unbridled tourism. Its biggest claim to fame was a patch of nearby desert that had been turned to "Dragon Glass" following a dramatic multinational missile assault on Dragon in the Seventies.

*I suppose they can consider that a failed mission since Dragon's up and about and burning everything in sight.* Zita studied the town, seeking the best entry point.

The center of the action seemed to be two large modern hotels, currently in flames. The irregularly shaped swimming pools they shared, enclosed by a high wall, were black with soot and bits of debris. Surrounding the flaming buildings, wide dirt plazas with toppled cardboard boxes and other debris suggested a lively street market under happier circumstances. Currently, men raced around trying to subdue the blazes. A handful in military gear fired dispirited bursts of gunfire at the circling lizard.

Her mind full of plans as she analyzed the bigger shapeshifter's televised flight, Zita tied on a half-mask of the same special material as her clothes, the latest update to her vigilante costume along with a hooded sweatshirt. Of course, her haste meant she'd left the sweatshirt at home. *You two figure out logistics. I'll go on ahead and try to lead Dragon away from the city. Join me as soon as you can, Andy. I know you're off in some weird place.*

*Not a chance,* Wyn sent. *You're already at my house, so just take me with you.*

Curiosity and concern sharpened Andy's questions. *Why are you at Wyn's? Is everything okay? I'm in Detroit. The city's not that strange given everything since we got our powers.*

Wyn's mental voice held the suppressed laughter that she hid behind her hand in the real world. *Zita canceled her cable subscription to save money. Since she couldn't get the live newscasts without floundering around on the Internet, she came here. You just missed her usual speed strip and dress routine.*

Andy's glee carried over their connection. *See? Detroit's great. I didn't have to watch the Live, Nude Zita Revue again.*

*You guys got issues,* Zita grumbled. *Andy at least I sort of understand. He probably blushes when he changes his own clothes and never looks down in the shower. Wyn, though, you're not afraid of a mirror, and you got the same equipment I do, so you've got no excuse.* She straightened her mask so it didn't obscure her field of vision.

Wyn ignored Zita's digression, instead choosing to argue her case to go with Zita, rather than Andy. "As I was saying, I can talk to Andy telepathically from anywhere, and once he's outside, he can be in Libya in a minute or two. Dragon just set both major hotels in the town on fire. They need me healing and you drawing Dragon away before he decides to incinerate that oil refinery the reporter just mentioned. If you take me with you, Andy doesn't have to stop."

"No can do, even if you were ready, which you're not. You don't even have shoes on, just those high-heeled slippers with the feathers shedding everywhere," Zita said. She picked a spot high above the television reporter's head on the horizon, where black striations of stone were just visible. To avoid surprising Andy with her actions, she sent the rest of her words over the party line. *I need to fly in as a bird so they don't catch me teleporting on camera, and I can't carry you like that. Not to mention, I have to come in some distance away. If I stick with you to protect you from Dragon, who knows how many more people he'll fry before we make it to town? Also...*

Wyn's eyes narrowed. She pinched the furrow between her perfect brows as if she could tell what was coming. "What?"

After shifting to a peregrine falcon, Zita teleported. Spreading her wings wide, she dove toward the town in the distance, using the gathering speed of the dive and the harsh, dry winds buffeting her to pick up as much speed as possible. *I'm already there.*

Wyn sounded like she was trying not to curse. *By the Goddess, Zita, you couldn't wait one more minute? Be careful. We'll be with you as soon as we can.*

*Teleported without you again?* Andy asked.

Wyn gave a mental snarl. *Yes.*

*Hey, I had good, logical reasons for doing so.* Zita tamped down the thought that it would've taken Wyn longer than a minute to get dressed and hoped that didn't leak into the telepathic communication. Aided by the fact that the dragon circled one spot, she pulled every trick she could to get there faster. Once she fought her way through the nasty black smoke that coated her throat and made it sting, she could see the city and her opponent better.

Other than the desperate swirl of activity near the fires, the streets were silent and empty, save for a goat bleating madly as it raced down a long road, trailing a broken rope. A pair of thin minarets rose near the elegant and untouched domes of some small mosques. Modern stores and converted homes with hand-written signs ringed the plaza periphery. Tiny cement walls outlined individual houses that had likely seen World War II troops garrisoned in them while the curving flourishes on larger buildings announced government offices and the occasional business. Palm trees and other hardy plants exchanged shade with buildings. A few roads were dark with pavement, but the majority were unpaved and blended with the ground, outlined mostly by the old cars lining them. A small television crew was set up and filming from the edges of the plaza.

Dragon swooped down and devoured the frantic goat in a single crunch. The dragon was as beautiful as a sandstorm; from a safe distance and in comfort, one could perhaps enjoy the sheer destructive aesthetics. Here, though, as he soared above the town and breathed fire upon the half-constructed frame of what looked like a factory, he was an odd and terrifying composite of animals. The head was that of a crocodile with an elongated jaw and sharp conical teeth extruding from it. Linked by a snaky neck, the head perched atop a lizard body with bat-like wings and four clawed feet. Red and bronze rippled down his body, shading to ebony stripes and spots on the rows of scutes that armored his back and along the tail. The finer scales of his stomach shaded lighter, a cloudy wash of variegated reds. The wings mimicked the same coloration, with the delicate arcing bones traced in the blackest shades, and the bottom edges fringed in reddish bronze. When he passed between her and the sun, a tracery of veins embossed the finer skin of his wings. Despite that, his flight lacked grace or any real dexterity; Zita suspected his large turning radius was the only reason the entire city was not in flames. As she watched, Dragon paused in flight to inhale, then exhaled flames again.

*I need to pick a different shape to get his attention before he goes after those houses. Guys, tuning you out to avoid being eaten. Dragon flies like a cow, but I've got to get him going fast enough that he doesn't have time to breathe fire on me, so I need to concentrate.* With a deep breath, she shifted to a pterosaur, a crested azhdarchid she'd seen once before in a magical land, and colored herself in vibrant shades of green, blue, and yellow to stand out against the paler sky and orange-tinged sands.

As Zita stretched her wings, she acknowledged the difference in sizes. *I'm the size of a giraffe with forty-foot wings, and he's the size of a professional basketball court. He's the only other person I've ever seen or heard of that's on par with Andy as a bird.*

Zita buzzed Dragon's head, diving and swooping by so close she could feel heat radiating up from the big form beneath her. To her surprise, as she closed in on the giant reptile, her sense of scent and instincts informed her of a basic error in the history books. Dragon was female, not male. Not that she remembered much about the bigger shapeshifter from her history lessons, outside of the eponymous form and the terrible swath of destruction that devastated two cities, multiple towns, and countless military units in North Africa and the Middle East. *Doesn't matter. She needs to leave these people alone.*

The great head jerked up, and beady reptilian eyes focused on Zita. Dragon roared a long string of syllables, her loud voice echoing like the low, rumbling exhale of a belching crocodile magnified a hundred times.

Pain slashed through Zita's mind, and her flight stalled for a moment. Blind with agony, Zita flapped her wings to rise higher and soared eastward, away from the town, praying she wouldn't hit anything.

Wyn and Andy both exclaimed as her torment slipped through the link to them.

With a flap of her wings, the dragon rose higher, head tilted, and her attention focused on Zita's struggling form. The building lay forgotten beneath her. "I said, this territory is mine, little interloper. Do you dare to challenge me when you cannot even fly right?" Her language seemed oddly stilted.

While the additional words brought another wash of pain, it was already receding as Zita wrestled the remaining dregs of it under control. She evened out her flight and headed toward the desert. *I really am the only shapeshifter who can't talk in animal form. Dragon's claimed this area as her own,* she sent weakly to her friends.

Wyn's concern poured over the link. *What was that?*

*Quick headache. It's over now.* Zita spiraled lazily to keep the larger reptile's attention and to give herself a moment to reorient. *I'll go north, maybe northeast and then loop around to avoid that mosque or village or whatever. West and south are more homes and the oasis. Those green, irrigated circles are probably farms. Maybe I can get her to the other side of the mountains.*

Dragon followed close behind, lower to the ground, flames flickering around her mouth. "Speak!"

*Oye, she'll regret telling me to talk,* Zita thought. *As soon as I get out of the city, I'll switch to a bird that can speak and keep moving away.*

*We're on our way, but Zita, we are only tabling the discussion until later about your denial of the fact that you get a headache and then know a new language whenever you hear people speaking in an unknown tongue,* Wyn sent.

*I give on the languages thing, already. Don't nag. Quentin and I tried to go to an international food festival in Adams Morgan. It was a painful education and hiding it from my brother was difficult.* The outskirts of the city passed under Zita, and she glanced behind to check on her pursuer.

*Oh, Zita...* Wyn sent, sympathy welling over the connection.

If she could have shrugged, Zita would have. Instead, she glanced behind herself. *I'm a grown-ass woman and can admit when I'm wrong. Happy?*

Wyn sent, *Not quite the adjective I would choose, but fine.*

"You cannot hope to stand against my power, so tell me why I should not eat you now?" the dragon said. She abruptly tilted sideways in a clumsy maneuver to avoid the minaret of a mosque.

Her throat shook, and her beak tapped rapidly as Zita tried and failed to contain a snicker.

Apparently incensed at the sound, Dragon lifted her head and dove at Zita.

*Well, at least I made it a couple minutes before she attacked. I think I'm getting more diplomatic... or not talking helped.* Zita whipped to the side, switching to a hyacinth macaw. The much larger dragon needed far more space to turn so Zita could get out of the way, but the rush of dust and wind stirred up by the other shifter's passage sent her small form hurtling farther away than she'd intended. And stung.

*Ow.* "You have to catch me first, lardbutt," Zita squawked in the same language, fluttering toward the vast empty reaches of desert.

As Dragon circled back around, she paused, inhaled, and spat fire at Zita.

"Just keeping it real, girlfriend! You ever think about an exercise program?" Once again, Zita evaded the attack, though not without a near-singe, and the wind sent her tumbling downward. Rather than fight it, she let herself tumble until she was close to the ground, then changed to a cheetah and ran full out.

The rhythmic thwack of wingtips on the ground and the heavy breathing behind her let Zita track her enemy with ease. She concentrated on speeding over the barren desert surface—packed dirt littered with pebbles, all in the same dusty orange-brown, broken up by the occasional stubborn plant. Spotting a distant rock spearing up out of the landscape, she angled toward it, even as a tremble in her muscles warned her that this form could not sustain an all-out run much longer. After forcing herself to run a half minute more, she turned aside at the last possible second from the rock, shooting to the side. Her lungs burned as her body protested the exertion.

Behind her, Dragon screeched, and stone snapped.

Laughing inside, Zita launched herself into the air, changing to a peregrine again and climbing higher. The pressure in her chest eased. *If I can just get high enough, this shape can sustain speed much easier.*

Flapping clumsily, the bigger shapeshifter brought her bulky body higher in the air and leveled out. Her snaky neck turned as she scanned the ground and then the air.

The rocky spire lay shattered behind her.

Some of Zita's good humor dropped away as she soared farther west, deeper into the desert. Below her, the earth softened, switching to the undulating waves of sand dunes. *Carajo. So much for that. She's not even a little hurt, and she pulverized that rock. Andy better get here soon because that was one of my best tricks.*

Below her, the sun touched the ground, turning it into a shimmering, gleaming sea of tiny reflective crystals. *Must be where the bombers hit her with the missiles back then, the famous Dragon Glass region. Pretty, and I didn't even have to pay for a tour.*

Dragon's shadow blotted out the direct sunlight, hiding the sparkle below.

*Fire-breathing, super tough, super strong, mythical creature able to destroy large buildings in a couple minutes versus a bunny-hunting bird that can be eaten by a fox if careless? Time to change up these rules.* Zita looped up, rising higher and higher, and then dove at her pursuer.

Dragon's jaw fell open, then she smirked. She slowed to a more leisurely pace.

*Chido.* Her speed building, Zita angled her body as if attempting to strike Dragon's back.

Dragon laughed derisively, smoke curling from her nostrils.

Right before she would have collided with a large scute on the dragon's back and died, Zita teleported the last few feet to stand on Dragon's back instead. Switching to her disguise form—that of the woman known as Arca—she scurried up the broad, armored neck to the head. She slowed until she stood between the two massive reptilian eyes. To distract the beast, she wrapped an arm around a protruding spike that overhung one of the thick brow ridges.

Dragon first shook her head like a muddy dog who had just come inside and then tried clawing at the spot, but her legs were too short to reach. Her claws scratched her own snout, though, and that only seemed to anger her more.

As she smothered her amusement that the bigger shifter's eyes crossed trying to watch her, Zita had a fleeting thought she should try to be diplomatic, but her mouth opened first. "Pendeja, please. I don't have to be the biggest badass here, just the one with the best plan. And I do, but it has nothing to do with your so-called territory, though, because I don't waste my time on that kind of shit. I'm here to give you a chance to chill and go back to not bothering the world like you were doing before."

Dragon hissed. "I slept, you vulgar creature. Now I am hungry, and the paltry meal of the fools who woke me is insufficient. They angered me—they stole the herders who should've been tending my food. I don't see my herds anywhere, and the girls are so poorly trained they can't even tell me where they are. I go to see, and there are no animals, only outsiders. They bring my flames upon themselves."

*Wyn, Dragon said someone was bothering her herders? What's with that?* Tapping on the eyebrow spike, Zita tsked. "Hey now, no need for name calling. You know, if you land and take human shape, I'm sure we could find you some breakfast if you didn't burn down all the restaurants. You like pancakes? Bacon? Everyone likes bacon except... maybe not bacon. How about cheeseburgers?"

Dragon did a barrel roll, presumably to shake Zita off.

As they turned upside down, Zita smiled, pleased that they'd left Al Jawf and the rocky mountains behind. Instead, they now circled over sand dunes that glinted peach and orange and gold in the morning sunlight.

*History says Dragon asked for a large herd of goats and cattle, tended by virgins for his harem...* Wyn sent. *I'll be dropped off at Al*

*Jawf since I'm more help healing than fighting. Let me know if you find anyone needing help out there.*

*Since Dragon's female, a harem's likely out. She must've seen someone out in the desert. Hope those poor people survived.* After another loose barrel roll from the reptilian shifter, Zita couldn't stop herself from making the request. "Can you do that again but faster? It'd be more fun, and I'm working hard not to fall asleep here. It's late my time, you know."

Dragon roared, and flames shot from her mouth, but the length of her neck and her long snout conspired to keep her from hitting Zita with the flames. "I am not a beast of burden! I am the Dragon, and I shall destroy you and burn your insignificant form to ash!"

Wiping her forehead with an exaggerated motion, Zita said, "Whew, and here I worried you would try to eat me. That'd be a problem for me because I don't lean that direction. I'm all about the dudes, you know? It's not you, it's me." She grinned and laughed.

Dragon rolled again.

Zita hung on and chuckled. "Again, again! People would pay good money for this, especially if you let them film it."

Her unwilling mount snarled and did a loop-de-loop.

This time, Zita turned to watch the bigger shapeshifter's muscles move under the thick skin. *She's got to be flying magically because she lacks the wing muscle definition she'd need to keep her culo up in the air, or maybe even that nose. Most of the flapping is to adjust her altitude and that sort of thing. If she weren't so flabby, I might have to work harder, but I can fly rings around her... if I choose fast flyers and concentrate.* "Hey, is clothing the reason you avoid being human? Listen, this new stuff is coming on the market so you can stay clothed when changing forms. I've got some on now and can totally hook you up if you need, but you have to stop wrecking the town first. It's good stuff, especially in a desert. The moisture wicking works great, and the boob support is actually both effective and comfortable."

Dragon seemed affronted. "You cannot make me dress like a whore! I am always modestly dressed when I choose to walk upon two legs."

Zita lifted her hands placatingly. "Oye, I was just offering to be nice. No need to bite my head off... seriously, no need. I haven't brushed my teeth yet today, and my breath stinks. How about you calm down, switch down into your person shape, and we talk this out, woman to woman?"

With a growl, Dragon pawed at herself again. She opened a small gash in the side of her snout, well away from Zita.

"Not much of a conversationalist? That's okay with me. We can just hang out and fly if you promise to try a few faster barrel rolls. Oh, and to stop snorting fire." From the direction of the town, thunder grumbled. Zita permitted herself a smile. *Glad to hear you guys are close.*

Not surprisingly, Dragon whipped her head from side to side in another futile attempt to dislodge Zita. Smoke curled up from broad lizard nostrils as she labored to climb higher.

Zita's next comment slipped out. "If smoke comes from your nose, is the fire burning snot then? That's super gross and unhygienic."

Dragon shrieked and dove toward a vast sand dune.

Leaning forward, Zita wrapped her arms around a spike. "Hey, no need to get suicidal. I'm just keeping it real, here. If that's the problem, I know an awesome witch who could whip you up magic allergy medicine."

The ground raced up at an enormous speed.

*Caramba, she's not playing. She's really going to do it.* Zita hurled herself from the dragon's head, changing in midair to a peregrine and coming up out of the dive as if she'd been the one to initiate it, instinctively using the speed to get away from Dragon and as high up as possible.

Dragon hit the ground with a massive boom, and sand exploded upward.

The spray hit Zita, scouring her body with tiny particles. She cried out and thrashed her wings to keep rising. Her eyes focused below. *Is she dead?*

As if in answer to her silent question, Dragon's huge body struggled out of the dune, shedding gleaming waterfalls of sand. She roared.

*Not dead, just the world champion of sand belly-flops, I guess.* Zita stretched her wings, checked the position of the sun, and tried to figure out her next move.

# Chapter Two

**Someone else struck first.** Andy's jet-sized bird form dove and clawed at Dragon, leaving a bloody furrow in the oversized reptilian back. When he pulled up and spoke, the words were English and reverberated, like a chorus of men's voices shouting their disapproval in unison. "Cannibal lizard!" Lightning coruscated around the eyes and shape of the gigantic golden eagle.

Switching to accented English, Dragon roared. "I am the monster of monsters! No one else shall claim my territory!" Apparently forgetting about Zita, she huffed fire at Andy and attacked.

*I'll just get out of the way, then. Wingspan, Dragon has to do a deep inhale before she breathes fire, and she's too out of shape to breathe while maneuvering,* Zita sent as she soared away. When she reached a safe distance, she circled and watched the two behemoths fight.

A brief wash of acknowledgment over the mental connection was her only answer.

In their winged shapes, Dragon and Andy were similar in size, with perhaps only a few minor differences. Dragon had more length from the tip of her elongated snout to the end of her wicked tail. However, Andy's wingspan was wider, a difference visible whenever the two behemoths closed on each other to fight. The high-pitched peeps of Andy's avian alter ego and the thunder of his wings surrounded Dragon's roars, punctuated by the rattling breaths whenever she paused and breathed fire.

Movement drew Zita's attention, multiple dark shapes in the sand not too far from the aerial battleground, and she drew closer to see more.

Closer to Al Jawf, near the Dragon Glass region, four vehicles burned. Splashes of dark brown stained the sand along with chunks of debris. Small forms clustered together, colorful whirls of fabric blending together. The two largest, black-clad figures stretched their arms over the smallest as if to shelter them. *Women and children? I think I found the so-called herders, Wyn. They're going to need help. Their rides are literally on fire. Hang on.*

After landing by the burning vehicles, Zita returned to her Arca shape.

Now she was close, she could see what she had taken for broken bits of vehicle debris were actually the gory remnants of people. One man's bearded, blackened head, sans body, stared at her from the sand a few feet away. The wind slapped her face with hot smoke, carrying the charred scent of burning plastic, meat, and chemicals.

She coughed and raised a hand to her mouth, stomach churning and throat burning with bile.

A black-clad form raised an AK-47 and pointed it at Zita. "Monster! You cannot have the children!" the woman shrieked. The gun shook in her hands. Behind the black veil and headscarf that obscured all but the top third of her face, one eye had swollen almost shut. Teary young girls hid behind her and the only other adult, another woman in loose apparel identical to the first. Most of the children seemed in the early stages of puberty, as adolescence had not thinned all the childish roundness from their faces, though a couple stood taller than Zita.

Jerking back, Zita raised her hands. "Oye, lady, I don't want to hurt anyone. I stopped by to see if you needed help. I can get to Al Jawf and find someone..." The words tumbled out in English. After a moment, she switched to the language Dragon had used and repeated herself.

Gesturing with the gun, the spokeswoman indicated the smoldering remains and answered in the same tongue. "Men—filthy migrants, by their accents—came to the school, took away the oldest students and the youngest teachers. They brought us out here and stopped to chastise us when the monster rose from the sands. It ate them, burned the vehicles, and demanded to know where the herds were."

"What herds?" Zita asked.

The teacher gave a shrug. While her eyes kept flicking to the action in the sky, she did not lift her weapon from where it aimed at Zita. "I do not know. Go away, before it or the new one returns!"

Zita glanced up at the sky where Andy and Dragon appeared to be doing an odd combination of wrestling and flying. A human shape, cape swirling dramatically, swooped in from the mountains and pulled the giant reptile's tail.

Dragon roared even louder, shot a blast of flame at the interloper, and slapped them with her tail.

Trailing flames, the human-shaped combatant sailed away with the force of the hit, tumbling end over end until they collided with the ground. They rose again in a ballerina-like pose and shot back toward the fight.

While Dragon was distracted, Andy ripped at one of her wings with his talons.

Dragon shrieked.

"My buddy's handling the monster, so hopefully she won't bother you all again. You want me to get someone to take you back to your school? I'm sorry, I don't have a way to carry all of you right now." Zita checked her position, doing her best to memorize landmarks. With the thick, black plumes of smoke confirming the town's location, she waved toward Al Jawf. *We got me, two ladies, and a bunch of girl tweens out here. Their kidnappers took them from a school and brought them to the desert. Dragon must've woken up when they started slapping the women around. She must not approve of that behavior because she ate the kidnappers.*

The woman nodded but did not lower her weapon. "Yes. They must fly the Libyan flag, or we will not trust them."

*That's terrible!* Wyn sent.

Wingspan sent a distracted growl.

Zita eyed the teacher's weapon, still aimed at her. "Could you trust me enough to at least lower your weapon?"

With a glance at her frightened charges, the woman tightened her grip. "No."

"Okay, not going to argue with the nice lady with the gun. I'll just go get help, then."

"Libyan help," the shyer of the two teachers interjected.

"Yes, Libyan help." Zita retreated, tilting her body sideways to be a smaller target until the bulk of a burning truck was between herself and the others. Shifting to a peregrine falcon, she took off and headed toward town.

***

A short time later, Zita landed near the chaotic main plaza in Al Jawf, changed to her Arca shape, and ran toward the bulk of the noise. Men still battled the fires at the former hotels, now recognizable mostly by the charred date trees and pools sullied with soot, but the flames seemed to be dying. A pair of ambulances and two buses were nearby, taking people on board. Sobbing and shouted orders filled the air. White sheets covered a row of motionless forms, guarded by a man with a gun. On the outskirts, a white van with a satellite dish and the logo of a news station parked crookedly, a side door hanging open. Two men with television cameras roamed the edges of the excitement.

*Dragon escaped,* Andy sent, his voice once more his own rather than the choral echo of his bird form. *We chased her around, but we lost her.*

The thought escaped Zita. *How can you lose a creature that big in a landscape of nothing? I have no idea what we'd do with her once you knocked her out, but...* She slowed, scanning the area for someone who seemed in charge that didn't have their hands full of equipment or the injured.

*Nice, Z. Our best guess is that she dove into the sand and then lay still. From above, all I can see is dunes, with the occasional bit of black sticking out. Once or twice I thought I saw her, but it turned out to be just rock beneath the sand. I'm above the group of girls now.*

*Bueno. I'm in Al Jawf trying to get help for them.*

Andy sent approval over the telepathic connection. *I'll guard the girls until they get back to town. If I thought they'd accept the offer, I'd give them a lift, but I assume they'd think I was Dragon coming back to finish them off. So, I'm floating around up here in man shape, keeping an eye on them from above.*

Zita snorted. *Wingspan looks nothing like that lizard.*

Wyn's reply seemed dry and distracted. *With the morning they've had, they might not be at their observational best.*

*Neta, they did seem trigger-happy.* Zita walked toward the man wearing a fire chief vest, guessing he could at least point her to whomever she needed to speak to.

As she passed a bus, an old woman opened the door and peered at her. Her face was weathered and wrinkled and wizened, but her dark eyes shone with warning. "Tourist! You come, be safe! This is bus for womans. If not see you, it not hurt you." She glanced around the street and tugged on the edges of her hijab, a patterned scarf in brilliant shades of yellow, white, and blue. "Hurry. Men not look you here."

True to her words, the armed guards surrounding the bus appeared very interested in looking everywhere but at Zita.

After a second, she jogged over to the vehicle. "I'm good," she said. "Tell me, who do I talk to about rescuing children? My friends found a bunch of girls hiding in the desert."

The woman blinked at her. "English not good. You come, safe." On the bus, scared faces peered out the window, their skin covered with soot and sometimes bandages.

Zita repeated her question, this time in the language she'd used with Dragon and the women in the desert. She raised her voice enough so the men nearby could hear her. One glanced her way while she spoke and then looked away.

Her eyes widening, the woman stared at her, then began texting on a small phone. "Despite your skill with our language, you must be a tourist as none of our girls would stand naked in public. I will give you some clothing. Your friends found them? We must phone the guard. Please, do you know any of their names? My grandchild goes to the girls' school. Come inside, quickly, before the demon beast returns. We will go to the hospital soon. They have found no more living in the wreckage." While she said nothing directly, her tone and expression were disapproving as her gaze swept over the shapeshifter.

Zita started to protest that a sports bra and capris did not equal nudity, but a quick glance at the enveloping, colorful clothing of the scowling old woman kept her mouth shut. "I am a foreigner," she admitted. "I can show the guards where the girls are if they could have a bus and..." She paused, eying the elderly woman again, "suitable escorts available for them? The dragon was injured and hid in the sands, so it should be safe to bring them home to their parents."

The men refused to look at her, although one snorted and wrinkled his nose. "All the men here are respectful of women, even Western ones who clearly did not mean to show disrespect by running around in almost nothing. If such a woman were to appear here, she'd undoubtedly be wise enough to accept any clothing offers so she could be regarded with respect and listened to. Al Jawf isn't cosmopolitan like Tripoli, despite the hotels." His words held a subtly different accent than the woman's.

One of his male companions and the old woman shot him a glare.

With an eloquent tilt of his shoulders, the guard gave his head a slight shake.

*Pues. I thought Andy was bad.* "Oh, fine, I'll take a bathrobe or something," Zita said. Belatedly, she remembered her manners. "Please and thank you, madam."

With a nod, the elderly woman disappeared into the interior of the bus, reemerging a second later with a ratty white robe. Once she had conferred the robe on Zita, she resumed texting, pausing every now and again to survey the shapeshifter.

It must've been a man's robe, as it was far too big for Zita, but all the men nearby relaxed once it engulfed her form. "Now I'm covered up, we need to help those girls. They're out in the sands. Dragon is injured somewhere. My friend Wingspan is guarding them, but he won't approach too closely unless it's necessary to protect them. They're scared out of their minds, and the teachers have guns they retrieved from the corpses of the dead kidnappers. Those ladies are badass and have promised to shoot anyone else who shows up without flying a Libyan flag."

The elderly woman raised a shaggy white eyebrow and stopped texting for a moment. Her tone held an all-too-familiar chiding tone. "I am trying to contact someone, but most are dealing with the fire. You should remain here until someone comes to deal with you." She closed the bus doors.

Zita glanced toward the main square. Even to her admittedly unprofessional eyes, the fire seemed to be under control, and the confusion had the regimented quality of organized chaos. She jiggled one leg, then the other, and began pacing, her robe dragging on the brown dirt.

One man turned away and pointed skyward. The other guards checked that direction too, though the one who had commented on Tripoli whispered into a handheld radio.

Antsy to help the girls, Zita turned to see what they were staring at.

A human shape descended from the sky, landing near the crowd. She (the figure was undeniably feminine) waved to the crowd and posed, then lifted off again. The television cameras focused on the newcomer.

It took a second for recognition to set in. Zita groaned and bit her tongue to keep from complaining out loud. *Why couldn't it be one of the African metahuman teams, especially that really hot guy, or the European squad? No, it had to be Caroline the grandstander, America's favorite flying tool of the Man.*

Caroline passed by overhead, dipping lower. Instead of the cheerleader-like outfit she'd worn all the previous times that Zita had seen her, this time Caroline's outfit resembled that of the local women. She still wore a tank top, but she had a loose, gauzy long-sleeve shirt over it, and she had exchanged the useless thigh-length skirt for a wider knee-length one. Below that, tall boots met the bottom of the skirt. On her head and flowing over her shoulders, a chiffon scarf hid most of her sunny hair and flared out dramatically behind her like a cape. Smudges and a few tatters marred her outfit, but all of it contributed to create an artistic effect. She called out in English, "Hail! Is there anyone who speaks English?" When she spotted Zita, she landed nearby. "You're Orca, right? Wingspan's sidekick?"

Zita gritted her teeth and turned around, fighting to wear a neutral face as she replied in English. "Arca, and I'm not a sidekick. We're a team." *I need to get these people to help the girls, but watch this tool suck up their time instead.*

"Right. Glad you survived. Does anyone here speak English? The U.S. government sent me on ahead once they got permission to assist, but I don't speak Arabic." Caroline fussed with the scarf covering her golden hair and eyed Zita, her attention lingering on the too-big robe. Up close, a bruise at the edge of her jaw, near her ear, was visible. "You clearly weren't expecting to be here."

"No, we weren't. I speak the local language but haven't gotten anybody to do much yet about the girls in the desert." Frustration and annoyance leaked, thickening the false Mexican accent Zita used to hide her origins.

The guards around the bus retreated closer to the vehicle after a burst of radio chatter.

Caroline smiled and bobbed a brief curtsey, her attention on a point beyond Zita. "Why don't you let me try it?"

A trio of men rushed over, their eyes on the blond. While all three wore the sand-colored uniforms and black berets of the military, two were probably officers, based on the unnecessary explosions of dangling braids and little emblems sewn on their spotless outfits. The third was likely an aide, given the way he adjusted his pace to stay just behind the men of rank. A loose circle of armed guards followed them. They bowed to Caroline, glanced at Zita, and then returned their attention to the other woman. Behind them, more heavily armed men marched and set up a protective perimeter.

The cameras followed, along with the graceful form of a tall woman, clad in a shimmering lavender pant set that looked like silk. Multiple scarves twined around her head, hiding her hair, neck, and the lower part of her face. A translucent veil hung over her eyes, obscuring their color. Even with fabric veiling every inch of the other woman, the grace of that walk was unmistakable. The floral, heeled sneakers were also familiar.

Zita said, "Muse?"

"Yes," Wyn said, her voice a sweet whisper. *My usual illusion would have hindered communication here. I created a costume appropriate to hide as much as possible since as I had time before Andy came to get me.* Her eyes narrowed accusingly above the gauzy scarf hiding her face.

Zita suppressed a wince. *I'm in trouble, aren't I?*

*Yes, and while I recognize the logic of your excuse, you will still need chocolate and an apology ready for when we have time. I've been very busy healing everyone who will accept my aid and was heading over here to handle the women,* Wyn sent. She nodded to Caroline, folded her hands at her waist, and knocked on the bus door. After a quick, whispered conversation with the elderly woman, she disappeared inside.

Caroline smiled at the trio of men, flashing her dentist-perfect pearly whites. "Do any of you speak English?"

"I do, Miss," the one with the least decoration said, his careful enunciation and accent revealing time at some British school.

"It's an honor to meet you all, and I look forward to proper introductions later. I'm sure you're already aware of the kidnapped teachers and girls in the desert requiring aid," Caroline said.

One officer whispered with the translator.

He said, "We had received a report of someone claiming such but were occupied with the fire. The safety of our citizens is our highest priority." His companions' eyes flicked to Zita in the bathrobe and then returned to Caroline.

Words burst out of Zita's mouth in Arabic. "It's not a tale. It's the truth. If the fire's under control, you guys need to get off your asses and send help. Two teachers and a handful of students, maybe ten total. Hard to tell with the burning Jeeps and corpses around them. Dragon apparently killed their captors and was incensed that they didn't have goats or sheep or whatever dragons eat here. She said she's hungry. I don't know. We don't have dragons in America. If we did, they'd probably eat fast food unless they prefer avocado toast or organic vegan or something." She stopped, realizing the others had fallen silent. Her stomach gurgled.

Everyone stared.

Zita collected her thoughts. "What? Just saying. Anyway, grab a bus or two to go get them and bring them home. Wingspan will ensure the dragon doesn't go after them, but they really need their parents right now. Oh, and if you don't fly the Libyan flag off the bus, the teachers will shoot you with guns they took from the dead guys. So, don't forget the flags."

The men seemed relieved when Caroline spoke next.

"Your country is allowing my government to assist with the issues you're having at least until your full forces can muster, so please, just let me know what you require. If necessary, I could show you or your chosen driver where the girls are for whatever plan you've made to help those poor children and their teachers," Caroline said.

The three uniformed men seemed to draw back their shoulders and puff out their chests. They whispered together for a moment, and then the translator half-bowed to Caroline. "Yes, we must collect another of our local leaders and then give you direction. Our rescue plans are already underway. Please come with us, Miss."

"Caroline Gyllen, civilian metahuman support currently attached to the United States Air Force," the blond said.

The speaker gave another partial bow. "Miss Gyllen. Right this way." Surrounded by his fellow officials and a group of soldiers, he strode off toward another section of the plaza.

Caroline winked at Zita. "See? I've got this. You may wish to head home before they complain about uninvited Americans," she said in a low voice. She followed the men, her posture a bit too correct, which may have been to cover the slight hesitation in her gait. Guards fell into place behind her.

Zita scowled and paced in front of the bus. *Seriously? They went for that? Not that I mind not dealing with government types, but they jump all over themselves with eagerness when she tells them the same thing I did. Caroline's taken over the issue with the girls, Andy, so she'll be leading the caravan to get them. Are you okay? Caroline's limping a little, and I think I saw a bruise.*

His reply was brief. *Understood. It's quiet out here. Pretty, too. I'm fine, though a couple of my flight feathers got plucked, and I feel a bit tender. I'd forgotten how that feels.*

Wyn's voice was dry. *It's not as quiet here. Zita used her inimitable flair for words again.*

Concern dripped from Andy's mental voice. *Please tell me she didn't insult someone important. Are we at war now?*

*No, but it's good Caroline distracted them before she could speak more,* Wyn sent back.

Zita scoffed and continued her circuit of the street. As her adrenaline faded, she felt the myriad of small cuts and weariness flooding through her. *I'm totally diplomatic, haters. How could you even hear me, Wyn?*

*The bus windows are open, and since you knew what you were saying, so did I. It was not an exercise in diplomacy.* The doors to the bus creaked open, and Wyn descended the steps. "I've finished the healing they'll allow me to do, so we can depart."

Heavy and insistent, the steady beat of helicopters filled the air, even as a pair of jets streaked by overhead, low and aiming toward the flaming airport.

"Were those things carrying huge missiles? Do you think they're planning on trying to nuke Dragon again? Maybe we should head out." Zita said.

Wyn shivered. "You'll get no arguments from me. Witches are not... favored here, even as healers."

Zita concentrated. *Government's showing up, mano, so watch for the jets. Where do you want to meet? Do you need me to teleport you?*

*I see them. I'll wait to leave until the women and girls get home. A longer flight to stretch my wings would be nice. Get some sleep!* Andy seemed distracted.

"Why were you up at one a.m. anyway? Not more nightmares, I hope," Zita asked.

Wyn dismissed her concerns with a wave of her hand. "Finishing a book. No worries. Shall we?"

"Sí, sí," Zita agreed. Taking the other woman's arm, they strolled down the narrow alleys between houses until they found a safe spot and teleported out. Behind them, the fronds of a date palm shivered in the breeze of their passage.

# Chapter Three

**The next evening,** Zita paced in the wide, faded lobby of the ancient government building, just inside the first security checkpoint. More guards blocked entrances to the interior of the building. Gray clouds obscured the sky outside the barred windows in a moody display that made the whole place seem even dingier.

While she was certain cameras recorded her actions, the bored guards at the metal detectors only watched her absently, their attention focused on people more threatening than a small woman who couldn't sit still. Her good work sneakers, the ones with the rainbow sequins to brighten them up, carried her back and forth across the drab tiles soundlessly. Other people slumped in hard plastic chairs nearby, their eyes glued to their phones. Nearby, two ancient vending machines clunked and hummed, fluorescent bulbs highlighting food of dubious freshness.

*You'd think an agent would at least invite me inside to discuss the case against the serial killer targeting my family, but no. I have to wait out here. Stupid DMS. Then again, the Department of Metahuman Services conference rooms suck even worse than the FBI ones.*

Finding loose coins in her pocket, she punched the numbers on the machine for what seemed like the safest snack and fed in her coins. The machine grumbled, groaned, and clicked.

"Where are my nuts?" Zita punched the button again with a finger. When that didn't work, she pushed against it, hoping to jar the food loose. The machine began a sustained, high-pitched wail. *If it isn't bad enough I had to spend all day sitting and doing taxes after a long night, now this thing won't even let me have a snack?*

"Miss Garcia?" A man emerged from the other side of the security checkpoint and strode toward her. Zita's eyes passed over the suit, which fit too well on a body where gym time was slowly losing to beer and donuts. The subtle brandishing of gold at his wrists and his gelled hair had Zita revising that to froufrou beer and gourmet donuts. His face had the tan lines she associated with sunglasses, and his nose was peeling.

One guard, a woman whose shoulders and walk proclaimed her passion for CrossFit or a similar program, waved. "Hey, Carter! Back from Brazil already? You bring me anything?"

He returned the wave and grinned at the woman. "Not this time, Daisy," he called over his shoulder, before stopping in front of Zita and refocusing on her. "Miss Garcia? You asked to speak to an agent?"

Zita withdrew a step as a flood of spicy chemical masculinity washed over her and made her nose itch. Smoothing out her expression, she tried to think pleasant thoughts and not gag on the man's cloying cologne. "Yes, I wanted to hear the latest on the Sobek—Tracy Jones case."

"My name is Carter Parzarri. I don't know if you remember me, but I was on the same task force as your brother before Miguel's reassignment to New York," he began, smiling down at her from a foot closer than she liked.

*Oye, how likely am I to forget the man who implied Quentin was dirty and deserved to be kidnapped and tortured to death by a psychopath? I was hoping for someone I haven't pissed off yet.* She hid her disappointment behind a smile and refused to retreat. "Yes, I do. Weren't you with the DEA before? Has there been any progress made?"

His eyes searched her again, pausing at her chest before lifting to her face again. "After the meta assault on a Brazilian military base, the Department of Metahuman Services received another round of recruits from other organizations, including agents from the Drug Enforcement Administration like myself. As you were told last time you called, that case has had no progress since late October."

Suspicion raced through her. Even though she feared the answer, she said, "Who's the lead agent on the case now? I want to talk to them." Behind her, the vending machine increased in volume, the high-pitched tone grating on her already frayed temper.

He cleared his throat. "Miss Garcia... To speak frankly, Mr. Jones is unlikely to have survived the blood loss, especially since he was supposedly shot in the torso and fell down three flights of steps—"

She cut him off, slashing the air with her hand like a knife. Zita's voice rose enough that guards nearest them glanced their way for a brief second. "I saw the shot and the wound. There's no supposed about it, and he didn't fall. He jumped and then ran off. Sobek's a meta and extra tough or something, you know that!"

Parzarri glanced around at the departing workers and then at his gold watch. "Miss Garcia. You and your family have been through very traumatic experiences, what with your brother's kidnapping and the later attack at your apartment, and I can understand your frustration. However, you need to realize that the odds of Mr. Jones still being alive are very low, and resources have to be diverted from less-active cases to ones with more immediate dangers to the public. You wouldn't want another family to suffer because agents focused on a case with no viable leads." He gave her a patronizing smile.

Zita fumed. *Smiling might work on some women, but it just makes me wonder if he would reward me with a dog treat if I give the right answer to whatever he wanted. Maybe I'll get lucky, and he'll offer a fancy donut.* "Tracy Jones kidnaps people and tortures them to death when he's not selling meth. How is that not an immediate danger to anyone in his vicinity? Who's in charge of this case? They need to talk to me. My brother Quentin and I have been getting condolence cards since November, and I know it's Sobek sending them!"

He cleared his throat and backed up a step. "Miss Garcia, the case against Mr. Jones is inactive. He's missing, believed dead, and no leads have surfaced for the past three months to indicate otherwise. Blank greeting cards are not evidence of life. I'm the head agent on the case should Mr. Jones surface. There's no one else to ask."

"I don't believe it! You fucking closed the case!"

As her voice grew louder, the closest guards changed position and watched her. The female security guard, Daisy, scowled at her and flexed. The vending machine whined again.

Parzarri narrowed his eyes and glared at her before his face fell back into a more neutral expression. He dug into a pocket and withdrew a business card. "It's inactive, not closed. Miss Garcia, I'll help you out. This card has the DMS tip line, and it also has my direct number. If you hear anything from Mr. Jones that can be verified as his work, call me, and I'll divert resources to it. If you don't have a concrete lead for us, please stop calling to request updates."

Zita inhaled and mentally counted to ten in four languages. She snatched the card. "Fine."

Before she could voice any more questions, he nodded. "Give my best to your brothers." He strode back toward the building interior.

"Wait!" She lifted her hand.

He disappeared through the internal checkpoint.

The thieving vending machine belched a puff of foul-scented air, then raised its pitch still more, as if gloating over her failure.

Zita kicked it.

Daisy took off her earrings and stomped over.

*Caramba.*

***

A couple hours later, Zita's ears still rang from the lecture she'd received for assaulting government property as she stood outside an apartment on the ground floor of her building. She shifted a too-hot paper bag carefully to one arm and pounded on the door. The tinny sounds of the television drifted out from inside.

"Señora Gloria, it's me." She heard no movement as she waited, just the too-cheery chirp of a show. Steam from the bag mingled with her visible breath, and she shivered, drawing the bag closer for its warmth.

She banged her fist against the door harder. "Señora Gloria! I know you're in there!"

The canned sound from inside cut off. Finally, deadbolts clunked on the other side. Zita stepped back.

"Zita? Again? Weren't you here yesterday? Come in. Why didn't you use the doorbell? Where is your coat?" The old woman's query was rough, as if she hadn't spoken for a while. She still wore her clothing from work, even the vest emblazoned with the logo of the retail store, though she'd exchanged her sensible shoes for slippers.

"Only strangers use the bell, and you don't open the door for them. It's been a week, Señora," Zita said, heading inside to the kitchen. Inwardly, she clucked her tongue at the mess, but she didn't say a word. "I didn't think I needed a coat to run down here."

Gloria closed the door, clucking her tongue. "It's snowing. You will catch a cold, and then what will your mother say?"

"Probably to wear my coat next time and to use some vapor rub when I get sick. How you doing? You eat dinner yet?" With relief, she set down her bag on a chair and started moving dirty plates from the table to the sink. *It's a good thing I brought soup because I think other than a couple of bowls, the only clean dishes are for dogs.* She glanced down at the two tiny, spotless matched sets that still sat on the floor, though they'd been unused for months.

The old woman shuffled into the kitchen behind her. "Fine. I'm not hungry." Her voice was flat. On the television in the living room behind her, a telenovela played, the sound muted.

Zita exhaled and grabbed a rag. She scrubbed the top of the table clean and began loading the dishwasher. "We been through this. You need to keep your strength up. You got work tomorrow, and didn't your grandniece want you to help with her new baby on the weekend?"

"Don't worry about me," Gloria said. "I'll get those dishes later." She flapped her hands, then stripped off her vest and folded it on a vacant seat.

With a shake of her head, Zita began their usual ritual with today's lie. "Quentin was sick, so I made a big batch of that soup recipe you gave me, sopa de pollo salvadoreña. Of course, he stayed instead of coming over because of the weather, so now I'm stuck with all this food. You'll do me a favor and take it off my hands? I can't eat all that." Her stomach grumbled.

Last summer, the old woman would've harrumphed and sent Zita away with more food than she'd come with, teasing her about it. Today, as she had done for the past few months, she grunted and plopped into a chair at the table. Gloria stared at her. "You think I don't know what you're doing?"

"What? I can't pawn off no leftovers anymore? I shouldn't eat this cake by myself either." Zita waved at the semita pacha on the table, hoping the sweet would tempt the elderly woman. She got a few more dishes loaded before her friend spoke again.

Gloria eyed the pastry. "Where'd you get that? It looks just like the ones back home." Her tongue darted out to wet her cracked lips.

*That's because I bought it in San Salvador. The soup I can do in my Crock-Pot, but I don't bake.* Zita smiled. "My job sends me to offices all over these days to translate tax forms. I went by a bakery and picked it up special."

Her eyes narrowing, the older woman harrumphed.

"For Quentin. He's got that sweet tooth, you know, and he sure loves pineapple," she lied.

Gloria sniffed. "I suppose he sent you on another date that didn't work out and you're buttering him up."

Zita piled most of the containers in the fridge, casting a quick eye over the contents... or lack thereof. *At least the soup will keep her fed for a few days until her grandniece can get here with some real groceries.* From a Thermos in her bag, she poured horchata into a clean glass and set it before the other woman. "Not yet. I'm storing up goodwill though, because Quentin's got me meeting somebody for lunch on Monday. He said the guy works in a gym, which means we might have something in common for once. Enjoy your food!" She set a napkin, bowl, and spoon in front of the other woman.

"How is your brother?" Gloria asked. She slurped soup and nodded for Zita to take the other seat.

Collecting a second bowl for herself, Zita sat in the indicated chair. "His injuries are all healed." She gulped down a steaming mouthful.

Eyes hooded, Gloria waved a spoon at her. "The man was kidnapped, tortured, and then assaulted again later in a second kidnapping attempt. How is he handling it?"

Zita shrugged. "He's had rough times, but he's been going to meetings with other veterans. That seems to help, even if they're just sitting around lying about how tough they all are. Support groups must work well when you've got something on your chest. Did the soup come out okay?" *That was subtle for me. Go, me!*

Her lip curled, then Gloria ate a bit more, her body relaxing. "Needs more mint, but not bad, considering." They lapsed into silence.

After they had finished the soup and cut the cake, Gloria wiped her mouth, set down her spoon, and watched the younger woman with a pensive expression.

Zita braced herself, knowing the question that would follow. On automatic, she began clearing the table.

"So. Have they caught Sobek yet? Or is he still loose?" Her aged hands clenched in the fabric of her long skirt, and the temporary ease of the meal was lost.

Even though she'd expected it, Zita flinched. "No, they think Sobek's dead, but I'll keep bothering them to make sure they keep working on it." *Inactive, my little brown culo. I'll try Jerome later tonight to see if his computer has turned up any trace of Sobek, and if that doesn't work, I'll call that fancy New York detective, Hound. Maybe he'll have more luck, though I got nothing to pay with. I wonder if he'd barter?*

The old woman exhaled as if it hurt to breathe. "It's not right. It's not right a monster like that can run around free! Children like you and your brother have to live in fear of his return, and my poor puppies—" Gloria gazed at a shelf on the wall, where a small statue of the Virgin Mary guarded a small collection of framed family photos and two tiny urns. She stood and shuffled toward the living room, her shoulders sagging. "I'm tired. It's time for my novelas now."

Zita scrubbed at the table harder than necessary, finished loading the dishwasher, and flicked it on. She glanced at the pictures, her resolve hardening. *I'm done waiting for other people to solve the Sobek problem.* "No worries, Señora. I'm going to do something about it."

# Chapter Four

**"My brother played me.** Again. He's probably giggling to himself in his office right now about setting me up with a crazy dude who claims he doesn't eat. Well, the joke's on Quentin. I went, so now I don't have to date again until next month when it's Miguel's turn to bore me to death with his choice." The map in her pocket crackled as Zita grumbled to herself and ignored the icy prickle of half-frozen rain on her face. Ghostly headlights parted the misty rain as she stomped down the deserted sidewalks and away from her latest failure of a blind date.

After a block, she noticed a railroad crossing and took a moment to peer at the tracks, eying the trees lining the area and the gentle curve that hid the rest of the rail lines from the road and surrounding buildings. She pulled out her map from her pocket, checked it, then shoved it back in before the paper could get soggy. Her spirits lifted. *Since lunch was a no-go, I've got an hour for a run before my afternoon appointment if I cheat and teleport part of the way. I'll use another form, so I don't mess up my work clothes, though.*

Gravel crunched under her good work sneakers as she trotted off the street and beside the railroad tracks. Despite the lingering exhaust from the trains, the muffling of the constant barrage of noise and scents along the busy streets was welcome. Leafless tree branches allowed peeks at windowless industrial buildings on one side, and little houses huddled together, trying to pretend the railroads didn't run through their backyards on the other. Raised several feet higher than the surrounding ground, two sets of tracks paralleled each other. The newer, less weedy set had to be part of an above-ground section of the Metro, given the telltale white covers over the electrified subway tracks.

She shivered and realized she'd already decided to run; she'd stripped off her clothing as soon as she could no longer see the road or the buildings through the trees, and now stood in her special gear, a matching purple set of capri leggings and sports bra/tank top. Once she'd stashed her shoes and clothes, she mentally sorted through shapes. Finally, she switched to a tawny German Shepherd Dog, one with thick enough fur not to be bothered by the weather and sufficient size to carry the bulging bag of her belongings. With her things dangling from her mouth, she began to run, leaping over obstructions and bounding partway up tree trunks for the sheer joy of motion. She was careful to stay away from the electrified rails. Her tail wagged, and she let it as no one was around to witness.

As she passed a building that sat close to the edge of the track, a whiff of sickness warned her of the presence of others. Zita slowed, ears perking, and paid closer attention to her surroundings. Following her nose, she came upon three unkempt men smoking cigarettes in a decrepit car. All the windows were cracked open, except for the missing one that had been patched up with duct tape and increasingly soggy cardboard. From what she could see, the vinyl seats had split ages ago, and rust accentuated every crack.

One man picked at sores interspersed among the patchy stubble on his face as he fidgeted in the back. "It's soon, right? Soon? Then we can go?"

His companions seemed just as twitchy. "Yes, soon. Once the train does our job for us, she said we get more," one of his friends told him, showing a smile made up of the most disgusting teeth Zita'd ever seen outside of a movie, rotten and brown. He twirled one end of the scraggly hair masquerading as a mustache on his face... or tried to.

The third man gazed at the tracks with an avid look, his pupils so wide she couldn't tell what color his eyes were. His mouth hung open in the filthiest goatee she'd ever seen, with the remains of countless meals dotting it.

*Druggies. Ugh. At least the car will keep them warm enough not to die of hypothermia.* Snorting with disgust, Zita returned to following the tracks. Once past them, she got only about a hundred feet before her nose announced the presence of fresh blood and death. As she watched, turkey vultures circled over the older railroad tracks.

"Here... puppy... puppy..." came a rasping whisper. "Come help the nice man..."

*Is someone injured?* Stashing her bag under a red chokeberry bush, Zita charged the buzzards, who had landed and were doing a creepy hop toward a bundle of rags on the railroad tracks. She barked, the sound reverberating in her chest. *Dios, don't let that be what I think it is.*

The birds scattered as did a rat.

Zita turned to check out the lump on the tracks and realized it was the shape and size of a man. Involuntarily, her tail crept between her legs, and she gulped.

"Puppy, here..." the whisper cajoled.

She blinked, eyes wide and ears flat against her head as she took in the details. Her sensitive canine nose wrinkled as the paper-thin reek of dry death and old blood mingled curiously with a garlic scent. Each step cautious, she padded closer. *That's...new.*

Pinned through his chest by a narrow three-foot-long piece of wood, the corpse of a man lay across the older railroad tracks. An orange and black braid of rope crisscrossed the body and secured the upper half to the rails, holding him in place. His head rested on the ground, with a metal train rail forcing his neck up at an odd angle. Strangely, a thick, woven strand of garlic sat next to his face. His skin was sunken, desiccated, and dry as if he were mummified, and his chest caved inward sickeningly. Dark purple eyes in a skull-like face tracked her movements. One claw-like hand tried to lift but fell under its own weight or the restraint of the ropes. "Come. I'm sorry, puppy."

*I can't believe that guy is alive, let alone conscious. I thought he had an injured friend nearby.* Zita shifted to her Arca form and dropped to her knees, trying to ignore the cold that lanced through her with the loss of fur. She reached out and tested the rope with her fingers, taking in the coarse fiber and loose weave, stiff with blood and ice. *Cheap utility stuff, but too thick for my multitool to cut. The knots aren't great, but he's bled all over them and the rope's swollen.* As she examined him, she tried to comfort him with a confidence she didn't feel. Her tongue tangled with her nerves, making her fake Mexican accent even thicker. "Hang in there, hombre. You're going to live."

She tugged on the rope to assess the amount of give, trying to be both careful and fast. Despite her caution, she bumped the stick in the man's chest, a carved and shaped piece of wood, like the leg from an old chair.

He groaned and coughed weakly. "Too late for that. Careful, I'm delicate. Pull...stake." Little white flakes drifted from his mouth, and after a second, she realized it was skin from the garlic.

"Sorry, just trying to get you to a hospital as soon as possible. I'm not moving the stick. Something's got to be stopping you from bleeding out, and that's as good of a candidate as any. Try not to die." Zita had loosened one of the man's arms and begun freeing the other when she heard a noise—the rapid patter of running feet skittering on loose gravel and rocks, and the low mutter of men's voices. "Call 911," she shouted over her shoulder, "This guy needs help."

The injured man's eyes widened, and he struggled against the ropes. Blood oozed sluggishly out of his wound. "Watch out!"

"Don't move, you'll make it worse," Zita told him. She caught a whiff of sweat and sickness and felt movement behind her.

On instinct, she whirled aside, hopping to her feet in a defensive position. "This guy needs a hospital! Back off unless you can help."

The druggies from the car surrounded her. Their motions were sharp and jerky, and none of them seemed to have any of the smooth movement she'd associate with any sports or martial arts. Stringy hair hung from beneath grimy knit winter hats with little pompoms on top, above too-thin bodies covered with ratty, stained winter clothing. They were indistinguishable in so many ways that she mentally labeled them by their facial hair—Mustache, Goatee, and Stubble Boy—just to keep them separate.

After a final yank on the hair on his face, Goatee withdrew a camping knife from a pocket. "Bad choice. He won't be the only one to lose his head today. Knives, boys." He managed not to stick himself as he unfolded the serrated blade, despite fumbling it several times.

Mustache giggled, unzipped his puffy coat, and groped around inside. The tip of a knife ripped through the grimy synthetic fabric of his coat and sent him off in a gale of laughter.

Stubble Boy pulled his weapon, struggling to get the long length out of his pocket. Alone of the trio, he did not carry a knife. Instead, he now threatened her with what looked like a sharpened piece of a wooden chair. Sweat dripped down his face and off his chin, despite the slush still spitting from the sky.

*Por supuesto, I didn't find an attempted murder victim. I found a murder-in-progress.* Zita slipped into a slow, defensive ginga movement as she waited for an opening and tried not to think about the sharp-edged rocks under her bare toes or annoying pinpricks of ice on her exposed skin.

The druggies' eyes caught the light and seemed to glow red.

*Oye, let's not make this creepy at all.* Zita cleared her throat and raised her voice. "Pues, I know you want to help the poor guy here, but you seem to have mistaken me for the rope. How about you put the knife down, and I'll get him loose?"

"Only if that means off with his head. We don't get our next hit until that happens, and it's harder to separate heads from necks than you'd think," Mustache said, freeing his knife from his coat. He waved the long, fixed-blade weapon at her. Light glinted off the serrated edge.

"Now, that might work. Don't worry, I'll give it back when I'm done." Zita stepped aside as Goatee attacked, his arms outstretched to grab her. Seizing the back of his coat as he passed, she propelled him into Stubble Boy, who was charging with his chair spindle raised. The men fell in a tangle of arms and legs.

Mustache jabbed at her, a raw, inexperienced thrust, and she darted backward, keeping to the outside of his knife arm. As he turned to follow her, she struck at his wrist, expecting the blade to fall.

It didn't.

She blinked and revised her estimates upward for the amount of drugs the men were on and their strength.

In the distance, a train whistle sounded.

"I hate to interrupt," the captive man on the tracks whispered, "but I believe a train is coming." He tugged at the ropes.

Switching to a gorilla, Zita charged at Mustache.

He slashed at her.

Jumping aside with a hoot, she seized the wrist of his knife-wielding hand and twisted, rotating his arm until he was forced to release the knife.

Mustache smacked her once or twice with his other arm, the blows more painful than they should have been, but eventually he threw himself to the ground to escape the lock she had on his arm.

After releasing him, Zita snagged the knife. She raced to the bound man's side, kicking Stubble Boy in the head before he could stand.

He fell again, tripping Goatee.

*Gracias a Dios that I've been practicing fighting as a gorilla with Andy.* Squatting low, Zita slashed at the rope with the knife, sawing at it with the serrated edge. The cheap blade bent under the assault on the rope, and she switched to her Arca shape for the added dexterity.

Mustache ripped a wooden post out of the ground and charged at her, swinging wildly.

"You're all metas? At least that makes this fight a little fairer," she said, sidling out of the way and letting him continue past.

His eyes seemed even redder than before, and sweat ran down Mustache's pocked face as he turned to face her. "No, we don't need to be freaks. Anyone can have powers now!"

"I don't think that's how it works. The path seems to be surprise coma, then powers, then being stalked by DMS," Zita said, dropping low under his swing. She slipped into an esquiva diagonal, dodging left under the post and feinting at his thigh before falling back into her ginga.

Bleating expletives, Mustache swung again at her.

She repeated the same defensive move, but this time she flowed into a gancho kick at the end. The heel of her bare foot connected to his jaw with a crack.

Her opponent didn't seem to feel it though his next words were too slurred to understand. Worse, his friends had recovered and now lunged at her as well.

*Chingada drugs. Three on one already sucks, and my hits don't phase them, plus they're all extra strong... I have to knock them out or disable them to keep them from continuing to attack, plus I need to get Almost-Dead there off the train tracks.* Her mind raced as her body went on autopilot to avoid their attacks. Zita hopped nimbly over the rails and hacked at the ropes again.

Mustache tried a sweeping blow with his post.

She ducked low, and Goatee got hit instead. While they were distracted, she rolled to the side and slashed Stubble Boy's Achilles tendon.

Goatee staggered back under Mustache's hit.

Stubble Boy tumbled as his leg gave out, falling atop the man on the tracks.

*Dios, don't let me accidentally kill anyone,* Zita thought as she twisted the chair leg from Stubble Boy's hand. She nudged him with her foot to keep him from lying across Almost-Dead. With the fixed blade knife, she blocked Goatee's stab at her. Following up with the wood, she struck the back of his knife hand twice before she spun away a few feet. *Since my weapons skills are rusty, I'm also lucky these guys don't know what they're doing.*

The folding knife fell from Goatee's hand

Zita kicked it aside, twirled the wood like a baton in her left hand and struck him across the face and ribs with it, driving him back. Knife in one hand, stick in the other, she faced the remaining two men. "Run for it," she advised, scowling. *Please don't make me cut another one of you. Be frightened and run from the loca with the weapons.*

Mustache jabbered something unintelligible to Goatee, and both shot her glances that seemed more annoyed than intimidated.

"I'd love to," Almost-Dead croaked, "but I seem to be tied up. Train's coming." He had most of one arm loose though his tugs to free his other arm were weak.

Zita backed toward the tracks, giving a quick slash to the ropes again. Another one gave. "You're mouthy for a guy who's half dead."

"Not half, but thank you for noticing," the man whispered. "Watch your back!" He pointed.

As she turned, Zita caught the flash of motion as both standing druggies rushed her at once.

Mustache still had his post, but Goatee outdistanced him, reaching out to grab her.

"Herd her closer so I can get her too!" Stubble Boy called out. He pulled himself into a sitting position.

*Pinche pendejos.* As quickly as she could, Zita danced toward Goatee, meeting his rush with her own. She slid underneath his outstretched arms and hammered a strike with the stick against the side of his neck, praying she'd judged her own strength right.

Goatee fell, unconscious, as she somersaulted aside.

Mustache charged at her, swinging his improvised club.

She retreated, watching for an opening. *He overextends and has to use both arms to swing that even with improved strength,* she noted.

"Hey, don't take that stake out!" Stubble Boy shouted, slapping at Almost-Dead.

Her phone interrupted, the screech of her manager's ringtone, loud despite the distance and the bag of clothing on top of it.

Mustache glanced toward the noise.

Zita swept in during his distraction and struck at his knees, hitting both with sharp cracks that had her wincing. Her stick broke in her hands, and her attacker fell. She tossed aside the broken wood.

A train whistled. Her phone kept ringing.

Stubble Boy made a choked sound.

Zita whirled, knife ready, and saw one of Stubble Boy's arms covering the mouth and nose of the man on the tracks. Jumping over Goatee and Mustache, she raced there and pulled him away with her free hand.

Stubble Boy landed between the sets of tracks.

Sawing on the ropes, Zita shook her head at the blood smearing the mouth of the tied-up man. "You bit him?"

The rail vibrated under her hands and a horn blew.

"Given his attempt to stab me again, it seemed the right thing to do," Almost-Dead said, working to pull off the rest of the restraints. His movements had gained some strength, but the wood was no longer in his chest.

She checked the injury, relieved to see no new blood appeared to be escaping it. Some corner of her mind noted the oddity, but she focused on freeing him. "Your stick fell out, but you're not bleeding."

He pulled away a rope and whispered his answer, "I fear my heart must go on, however ignominious the circumstances and useless the organ."

Zita cut through the last rope, glancing over her shoulder to ensure the druggies weren't up again. "Big words, but apply pressure to your chest wound, or you'll bleed out!"

The injured man set a hand over his chest. "Must you taunt me with my worst nightmare?"

"You are the weirdest dude I've ever rescued." She dropped the knife and shifted to a gorilla. Gathering him up, she cradled him as carefully as she could.

"Thank you." His voice was quiet.

Stubble Boy shrieked. He began to shake, and his hands glowed red. He sat up and held out his hands as if he'd never seen them before, his face turning an ugly shade of unhealthy red. "What? It hurts! It burns! it burns!"

The train was now visible, the horn a constant, panicked blaring sound that told her someone saw them.

Hair prickled on the back of Zita's neck. Still carrying Almost-Dead, she jumped off the tracks and brought them both to the ground, shielding his form with her temporarily larger one as much as possible. Mindful of the hole in his chest, she tried to keep as much of her weight off him as possible.

Fire blasted out of Stubble Boy's hands and hit where they'd been with a whoosh, a boom, and the scent of scorched nylon. He flew backward toward the newer tracks.

The train whooshed by, brakes screeching, horn repeatedly blasting, almost covering the incoherent screaming from the other side of the vehicle.

Zita flinched and hooted as tiny flecks of burning fiber from the rope still on the tracks hit her.

Beneath her, Almost-Dead hissed as a few flakes caught him. "Fire. Why is it always fire? I am not a fan of fire. Why is it never scented bath water at just the right temperature?"

Rolling off the man, Zita returned to her Arca form. "As if we're that lucky." After she glanced at his gruesome chest injury to ensure it was not any worse than before, she settled into a defensive crouch. *The knife is on the other side of the tracks. If I'm lucky, I can reach them and knock out Stubble Boy before he can shoot again.*

When the last train car passed, she darted forward to reclaim the knife... but paused.

Stubble Boy had stopped screaming and instead choked and gurgled. A circle of scorched earth lay around him, and spasms shook his body.

With an incomprehensible exclamation, Mustache staggered to Stubble Boy's convulsing form, clumsily hopping over the rails. He tripped and reached out to pull himself up using the closest rail. The white one.

Zita's eyes widened, and she shouted, "No! Don't touch the—"

Mustache's body jerked, his muscles stiffening. His mouth fell open and stayed that way.

*Can't touch him directly. Need something nonconductive...* Zita stared at the bloody chair leg for a second. Spotting the post that Mustache had attacked her with, she ran to it. After shifting back to a gorilla, she snatched it and used it to shove him off the rail.

A spark arced between his hand and the rail as he detached.

Once he was free, she moved him off the tracks and bent over him.

His blank, staring eyes and gaping mouth told her already what his state was. Wisps of smoke rose from his too-warm body, carrying the stench of charred flesh.

She stepped back, her stomach churning. "I guess I could try CPR."

A hand touched Zita's shoulder. Almost-Dead stood beside her, holding his own chest. "Nothing cures true death." His voice was raspy, raw, and strained.

Zita gave a brief nod, fighting the rising nausea. "You need a hospital."

He coughed, a harsh, hacking sound that made her lungs ache just to hear. When he spoke again, his voice had acquired a thick Eastern European accent that had been entirely absent before. "It's far too late for that."

Stubble Boy moaned and gave a final convulsion before going limp. Afterward, his breathing was loud and harsh and uneven.

"You killed them. You're monsters! Both of you!" Goatee shouted.

Almost-Dead stumbled away from the Metro tracks, his head tilting as he surveyed the area. "Technically, your one friend is still alive, and the other chose to grab an electrified rail. Even if she had somehow convinced him to do that, you were trying to murder us, so it would be self-defense." Another painful-sounding series of coughs ripped through his frame, and he clutched at his chest.

Going to Stubble Boy, Zita moved him farther away from the tracks and propped him up against an abandoned crate to help him breathe. *That should be far enough to stop him from touching the third rail even if he has another fit before an ambulance gets here.* With a frown, she noted the thready beat of his pulse under her fingers. Exhaling deeply and touching as little as possible, she dug through his pungent pockets. She found and discarded his wallet and keys before locating the object of her search. Touching the phone as little as possible, she called emergency services.

After a brief conversation with the operator, she wiped the phone and dropped it next to Stubble Boy. Lifting her voice to carry to all the others, she called out, "Ambulances are on their way with... Where's the injured guy?" She glanced around.

While she had been absorbed, Almost-Dead had limped away into the shadows between two warehouse buildings.

Hurrying, she slipped through the hole in the chain-link fence and chased after him, ignoring the foul threats Goatee shouted after her. "Hey, you need help. You should rest until they can get you to a hospital."

Farther down the track, her manager's ringtone shrieked again.

The man she had rescued gave a harsh laugh. "Not that I'm ungrateful, but I must go. The hospital can't give me what I need, and the police do not like my kind."

"No mames. Hombre, you have a chest wound and were chingado tied to the rails. You need a hospital and to make a police report. Especially the hospital part of that." Zita seized his arm, careful to be gentle, as his skeletal face was corpse-pale and lined with deep pain-filled creases.

Her phone kept wailing, but blissfully, Goatee Boy's imprecations ended so the words that followed practically echoed in the near-silence.

Almost-Dead tried to pull away, his entire body listing at an odd angle. His breath steamed the air far less than it should and far too rarely. "Please. I cannot. If I go there, I'll die. A friend lives near here and he'll help before I lose what little self-control I have left. Didn't you hear those men? I'm a monster and a danger to everyone if I snap. I'll survive this. If you insist on checking on me, meet me at the Danz Mizer club tomorrow. Ask for Dmitri inside."

*Sobek's old club? Maybe I can get some information on him at last, assuming this guy doesn't die first. I know what I'm doing next to find him.* Hands on her hips, Zita shook her head. "Don't be stupid."

Almost-Dead—Dmitri, she supposed—snorted and met her eyes. "I'll get what I need, no worries. I'll be fine. Are you going to answer your phone?" An elongated fang peeked out coquettishly from his mouth.

Zita blinked as her cell fell silent, finding herself back at the railway tracks and halfway to her bag of belongings. Her feet ached with cold. *What was I doing? Oye, the injured guy! I can't believe I let him walk away without help.* She turned back to where she'd last seen him.

He was nowhere in sight, though Goatee spotted her and tossed another curse at her.

"I'm bringing a healer too, Dmitri!" Zita shouted, confused. She rubbed her hand over her hair, forward and back. *I must need lunch and a nap if adrenaline wearing off is making me this stupid and sloppy.* Sirens howled nearby, and she swore and raced back to where she'd left her things.

# Chapter Five

**Later that night,** Zita stood still, trying to untangle Siamese cats from her legs while balancing a bowl of food from home and a cup filled to the brim with tea. Seated nearby, Wyn and Andy watched with amusement. Wyn's living room was much like the rest of her house: a modest place made dramatic with splashes of color, elegant furniture, and a staggering number of books. Lilacs and tea permeated the air, mingling with the scent of the bookshelves.

"I confess, Zita, it surprised me that you would elect to meet so close to your usual bedtime," Wyn reclined on the velvety red couch, another dainty cup of tea of in her hands. Her cats' abandonment of her seemed not to bother her.

Andy sipped his hot chocolate in a nearby chair, an overstuffed white creation with crimson stripes matching the sofa. "It's ten. It's past her bedtime."

One cat yowled and headbutted Zita's leg.

"No," Zita told the animal, clutching the snack to her chest and inching closer to a chair. "Don't you feed them?"

Wyn giggled. "Yes, they had salmon tonight. What are you eating?"

"Tuna salad, but with cottage cheese and vegetables." Zita lifted the food a little higher and set the astringent-smelling tea on the fancy glass-topped Celtic coffee table, hoping the felines would go for the drink so she wouldn't have to have any.

"Oh, well, that's all your fault, then. Perhaps if you shared some, they would go away. It works with Cupcake," Andy said, referencing his own giant, spoiled tom. While he had originally only agreed to provide a temporary home for the animal, the cat now had his own embroidered bed, Christmas stocking, and Instagram account.

Zita rubbed a hand across her forehead. "I refuse to reinforce their bad behavior. You're right. It's late, but it's tax season." She gestured at the front window of the house and the snow piling up on the outside window ledge. "I only got home an hour ago even with teleporting. My lunch got cut short, and my dinner break almost didn't happen."

"Rough day." Wyn clucked her tongue and sipped her tea, ignoring the issue of her cats entirely. "Drink your tea. It'll relax you. Shall we cover vigilante business quickly so we can all sleep at a reasonable hour then?"

"I've got a furnace to help install in the morning, so yes," Andy said.

"Works for me. Right then. We drove Dragon away from Al Jawf for now. Do you think we have to check back regularly to see if she returns? The locals didn't seem crazy about us." Zita took a bite of tuna salad.

A cat gave a mournful cry and flopped at her feet as if it had taken a mortal wound.

Andy's expression sobered. "Libya, Egypt, and every country along the Saharan Desert are on high alert, and the U.S. and other concerned nations are negotiating to give them military aid. We've been officially requested to stay out of it unless we want to turn ourselves in and join up the way Caroline Gyllen has." He coughed. "That said, I've been informed privately that should I perform discreet flyovers, non-Libyan forces would appreciate it."

"Become a tool like her? No, thanks. The last thing we need is to be hit by a nuke intended for Dragon, so I'm okay with hands off unless she starts slaughtering people again when nobody's stopping her." Zita shuddered.

Wyn cleared her throat. "As much as I believe we could aid with rebuilding, healing, and so on, I concur. While the news appears to be inaccurate otherwise, they did announce that the African metahuman groups will keep a closer eye there as well."

Zita grinned. "What are the reports saying now? Are we now all supposedly strippers? Did Wingspan shake his booty to shock Dragon into submission or Muse fly in on a broomstick?"

"Not funny, Z. I hate that video," Andy muttered. The tips of his ears flushed red.

Wyn coughed and circled the rim of her teacup with a finger. "Actually, they're saying that Caroline distracted Dragon until brave Libyan forces drove off the beast. Wingspan assisted Caroline. Libyan medical resources accepted my minor and unnecessary aid. Additional American reinforcements helped with cleanup until additional local support was available."

Blinking, Zita felt her smile fade as annoyance took over. "Ni modo. I don't usually mind when the news gets stuff wrong because that only helps keep our identities secret, but seriously? Caroline and the Libyan army? I mean, they didn't see much of me busting my culo to keep Dragon out of the city, but you guys deserve more credit than that. How did they miss the giant bird kicking Dragon's ass?"

"Did you expect them to spin it any other way? Doesn't matter. We didn't do it for the credit, and we know what we did. Caroline tried to set them straight at first, but they didn't show that in the televised clips." Andy shrugged.

Honesty forced Zita to admit the truth in his words, but she growled, nonetheless. "You're right, all but that bit about Caroline. That publicity hound never lets go of a scrap of attention."

His shoulders hunched, but Andy didn't say any more.

Fussing with her hair, Wyn released it from its bun as she removed a small stylus. She plucked her tablet from the coffee table. "Right. This is where we all reiterate that we're on your side of the feud with her, even if she seems oblivious about the vendetta. Since we're in agreement on the falsity of the news reports, why don't we take this opportunity to cover what we've been doing as our alter egos and what we should watch for?"

Andy nodded.

With a sigh, Zita plopped onto a chair identical to Andy's and shoveled in a bite of food, refusing to feel guilty despite the cats complaining near her dangling feet. Neither animal had made a move toward her tea. *It's silly how I can't sit anywhere in here without feeling like I'm five.* "What's up? How've you been keeping busy?"

"As Wingspan, I've spent a fair amount of time helping with overseas storms, but I don't think I need to continue. I'll keep an eye on them in case something catastrophic blows in, but others have had it handled, even Typhoon Haiyan, which was slated to be a big one. It was a real relief as I'm still not certain what I'm doing when I mess around with weather, and it's risky to practice." Andy shuddered.

"Speaking of inclement weather, if anyone wants to clear my sidewalks, I'd appreciate it." Wyn's long lashes fluttered as she glanced up from her electronic device and smiled.

Zita wrinkled her nose. "Sorry, I can maybe get to it around lunchtime, but my apartment building's all old people who get up early. I have to clear the walks before I head into work or it'll be like a senior citizen hockey pileup, but with worse language. Of course, if work cancels my appointments, I can stop by earlier."

Setting down his mug, Andy lifted a hand. "I've got it. I'll stop by around dawn and do your walks and driveway before that install. I almost forgot to mention I've got another job interview this month."

"Cool! Where at?" Zita asked.

Wyn beamed. "Excellent! Where?"

He took a deep breath and picked his hot chocolate back up. "St. Louis. That and the one in Detroit I went to last week have been the only two listed lately. Physics professor positions, even assistant ones, aren't easy to find."

All three were silent a moment.

"Well, that'll make hanging out more difficult, but good luck!" Zita said. "No hay bronca, mano, you'll be complaining about me teleporting in to visit before you know it."

Wyn hummed. "It is unfortunate they're not closer, but we'll both be happy to see you able to pursue your chosen vocation."

He fiddled with his cup. "Thanks. I'd rather stay near here or near my mom, but so far, no luck. There was a sweet research position in southern Maryland, but someone else got the job before I could even apply. Detroit seemed to have someone else in mind, so St. Louis is my best chance right now."

Zita winced. "That sucks, mano. It's not close enough for you to visit either family without giving away your secret, though I've always wanted to climb and parachute from the Gateway Arch."

Pinching her brows, Wyn murmured, "Yes, let's have him plan his move around the landmarks you can climb."

Andy sighed. "I need to find something before Dad gets his hopes up too high that Cristovano and Son HVAC could be a long-term reality. For Christmas, he gave me a card saying he'd pay for my CFC certification—that's required to service air conditioning units—and showed me how he's been keeping track of my hours so I could apply to be a journeyman this year."

Waving her fork at him, Zita listed the benefits of the gift. "That's real sweet of your dad, even if you would've preferred another video game. Certification means more money in any profession, so getting it will help you pad your savings. Plus, you'll have a side hustle to fall back on. Quentin paid for me to get locksmith certification a few years ago, and that's the only reason I still got a place to live."

"That, and your other brother is your landlord," Wyn murmured.

Zita dismissed the comment with a wave of her hand. "Details! Andy gets what I'm saying."

Andy ventured a halfhearted smile and rubbed the back of his neck. "Yeah, I know. I just don't want to break his heart. HVAC is an honest living, but it's not what I enjoy. How's your aunt and the lawsuit, Wyn?"

Wyn smiled, but it didn't reach her eyes. "Thanks to my spells and the care she gets in her nursing home, her Alzheimer's isn't progressing, so she's... well, she's happy, even if she doesn't always remember me. Because she's doing so well, the judge denied the motion to move her to someplace cheaper until the case is resolved. My parents have also been barred from visiting her given the nasty trick they played around the holidays even if I can't prove their negligence legally."

Zita stuffed food in her mouth to keep from commenting on Wyn's parents.

Andy's expression revealed he was doing something similar.

Smoothing the satin pajamas over her knees, Wyn took a deep breath and ran her fingers through a decorative bowl of polished rocks. She plucked one out, considered the translucent pale blue crystal, and said, "It's over, and she's safer now, so why don't we finish up with the vigilante news. Has anyone had any notable rescues since that fire at the Canadian eldercare place?"

"Stranded motorists and toppled sixteen-wheelers, mostly," Andy said. "I'm getting a good sense for that kind of thing."

Zita poked at her food. "I interrupted a murder today, but the attempted victim ran off before I could get him to a hospital. I'm supposed to meet him at Danz Mizer tomorrow night to ensure he's okay."

"Isn't that the club where Sobek was kidnapping people?" Andy asked.

She nodded. "Sí. I want to see if the guy knows anything about that, but at a minimum, he might need Wyn's help. The old geezer was in rough shape when I saw him last, but he had fangs, so he might've had a meta trick to survive. Would you mind?"

Sympathy on her face, Wyn's answer was immediate. "Of course, I'd be delighted. He can't have been that old. The latest studies have shown the comas that gave us powers only impacted people between the ages of twelve to fifty. They can't rule out younger children, but so far, no one has reported anyone outside of that range."

"I didn't ask what his birthday was. It was weird. Bunch of druggies tied a dude to the railroad tracks." Zita shrugged.

Wyn's eyebrows shot up. "How... traditional. That explains why I had to heal you earlier."

"Did any of the would-be killers twirl his mustache?" Andy asked. "If they didn't, I'm losing faith in mankind."

Wincing, Zita nodded. "Yeah, actually, one did, but not well."

Andy wiped pretend sweat off his forehead.

"I don't want to think about it," Zita said. She clenched her bowl, the cool plastic bending under her fingers until she forced herself to loosen her grip.

The others winced.

Concern on her face, Wyn hesitated.

Zita shook her head, fighting queasiness. "No. No details on this one."

Wyn held up a finger and took a deep breath, her eyes searching Zita's face. She nodded and tapped her tablet. "That explains why the Internet says you're wanted for questioning by the police. Supposedly, Arca lost it and beat up three random stoners. It did seem unlikely."

Andy snorted. "No way. Not Z."

"At least you guys believe me. Those guys were so high that one grabbed the electrified rail... It was bad." Zita grimaced. "I'll have to get the old man to tell the cops what happened, but he'll need convincing. He really didn't want to do that."

"You need to resolve that soon before it escalates," Andy warned.

Wyn scribbled something on her tablet. "Agreed. I'll help you persuade the victim to testify on your behalf. Let's move along, then. Zeus and his God Kings gang are unaccounted for so we can assume they have grown either much more discreet or are struggling to reorganize with the losses of Janus and Pretorius. We can only hope their inability to force Janus to open portals for them means their crime spree is over or at least curtailed."

"Hope the kid has the good sense to stay missing, presumed dead," Zita muttered, remembering the scrawny, unhappy teen.

Andy grunted. "For his sake and for his family, I'd agree. However, I have a strong suspicion the government's hiding him."

"How so?" Wyn lifted an elegant eyebrow.

Andy rubbed the back of his neck. "When I asked Caroline how she got to Libya so quickly, she claimed to be in the area already for reasons she couldn't share. If the kid went to the U.S. government to check on his family..."

It was Zita's turn to grunt. "They wouldn't let a teleporter walk away. They'd figure out some way to use him. Poor kid. If that's the case, I hope they're kinder to him than Zeus, and we should expect to be ambushed at some point."

"Ah, there's that Zita optimism we all know and love," Wyn murmured.

Zita raised her eyebrows. "You don't agree they'd draft us if they knew everything we could do?"

Andy exhaled noisily. "While most of my powers are more obvious than yours, I have to side with Zita on this one. Caroline said her handlers wanted to talk to us, or to Wyn, anyway, though they wouldn't mind if I tagged along."

"Am I disappointed or relieved that they don't want to talk to me?" Zita paused and contemplated. "I'm not surprised. The Man knows I know." She ate a bit more.

"The government knows you know what?" Andy asked. "Wait, there's no way that answer isn't going to keep me awake later. Forget I asked."

Wyn raised an eyebrow. "Not unexpected, given how busy we've been trying to assist everyone this winter. Did they have a specific topic in mind? And why me?"

He coughed. "Caroline didn't say. They probably didn't tell her, and we didn't have much time to chat once the rest of the American forces arrived."

Zita waved her fork at Wyn. "Can we agree that dealing with Caroline or the Man directly will only cause trouble for us? If you meet with them, Wyn, promise me you'll take Andy or me to cover your back?"

After a moment of silence, Wyn nodded. She coiled a chestnut ringlet around her finger and then released it. "Very well. I have no wish to be imprisoned or forcibly impressed as other countries have been doing. Our government has a mandatory registration bill pending as it is."

"See? Governments. Can't be trusted." Zita ate another mouthful.

"Did any of the studies you read have a cause for powers yet?" Andy asked.

Wyn shook her head. "They're speculating that it's a genetic mutation triggered by one or more unknown events, as it rose without any clear infection vector other than the age limitations. One study noted industrialized countries had higher numbers of metahumans but couldn't eliminate the possibility that countries reporting fewer either weren't sharing or didn't have accurate numbers."

Zita took a moment to sort through that. "So, they don't got a clue."

"Not really, no." Wyn lifted her hands in surrender.

Andy shrugged. "It was worth asking. So, does anyone have plans other than watching weather forecasts?"

Wyn turned off her tablet. "Rani's in the area until next Wednesday. We've got a date tomorrow night that I'll have to reschedule to go to the club with Zita. I'm still trying to decide when the right time is to tell a girlfriend that you're wearing an illusion."

"Why don't you just have fun, and if it looks like it'll get serious, then start thinking more about it. If you're waffling over it in front of us, you're not ready yet. Just don't go sexing her up until after you tell her, unless you want to screw things up," Zita said.

Andy coughed. "Even if I lose my man card for discussing this, I agree with our resident expert in destroying relationships. You won't want to get serious without telling her. Let us know when you do because we'll need to stop hanging out as a trio out of costume or at least avoiding it around Rani."

Nibbling on a fingertip, Wyn nodded. "True. Giving her my identity increases the danger to you two, and I don't think I'm ready to risk it. Perhaps I'll hint that I'm using an illusion when we're a bit further along in our relationship. Zita, how's the training going with that young shapeshifter?"

"The one with the bad heart? Yeah, how's that going, Mr. Miyagi?" Andy said.

Wrinkling her nose at Andy, Zita said. "I'll assume that's a lame reference and let it pass. We made some progress before lessons had to go on hold until after she gets some new medical treatment. I don't want to kill the poor kid by overstressing her when she's sick, and yes, your healing helped."

Wyn smiled. "That sounds hopeful."

"Let's hope nobody pisses her off in the meantime." Andy's words were soft.

Zita paced. "The government gave her a special inhaler that stops her shapeshifting. I'm a little concerned about the Feds being able to produce that kind of chemical. We'll need to watch any gases people hit us with carefully if they've figured something like that out."

Andy flinched and nodded.

"It inhibits powers? That is concerning." Wyn frowned into her weedy tea.

"As far as Elle, it's for the best she's getting help from somewhere else. The kid was starting to act like I'm a role model." Zita shuddered.

"Oh, we can't have that." Andy laughed.

Wyn leaned forward. "Why wouldn't she look up to you? You're accomplished in your own way."

Andy said, "Of course, there's also the death wish to consider..."

Zita scoffed. "Oye, I don't have a death wish. Anyone would have done the same stuff as me given the chance or enough practice. It's just..." She fought for the right words, stopping and jiggling her leg before abandoning the entire effort. "I'm not a role model."

After a deep breath, Andy eyed Zita. "I'm almost afraid to ask, but any news on Sobek? You know we've got your back if you're still going after him."

Sourness filled Zita's mouth and colored her tone. "Oh, I am. DMS claimed his case since he's a meta as well as a psychopathic murderer and drug lord. They've classified it as an inactive investigation because they think he died when Quentin shot him. They also have no leads, according to the agent I spoke to, but that guy's shifty."

Wyn raised an eyebrow. "Personal animosity is dripping from your tone. Is the DMS agent another one of your disastrous blind dates?"

"Do you think the government would mind if we only talked to women and married men given the rate that Zita's alienating all the bachelors?" Andy's question seemed sincere, other than his evil smile.

With no real animosity toward her friend, Zita made a rude gesture at him. "The DMS guy, Parzarri, was on the joint task force investigating Sobek when my brother got kidnapped. He's the drug cop that claimed Quentin was a dealer who pissed off his boss."

Wyn groaned.

Honesty propelled Zita to admit her own contribution. "I maybe let him know what I thought when he badmouthed my brother, and we haven't gotten along since."

Andy whistled. "Nice to see you can change up your game and aggravate them without dating them first."

Zita rolled her eyes. "Anyway, Jerome hasn't found anything either for all his computer games. All of Sobek's known bank accounts are frozen, and nobody's even tried to touch them that he could find. Whatever Sobek's up to, he's keeping himself below the radar. I tried Hound, but he and his partner were tied up with missing kid cases and couldn't help, though he said he'd talk to some contacts to see if they knew anything."

"You're not thinking he's going to call in those mercenaries?" Wyn wrinkled her nose.

Zita hummed for a moment as she considered it, then grunted. "Sadly, no. Investigating seems like something they'd farm out to Hound."

Andy eyed her over the rim of his cup. "Sadly?"

"She means happily," Wyn corrected. "Though if you meant what you said, you can handle the android with all the guns. Kodiak or Vaudeville are personable enough, but Freelance is creepy."

A grin slipped out, and Zita flexed her fingers. *I'd like to handle him, all right. And his grapple gun. Oye, maybe one in each hand?*

Whether Wyn was cheating and skimming Zita's mind or just reading her expression, her friend made a moue of distaste. "Ugh. No wonder your brothers have to pick dates for you. You have the worst taste in men."

Zita shrugged. "Do not. Why does not sensing his mind bother you when you went your whole life before without being able to pull that trick? You healed the guy, so you know he's not a robot. He's just a dude who sneaks around all competent and sexy and with the sweetest toys."

"How can you drool over him like that?" Wyn's headshake was so violent her curls bounced.

Hoping to end the discussion, Zita kept her tone light. "Have you seen the man? At least give him respect for all the hard work that went into that fine body."

Her friend wouldn't let it go, setting down her teacup with enough force to make the china clink. "He is a murderer."

Zita could feel herself sweating as she struggled to find the right words without touching on parts of Wyn's past she knew the other woman wouldn't want to dwell on. "There's worse. Sometimes violence is necessary, even killing. I know your religion doesn't let you do violence with magic, but you clobbered that drug dude just fine with the pan when you had to. Andy and I have been in a bunch of fights. Are the three of us bad?"

Wyn's chin jutted out. "No, those were all justified—we were saving people, and we don't kill. Mercenaries kill for money."

*She killed someone once in self-defense...she doesn't remember or doesn't want to? I'm not going to remind either of them of their accidental kills when we first found our abilities. Her Southern accent has already gotten stronger, and that's one of her tells when she's upset.* Biting her tongue to keep the words from escaping, Zita lined up her words like soldiers. "I agree it shouldn't be done lightly.

We're lucky our powers give us the option not to kill. Not everybody has that choice. My brothers are both veterans. Are they murderers?"

Andy slurped his hot chocolate. "Danger, danger, Will Robinson," he muttered. When the women turned their attention to him, he eyed his feet. "Don't mind me. I'm just having cocoa, thinking about classic sci-fi, and not getting involved in any way, shape, or form."

Wyn returned her focus to Zita and began her protest. "No, but that's different. Military service—"

Zita exhaled. *Logic. Wyn likes logic and truth and sharing squishy feelings stuff.* "My brothers joined the military because that was their best chance to get a foot up and out of where we were." She squelched her own guilt, knowing her youthful cancer had made the military a necessity rather than an option for Miguel.

Before Wyn could protest, Zita continued, "Not that they didn't want to defend our country, too, but they wouldn't have done it for free. I don't know if all the mercenaries' kills have been fair ones, but at least they have a policy of avoiding collateral damage. They stepped up to stop people from getting slaughtered in Brazil and at the New York museum. The sniper you hate went out of his way to help that old guide escape in Brazil. I'll give them the benefit of the doubt for now."

Distress radiated from Wyn's face and body. "Still, I don't see how you can salivate over the man."

Zita patted her shoulder. "No hay bronca, amiga. He's hot. That's all. I'm not dating the guy, and nothing's ever going to happen, any more than with Bruce Lee, Eduard Folayang, or Cesar Millan. Who knows if we'll ever see them again anyway? If we do, hopefully, we can all play nice, and I'll just be subtle, so he doesn't catch on and feel uncomfortable."

"You, subtle?" Andy blurted. "Never mind, I'm not here."

Wyn blinked at her. "Are we talking about the same frightening individual?"

Zita waved her hand. "He's still a person who might be uncomfortable at some stranger admiring his fine self. When we hiked back from the temple, his quiet was relaxing." She cut herself off before she said the rest of the thought. *All I had to do was not get eaten by a dinosaur and keep a few million secrets. It was nice not to worry about saying the right thing all the time to avoid upsetting friends or family or people who give me paychecks. Like right now. I'd rather find a path through a literal chingado minefield than distress Wyn.*

Andy gave a half-smile and offered her a way out. "Fewer expectations?"

Seizing on the opportunity, Zita made a face at him. "Look at you, all psychoanalyzing and shit. Is that what happens when you have a doctorate in physics these days?"

He wrinkled his nose at her and stuck out his tongue.

Wyn's tone softened. "I'd hope you don't include us in the list of people you can't talk freely around. Most people use the Internet if they want to speak without fear or repercussions."

"The Internet doesn't have a fine culo to look at while chatting," Zita said. *It's way too late, and I'm too tired for this conversation.*

"Why don't we just abandon this incredibly uncomfortable discussion and get back to the Sobek business?" Andy said, somewhat desperately. "Could he be dead?"

Zita barked out a laugh. "I doubt it. Sobek's extra tough and strong, in addition to being able to hold his breath for a long time. Quentin's shot hit his torso, but Sobek's big and it could've missed anything vital, or he could've gotten help under an alias, which is my guess. He was drug lord enough for the DEA to be in the original task force, so an underground doctor makes sense."

"I concur that he could locate medical aid, but we have to consider that his wound might've proved fatal." Wyn sipped at her tea, an odd expression on her face.

Watching her friend, Zita worried she'd made a misstep for a moment before plowing on. "Considered and rejected. The cops aren't taking it seriously, but Quentin and I have both been getting blank 'Thinking of You' and condolence greeting cards in the mail. I can smell Sobek's hands all over them."

Wyn still seemed dubious. "It's odd, but it might be someone else doing it."

Zita grunted. "I can literally smell his nasty ass on the paper, but I can't tell the cops that. I'm not going to risk Sobek harming my brother or those around me again. Everyone else has given up, so I need to step up and handle it."

Brown eyes wary, Andy said, "How are you planning to do that?"

She lifted her hands in the air. "Find him and hand him over to the cops again. Being locked up is far worse than death, and my family needs to be safe. He ran his kidnappings out of that nightclub, so I'm hoping to get some tips when we go check on old Dmitri from the tracks. Maybe he'll know something. It'll be a late night tomorrow. You want to come with, mano?" Zita paced.

Andy coughed. "I'm...I've got plans to hang with another meta and talk about living with super strength, but if you need me at the club, I can cancel."

Zita beamed, glad he'd found someone to commiserate with. "Who? Do I know him?"

"Just someone I met. Nobody important, but they haven't had another meta to talk to either..." Picking up his mug, Andy chugged the remains of his hot chocolate and scurried into the kitchen.

Wyn leaned forward, watching him go, then sat back. Blinking, she sat very straight and shot Zita an unreadable look. "The friend doesn't matter. We're both happy you found a sympathetic ear on the subject. Aren't we, Zita? I'm certain the two of us can handle talking to an elderly man without you." Her shark-like smile and narrowed eyes told Zita what her answer should be.

"Yes, very happy, practically orgasmic," Zita said.

"Not comfortable with you using that word around me," Andy called out.

She waved her hand, dismissing his comment. "We got this. Wyn and I will go see if the guy's okay. He wanted to meet at Danz Mizer, so we can hit up the bar employees too while we're there and see if anyone at the club can point us in Sobek's direction. If Dmitri loses it and gives us trouble, he was in rough enough shape that even Wyn could take him. Pan comido."

In the kitchen doorway, Andy winced as he returned. "I wish you wouldn't say that. It always goes badly for us."

Wyn seemed very interested in her teacup, tilting it back and forth.

Unease spread in Zita's mind, and she ran through everything she could remember saying or thinking. Her voice more tentative than she would have liked, she said, "Wyn? You okay? You've got that expression which means something is bothering you."

When Wyn's gaze lifted from her cup, she still did not meet Zita's eyes. "I think you should be prepared to not find anything. After yoga with you last Saturday, I tried a tracking spell on Sobek."

"You can do that?" Zita said, rising to her feet as excitement escalated.

Andy just nodded.

Wyn bit her lip. "Yes. It seemed like it would be a useful spell, given my aunt's Alzheimer's. I've gotten it to work with either a full name or something of theirs, preferably both. Hair or an actual part of the body would work best."

Setting down her food and drink, Zita bounded over to her friend and squeezed her shoulder in excitement. "Why didn't you tell me you know where Sobek is? We can go there, confirm his exact location, call in a tip, and get that pinche pendejo put in jail for the rest of his life! We don't even need to bug the old guy at the club." She broke out in a broad smile.

Wyn lifted her gaze to meet Zita's. "I don't know where Sobek is. The spell failed. I've only used it on living people before, but death might explain the odd results. It should've given me a location and allowed me to track him. However, while I could see the magic working, it never showed anything. It's possible I got his name wrong from the news, but they seem to be consistent, so the only thing I can think of is that he's dead."

"Maybe it was the spell. Have you used it before?" Zita said.

Her friend avoided her eyes. "Yes, the spell works. I've tracked my aunt, my cats, and a... few other people."

Oddly, Andy seemed immersed in studying the drapes covering the window.

Suspicion rose, but Zita couldn't figure out why her internal alarms were ringing. She flexed her shoulders. "Sobek's a meta. Maybe you need to adjust it to work on a metahuman."

Wyn licked her lips and removed a small flask from her purse. She poured a generous dollop into her teacup. "I've tracked a meta." Her eyes darted to Zita and then away.

The scent of alcohol in the cup stung Zita's sensitive nose, and realization hit. "Wait. You been tracking me? What the fuck, Wyn?"

Her gentle friend's hands tightened on her cup. "One of the times you were hurt, back when we were having issues, I may have appropriated a little bit of a bloody bandage. I just wanted... I wanted to be able to find you if you needed help. We've sorted all that out though, and I haven't used it on you since then."

Andy still seemed far too interested in the curtains and was biting his lip. His shoulders were braced, and his hands were buried in his pockets.

Zita narrowed her eyes, her mind working. "You knew? Mano!"

He flinched, his face sheepish. "Yes. Sort of. I mean... I saw her take the bandage, and she said what she was using it for. We were worried you were going to get yourself killed and we wouldn't be able to save you in time. I told her she should ask you and work things out. I really did."

Turning her head toward the other woman, Zita demanded, "Do you have something to help you find Andy?"

That got Andy to stop staring at the carpet. His eyes wide, he stared at the witch, his face pale.

Wyn pursed her lips. "No. He's nearly invulnerable, so the odds of him requiring my aid are low."

Andy's shoulders relaxed, and his breath was audible as tension left him.

"I notice you're not as blasé about spells on you, mano. You two know I'm not helpless, right? And I should get the same rights as other people?" Zita shouted, her anger getting the better of her.

His shoulders drooped. "You're right. I'm sorry."

Switching her attention back to Wyn, Zita took a moment to regain control. Her voice still held an edge when she spoke again. "Are there any other invasions of my privacy I should know about? Not that I'm ashamed of anything I've been doing, but I'd like to know now so I can digest it all at once."

Wyn's hands trembled, and her face was red. "No. I'm sorry. It seemed harmless, and I didn't intend any wrong..."

Zita folded her arms over her chest. "You knew it was wrong or you wouldn't be so embarrassed. If you'd asked, I might've given you something, something without my blood." She struggled to keep from saying more. *They meant well*, she reminded herself.

Wrapping her arms around herself, Wyn rocked on the couch. "I was wrong. I'm sorry. I didn't mean any harm, and I only checked on you once. It was before that big talk we had at the museum, and I haven't tracked you since, I swear. I've been respecting your privacy."

"I'm sorry too, Z. I should've stopped her or said something," Andy said.

Running a hand over her short hair, back and forth, Zita inhaled, forcing her breath into a regular pattern. "You know, I'm tired and mad at both of you. I'll forgive you tomorrow, but I got to get some space. Wyn, you still in for the club?"

"Yes, and for what it's worth, I'm sorry." Wyn rose and hugged her.

After thumping her friend gently on the back, Zita released her. "I know. My family would pull the same shit if they could. I just need breathing room. You want a teleport back, mano?"

Andy stared out the window, and his eyes glowed white. "I'll fly back as me."

Zita nodded. A thump caught her attention, and she glanced down.

Her empty bowl rolled on the carpet, and the cats licked their whiskers, looking smug. They smelled like tuna.

She swore.

# Chapter Six

**The biggest problem with questioning people** at the Danz Mizer nightclub was that nobody would let Zita in.

Grumbling under her breath and wearing her Arca form, Zita jiggled her leg and scanned the street again. While the streetlamps seemed anemic, a flashing neon sign, a billboard atop the club, and a strobe light nearby provided sufficient illumination to see. Little had changed from the last time she'd seen the two-story club in the summer, other than the beefy no-neck bouncer now wore a black jacket with the club's logo instead of just a t-shirt. Several partiers wobbled in the long entry line or minced their way down the sidewalk, trying to avoid icy patches and the dirty gray snow lining the street. Despite the wide variety of coats on display, most were open to show off the tight clothes beneath.

Zita was the only one shivering in her Spandex-like costume and hooded sweatshirt. Burrowing her hands into her pockets, she touched the comforting weight of trail mix and the phone she'd designated for vigilante-related calls.

Beside her, a fit, bald man smiled, sympathy in the expression. "Friend running late still?" He had the broad-shouldered, toned build of a serious swimmer and held his body in a relaxed, loose position, except for his face, which he kept slightly turned away. His bomber jacket yawned open from where he'd tried to offer it to her earlier.

"I have no idea why. She was pretty much ready when I spoke to her earlier," Zita replied. Perhaps because she always used it when she wore the Arca shape, her words held the music of her fake Mexican accent without her needing to consciously add it. *If you're covered in an illusion anyway, why take the time to dress and do makeup? If I weren't waiting for her to join me, I would've just snuck in. Then again, if I'd done that, I might not have been able to talk diving with Ben here.* She stole another glance at him, admiring the defined chest outlined by a form-fitting shirt.

"Do you think she's okay?" His brow furrowed.

*One good thing about being friends with a telepath is you can always hear her when she shouts for help.* Zita nodded and sighed. "She's just taking her own sweet time, I guess. So, we've both dived in the same cenotes in the Riviera Maya. Do you rock climb as well as dive?"

Ben shook his head. Light caught the side of his face that he'd had turned away, glancing off a wide, raised burn scar that ran from his ear and cheekbone down his neck. "No."

She forgot about the scar almost as quickly as she'd seen it, but her interest fizzled at his words. *Oye, nobody's perfect. I can't expect him to share all my interests.*

"I'd like to try it though," he continued. "It seems like it could be fun, and diving isn't the challenge it used to be."

It was her turn to tilt her head as her hormones surged back to life. "Why's that?"

He shuffled in place, his hands flexing. Finally, he answered, "For full disclosure, I'm a meta. I can breathe underwater, and the cold and pressure don't bother me. It's actually useful since I'm an inland diver, which means I fix or find stuff underwater professionally. My work's great, but sometimes I like a challenge."

*I wonder what qualifications I'd need to get that job? It might hold my interest more than translating tax forms or locksmithing.* Zita grinned at him. "That's one of the better abilities I've heard.

Theoretically, my friend should get here anytime, so I'll just ask now if you want to get together sometime? Maybe go rock climbing, and I could show you the ropes?"

He blinked twice, and his smile returned.

A second later, she realized how he could take that and specified, "The ropes for climbing. Not kinky ones." Her ears burned. *Smooth as usual, Zita.*

Ben grinned wider, and years fell away from his face, making him look closer to her age than the five to ten years older she'd originally guessed. "Sounds good. Let me give you my number. What should I call you?"

"Arca. Give me a sec," she said, her smile spreading as she dug in her sweatshirt pocket for her vigilante cell phone. *Sweet! Maybe my luck with guys is changing.*

Wyn emerged from a cab, her Muse illusion firmly in place. Her friend waved gaily, then paused to pay the driver. Picking her way carefully over the terrain, she headed toward the pair.

"Oh, hey, there's my friend. I've got to go with her to talk to someone about this thing we're looking into, but first, let me get your info." Zita held up a hand in a quick wave and glanced at her companion as she flipped her phone open.

Ben had lost his smile.

"Dude, what's up?" she said. Tension crept through her, and she scanned the area for obvious threats. Her body moved, turning sideways to present less of a target. *Seems safe enough.*

He rubbed his head and frowned at the sidewalk. "I'm going to hate myself in the morning. Listen, you're the real Arca, aren't you? I thought you were just playing dress up, but then I saw your friend. She's kind of unmistakable."

Zita glanced at the ghostly blond woman in a short, shiny silver dress that exposed her slender arms and miles of leg. She smiled. "Muse is like that. We try not to hold it against her. Sí, I'm the real Arca. What about it?"

His words slow, Ben said, "Yeah, I'm sorry, but I thought you were just dressed up like Arca, not actually her. A date's a bad idea—I work for the police, and you're a vigilante. You seem great, but I'm going to have to bow out."

She straightened up to her full five feet of height and held her smile by force of will. Her leg jiggled as she shoved down the familiar disappointment. *Probably wouldn't have worked out anyway.* "I get it. Respect for telling me straight out and not trying to get into my pants first."

He shrugged. "I try not to be a dick. Sorry."

Zita offered him her hand and forced herself to keep smiling. "I understand. We're cool, hombre."

Ben smiled weakly and shook once, his hand hot and dry against her skin. "Thanks. I think I'll get my pal and see if I can stop him from doing anything stupid. My phone keeps sending me winter storm alerts too." He scurried toward another man.

She watched him go, letting her face relax into its normal expression. *Ah well. No real loss. It definitely wouldn't have worked.*

Wyn glided over. "Where did your friend go and why were you baring your teeth at him that way?"

"His buddy needed him. You ready?" Zita shrugged and headed toward the door.

Licking her lips, Wyn eyed the entrance. "Yes, work was tedious and annoying. I'm so ready for a drink and maybe a little dancing."

Zita stopped and tilted her head at her friend. "We're here to question people about Sobek, not party."

Wyn peered at Zita through thick eyelashes, her eyes intent and a stubborn expression on her face. Her elegant hands curled into fists. and her whole body was tight. "Yes, and once that's done, there's no reason we can't blow off steam for a few minutes. Have I mentioned recently the amount of overtime I've been working or the fact that my parents haven't dropped the lawsuit against me yet so they can throw my aunt to the wolves and use her money to fund offensive protests? Not to mention the fact that my two best friends and I regularly endanger our lives and freedom?"

With that, Zita exhaled and glanced away, wistfully abandoning her plans to go home and sleep as soon as the talking was done. "Fine. But remember the rules. Never drink anything you don't open yourself. You know I'm available if you ever want to work out some of that stress with exercise." Her tone may have been gruffer than intended.

Her friend beamed, her muscles untensing. "Yes, Mother. I recall the last time I invited you to go clubbing, so I came prepared. Hold out your hand."

Not bothering to hide her dubious expression, Zita complied.

Wyn withdrew a small crystal obelisk from her purse, like a tiny purple Washington Monument, and dropped it into Zita's hand. A thick silk thread hung from the stone. "See this? This amethyst will instantly sober up anyone who touches it, so you hang onto it. If you have any concerns about a spiked drink, you can tap yourself or me with it, and it'll clear up any alcohol or drugs in our systems. The enchantment's only good until sunrise, but I assumed that would be sufficient for our purposes."

After accepting it, Zita's shoulders relaxed, and she tucked it away in a pocket. "Thank you." *Not that I'm going to be any less alert until she's home safe. Nobody's victimizing my friend if I can help it. She's been through enough.*

Tilting her head, Wyn said, "You're going to tell me why you're so paranoid about people dosing drinks sometime, right?"

After a moment of wondering if her friend was stealing peeks into her mind again, Zita harrumphed. "Yes, but not right now. I'm freezing. You think you can get us into the club, or should I pick our way in around back? For some reason, the bouncer said I wasn't dressed right." She wrinkled her nose and glowered at club security. Since her last unsuccessful attempt to get inside, a second security person had shuffled out to join the first. While the first one interacted with a gaggle of college girls, the new one, a short, thick-set woman with a small head, bristly hair, and an unfriendly expression in her beady eyes, glared impartially at everyone.

Wyn laughed, a musical, lilting sound that had people nearby smiling involuntarily. Even the surly new guard lightened her expression. "I am shocked and appalled by their excellent judgment, but yes, I can get us in." She regarded the bouncers, and her lips tilted upward as she sauntered toward the front of the line, her hips swinging.

A second later, Zita jolted into action and scurried after the taller woman. "You know you suck, right?"

*** 

The bouncers let them in.

The first floor held a coat check and restroom, followed by a dance floor with a bar and glassed-in DJ booth on the far wall. A door that led to the kitchen sheltered beneath an ornate, sweeping wooden staircase next to the bar. All other sides were lined with tables and chairs and had full-length gold-framed mirrors that seemed to vibrate with the colors of the dancers' clothing. Indirect lighting and the warmth of so many bodies gave everything a dreamlike feel. People moved and throbbed in a choking cloud of artificial fragrance, sweat, and alcohol, spiked with the scent of the fake fog that spilled out around the DJ booth.

With a few words and a flutter of the witch's eyelashes, Wyn and Zita were through the velvet rope closing off the staircase and up to the VIP area, which took up most of the second floor. Built like a long square balcony floating above the dance floor, it had a collection of small tables and luxurious booths on three sides. The fourth held another lengthy mirror and a polished bar, behind which the requisite bartender stood. Hanging from the ceiling in the center of the room, a chandelier the size of a table sparkled like a thousand tiny suns or disco balls, as light reflected from the crystal drops hanging from tiny crimson ropes. Here, rather than gathering as a massive horde, patrons clustered in small groups around the seating, and conversation hummed under the music from below.

"How about one of those booths?" Wyn said, collecting a drink from the bar and sipping. After making a pleased noise, she said, "The bartender said he'd let Dmitri know we were here." She led the way toward a booth.

Zita grumbled and followed.

Then the waiting began.

"Arca, stop fidgeting. It's only been about fifteen minutes," Wyn said, using Zita's vigilante name with only the slightest pause. "I told you that you should've ordered something." Her lips curled into a slight smile as she lifted her drink, a concoction that varied in shade from deep purple to pale lavender. She laughed. The amethyst eyes of her illusory form sparkled. Unlike Zita, she relaxed back in her seat in their corner booth, stroking the velvety fabric of the curtain that half-hid their table. "More clubs should have these curtains. They add such a lovely, dramatic feeling and a bit of privacy. The VIP section was nice before, but it's even better now."

*She's just happy that fewer people can stare at her since we pulled the curtain. While I've told her that she's more attractive as herself, the ice queen look seems to work for most people. Would the illusion update if she actually followed one of the exercise regimens I've given her to reflect more toned muscles?* Zita yanked her mind away from designing another workout for her friend; it was probably a waste of time though it had to be more interesting than a sitting around. "You know I don't drink. Did you order that because it matches your... well, Muse's eyes?" She scrutinized her friend's drink with no enthusiasm.

Wyn sucked a strawberry off the end of the weird fruit kabob decorating her drink and pointed the little plastic sword at her. "Telling would be cheating. You'll have to determine that for yourself. So, why are you so prickly about drinking in clubs? You don't seem upset when people drink at home. You even have a box of liquid impersonating wine in your refrigerator for me." Discreetly, she checked her phone.

Zita watched a pair of people cavorting below and gave the easy answer. "I have a fast metabolism, I'm five foot nothing, and drinking prevents any of the most fun workouts, like the aerial stuff or climbing."

Her friend dissolved into giggles. "Bless your heart, you're a lightweight, and it cuts into your exercise routine."

Grunting, Zita agreed. "You say that like it's a bad thing. It isn't. It just is."

Wyn sobered and circled the rim of her glass with an elegant finger. Her words dragged out of her. "That only answers why you don't drink. What's the story on your dislike of drinking any beverages at bars? Drinking only unopened bottles of nonalcoholic beverages is overkill."

"Not if it's justified," Zita said. She concentrated on holding her shoulders straight. *Where is that Dmitri guy?*

Wyn pursed her lips. "Normally, I'd insist it was paranoia, but..." Her face softened, and silver gleamed at the corners of her eyes. "It happened to you? I'm so sorry."

Zita looked away for a minute, and when she spoke again, she was gruff. "No hay bronca. I got away before he could do anything and then passed out in a bullet ant nest. Whoever it was didn't want me bad enough to risk getting stung by the whole colony. Those things can take you down fast." She brushed at her arms a couple times before she caught herself and stopped.

Wyn's eyes were very wide. "Bullet ants? Were those the ones with the very painful stings you warned us about when we were in Brazil?"

She nodded. "Sí. The ants got me a bunch of times, but since I wasn't moving, most ignored me. I was out for hours, which was a blessing. Once the drugs wore off, though, I was in a lot of pain and partially paralyzed."

"Paralyzed? You hate being restrained. Always have." Her friend winced.

Squaring her shoulders, Zita shrugged and tried to seem nonchalant. "It wore off." After she opened the curtain, she checked for the old man they were supposed to meet, then let it fall closed again.

With a deep breath, Wyn said, "That's terrible, but at least he didn't..." She ducked her head, hiding her face for a moment behind a veil of silvery hair.

Zita offered her a half-smile, paused, then reached over to squeeze her friend's upper arm.

"How did you get out of the nest?" Wyn's hands pressed flat on the table.

Her mouth was dry after the retelling, and Zita considered ordering a bottle of water, then reconsidered given the probable price tag. "A few locals lifted me out, and one nursed me until I was back on my feet. Remedies for bullet ant bites are pretty common there, but I was shaking for days thanks to the bites. Lost the job."

Wyn winced though her customary composure seemed to be restored. "Ugh, that sounds dreadful."

Zita shook her head. "My nurse and I got to be friends so I hung out in Brazil awhile afterward. Avoided those nests though."

Wyn smiled, though it was shaky. "That's a nice ending. Do you keep in touch with her?"

Now Zita wished she did drink since their conversation had veered further into territory she didn't want to talk about. "No. I wonder where that Dmitri is?" *I hope he didn't die because he insisted on wandering off without letting me get him help. Why did I walk away? That's not like me.*

Tucking a curl behind her ear, Wyn said quietly, "New leaf. It's a simple question, and it can't be any worse than what you've already told me."

With a deep inhale, Zita mentally wished she'd put more limits on the promise to share more. "She was the friend that you remind me of, the one who died. When she died, the rest of her tribe banned me as major bad luck. Anyway, I don't drink anything but bottled stuff in bars and nightclubs unless I see them make it and never let it leave my hand. You shouldn't either."

Her friend didn't seem to know what to say about that, and took a slow pull of her purple concoction, her eyes downcast. After a slight pause, she gulped more.

Squirming at her friend's slumped, tense posture, Zita tried for a joke. "Órale, it's for the best. I can't afford no prices at a place like this anyway, and I don't think these people are ready to hear me talking drunk."

After a moment, Wyn smiled, leaned forward, and squeezed Zita's arm. "True. If your usual speech is you filtering your commentary, the world is unready to hear the truth unfettered and quite so real."

"You know it." Zita stuck her head out and scanned the room for Dmitri again.

Eerie music still played, unearthly voices rising over pulsing electronic beats. Fog rose from the base of the bar, spilling out and over the floor before sneaking under the railing to cascade down toward the first floor. Robust railings, chest-high even on tall people like Wyn, allowed the VIP patrons to watch dancing partiers in the more conventional club below without risking a fall. Although this section was not crowded, it was still busy with people dressed in a variety of shades of black, with the occasional jewel tone to break up the monotony. The deep plum of her sportswear and dyed-to-match dollar store sneakers fit the color scheme, though she had none of the requisite embellishments adorning anything. While she had no problem with most of the outfits, a few seemed particularly impractical. "Is that clothing or duct tape on that guy? We're certain this is a dance club, not a weird bondage place, right?"

Wyn shrugged, her body uncurling and shoulders straightening. "Does it matter? The gentleman behind the bar said he'd send Dmitri our way once he arrived."

"Not helping." She went back to scowling at the increasingly drunken crowd.

Wyn hummed a little. "Perhaps I should order another of these. I won't object if you want to observe them making it this time."

Squinting at her friend, Zita noted the rosy tinge in her cheeks. *The illusion changes to reflect the woman beneath, without changing the face or outfit.* "That's your second... purple drink. Are you drunk while we're on an information-gathering mission?"

"I'm not drunk, just warm. Is it really a mission? It seems more like a long shot than anything. What are the odds that the old guy you rescued will show up here, especially if he's half dead?" Wyn read a text on her phone and giggled.

*Definitely tipsy.* Zita palmed the magic rock, rubbing the soft thread of the necklace in her fingers. She folded her arms across her generous chest and wrinkled her nose at her friend. "Seriously? I'm sorry, how is hunting the psycho who wants to torture me and my family to death a waste of time? Sobek used this club for drugs and human trafficking. Why is it a long shot that the current owner and employees or a regular might know something about his whereabouts?"

Her friend held up a hand. "Whoa, I'm sorry. I didn't mean to imply finding Sobek's a bad cause. That's fine. I'm simply pointing out the reality that if anyone here knew anything useful, they would've told the authorities during the investigation here last year."

"Maybe they were too afraid to tell the cops. The guy I rescued might be the janitor, and maybe he'll help. Cleaning staff knows all the dirty secrets." For a moment, Zita wished Andy could've come with them, knowing he would've appreciated the joke about the janitor. *At least one of us will get to relax tonight. Maybe he'll spar with his super-strong friend or do something else fun.*

"One can hardly blame anyone for failing to be enthused about introducing themselves to masked vigilantes, especially if you were your usual self when you asked to meet earlier," Wyn said, taking another sip. She leaned out to peek around the scarlet veil of the curtain. Her friend laughed at something, a sound like silver bells chiming, and her lashes drooped over her eyes.

Zita touched the crystal to Wyn's hand.

Her friend's eyes shot open, and she pouted. "That was completely unnecessary. I was just relaxing, for once."

The music stopped.

Zita found herself crouching in a ready position on the bench seat as she tucked the stone away. "Hear that?" she whispered.

"No," Wyn said, drawing back the curtain.

A second later, a different, peppy song about a monster mash rang through the club. The DJ's voice, amplified by the sound system, broke in. "Ladies and Gentlemen, Dmitri Tepes, the Dark Prince of D.C., is among us!" Some of the crowd cheered. The visible club patrons resumed their previous activities.

"Oh." Zita let herself drop back into the seat. "I guess it won't be a fight. At least we know he's here, but what's with the silly title?"

Wyn shook her head. "You're the only person I know who's crestfallen when there isn't danger." She took a swig of her drink, her eyes daring Zita to say something about it.

Zita sank back into a welter of silent impatience.

"You sought Dmitri? You have found him," came an amused baritone, a heavy Eastern European accent dripping from the words.

Wyn squeaked, fumbling her glass, and seized Zita's arm.

Less surprised, Zita turned as well. Something tickled her sensitive nose, and she wrinkled it as new scents joined the overload of the club. *Dead thing, not quite right, incense, cologne, and makeup.*

A man stood at the far side of their booth, by the section of the bench that had been empty. A single spotlight shone on him, and then it faded out until the booth returned to the dimness of the rest of the club. Slim and lithe, he lounged for a moment, allowing them to get a good look before he sat across from them and closed the curtains. His silky shirt stretched across a defined chest and flirted with well-developed biceps, before tapering to a narrow waist and pants of plum purple. He wore a floor-length black cape that flared with every movement and had a silly high collar framing a striking face decorated with dramatic cheekbones and sparkly eyeliner. "My savior! And you brought a friend! How lovely. Dmitri is delighted to make both of your acquaintances."

Zita approved of his shape; his musculature complimented his physique, underscoring the benefits of a finer build without bulking up into caricature or seeming weak. His movements, though graceful, lacked any of the patterns she would expect in someone that perfectly fit. She frowned, disturbed by the niggling sense of wrongness about him. His body was too still. "You got better."

"Perhaps I was merely pining for the fjords?" he offered with a expectant grin.

While she recognized the expression as one she'd seen on others' faces after a reference she failed to get, Zita didn't know what to say. "Fjords?"

Wyn slanted an accusing glance at her. *I thought you said the man at the railroad tracks was a hideous old man and might die before we met? I may have to hate him though. I can't do smoky eye makeup that well.* Aloud, she smiled at the so-called Prince of D.C. and said, "Delighted to meet you. Do we need to call you by your title?"

He winced, and a fang peeked out as his mouth turned down. "No, please do not. It's a conceit of the club owner to have me introduced that way. Even if it were not, neither of you would fall under my jurisdiction, so to speak."

*I did say he had creepy fangs, but now that he's healed, it's more than just his teeth. Maybe it's all part of his meta power? He did seem less concerned about what should've been a fatal injury than I expected, and he doesn't stand like a martial artist or dancer, but he's got the body of one. His fitness might be an aspect of his powers.* Zita concentrated on remembering Dmitri as she'd seen him at the railroad tracks and sent the image to her friend. "I guess you weren't kidding about not needing a healer. So, what are you?"

Wyn flinched, instinctively drawing away. After a moment, her body uncoiled. *Oh, disgusting. It's amazing that he survived! Though I do have to wonder, Zita, why you bothered to check the derriere of someone who looked like that.*

*Habit,* Zita sent back.

Dmitri tucked a strand of his shoulder-length hair behind an ear. "I'm merely a friend of the owner and a frequent patron here."

The women glanced at each other.

*He still might be useful if he's a regular,* Zita sent. She sniffed the air and watched him, trying to figure out what bothered her. The dim lighting didn't help. *No sweat or food odors or anything like that on him.*

Dmitri eyed her. "If your question was the baser sort, yes, I am a vampire. Perhaps I could wear the more classic tuxedo to assist in identification, but that does restrict one. No, I am not planning to dine on either of you and no, my teeth do not come out."

Distracted for a moment, Zita said, "Do people actually ask you to take your teeth out?"

Running his tongue over the fangs, he nodded.

Doubt mingled with curiosity from Wyn's half of the mental connection. "So how did you survive all that? It must've been traumatic, especially in the daytime."

His tone flat, Dmitri said, "It was torture." After a second, he flashed a smile, and his voice lightened to its original soothing music. "It was only my enormous strength and the terrible vampire puns that enabled me to survive the ordeal. Arca set the jokes up so beautifully, it would've been a sin against my nature, perhaps even my soul, not to respond. You have saved my life, and I thank you." He touched his fingers to his forehead and then tipped his hand toward Zita.

She shrugged. "No big. Why would they do that to you?" *Other than the creepy undead thing. I get it now. He doesn't breathe unless he's talking, and he smells...off. Dead, but not.*

He raised his hands. "As far as what they wanted, I do not know. I was sleeping at my friend's home, and when I awakened, they were doing rude things like staking me. When they could not rip my head off, and my friend lacked any cleavers, they stuffed me into an odoriferous and poorly appointed trunk. Now," the vampire said, "did you require anything else? If you have come for my charming conversation, I can indulge you for a time, but I do have obligations this evening. Such things come with being the heir to an imaginary throne as you might guess."

Wyn tugged on a lock of her hair and stared at the table. "We're looking for a man..." She paused.

Dmitri pursed his lips, then gave a grin, his fangs flashing. "I'm flattered, but I prefer to get to know my partners first."

Zita made a disdainful sound. "Gross."

"And now I am less flattered. Who is this lucky or unlucky man you seek?" Dmitri laid his hands flat on the table.

After a deep breath, Wyn held out her hand, palm upward. A small illusion of Sobek appeared.

Dmitri hissed, his fingers arching into claws for a second before he recovered. His mouth tight, he leaned away. "I have seen enough. Put him away. You seek drugs? They are not sold here."

The illusion winked out.

Zita shook her head and shoved the long hair of her disguise out of her face and over her shoulder. "No! We're trying to catch him. He's not just a drug dealer. He's a sadist who uses drugs to bankroll his hobby of kidnapping people and torturing them to death while their loved ones watch."

Wyn made a face. "Then he tortures the watcher to death and leaves the corpses in public places. Additionally, he kidnapped metahumans for a while and sold them while trying to join up with a terrorist gang."

Zita took up the thread. "DMS had him, but he escaped in October. The cops think he died, but nobody's found his body."

Dmitri crossed his arms over his chest, glaring stonily at the curtains. He withdrew a phone and texted, barely glancing at it as he stabbed at the screen. "Quite the criminal resumé. I asked Danz Mizer's owner to join us if she's here. Your Sobek is neither dead nor undead... yet."

"What?" Zita and Wyn chorused.

"He was here a night or two before my adventure with you at the train tracks. Had I known of his depravity, I would have summoned the police," Dmitri said. "And we have a very big problem." His full lips drew down into a scowl.

Torn between being happy about being right and being disappointed that Sobek was still a threat, Zita tensed at the vampire's bad mood. She moved closer to her friend so she could shield Wyn, angling her body to fight if he attacked. "What's that, besides the confirmation that he's alive?"

Dmitri glared out into the club, his skin somehow paler and his expression flat and lifeless. Red flared within his eyes. "It all makes sense now. The attack on me must've been because I told the others... someone must've warned him." He seemed to notice Zita's posture and shook his head. "I am no threat to you."

"Warned him about what? That's a pretty good murder face you got going on right now, just saying," Zita said.

The vampire sighed and massaged his forehead. "Someone strong enough to make progeny—a rare ability—has been feeding him their blood. He's had enough of it..." When he opened his eyes again, they had returned to normal.

Zita waved her hand. "Can you lose the dramatic pauses and finish the sentence?"

With a curt nod, Dmitri continued, "If he has much more blood or dies, he will become a vampire. While I can't tell exactly without meeting whoever was foolish enough to give blood to a metahuman, he may be able to break away from their guardianship. If he is the man you say, vampiric hunger will only augment his current bloodlust. Not to mention, he may be able to make more if he's powerful enough. Fledglings made by a madman would be a recipe for disaster."

Wyn went pale and gulped her drink. "Could you be wrong?"

Dmitri shook his head. "I'm a savant of sorts. One of my abilities allows me to know all undead, at least vampiric ones, when I see them. I know their strengths, weaknesses, powers, et cetera." He waved his hand.

Zita swore in a few different languages, her body going cold. *My family. Dios, protect them if Sobek gets even more powerful. I told everyone he wasn't dead, but the biggest danger comes if he is dead. Undead. Whatever.*

*We'll catch him,* Wyn promised silently. Waves of reassurance came through the link.

*It'll be a lot harder if he's some kind of unnatural walking dead,*
Zita groused mentally.

When her audible cursing subsided, Dmitri picked up the
conversational thread again. "Right now, he's under his maker's
thrall. I sensed their control over him, but I do not know what they
are compelling him to do. Given all that, I will help you find him.
The more monstrous metahumans will only speak to their own,
and I have met most of the locals. We have something of a
reputation as a haven here."

Sympathy welling in her eyes, Wyn covered his pale hand with
one of her own. "You're not a monster."

Zita cleared her throat and tried to explain. "He's dead like a
ghost, but solid and with fangs and he eats people. Also, he smells
funny."

He rolled his eyes. "The words you seek are undead and
vampire. Dead is a gross corpse putrefying in a grave. Undead is
sexy and mysterious and looks appealing on my online dating
profile. Perhaps I am not a monster, but I do feed on humans to
survive."

Struggling to keep her face blank, Zita scooted away in her seat
a little.

After a glance at her, he lifted a placating hand. "I do not kill or
do more than sip from the willing, in part because I am careful not
to extend my powers so far as to require a deeper drink. It is what
it is. If nothing else, believe that villagers with pitchforks and
torches are hard on the wardrobe and make it difficult to read in
peace. As it happens, others here agree with me, and we have been
working on ways to balance vampiric needs with keeping
everyone, including regular humans, safe."

Zita eased back more. Although she tried to keep her voice
neutral, suspicion still slipped in. "Everyone just agreed to play
nice?"

Sadness touched his eyes before he turned them toward the table's surface. Withdrawing his hand from beneath Wyn's, he traced a whorl in the polished wood with the black-painted tip of a fingernail. "More or less. Some would prefer fewer rules, but we've been firm. As far as Sobek, I will assist you in finding him. Once we've located him, I'll unmake him so he returns to whatever he was before being turned."

Curiosity gleamed in Wyn's face, a familiar scholastic eagerness, as she swirled the liquid remnants in her glass. "You can do that? That's quite unusual. In most mythos, there's no cure."

His eyebrows rose, and Dmitri studied the witch. "Not just lovely, but familiar with the legends? Truly, you two are full of surprises. I cannot remove the vampirism from anyone that woke from the coma as vampires, like myself or Domina, only those who are second generation or later."

"How do you even know that? Did you make a vampire and then undo it for kicks?" Zita asked. Her stomach curdled. "That sounds pretty perverse. Does unmaking mean you kill them?"

He frowned at her. "Despite your desire to believe the worst of me, no. As I said, I am aware of any vampire in my vicinity and their capabilities. That includes myself, so even if I've never had cause to use it, I know how to do so."

"I apologize for my friend. She enjoys wallowing in her own idiocy from time to time," Wyn said, kicking Zita under the table. Whatever shoes she wore under her illusion were pointy and stung.

"Harsh," Zita said, pulling up her legs to avoid future punishment.

Wyn quirked an eyebrow at her as she daintily stirred her drink with the plastic drink sword. "Though that reminds me of something... a vampiric race in a series of novels I read..."

Dmitri looked away. "While I'm certain you read nothing but the finest works, one cannot depend on fiction for factual accuracy." When his phone buzzed, relief flashed across his face as he withdrew it and scanned the screen. "Excellent. Victoria's on her way now."

Wyn's brow furrowed as she replied, "Of course, credible primary or secondary sources are preferable, but that phrasing and collection of abilities seems familiar."

"Speaking of accuracy, you got to tell the police what happened at the railroad tracks. They think I just beat up those guys for no reason, and I'm not like that," Zita said.

The vampire frowned and shook his head. "I prefer to stay away from the authorities. Right now, I'm a nonentity to the DMS and the police, and I'd like to keep it that way. I'll try to figure out a way to assist you if there's something I can do that won't expose my...state."

A few seconds later, someone knocked on the wood of the booth. "Dmitri?"

Rising to his feet, Dmitri drew back the curtain.

On the other side of the fabric, a tall, stocky woman gazed at them, curiosity gleaming in her faded gray eyes. She stood very erect with her hands folded in front of her long, bullet-shaped torso. Other than the glint of blood red stones and gold from the rings in her hands, she was clad entirely in black from head to toe, save for a short white mantilla covering snowy hair and the lace cascaded from her sleeves. Pearls dripped from her wrists, neck, and ears. She smiled, revealing tidy, rounded teeth.

Zita had a second to breathe a sigh of relief. *No fangs. Gracias a Dios.*

In dramatic, ringing tones, the stranger said, "Dmitri? I thought you were going to keep close to home until after—" She cut herself off and slid a sidelong glance at Zita and Wyn. "Who have you brought to my court? Do they seek an audience?"

Wyn gaped at the old woman for a second before she closed her mouth.

Dmitri bowed to the elderly woman, lifting her hand and kissing her rings with a flourish. He gestured toward his seat, offering it to her. "Your Majesty, I bring you the ladies known as Muse and Arca. They brought disturbing news I thought you needed to hear. Ladies, this is Victoria, Queen of the D.C.-area vampires and owner of this fine establishment."

"Ah, if only everyone had your manners, Dmitri. The world would be a more civilized place." Victoria favored him with a smile before her features settled into dignified neutrality. Her movements stiff, she slid into the empty side of the capacious booth.

*Gout or knee problems, following a sedentary history,* Zita assessed.

Dmitri reseated himself beside his friend.

Wyn inclined her head when introduced and murmured something. *She's a dead ringer for Queen Victoria. That's a famous British queen who died in 1901. The entire Victorian era is named after her.*

*Why do you assume I never heard of Queen Victoria? At least part of the resemblance is makeup. You can see the edges of it around her ears. If she's pretending to be a British queen, you think she'll serve tea and cookies? I'd be fine with that provided there's no blood in anything. Is she a vamp?* With a cautious glance at Dmitri, Zita leaned forward and tried to discreetly sniff as she held out her hand to shake. Her attempts at subterfuge failed when she sneezed four times in rapid succession. She wrinkled her nose and shook her head a little, trying to dislodge the musty herbal odor.

Victoria smiled and patted Zita's hand. Her fingers were dry, soft, and warm. "Odd how many shifters do that. Good to see my perfume still works."

Surprise had the question spilling out of Zita's mouth. "You meet a lot of shapeshifters? Really?" *She's warm, fangless, and breathing. No matter who she's pretending to be, she's not dead like him.*

Wyn's reprimand came fast. *Undead. She doesn't have any magic either, unlike him. Forget about cookies and at least attempt not to alienate them. We could use allies who know the circles Sobek's been running in. In case she's lying, I'll skim her while we interview, just to ensure she's not hiding Sobek in her office. Don't worry, it'll be surface thoughts only, not a deep scan.*

Her chin rising, the old woman nodded once. "I've met my share. Very nosy sorts, but excellent for the kitchen's bottom line."

Wyn smiled and sipped her purple drink. "That does describe our Arca."

Zita made a face at Wyn. *As if you need my permission to do your brain thing.* The warm link to Wyn faded, and she was alone in her own mind again. "Fast metabolism and high caloric needs. You'd think you'd remember by now."

Dmitri hid a laugh behind a cough.

"Since you rescued Dmitri, Crown Prince of Vampires, I am in your debt. What did you need to speak to me about?" The elderly woman pinned Wyn with her gaze, apparently having (correctly) deduced who the people person was.

Zita watched and smothered a smile. *Fine with me. I get away with more when people ignore me.*

"They need to know more about Mr. Jones, that man you had here last week. Given what they had to say, I'm concerned the attack on me was because he's far worse than we feared." Dmitri set a hand on Victoria's shoulder. "I know you'll be shocked, but he's a murderous psychopath who escaped jail a few months ago."

While Victoria's mouth rounded in an O and her hands flew up, she squinted and seemed more uneasy than surprised. "That's terrible. How can I help? The police never said what he'd done when they came by asking questions in the summer."

"I don't pry into your business associations, but would you know where he is?" Dmitri stood, his hands clasped behind his back.

Shaking her head, Victoria said, "Our business is concluded. He had loaned me some money to get this place going, and I was able to pay him back recently. He only came here to sign the last of the paperwork releasing his claim. I will likely never hear from him again and certainly will not make the mistake of doing business with him again. He made it clear that if he had not required the money for some trinket and an upcoming trip, that he would not have released my club so easily."

Wyn leaned forward, a furrow appearing in her brow. "Dmitri said you were queen of the vampires. Doesn't that mean if he's an incipient one that he'll appear here someday?"

If possible, the elderly woman paled further, almost matching Dmitri's unhealthy pallor. She clutched at his forearm and stared up at him. "He's... turning? You said he had taken blood, but I thought... He's that close? Who turned him?"

"He is. I don't know who's behind it, but I intend to find out and reverse it." The vampire's tones were grim.

With a deep breath, Victoria regained control of herself, and a neutral mask settled over her features again. "Good. See to it. Monsters threaten us all."

Dmitri inclined his head.

"Can you tell us anything that would help us find him?" Zita said.

The old woman's eyes grew distant, and she studied the curtains, her eyes unfocused. "Not much, though I will have our accountant forward you the address he put on my copy of the paperwork and his lawyer's contact information. I will also allow you to speak to the staff in case they noticed something, provided you do not inflame their fears with incendiary talk. I regret I focused on other things last year and missed seeing how he had influenced my club until after the police came around."

Dmitri cleared his throat, and when he spoke, his tone was gentle. "What about Boris? Do you have any way to contact your grandson?"

Victoria lifted her chin, but some of the tension leaked from her shoulders. "No. He's in witness protection, and I have had no contact with him, nor will I until the police inform me that the risk to him is past."

*Grandson? Does she mean that moron Boris who was kidnapping people until he decided to turn witness against Sobek? Guess that explains how he got the manager job here,* Zita thought.

Wyn cleared her throat, and her tone was sympathetic. "I'm sorry you had to be parted from your grandson. That must've been very hard for both of you."

The elderly woman seemed smaller somehow, and her eyes sought out the vampire. "Thank you, dear, but it was for the best. He's safer where he is and far from the temptations of his former lifestyle." She inhaled deeply and folded her hands in front of herself as she squared her shoulders. "Oh, and before I forget, feel free to stop by on a Wednesday night. The front door may say the club is closed, but we're open to a select clientele, metahumans and humans friendly with them, via the back entrance. We offer a safe place to relax and find others of a convivial nature, provided basic conduct rules are followed. Your third is a shifter, correct? He may come too, but no humans until we get to know you better."

"Vic," Dmitri moaned.

Wyn's lips twitched. "We're honored by the invitation."

The old woman raised her brow archly at the vampire. "What? It will not harm our court if they sometimes attend Sanctuary Night. It may even keep you safer, my young friend. A prince requires allies, after all." Switching her attention back to the other women, she continued, "You will always find Dmitri or myself—or both—here and visible on Wednesdays. Other nights, I stay in my office, and Dmitri has that artistic temperament, always unpredictable."

The vampire licked his lips. "Vic, can we drop it for a few?"

"Of course. Why don't you take your new friends and see if the staff can help them more? If anyone gives you a hard time, come to me. I'll be in the office with some paperwork that requires my attention," Victoria replied.

The curtain was yanked aside. "I'm heading home. I feel ill," a curvy brunette in a short, tight black dress complained in a sultry voice. She studied Wyn and Zita through black-rimmed eyes and pursed her lips, a vibrant crimson slash against the unnatural pallor of her face and the glossy ink of her hair.

Zita could not help but notice that the newcomer only breathed when speaking. Despite the cloud of musky perfume, heavy with cloves, and thick makeup surrounding her, faint metallic undertones underlay the unknown brunette's scent. *Another vamp.*

Irritation crossed Victoria's face before it disappeared behind an expression of regal benevolence. "Get well soon, then, child. We might have to close early anyway given the weather. Dmitri and his friends may come by to speak to you on your next shift. Be honest and please knock next time," Victoria said, giving a regal wave. Lace fell away from her wrist, revealing two small healing wounds.

Zita fought to keep from scowling at Dmitri. *Somebody's been biting the old lady, and I can guess who. No wonder she's tired.*

"It shall be as the queen wishes," the other woman replied, an edge to her voice that could have been mockery or laughter. The curtain rings squealed in steel protest as she yanked them half-shut.

The waitress sashayed away. She touched the arm of the bald man waiting there for her and leaned close to murmur something intimately in his ear. With a wink, she glided through the door.

Recognizing him as the man she'd chatted with outside, Zita's breath caught. *It shouldn't surprise me that someone else noticed his hotness, but goth vampire skank is way different from... whatever I am. Sporty, maybe.*

Victoria whispered something to Dmitri in a querulous tone.

Dmitri patted the old woman's hand and smiled at her.

As if he felt the weight of her gaze, Ben turned his head. No recognition flickered in his gaze when their eyes met, and he turned away to follow the waitress.

Zita returned her attention to the table though she wanted to run over and make sure he knew his date was dead. *Hope she's cooler than she seems for his sake and keeps her fangs off him. Unless that's how they both like it, I guess.*

Warmth ran through Zita's mind as the mental connection between herself and Wyn slid back into place.

Dmitri again patted Victoria's hand. "I'll check on you later," he said, fondness apparent. "Rest up."

*Clubs can't function without people to run it. Maybe we should talk to whomever got Boris' old manager job?* Zita sent.

Assent hummed through the line. *Dmitri might be able to give us that name. Victoria's feelings for Sobek are a tangled mess, though she was largely truthful. She knows more about him than she's admitted, and she's far too relieved that Boris is in witness protection to have been ignorant of Sobek's predatory preferences. Well, that and she's more than a little annoyed that Dmitri and Sobek know anything about each other. Apparently, she scheduled the paper signing for when she knew Dmitri would be absent, but Sobek showed up with his lawyer on a different night. She tried calling in a tip to DMS about the property he took in exchange for giving up his share of the club, but as far as she knows, nobody's followed up on it.*

Zita struggled to keep from reacting. *Stupid-ass DMS, making the rest of the government look like geniuses. Can't they do anything right? Pues, when I call in a tip tonight, I'll ensure I mention it and that they should talk to Victoria again. Anything else good?*

The shared mental link hummed for a moment as Wyn thought, and then her friend added, *She's not a fan of the waitress who just left and will fire her if she doesn't lose the entitled attitude?*

Dmitri stood and held the curtain open. "Ladies, why don't we let Victoria go about her business? We can speak to Incubus. He's the member of staff that's been here longest and might be able to direct our inquiries to the correct people."

Exchanging glances, Zita and Wyn murmured their farewells to the old woman and trailed after the vampire.

# Chapter Seven

**Dmitri led Zita and Wyn** to the VIP bar. He stopped at the edge of the polished mahogany wood and lifted a few fingers. "Incubus, my friend! Would you spare a moment?"

At the other end of the bar, the bartender waved. "Sec," he called out, dumping straws into a container. When he turned, Zita stifled a gasp. *That's the guy Quentin set me up with the other day, the yoga instructor who wanted to help with my sack of chakras or something.*

A second later, she felt Wyn's amusement. *Oh? He must be quite fortunate to have survived a date with you unscathed. What's wrong with him? He's athletic and quirky looking. I'd expect you to be drooling all over him like a burger. Sack of chakras?*

*Órale, I appreciate a fit man, but he's all... he was all over my aura this and balancing my spirit that. Plus, my sack of chakras is all neglected or something. He said he didn't eat food, but I didn't believe him, especially since he smelled like weed. Still does.*

Today, her former blind date had anchored his frizzy brown bun with ornate red chopsticks, decorated with golden characters and art. A sleeveless tunic with a Mandarin collar showed off his tight limber form. With quick, flowing steps, Incubus crossed to their end of the bar. The eyes of the golden scrollwork dragon on his outfit seemed to wink at the women. "Dmitri! You must have recovered! You're practically pink."

Dmitri scoffed. "You flatter me, my friend. Might I borrow you? We're helping Victoria with an issue."

Wyn snapped her fingers. *He meant sacral chakra! He was either hitting on you or going to suggest you do something artistic. Given what an incubus is, I suspect hitting on you. It's well that you ruined it or whatever else happened to prevent the date from happening.*

Zita huffed. *Why does it have to be my fault? It wasn't going to work out for so many reasons anyway, including the pot. I can't forget that after I said no thanks, he tried to lure me into attending his advanced yoga class on Saturday morning.*

A half-smile on her lips, Wyn shot a sidelong glance at Zita. *Are you going to the class?*

*Well, not now. Unless maybe I should go to make certain he's not eating people... He did say it was hardcore.* Zita pursed her lips thoughtfully.

Wyn's amusement rang through the mental connection.

Incubus glanced around the club. "Sure, it's pretty dead up here tonight, no offense, other than the reality show chick. She's been spending most of her time closer to the dance floor and only retreated up here recently to preen for her admirers. Not the healthiest of ways to improve your karma, but at least they're paying for their drinks."

"Ah, you hold fast to that ancient chestnut still. Things are slow again?" Dmitri asked.

With a wave of his bar rag, Incubus shrugged. "You know how it is in this business. Are you really Muse and Arca? Perf. I loved your video! That song totes gets people on the dance floor. Movement is great for cleansing the body of negativity and raising a sweat."

Zita snorted. *It's a dance now?* She couldn't stop herself or the dryness in her voice when she added, "And increasing their thirst."

Incubus grinned. "That too, but the VIP area is slow tonight. It is what it is. What'd you need? Another drink for the lovely Muse?"

Wyn smiled graciously and nodded to Incubus, setting her empty glass on the bar. "Thank you, I'd love one. We had very little to do with either the video or dance other than being in the clips." *Another reminder to watch what we say—or at least what you say—in public. The next unauthorized song and video created from footage of us might be less flattering. It's been three months, so at least Andy shouldn't still despise it as strongly.*

Zita shrugged, unrepentant. *Someone may have taped an image of him patting his own butt on his computer monitor and bathroom mirror, so no.*

*Oh, Goddess.* Wyn sighed mentally.

*He shouldn't have messed with my snacks last time we sparred.*

Unaware of the silent conversation, Dmitri focused on the subject they'd come over to talk about. "A week or two ago, you witnessed Vic and a few gentlemen signing some paperwork? She said for you to tell us anything you can to help us."

Incubus' whole body tightened, and he pressed his lips shut. He nodded.

"What can you tell us about the man who signed the papers? I know he's been here before, and I've seen you speaking with him. These ladies need to talk with him."

"That guy is like a walking black hole, so I avoided him. He only spoke to me to order drinks, so I filled his cup and let him be. The queen said his drinks were on the house and to keep him happy enough not to notice me. I can do that." Incubus slapped a rag on the bar top and started wiping it.

*Funny, Victoria told us she didn't know a lot about him. Between that and keeping Dmitri away from him, it sounds like she had a good idea of Sobek's sick idea of fun.*

Wyn flashed him a smile. Her eyelashes might have fluttered. "Yes, but the best bartenders always have the scoop on their own place."

Relaxing under her approval, Incubus beamed and reached out as if to touch her hand, but Dmitri gave a brusque shake of his head. After a second of hesitation, the bartender fiddled with the sticks anchoring his hair and licked his lips. "The papers were legal stuff. Releases and property notices and such. I did hear him complain to his lawyer about the cost of a knife and airfare, but I doubt that's important. The only one who could maybe tell you more other than the queen is Domina. She might've fixed him a drink once or twice and done her usual flirty thing with him."

Zita wrinkled her nose. *This Domina has seriously dangerous taste in men.*

Quiet agreement came from Wyn through the party line. *It's got to be abysmal when even you think so.*

*If I didn't have good taste in men, I'd be dating one of the losers my brothers have thrown at me.* Zita forced herself to focus on the men's conversation.

Wyn had to have the last word. *I am certain you will continue to console yourself with that, however untrue it is.*

Dmitri frowned. "He doesn't seem like her type."

Incubus raised his hands. "That's the best I can do. I've never seen him here during working hours, and those few times I saw him, he generally was talking to the higher-ups—you know, Boris, Tiger, or the queen herself. Boris disappeared over the summer, Tiger quit, and you already talked to Victoria. Any worker bees who dealt with him more are gone except Domina and me. Turnover is real, you know."

His eyes widening, Dmitri said, "Tiger left? But I could've sworn I saw him downstairs earlier." He tapped a finger against his mouth.

After checking their immediate vicinity, Incubus leaned toward Dmitri and lowered his voice. "He might've stopped by to pick up his final paycheck, but he won't be here now, not with

Sheriff itching to kick his butt now that he's no longer a manager. Between you, me, and the bar..."

Zita and Wyn leaned in to listen.

"Gossip is bad for spiritual equilibrium, but Tiger was not purring when he left. The new accountant caught something wrong with the books, so Tiger ditched this place before they could pin it on him. He was talking crazy, but Domina had him under control, so I didn't listen to more than that. I avoid people who are too negative, and Tiger kept a lot of anger inside. Domina is... Domina." Incubus straightened. A waitress called out from the other end of the bar, and he excused himself for a moment to mix drinks. When he returned, he rubbed his hands with the bar towel.

"What did you mean about Domina? Is she here?" Zita asked.

The bartender shook his head. "No, she left early tonight. The special guest for tonight's event got into it with her earlier, the reality star chick in the red over there. Too much ego for one room, I guess, and Domina decided it wasn't worth her time to do her job, as usual. She ducked out the back." He nodded toward a cluster of people, before frowning and glancing at Dmitri. "As far as what I meant, Dmitri was closer to her than me. All I'll say is that Domina's focus on physical gain harms her inner balance and that of people who remain with her too long. She can also be less than discriminating in her conquests if they serve a purpose."

Zita took a moment to puzzle out his description. *Did he just call her a gold-digging slut?*

*Yes, I'm waiting for him to say bless her heart or her heart chakra. She must've been the waitress we saw,* Wyn sent back.

Dmitri gazed at the bar, his finger tracing whorls in the polished wood. "Don't judge her too harshly. She... sees the world as she wishes and has little patience for those who do not share her vision. Thank you, Incubus. So, it's of no use talking to anyone else?"

Spreading his hands wide, Incubus said, "Sorry, that's my take." He slapped his rag on the bar and began wiping it down again.

The vampire glanced over the club, rubbing his chin. "Of course, Domina chose to leave early tonight. Perhaps I could perform inquiries... Speaking of which, did you ever figure out who knew I was crashing at your place on Monday?" Dmitri asked.

The bartender shook his head. "No, I didn't mention it to anyone. It's possible one of the others who closed up here might've noticed you getting into my car or maybe they just followed us from here."

Dmitri folded his arms over his chest. "It was worth asking. Thanks. Did you get the door fixed?"

Incubus nodded.

Ignoring the door repair conversation, Zita focused on Wyn. "How do you want to handle this? Any suggestions for our next move?"

"Handle what?" Rani said, coming up beside them and linking arms with Wyn. "Hey, beautiful! Hi, Arca. Who's this?"

After hiding her surprise, Zita forced a smile and waved. "Hi, Rani." On party line, her tone was less jovial. *Seriously? You brought your girlfriend on a mission? I thought you canceled your date tonight.*

*Postponed, not canceled. It's a few interviews, not a mission. A piece of cake? Remember telling Andy that? We're done anyway if the only people who know anything have left for the night. Besides, didn't you ask someone to a stakeout once?* Wyn patted Rani's arm. "Don't worry about it. We just wanted to talk to a few people, like I told you, and I think we've run out of subjects. This is Dmitri. He's assisting us with the case."

Dmitri's eyebrows rose, but the vampire took up the thread of conversation. "Yes, I am their dark assistant, languishing in the night until you three bright flowers deigned to shine upon me. Would any of you like a drink?"

"Isn't that my line?" Incubus said.

*Fine. Point made. Don't drink anything poured by the bloodsucker.* Trying to smooth over the momentary discord with her friend, Zita jumped in. "I could do with a bottled water. Does anyone want a snack? Is anyone else hungry?"

"I already ate. I'll order one of those purple things Muse has later," Rani said, with a stiff smile.

Incubus nodded, setting a sweating bottle of water in front of Zita before scurrying off to another patron.

Dmitri gave them a tight smile. "You will, I trust, excuse me that I do not join you, but I have dined already, and I do not sup."

Wyn blinked at him, her eyes going distant for a moment. When her attention returned, she said, "Did you just quote *Dracula*?"

"I do adore a woman of spirit, intelligence, and excellent literary taste," the vampire murmured, inclining his head to Wyn.

Zita narrowed her eyes at him. "No eating anyone else."

"You don't date much, do you?" Dmitri said.

Wyn and Rani giggled, their fingers over their mouths.

"What?" Zita put her hands on her hips. After a second, she caught the joke and groaned. "Seriously, guys?"

Dmitri gestured as if zipping his lips closed. "I said nothing. Please continue issuing directives for us helpless lambs."

"Lambs, my little brown culo." Zita twitched and pointed at her eyes with two fingers, then at the vampire.

He grinned, oversized canines peeking out. "Truly, I shake in my boots. I dined earlier and require nothing."

Wyn smiled. "I've got my drink and excellent company, so I'm good," she said, glancing at her date with lowered lashes.

Her girlfriend made eyes at her.

Zita tried not to roll her own.

Victoria paused in the doorway, scanning the room, and then swept over to the bar. Her lips were in a tight line as she seized Dmitri's arm, tugging him away from the women. "Dmitri? You need to handle something."

"Pardon," Dmitri said, allowing himself to be led a few feet away.

The old woman whispered something in his ear and then squeezed his arm. Her sober expression deepened the sorrowful lines of her face.

Fear slid across the vampire's face for an instant before he pulled his cape closed and stood up straighter. Glancing at his watch and then at the bar, Dmitri said, "I am terribly sorry, but I find myself called away to handle an emergency."

Tucking her arm into his, Victoria said, "I'll drive. Good evening, ladies."

Incubus waved at his boss. "Got it. With Tiger gone, I guess I'm playing manager. I'll get Laurie to play waitress instead of barback since Domina lit out."

"Excellent," Victoria said. She and Dmitri rushed away, the vampire almost dragging the elderly woman.

After he exchanged a few words with the bar helper who'd been restocking the bar, both staff members glanced over at the loud table of patrons surrounding the reality starlet Incubus had indicated earlier. Said woman, wearing a dress that reminded Zita of a licorice twist, currently swayed on top of her table with a drink. At her feet, her companions whooped and waved their glasses.

The bartender shook his head. "Special guests and theme nights. Good luck, Laurie."

With a pained expression, his coworker nodded, straightened her uniform shirt, and slapped a smile onto her face, heading toward the rowdy group.

Rani beamed and squeezed Wyn's shoulder. "Sounds like you're free now! Want to dance? Downstairs is just calling our names to show all those people the right way to do so."

Somehow, Wyn managed to make chugging the dregs of her drink seem graceful. "I would adore it." She giggled and clasped Rani's hand.

Zita hurried forward, pressing the purple rock against Wyn's arm. "At least take your good luck charm," she said.

With narrowed eyes, Wyn dropped the rock in her purse. Ice dripped from her voice. "Thanks. You're not getting that back." Turning deliberately away, her tone lightened. "Shall we go, Rani?" They sashayed to the stairs.

Someone behind Zita tsked. "Your friend is busy, and given your epic crash and burn outside, I'm guessing you're not. Boss man wants to talk to you."

Zita stepped sideways, angling her body defensively, even as her mind caught up and identified the speaker. *Trixie. She gets around for a doctor with a side job as a mercenary. Or vice versa. I can't ask without revealing I know her real name, which might expose mine.* "Wow, and people say I'm tactless. Hi, Vaudeville."

Setting a finger on her chin, Trixie cocked her head. "Too much? Don't you want to malign that guy's character now he's turned you down? With a face like that, he's going to have slim pickings. I mean, those were some nasty third-degree burn scars. Healed a few years, but still." She moved to lean against the bar beside Zita. Despite her insouciant attitude, her posture still held a hint of military training. Her flapper-style spangled dress did not seem to include any pockets or bulges hinting at items that could be used as weapons. The pineapple slice on the rim of her martini bumped her nose as she raised it for a sip. She grinned at Zita.

With a wave of her water bottle, Zita dismissed the idea. "Oye, no. Leave the guy alone. I asked. He said no. No big. Even if he was a hot meta, a pro diver, and a former firefighter interested in trying rock climbing." *He's also already moved on with someone else, hopefully only for a short time given her deadness, so it's good we skipped all the hassle of failing at the relationship thing. Realizing* she'd let herself trail off, Zita tossed in, "I prefer guys with more self-confidence. Probably wouldn't have worked anyway."

Trixie fluffed her bob—obsidian black, so she had to be wearing a wig or had dyed it, though she hadn't bothered to do anything with her blond eyebrows—and blew a kiss at herself in the mirror behind the bar before answering. An almost invisible earpiece rode in her right ear. "Aw, I just thought you could use the usual girlfriend backup trashing him, but that's so sweet and naïve and altruistic of you to be nice about it. I think you could do better than him." She paused and laid a finger on her crimson lips. "Maybe not better. Maybe just stranger."

Even if she suspected she knew the answer, Zita asked anyway. "Is there a reason you're here eavesdropping on me tonight or did you just want to see how the interesting half lived?"

"Hound sent us. Boss man wants to talk to you, and whichever of your friends have gotten good looks through the God-King portals." Trixie laughed. Lines crinkled at the corners of her eyes.

Zita took a swig from her water and screwed the cap back on. "That's mostly me, but I'll check with my friends. Where's Freelance?" She scanned the room, wondering how a man dressed like a cross between a SWAT officer and a ninja could hide even in an inebriated crowd. Curiosity rose. *Did he actually take off the mask? I wouldn't mind checking him out when he's not wearing Kevlar.*

Trixie dashed her hopes. "Looming ominously behind the club, of course, in a patch of shadows he might have imported for the task. Perhaps even doing some atmospheric brooding from atop a gargoyle. Sadly, I have yet to get him to wear a cape when he does that. You want me to hold your drink?"

Surveying the other woman, Zita shook her head. "No, I'm good. He's what on a what?"

"You don't trust me with your drink? I'd be hurt, but that's a wise decision on your part. The gargoyle was a joke, this time. So, you going to go see the boss or hover around and wait for the trashy oxygen thief over there to notice you? Reality TV stars can be fickle, but she might glom onto you. Muse would make her look bad, but you're just Internet-famous enough to give her a boost." Trixie flicked her crimson-tipped fingers toward where the woman in the licorice dress held court, then drank most of her drink in one extended, loud slurp.

With a nervous glance at the woman Trixie indicated, Zita said, "I'll see if my friend has anything to add about the portals before I meet Freelance out back. How did you get in the VIP area anyway?"

Trixie sniffed. "We get in anywhere we want, like roaches, since we specialize in collecting bounties and rescuing kidnap victims. Kodiak's a sexy bear, but not a talker, and nobody ever accused the boss of being a people person. Clearly, I ooze with humor and charisma, so doors open to me."

"That makes you sound contagious." Zita wrinkled her nose.

With a laugh, Trixie touched two fingers to her forehead in mocking salute. "It also doesn't hurt to throw a bit of dough around. A little casual bribery goes a long way. How did you get in here with that on?"

Zita snorted. "Muse. They wouldn't let me in the club without her."

With a laugh, Trixie nodded. She lifted her empty glass over her head, giving it a shake once she captured Incubus' attention. "Works for me. Tell the boss man I'm taking fifteen for R and R and turning off my ears, so he has to wait to be a killjoy. Hey, barkeep! Got any more good hooch?" Detaching her earpiece, she tucked it into a pocket in the small cleavage of her dress.

With her water in a death grip, Zita left the other woman negotiating drinks and continued to the first floor. She stopped near the wall of dancing bodies and scanned the area for her friend. Despite their narrow head start, Wyn and her girlfriend already danced in the center of the floor. A small circle of space was cleared around the two women as if no one wanted to intrude on their moment together.

Focusing her thoughts, Zita sent, *Got a sec?*

*What's up?* Wyn continued to undulate to the music.

*Freelance and company are here and want to talk about the supposedly deceased Janus. I guess when Hound said he was too busy to help find Sobek, they were the ones he said he'd talk to about it.* Zita paused behind a group of sailors and gulped water.

*They're here? I can't add much other than to say the portals weren't magic, but I'll go with you if necessary,* Wyn sent back loyally. Unease and dismay drifted through the link.

With that reminder of her friend's dislike of the mercenary leader, Zita changed her plan. *No, I got him. You enjoy date night.*

Relief sang in Wyn's mental voice. *Thanks.*

At the edge of the dance floor, people also avoided a plump redhead dancing alone. While her dress emphasized serious curves that otherwise might've won admirers, one of her flailing legs narrowly missed kicking someone, explaining the caution of those nearby. "Come on, come dance, Miguel!" she called out, all of her attention on a table nearby.

Zita glanced that direction casually, only for her eyes to widen when she recognized the aristocratic features of the tall Latino the woman was beckoning. She turned away, panic blooming and hid behind the sailors again. *Why is my brother here? What if Miguel guesses I'm Arca? Wait, is he here on a date or for work?*

Curiosity warred with concern. Screening her face with her hair, Zita edged to the farthest corner of the bar by the kitchen, watching him. For once, her brother had relaxed his usual attention to his environment and paid more attention to the dancing girl than to those around him, though he still kept a wary eye on his surroundings. And Wyn.

When her brother noticed her, Zita sidled up to the bartender and asked if she could use the employee exit. She fought to keep from fidgeting. *I need out. Miguel's here flirting with a girl, the redhead in the blue dress who's mixing up the Zumba and kickboxing moves at the edge of the dance floor. He's spotted you and me, but if he guesses who I am, we've got trouble.*

Without pausing in the construction of what seemed to be a complicated drink, the bartender gave her directions about how to go out the back entrance.

Wyn casually glanced around until her gaze landed on Miguel's date, never pausing in the synchronized swaying she and Rani were practicing. Her eyes grew distant for a moment, and the mental link disappeared.

Zita waited, inching toward the door.

Someone moved so Wyn couldn't be seen, but the connection returned a moment later. *It's the vet you rescued at the zoo. Linnea Bagley? Interesting. She came here with Miguel and no, her intentions are not all platonic. Shall I observe them for you and determine if tonight is business, pleasure, or both for your brother?*

After thanking the bartender, Zita paused by the kitchen entrance, watching the swirling mass of people. When she tried to drink more, she was surprised to find her water empty already. She tossed it in the trash. *Could be, and sí, give me the deets about them later if you can. Don't eavesdrop though. I'll be just outside if you need me. I'll talk to Freelance, then hang out in animal form so the snow isn't a problem.*

Wyn's tone was dry. *I'm on a date. Your presence is not necessary. In fact, as much as I love you, I'd rather you just went home. Rani and I are grown women and might like alone time.*

Zita watched her friend and Rani dance as she snuck a glance or two at her brother.

He now stood talking to the woman who'd been calling to him.

Zita slipped out through the kitchen. The cook and helper flirted with each other with good-humored fondness as she moved past. Zita felt a twinge as she slipped unnoticed outside—not loneliness, because she kept far too busy for nonsense like that—more the wistful thought that it'd be nice to share time with someone who understood, rather than someone who tolerated.

She picked her reply to Wyn carefully. *Not until I see you safely out of this place and away from my brother. No hay bronca, you'll have as much privacy as a crowded club affords. I'm not the mind-reader, remember? I'll just sit outside until you're ready to leave. You're not willing to unmask yourself to Rani, so it's not like I'll mess up your sex life.*

Wyn sent a wave of annoyance. *Fine. I understand, but I don't have to like it.*

***

After leaving a succinct message on the DMS tip line to talk to Victoria and Domina regarding Sobek, Zita exited the back door of the club with relief. She inhaled deeply, enjoying the relative quiet, even if the air was redolent with exhaust, tinged with food, garbage, and cheap perfume. Cold fogged her breath and bit at the back of her throat. The door snicked shut behind her. *Now, if I were a hot mercenary who liked skulking and sniper rifles, where would I be?* She surveyed the alley.

The massive planters by the exit held mostly cigarette butts and dirty snow. Most of the old liquor boxes and old debris were gone, but new trash had begun to accumulate in the corners and at the base of buildings. Fragments of music and pulsing bass rose and fell, and Zita twisted to check behind herself. Navy blue paint still covered the wall and door of the nightclub though someone had added flecks of silver paint glinting like stars to it. A harsh LED bulb now shone above the Employees Only sign, the piercing illumination showing time's wear and tear on the building. More gently, a billboard facing away leaked light from atop a neighboring building, but only where a yellow glow escaped the edges of the ad.

The strobing spotlight of her previous visit was either gone or not turned on. At the end of the alley, about a block away, an old white pickup had been backed into the alley and parked.

While she suspected she knew where he was, she decided to check where boring people would wait to talk to someone first. After stepping onto the cracked pavement, she scanned every patch of visible shadow for the elusive mercenary. "Sí, sí, not ground level."

Zita ran to the closest pot, leaping into it and using her momentum to get higher up the wall. Her cheap sneakers squeaked and slipped a little from the wet, but she caught the edge of the roof with her hands and pulled herself up in a single smooth move, flipping to her feet. She scrutinized the rooftop, her body crouching low from habit. The lit billboard faced away from her, and the charcoal-colored asphalt roof was mostly hidden beneath a light coating of snow. Someone had added an illegible graffiti symbol to the cement shelter of the stairwell since her last visit here.

A familiar dark form stood in the shadows thrown by the billboard, a long gun resting casually across his back. Body armor blurred the lines of his form but failed to hide his taut, muscled shape or the economical, predatory grace of his movements. The tinted glass of his goggles glinted despite the poor light and hid his eyes even as layers of cloth disguised the rest of his face. His hand hovered over a handgun in a waist holster.

Zita angled her body sideways to provide less of a target and prepared for a rapid shift or jump off the rooftop. Her pulse quickened. "Don't shoot!" She raised her hands over her head.

Freelance let his hand drop a few inches from the weapon.

"So, what brings you to my neighborhood?" she asked, even if she suspected she knew the answer. While her tone was casual, even cocky, she kept her stance defensive just in case she'd been wrong about him.

The same robotic tones of a mechanical voice changer answered her question. "Working."

She shivered, the cold prickling her bare lower legs as she drew closer. "Obvio. What did you want?"

"God Kings?" he said. The goggles that obscured the upper half of his face tilted her direction briefly before returning to focus on the street.

She shook her head and allowed her stance to relax a little. "Let me guess... Hound told you they might be here? Are you still chasing poor, crazy Jennifer Stone? Why?"

He tilted his head.

Zita rolled her eyes. "For money, right. Silly question. Haven't seen any so far. It's been mostly borrachos and staff. We're here because we're chasing a meta who escaped in October and heard someone inside might have seen him."

His hand moved away from the holster almost hidden against the streamlined strength of the taciturn mercenary's side. "Sobek."

Her body warming as she followed the motion, Zita blinked. She started to jog in place and forced her attention away from his body. "Yeah. You here to help?"

"He worked for them."

She rubbed the back of her head. "Not anymore, I don't think. The God Kings burned him pretty bad when they freed Tiffany and left Sobek behind. Pretorius told him he was nobody to them unless he could bring them something real valuable. The tips we got today mentioned Sobek needed cash for a knife and a trip. Did Tiffany ever pay you guys for the mission where she tried to leave you to be eaten by the dinosaurs?"

He did not deign to answer.

She assumed that meant no. "So, you want to exchange info? You got anything on Sobek?"

"Outside resources. Same distributors for his meth, but new routines. Rumors of changes to the drugs. Where do the portals go?"

Zita strolled closer. Slowly. The last thing she wanted was to spook the man with the killer body and an endless supply of firearms. From here, his subtle, basic scent teased her, masculinity mingled with the woods and gun oil. She told her hormones to shut up and forced herself to focus. "I don't know exactly, but I'd guess their stronghold's in Central or South America, near the equator. I was close to a few portals. I heard howlers in the background, and they're only native to Central and South America. The building I saw was clearly built for the tropics, and it had dirt, not sand, so not on a beach. Someone who escaped said their compound is in the rainforest somewhere, too, and the jungle I saw was definitely Central or South American."

His head lifted. "Compound?"

"Sí, my source claims they kicked out some drug lord, so I'd assume it's got walls and maybe a pool. Big-time narcos always got one of those, right? So they can pose by it with their honeys?" Zita stopped a few feet away from him, at a distance that would permit her to keep her voice low but still let her watch his whole form so he couldn't draw without her seeing him.

"Name?" Freelance didn't seem willing to speculate about the existence of a pool.

She waved a hand. "He didn't say. It was a few seconds of conversation with a very scared person. The only other thing that might help you is that the compound had problems with 'disco monkeys.' I checked a lot of books and didn't see any monkeys with that name, so they might be endemic to the area. If you find them, you might have your compound."

Zita drummed her fingers on her hip, disappointment rising when Freelance didn't speak again. "Well, if that's all you wanted, everyone who knows anything about Sobek has already left here tonight, so we won't get more info today." An icy breeze swirled over her, raising goosebumps on her bare skin, and she shivered. "Next time you want to chat, pick someplace a little warmer, sí? You always snag the best observation points, but it's a sucky place for a meet. I can't wear real clothes and shift, so I'm freezing over here."

Air huffed through whatever mechanical voice changer he used. Reaching down, he dug through the dark pack she'd overlooked near his feet, and tossed a small, bright orange bag at her.

Snatching it out of the air, she squinted at it in the poor light. Black block letters read EMERGENCY BLANKET on it. "I'll just shift to something warmer. That way you don't got to fold this back up. Thanks, though." She winged it back at him with a smile.

Although Freelance turned his body away slightly, he caught the flying object and gave a curt nod.

Remembering Trixie's comment, she said, "Oh, Vaudeville said to tell you she was taking fifteen minutes off, and she took out her earpiece so you'd have to wait to yell at her."

His shoulders twitched, and he almost shook his head. "Drinking?"

She nodded. "Yeah, but she didn't seem drunk if it helps any. One of my friends is relaxing here tonight too, so I'll keep watch from up here. Wouldn't be my choice for a good time, but hey. You got a team. Everybody likes something different. Maybe not as different as Vaudeville, but you know how it is, right?"

His head tilted, but he said nothing. He did, however, turn his head to watch the front of the club.

Since he wasn't talking, she peered over the edge. The same two bouncers were still there, the female one glaring at the line while the bigger one, who had refused Zita entry, handled the actual talking. She vented a little. "I'd rather be sleeping or scoping out my next free climb, but even sitting in snow beats staying inside the club and being bored to tears. You heard of the Bassiter building in New York? I'm going to climb that. My goal is to hit the top before the sun does some morning. I'd have modified my plans if my friends were coming, but they declined. That's for the best, I guess. They'd have wanted to talk or something, and I'd have to make things easier for them."

To her surprise, he broke the silence first, a moment later. "Why climb?"

Forgetting he (probably) could not see her expression, she made a face, and her answer spilled out of her mouth. "Duh. For the challenge. It's more fun if I don't cheat."

He continued to watch or sleep or whatever he was doing. "Which parapet?"

"West, it's got the least street activity. I'd race you up it, but I doubt you're into it," she answered as she eyed the edge opposite, trying to decide on a spot to observe the alley. Cold seeped into her hands, and she shivered.

"Accepted," he said.

She blinked at him. "What?"

Freelance made a minor adjustment to his goggles and studied the street. "Race when?"

Zita scrutinized him, but the mask gave nothing away. "You actually want to? Muse, Wingspan, and I can get away if we're seen before we're arrested. Not that Muse would ever want to go climbing."

He tapped his grapple gun.

Remembering past issues with other climbs, she decided to be clear on the rules. "No grapple gun either. Just free-climbing. Pee before you go. If I need help, I'll ask for it, and you do the same. This is about the climb, not anything else," she blurted.

He answered with another of his small nods.

She grinned like a fool, lapsing back into silence and contemplation of the area. A thought struck her. "There isn't enough space for a pteranodon there, and none of my other flying forms are big enough to catch and carry a falling person. I can't stop you if you fall," she lied.

His head inclined. He didn't sniff, but even his mechanized voice conveyed his certainty. "I won't."

Zita eyed him. "You don't need to scout it out first?" She'd scoped out the Bassiter in multiple forms, checking to see the building had sufficient holds and selecting the rough route she'd take.

"Done it before." He made a minute adjustment to his goggles.

She bit her tongue to keep from laughing. "This race is getting more interesting by the second. Is your friend Vaudeville ever going to give that phone back, the one she stole from Wingspan?"

Freelance shook his head almost imperceptibly.

"Didn't think so. I'll text that number if a day seems good for the climb. You can let me know if it works for you. I didn't set a date yet."

He nodded.

*An illegal, challenging early morning climb with eye candy? Sweet! He's got a lot of reach on me, but there are some overhangs where he'll have to jump or fold that magnificent body up pretty tight. I've got a chance at winning, but it'll be hard.* Exhilaration lanced through her at the thought. "Fine. You're on, then. We start at one in the morning, as shift change puts the guard at the farthest point away."

He made no comment.

She ran a hand over her hair, forward and back. "In the meantime, I've got to figure out the Sobek thing. We know he was here at one time, but everyone's claiming they don't know where he was going next. And why would anyone lie about it to us?"

As always, Freelance was succinct. "Money."

Zita blinked at him. "Money?"

"Or fear."

After a moment, Zita had to agree. "That is his preferred motivation for others, isn't it? Love's possible too, but unlikely given Sobek's psycho personality. Whatever the case, DMS is here, so outside's the place to be. I don't know how they knew we'd be here. It could be coincidence, but that agent's stationed in New York, last I heard."

Her companion tilted his head. "Wingspan."

"Yeah, right. Why would he do that?" Zita snickered and tucked a strand of hair behind her ear.

At first, it seemed as if he wouldn't answer, but the mechanical words emerged eventually from the taciturn man. "With Caroline Gyllen in New York."

She waved a hand at him. "She's probably following him around to steal credit for all his hard work. He's been crazy busy rescuing people trapped in cars with all the snow we've been getting. Knowing her, Caroline's also nagging him to bow to the Man's every whim and be a tool like her."

"How then?" The mechanical rasp of his voice stole any emotion from the words, but they still lay between the pair like a declaration.

Not because she doubted Andy, but rather because she wondered how her brother had known to be there, Zita considered his question. She stepped out of her shoes, then positioned her feet atop the cheap sneakers. *Could Miguel have chosen this place for a date as a pure coincidence? If he were on a date, he would've called or picked somewhere closer to his new home. He always calls if he's going to be in town off duty. Who had known she would be here? Dmitri, her two friends, Hound, and his partner. Freelance and his team were here because of Hound.* "Could Hound or your team have told them?"

He shook his head. His goggles focused down toward the street, and he took a step closer to the edge.

Zita's mind raced, coming up with the same short list. "My friends would never say anything, and you claim your team and

Hound wouldn't, so that leaves the guy I came here to meet... He tore out of here earlier on some mysterious errand."

Freelance said nothing.

She ran a hand over her hair, smoothing, then rumpling it. "Our talks are always so fun. Since I need to keep watch to ensure my friend gets home safe, I'm going to slip into something more comfortable."

His head turned toward her so fast that she blinked.

"What?" Zita shifted to a snowy owl, figuring the artificial light would provide enough light for the diurnal owl form to see clearly. When she settled into place atop her shoes, she fluffed her feathers and turned her attention to the street. The bouncers were no longer outside, and the line to get inside was dispersing. *Odd.*

Whirring came from her silent companion as he touched the side of his goggles. His attention seemed zoomed in on the entrance.

As she watched, a pair of young women approached the front door and tugged on it, fruitlessly.

*The door shouldn't be locked.* Unease ran through her.

A second later, Wyn's voice rang out in her mind. *Zita! Someone's taken the club hostage and is demanding you—Arca—come right now or he'll start killing people.*

She switched to Arca long enough to fill in Freelance. "Someone's taken over inside and is holding the place hostage. Did Vaudeville get out? Muse is in there. Wingspan's not."

Her rooftop companion readied a shotgun.

"I guess she's still in there too. Don't kill nobody." Without waiting for an answer, she hurled herself off the edge, shifted to a snowy owl in midair, and flew to the side with the employee exit. Landing by that, she switched back to Arca, withdrew her picks, and worked at the lock. Finally getting the door unlocked, she yanked it open.

A man lunged for her throat, his eyes glinting red.

# Chapter Eight

In the Danz Mizer employee entrance, a tall man in a sweat-soaked silk shirt and dress pants swiped one lengthy, meaty arm at Zita. Rings glinted on his fingers like colorful brass knuckles, and his face was curiously blank.

She danced backward, reflexes reacting to get her out of the path of the clumsy haymaker before it could land.

Her attacker staggered a couple of steps when his fist met no resistance.

Before she could do anything else, a shotgun boomed.

Her attacker jerked as a slug hit him with a buzz. His body stiffened, and he fell to the ground, his muscles twitching.

Turning around, she saw Freelance slide down a rope to the ground, a shotgun cradled in one arm. "Good timing."

The mercenary trussed up the man still shivering on the ground and set him aside where he would not impede access to the building. "Plan?"

"Get the hostages out and tie up the attackers long enough for the cops to arrest them?" she said.

Freelance rubbed his forehead above his goggles.

In a nearby doorway inside, she could see the kitchen staff peering out.

When she went to speak again, an artificially magnified voice boomed out from inside. "If Arca doesn't appear in the next minute, who'd like to die first? Volunteers?"

Zita swore and gestured to the cook and helper to exit. "Get as many out as you can and don't let them block this exit. I'll herd people through as much as I can on my way to my guest appearance." Without waiting for an answer, she ran into the building.

***

Once Zita reached the kitchen, waving people hiding in the restrooms out along the way, she peeked into the main area of the club to survey the changes made in her short absence.

The broad backs of two men blocked the kitchen doorway. Both hefted broken beer bottles. Most of the patrons, unhappy and disheveled, huddled against the walls, Rani among them. Bright overhead lights dispelled the dim glamor of earlier and highlighted every sticky spill and imperfection. The center of the dance floor was empty. Pairs of people, most of whom seemed dressed to party rather than kill, stood in front of the stairs and each exit with a variety of improvised weapons. Their expressions were empty. Their eyes gleamed red. Down by the cloakrooms, a couple with blank expressions stood over the twisted, immobile bodies of the bouncers.

Behind the bar, Wyn held out her hands toward the man in the DJ booth a couple feet away. "Please, no!" she begged. "Tiger, please don't hurt anyone. Give Arca time to get here." A glassy-eyed woman stood beside her, a wine bottle gripped like a club in her hand.

"Shut up. You're worth money, but nobody said undamaged. We know she was here with Count Dracula." In the DJ booth, a man with a microphone—Tiger, presumably—scowled at Wyn, pulling a long-barreled 9mm pistol from his waistband. His Danz Mizer t-shirt exposed ropy arms covered in tattoos, with the most prominent ink being the tigers on each forearm. For some reason, he had shaved the sides of his head but left the top longer, so it flopped to one side. A scraggly beard hid his chin and neck.

Four people surrounded him, clearly stationed as guards, but they had the glazed expression common to the people on the doors. A couple of blood-spattered forms lay at their feet.

"Is this the spot with the pizza party? Because I heard someone wanted to see me, and I know it's got to be for free food, right? 'Cause I'm all about that, you know?" Zita drawled, shoving open the door and sidestepping the two big men. She kept her posture insolent and relaxed, despite wanting to grimace at the way her bare feet stuck to the floor as she walked. Her skin crawled at the situation. Had the lights been lower, she would've tried to knock the kitchen guards out so others could escape through the rear exit, but she didn't want to risk the hostages or her friend. *You okay? Do you know this loser?*

*The lady bartender on this level shouted Tiger's name and told him to get lost. In return, he had his minions bludgeon her. Then he pulled his gun...* Wyn glanced down at her feet where a woman in the club's uniform lay.

Tiger gestured with his gun in an appalling display of poor muzzle discipline. "Finally. Let her through. I suppose I don't need to kill too many people then."

The hostages let out a collective moan, punctuated by a few sobs.

Stepping out from behind the glass shielding the DJ booth, Tiger gestured to the smallest of his guards, a woman wearing little more than artistically draped pieces of cloth. He shoved a camera into her hands. "Hold this and film. Pan out over the whole club and then focus on Arca."

When the camerawoman obeyed, Tiger began to intone into the microphone in his hand, "It's time that humanity takes back the world from the scourge that has infected it. With this new performance enhancement drug—"

Zita broke in. "Wait, is all this so you can sell dick drugs? Dude, just spam email like everybody else. Hostages are overkill."

While the surly man glared at her, he didn't reply and instead continued his speech. "With the Achilles drug, anyone can be a meta for a time. Worried about them going mad with power? No problem. Use Myrmidon instead. It embeds obedience in the pills so anyone can be your slave. For tonight's show, certain individuals in the crowd tried the pill. Some knew they were taking a drug, others simply left their cocktail alone too long. None knew it was Myrmidon or knew they'd get to tear apart a meta tonight."

*Nobody's murdering Wyn or me tonight. Hopefully, I can keep everyone else safe too.* Zita looked around. "You drugged these people?"

"Why, yes, thank you for asking. For a reasonable price, your enemy's men can be your men for a while with Myrmidon. You, go stand by Arca." He gestured at the people near the DJ booth and one of the women by the restrooms exit. Grabbing the arm of the camerawoman, he added, "Not you. Keep filming."

Two men and two women pushed their way to the edges of the dance floor. All were taller than Zita and dressed to dance. Their eyes glinted red, and one woman took off her shoes, holding the stiletto heels like weapons. The men and the remaining woman simply clenched their fists.

Once she was surrounded, Tiger tucked his gun back into his waistband and hit a switch in the booth. "Kill her! Rip her apart!" Spotlights flared, focused on Zita.

Involuntary tears sprang to Zita's eyes from the sudden assault of light. She heard and felt, rather than saw, the movement as people advanced on her. Dropping low, she rolled back to where she remembered the bar being and wiped her eyes. After grabbing two beer bottles, she flipped the drinks to improve her grip on the sweaty glass necks and said, "You all should attack one at a time, like in the movies. It'll show off your mad skills better."

Her attackers ignored her advice and rushed at her again in a swarm.

"Cheaters," she swore, and bashed the two men in the face with the bottles, spinning to smack the shoes out of the woman's hands before they had her retreating. No one reacted to the hits. *They're idiots who wanted to party and got dosed with something nasty. I don't want to pull my usual tricks on them because they don't deserve to be hurt for his deception, but they're so high they're not feeling any pain.*

As if to add insult to injury, Tiger's magnified voice rose over the scuffle. "And remember. If you find our fine products intriguing, subscribe to our channel and upvote. The full line will be available to interested organizations soon."

*Sorry. He's so close to me that I can't use my sleep spell without including myself in it. If I try to start a spell, my guard hits me, and then I lose the spell and have to start over.* Wyn glanced down again at the bartender at her feet, her mouth set in unhappiness. A bruise was just beginning to bloom on one perfect cheekbone.

As multiple hands grasped at her, Zita shifted to a capybara and bolted between legs to get free of her attackers. Deliberately, she drove her relatively heavy body against a knee as she passed.

Her ploy worked, and the man she'd rammed fell, taking down one of the others with him. Eerily, none of her attackers made a sound, so the only noises were panting, the misery of the hostages, and Tiger's occasional command or sales pitch.

Shifting back to Arca, she seized a barstool by the seat and whipped it in a wide arc to slam it into the quicker of the two attackers still on their feet. She connected once with a loud crack, then drove the woman back and caged her between the stool's legs. "I'm super sorry about this."

Her prisoner grabbed Zita's impromptu weapon with both hands and unnatural strength.

Shifting up to a gorilla, Zita pulled the stool first to one side, and then to the other rapidly, slamming the first attacker into the second.

They went down in a jumble of limbs, but the ones who had fallen before had gotten to their feet.

Zita changed form again to a large capuchin monkey, modeling it after one she'd seen her last time in Brazil, and scrambled up onto the bar. Her mind raced. *If they weren't drugged, they wouldn't attack...* An idea sparked. *Wyn, use the sober-up rock on your guard and then on the guy by the kitchen. Then toss it to me, and I'll use it on my attackers. I should be able to dodge them until then. Let me distract them first.*

Wyn's eyes widened, and her head inclined. Her body tensed. *Will do. I called Andy. He's on his way.*

Zita hooted and flexed her fingers. She raced down the bar, hopping over an abandoned anchovy pizza, toward Tiger. *Good. Guess that's my cue to be my awesome distracting self.*

Picking up a pair of maraschino cherries as she passed a bowl, she tossed them up and caught them in her mouth. Then she waited for the drugged partiers to march close enough. As soon as they did, she pressed a couple of buttons on a pair of soda guns, and hosed them all down, focusing on Tiger as much as possible.

A tang of sugar and lemon filled the air as the carbonated liquid splattered all over Tiger and the camerawoman. He wiped his face, sputtering.

Taking advantage of his distraction, Zita dropped the handles, darted in close, and then shifted to Arca to deliver a solid heel kick to Tiger's chest.

He staggered back, propelled by the strike and sliding on the wet floor. His shoulder hit the edge of the DJ booth, and he cried out.

Seizing the gun from his waistband, Zita glanced around.

The drugged partiers had almost reached her.

Zita vaulted back up onto the bar, then to the counter behind it. She shifted back to the capuchin again, though the gun's weight meant her one arm was useless for anything other than dragging it with her.

The guard beside Wyn crumpled, and her friend darted toward the kitchen guard.

Drugged partiers started climbing over the bar.

From above, someone cheered. It sounded like Trixie, but Zita didn't dare take the time to see. She leapt onto a shelf, and then catapulted herself onto the massive chandelier. Her leg muscles tensed as she clung to the fancy lighting fixture and watched.

"That's quite enough!" Tiger roared into the microphone as he struggled back to his feet. He growled and yanked his shirt sleeve up to bare a bicep. Scratching at his arm, he peeled off something and tossed it up in the air. A grinning skull popped into existence, with flames glowing in the mouth and eye sockets as it floated above the floor.

From her peripheral vision, Zita could see most of the people on the VIP floor had gathered near the stairs, her brother, Linnea, and Trixie among them. Miguel and Trixie were closest to the center railing, but several patrons had their phones out and focused on her. A limp form hung over the bar, and Incubus crouched behind it, whispering into a phone.

More importantly, the skull drifted below, then tilted up, jaw opening. A ball of fire rocketed out at Zita.

She swung from the chandelier and landed on the railing, toes and tail curling around the black metal and hands gripping the top rim. Her other arm still cradled the weapon as she pulled herself up to balance on the top.

The attack crashed into the chandelier, sending it spinning. Tiny flames ignited on the ropes.

Incubus swore and ran over with an extinguisher. He sprayed the chandelier and the skull.

The skull coughed, going dark, but continuing to float.

"Arca!" Wyn waved the rock.

Changing position to grip the rail with her gun hand, Zita shifted to Arca and held out her empty hand.

Wyn threw.

The rock arced through the air, cord trailing behind it... and rose no more than half of the distance before falling to the ground.

The words slipped out before Zita could stop herself. *Still skipping arm day, huh?*

"Get that thing and tear Arca apart!" Tiger shouted. He stormed forward and pushed Wyn out of his way toward the wall where hostages cowered.

Wyn tripped.

Lights flickered back on in the skull. It spat another fireball at Zita.

The frantic jump to avoid being burned left Zita face to face with her brother. She froze and stared up at him for a millisecond, then shoved the firearm into his hands. Her nerves rendered her fake accent so thick as to garble her words. "Get people to safety. Back entrance through the kitchen's open." As soon as his hands closed around the weapon, she backflipped onto the chandelier again.

Slimy with foam, the battered chandelier jerked and groaned under her weight, and one of the damaged ropes snapped, though the main chain held.

*Can't stay here.* Zita checked below for a good landing spot.

Tiger's minions scoured the floor for the magic rock. A woman in a very short dress grabbed the necklace from where it had snarled on a spigot. She held it up, then collapsed. The necklace dropped from her hand and bounced under a table.

Zita swung back and forth, leaping from the chandelier at the farthest extension of her swing to land on the bar. She kicked one of the drugged people standing guard there in the shoulder and then vaulted over them, landing as a capybara. She sidestepped two goons and darted under a chair. *Wyn? You okay?*

*I'm fine. I tried to exorcize the flying skull as I did Tiffany's magic mud creatures, but it didn't work. I can only put out the flames or... yes, that might work.* Before Zita could protest, her friend stepped between her and the skull, and lifted her hands, tracing invisible shapes. A translucent bubble formed around the floating skull.

With a hiccup, the skull breathed fire again, but the bubble contained it.

A hostage hiding under the table kicked the rock away. It skittered across the floor and stopped against a motionless bouncer near the cloakroom.

Zita reversed direction and ran for it.

On the stairs to the VIP floor, her brother and Incubus crept down. Trixie, Miguel's redhead—Linnea—and several other people followed close behind.

His face unhappy, the bartender reached out and grabbed the arm of one man guarding the steps.

Instead of attacking, Incubus' guard moaned, and his whole body went slack. His mouth dropped open, and a thin line of drool ran out. He groaned, but not in pain.

Incubus licked his lips. Sweat beaded on his forehead. Light spilled from his eyes, and he panted, faster and faster in unison with the guard.

*I do not need to see that.* Zita checked on the rock.

One of the drugged people, a woman in a tight orange dress who had been guarding the front door, grabbed it. With a groan, she passed out, and it tumbled to the floor.

"Leave that thing be," Tiger shouted before the other guard could get the object.

*Guess I can't count on them continuing to knock themselves out with the rock.* Zita switched to her Arca form and snagged the rock's necklace. She scanned the room.

Wyn stood stock still, her attention on the bubble containing the skull.

"Don't hog all the fun!" Trixie called out from behind Miguel, who was grappling the other stairway guard. Sliding down the polished banister, she cackled as she landed on her feet at the base of the stairs. She glanced around and her eyes caught on the discarded pizza, lighting up. "Oh, sweet." Stripping something off the pizza, she snapped it like a towel. It unfolded into a large fish, a three-foot-long trout in brilliant speckled shades of green and gold and red. Laughing maniacally, she rushed at the second stairway guard and swung it like a baseball bat.

The fish hit the guard in the face, and he released Zita's brother to swing at Trixie.

With both guards occupied, Miguel motioned to the others behind them, and they streamed toward the kitchen exit.

Tiger shouted. "No one is leaving until I say so!" Tearing at his arms, he hurled something at Miguel. Orange swirled and elongated into the form of a nine-foot-long tiger.

Miguel reached back as if to draw a weapon and patted the small of his back. "Where did it go?" He swore in Spanish. A second later, his eyes widened, and he cried out, "Linnea!"

His date had pushed past him and now stood between Miguel and the tiger. Linnea held out a hand in front of herself, shivers wracking her frame and sweat pouring down her face. As if summoned by the drama, her hair had bounced loose of her chignon and now exploded out in a bright red halo of tight curls around the veterinarian's face.

The great cat snarled but stopped.

Trixie's fish sailed by and smacked into the camera. The device and fish fell to the ground with a crack and a squish.

The drugged man remaining by the cloakroom stumbled over the smaller bouncer and then grabbed for Zita.

She backed up, letting his charge carry him past her. Zita slapped his bicep with the rock. "Sorry," she said.

Her attacker fell.

Zita sprinted to the main entrance doors and unlocked them. "Front's open!"

Tiger howled. "Why won't you people just die?" Tearing at his other arm, he pitched that tiger at a cluster of hostages by Wyn. "Kill everyone but me!"

Another tiger appeared and stalked toward the hostages.

Wyn managed to keep on her feet as the crowd shoved past her in a panic to get away from the second beast. She held her hands out. Desperation shone as she waved her hands at it. Multiple copies of the tiger, only sparkly and purple, appeared between the tattoo animal and the crowd. "Arca, I can't get the cat and the skull. Help!"

The new tattoo tiger pounced on one of Wyn's illusions and mauled it until it dissipated in a puff of glitter, then continued to the next one.

The short, surly female bouncer staggered to her feet. "Who struck me? Nobody messes with Sheriff!" A rank odor, somewhere between feces and skunk, rose around her and then disappeared. She shrieked and writhed, her clothing ripping as her body contorted. Coarse black and white fur rippled across a muscled body as it stretched impossibly.

As the bouncer convulsed, Zita paused for a second at the spectacle and took a few steps back. *That looks painful.* Her hair rose on the back of her neck, and she somersaulted away in time to avoid a fireball from the newly freed skull.

Zita ran past holding the necklace while the bouncer was busy. Catching Trixie's eyes, she shouted, "Vaudeville! Touch the drugged people with this!"

Setting down the jar of cherries she had been spitting to knock attackers down, Trixie held out her hands. "Throw it! I'll get on with some bad touching!"

Forcing herself to focus, Zita tossed the necklace to Trixie and hopped onto a chair. Shifting to a snowy owl, she soared up toward the floating skull.

Below her, the crowd swirled in a confused mass. Linnea had dropped to her knees, but still held off the first tiger, and Wyn's healing spell glowed green as her friend tended to someone on the ground. Rani shepherded injured patrons toward the rear exit, her regal features drawn and tight. Vaudeville skipped in and out, running the sober-up stone across everyone she could see. All the drugged partiers seemed to be unconscious.

As the skull glowed in preparation for another shot, Zita seized it in her talons and yanked it upward, so it blasted a wall. *Andy, I hope you're on your way. We could really use you.*

*Incoming. Having trouble finding the place,* he sent.

"Who wants some? I'll kill you!" A human-sized honey badger shrieked from below Zita where the bouncer had been. Her beady eyes scanned the room until they fixed on the closest tattoo tiger, the one rapidly depleting Wyn's illusory copies. The honey badger snarled and launched herself at it.

*Seriously, even berserk honey badgers can talk in their animal forms, but I can't? I hope she's not as rabid as she seems.* Zita grumbled as she flew to an empty section of the VIP area and dropped the skull on it. When she landed beside it and shifted to a gorilla, pain jolted through the soles of her feet from where she'd burned herself grabbing the flaming monstrosity. *Going to need you to heal my feet later, Wyn.*

Her friend sent wordless assent back.

She risked another glance below. Blood and a black chemical—*ink?*—splattered the floor by the ongoing fight between the honey badger and tattoo tiger. The snarling, grunting ball of fur wedged in the space between coat checks. Tiger and Miguel wrestled by the bar, blocking the kitchen door. A trickle of people ran for the only remaining exit by the restrooms, but most could not get past the various battles.

Zita smashed the skull against the brick wall. While it didn't break, the fire snuffed out. She checked below again.

Miguel dropped, and Tiger rose above him, a jagged, two-foot-long knife dripping blood and glowing lime green in his hand. He smirked.

Wordless protest escaped Zita, and she gaped at him, panic and disbelief warring within her. *Miguel? Not my brother...*

*Don't worry. I'll heal him,* Wyn sent, fighting through the crowd in that direction.

Tiger stabbed at Wyn.

From behind, Miguel staggered into a rough lunge and knocked him down. A dark stain spread on his left side.

Tiger fell, dropping his cartoonish weapon.

Relief soaring through her, Zita bashed the skull against the wall again as she kept an eye on her brother.

Miguel slammed the hilt of the blade into the back of Tiger's head.

Tiger collapsed.

Knife in his good hand, her brother headed toward the animal menacing Linnea.

Zita shifted to Arca and called out, "Don't get cocky, DMS man!" Inwardly cheering, she checked to see if she'd broken the skull yet. *Still no cracks. Maybe crack it as a hyena? I don't want fire down my throat though.*

An upstairs window exploded inward, glass shattering, as a man flew inside. Pausing in midair near the wrecked chandelier, Andy brushed off snow and bits of window like dandruff. He wore his Wingspan costume, including a cape. His gaze skimmed both floors, briefly stopping on Wyn and Zita before sweeping back across the rest of the room.

"Tigers? Who brought tigers?" he said. "What's going on?" He landed on the dance floor by Linnea and her beast.

"The doors are unlocked! Tigers are evil tattoos. This thing and the mangy dude with the tats are bad too. Rabid badger's on our side... probably. Anyone else attacking is a drugged innocent." Zita rammed the skull against the wall again.

Andy turned and saluted Zita, his cape swirling as he did so. "On it!"

"Watch out! I lost it!" Linnea cried out.

Her tiger whirled and pounced on Andy. Or tried to. The massive creature bounced off his back, its claws ripping his cape into tattered strips as it fell to the ground. The great cat stood up again, shaking its head.

Surprise on what little of his face was visible, Andy jumped and shrieked, spinning around. He grabbed the animal and broke its neck with a loud crack. *SWAT team outside and a bunch of DMS guys. Good job disabling their getaway SUV and tying up the driver for the cops to find.*

Linnea sagged with obvious relief.

"Oye, Wingspan, since you're here, smash this chingado thing!" When Andy glanced at her, Zita threw the skull at him. *That wasn't me. Freelance was outside though.*

As it relit, Andy snatched the object from midair. "Oh, gross!" He crushed the skull between his palms, but not before it breathed fire on him. While the rest of his costume was fine, his battered cape ignited. With the sound of Velcro ripping, he tore it from his neck and dropped it on the ground, stamping out the fire.

Shifting to a peregrine so she wouldn't have to walk, Zita flew down to the dance floor.

Wyn stood by Zita's brother, with the gentle green of her healing spell covering his injury. Miguel gestured toward the kitchen with his free arm, his tone urgent but too low to be intelligible. Linnea shook her head at him and snapped something back.

*You go, girl. Don't let him boss you around,* Zita thought with amusement.

Unable to reach the front door due to the increasingly blood and ink-smeared battle between the badger and the tiger, the remaining hostages stampeded—in a panicked mess of sweaty bodies, random violence, and screams—to the kitchen door where no one was fighting now. A trio of women mowed down a fourth.

Zita dove into the crowd of exiting hostages, shifting to Arca right before reaching them. She took a few elbows and rude shoves as she retrieved the trampled lady. After dragging her to a seat, she poured the injured woman's unprotesting body into it. "Hold on. We'll get you some medical help."

When Andy was done extinguishing his clothing, he frowned at the remains of his cape and headed toward the continuing battle between tiger and badger. "Crap. Now I've got to get another cape. Was that a trout?" He paused at the remains of the fish before continuing across the floor.

"Vaudeville was slapping people with it," Wyn called out from where she was healing someone.

Trixie cackled, stepping out of the kitchen. The last vestiges of the crowd parted around her. "I know, I'm hilarious, right?" She hauled out a long-barreled 9mm from her cleavage—how, Zita couldn't tell, as the gun was far too large to have been hidden there, especially in a tight dress—and wrapped both hands around it.

"Retro, more like, and showing your age," Andy muttered, but he grinned.

After ensuring the woman she'd rescued would stay upright, Zita checked for other injured. Dismay grew as she counted several motionless shapes lying on the floor.

Tiger started to get up.

Trixie tsked. "You young bucks got no respect for a lady with a little seasoning." Altering her stance to brace herself, she leveled her gun at Tiger and gave him a saucy wink. "Now, mister, don't go making me sprain my wrists using your bean-shooter here. That'd put a real crimp in my shimmy, you know, what with the fuzz over there playing witness. Just sit there and don't move."

He remained still.

Striding over to where the tiger and badger thrashed around, Andy reached in and yanked them apart.

*Por favor, don't all be dead.* Steeling herself, Zita checked the shapes one by one for survivors. To her relief, most still breathed. She called out the injuries so Wyn could choose the most injured to heal first. Zita's feet throbbed with each step.

Andy snapped the neck of the tiger.

It melted into a puddle of ink, and then even that dissipated.

"Most of the drugged people have some kind of serious internal injury, like burns on the inside," Wyn fretted. Despite her tone, she hurried to the next patient.

The giant badger clawed and bit at Andy.

"Are you sure it's on our side?" Andy flipped the badger around, so the head and claws faced away from himself, and drew the other shifter close, his face red beneath his olive skin. "It tried to castrate me!"

The badger snarled.

"Don't take it personal, Wingsy, everyone loves a ball shot! Cops are closing in, so clear out if you're going to," Trixie announced, one hand touching the earpiece, once again in her ear. Wiping the gun handle with a bar rag, she kept the weapon trained on Tiger but held it out so Miguel could take it. "You dropped this. I found it. I would've shot Tiger, but the kick from these is nasty, and I don't have the time for sprained wrists. Plus, I don't want to risk shells down the neckline of this dress. It's not made for underwear, and my boobs are too pretty to scar."

Andy grumbled, "Way TMI."

The badger's skin rippled disconcertingly, and she shuddered. Her head cocked to the side, and her front legs stretched impossibly out in front of her, turning to bare skin. She writhed.

Zita shrugged at her friend as she helped an injured man sit up. "She's got a point though. Anybody in a low-cut shirt on a gun range is either a newbie or stupid."

"You stole that from me," Miguel said, his tones cold as he strode over to Trixie. He swiftly accepted the weapon.

The doctor wiggled her fingers and disappeared out the back door. Her last word drifted behind her. "Borrowed, cutie, borrowed!"

A couple of moments later, Andy squeaked and dropped the nude, now-human bouncer. "Eep!"

The bouncer fell to the ground. "Hey!" Yawning widely, the woman glanced down at herself. "This again?" She squinted at Andy. "Oh, hey, are you the real Wingspan?" Not so subtly, she craned her neck to check his rear.

The tips of Andy's ears turned pink.

Something banged on the front door, followed by a pair of loud thuds. "Police! Everyone down! Down, down, down!"

Verdant light swirled around Wyn's fingers and died. She rose from where she'd been healing someone and ran toward Andy. "Wingspan!"

"Right. Arca, can you get clear?" Andy ran to Wyn and scooped her up in his arms. He paused.

Zita nodded. *Meet you at Wyn's house.*

Assent echoed down the mental connection as Andy flew out of the club the same way he'd entered.

From where he stood guarding Tiger, Miguel said, "Wait! You should allow the police to question you."

Zita snorted. "Not likely, hombre. Make sure they know we didn't start this." She shifted to a South American horned owl and escaped out Andy's window. As she soared away, she sent one last thing over party line. *For your next date with Rani, Wyn, can we go climbing?*

# Chapter Nine

**The next afternoon in northeastern D.C.,** Zita stood in her Arca guise by the front door of Dmitri's house, feeling very out of place. Leafless trees stretched overhead in a tiny lot that struggled to contain a large fanciful house. Real stone, rough to her bare fingers, supported siding and numerous oddly shaped windows. Stained glass ran the entire length of one of the two towers on one side. A ramp wound up most of the sloping front yard, lined with rectangular boxes that probably held flowers in warmer months, but now just provided geometric frames for the bare soil and leftover lumps of snow.

While she tried to ignore the feeling that this was truly a bad idea, her mind sped along, planning her next moves. *I'll knock first, in case someone is home. When nobody answers, I'll slip around back and pick my way in through one of those upper windows. When I crashed Incubus' class to question him about how people knew we'd be at the club, he mentioned the cops have been unable to reach Victoria and bugged him about it. I know she left with Dmitri right before the chaos started. If the vampire isn't the amiable drama prince of darkness that he seems, I can't afford to waste time saving her. It took forever just to get his address. If she's visiting here of her own free will, I'll just leave.*

Zita snorted, annoyed with her own hesitation and her fist hit the door in three sharp, brisk thuds as she kept a wary eye out for witnesses. Most of the street was deserted. She checked the address again and slipped a hand into her sweatshirt pocket to touch the lockpicks there.

The door flew open.

Her body slipping into a defensive stance, Zita took a step back. *Incubus said Dmitri would be dead to the world until sunset. He probably meant literally. Who's this?*

"Oh, you must be one of David's little friends. You must be freezing in that clothing! Wait, are you his new personal trainer and lifestyle coach? Come on in out of that cold. I've got to get back to the hospital, but I'll just wake him up so he can talk to you," the woman said. Tight salt and pepper curls, still glistening with water, bounced as she waved Zita inside. Despite the dark circles and redness around her striking purple eyes, the same color and shape as Dmitri's, her motions held the energy of a woman half her age and weight.

*Fit but not any recognizable exercise. Perhaps aerobics and manual labor,* Zita assessed and then blinked as the barrage of words sank in. Her hand slid from her tools. "Ah, sure. Does Dmitri live here? Do I have the right place?"

Beaming, the older woman patted Zita's shoulder and steered her to a seat in a living room done in white crocheted doily and shades of blue. She seemed to completely ignore the mask Zita wore. "Yes, dear, he likes to go by his middle name, but I'm his mother. I brought him into this world, so I believe that those forty-seven hours of hard labor buy me the right to call him anything I want. You can call me Yana." She paused and eyed Zita.

*He lives with his parents? Do vampires do that? Not like they don't have the room, given the size of this joint, but it seems wrong for the whole prince of darkness thing.* Bemused, Zita realized she was supposed to say something. "I'm Arca?"

"Lovely! Let me get you some hot tea to take the chill out of your bones. Why on earth are you out in this weather without a real coat? You do drink tea, right? The kettle just boiled, so you've come at the perfect time." She pulled a rope on the wall.

The muffled sound of a foghorn resonated through the polished hardwood floor. Chatter trailed after Yana as she bustled around. Leaving the room only resulted in her raising her voice to be heard, and she seemed to pop her head back in every few seconds to ask Zita a question that she'd then answer herself.

*Well, this isn't how I expected it to go at all,* Zita thought, studying the house.

Despite the expensive neighborhood, high ceilings, and fancy wall architectural flourishes, the furniture was the same prosaic stuff Zita would've expected in any middle-class senior citizen's home, other than the layers of heavy drapes blocking what she guessed were windows. The decor and furnishings seemed a little too small for the space as if it had been moved from a much smaller place and put into the same configuration as before. Her shoulders relaxed with the absence of museum-quality pieces, and she prayed she wouldn't have to fight this nice woman's son. Even if Yana never stopped talking.

Within minutes, a small plate and mug were thrust into her hands. While Zita never minded a snack, the cookies smelled like damp baking soda. She tried to tune back into the endless stream of babble.

"I can't tell you how happy I am that you're helping David with his new regimen and how well it seems to be working! Why, he hasn't had to go to the hospital in a year, so it's a record! Of course, a mother would like this miracle recipe so she could prepare a meal for her boy again, but I understand it's a new proprietary formula." Yana beamed at her, almost dancing in her sensible beige shoes.

Zita shifted, the plastic cover on an aggressively floral sofa squeaking beneath her. "Thank you," she said. *Hospital? The food comments make sense. Nobody wants to tell their mother they've become a blood-sucking undead unless they have an unhealthy relationship. If he did feed on Victoria, the odds have gone way down that she's here.*

"Your help has made such a difference in my boy. Why, he hardly looks like the same man. This was my favorite from when he was sick. It was taken just last April after his most recent bowel surgery. Ignore the puffiness. That's just a peristomal hernia, long healed now. Isn't the difference amazing?" Yana selected a framed photo from the horde surfing on their own individual doilies and passed it over. She beamed, laugh lines crinkling at her eyes and mouth. A familiar antiseptic hospital scent clung to her cardigan.

Zita struggled to keep her face neutral and bit her tongue hard.

Dmitri—or David, as his real name apparently was—stood arm in arm with Victoria and his parents in front of a snowy mountain and a log and stone house gleaming with dramatic windows. While his crooked smile, basic bone structure, and limpid purple eyes were the same, the man in the photos was cadaverously thin and wasted, save for a grotesque bulge on one side of his waist. For all he dressed neatly in an old-fashioned suit complete with a pencil-thin bow tie, his shoulders were bowed, and his skin was an uneven, translucent white where sunken blue veins stood out against his pallor. His pained stance held the unnatural fragility she'd seen previously in only the very ancient or dying, nothing like the urbane undead with his gym-perfect body that she knew.

"I think there's been a mistake. I'm not a personal trainer. I was here to…" *Search through your son's things to see if he set my friends and me up to be killed? See if he's holding his best friend prisoner as a snack? That wouldn't fly. She'd strangle me with a doily, and there wouldn't be a sign because she'd just change the plastic on the sofa. Props to her for cleanliness though.* Zita wracked her brain for an innocuous excuse and set the picture in her lap.

Yana gasped and clapped her hands together. "Are you his date? Has he finally gotten over that awful girl? She never appreciated my sweet boy and then had the terrible taste to leave him for that doddering idiot with the money once she found out about the house."

Zita had the bizarre image of the woman going house to house, preparing tea and cookies in the kitchen and leaving behind a living room stuffed with doilies as the only sign of her presence. She bit her tongue before she could ask if the ex-girlfriend had been frightened by the doily invasion. *What would Wyn say?* "We're just, uh, friends. It seems like a lovely home to me."

Clucking her tongue, Dmitri's mother said, "That's a pity. He could use a nice girl. She was upset that while the house is David's— he bought it—he put his father and me on the deed during a health downswing because he didn't want us to pay inheritance taxes on it. We live here because he used to need our help with all his health issues..." Her face grew sad before it brightened again. "But he's doing great now, other than the photosensitivity. It's a shame he has to stay inside all day now that he's able to move around normally otherwise."

Nodding, Zita took a bite of her cookie to give herself a moment to process, then choked on the gluey tasteless object. Feeling as if she had accidentally begun eating a paper-mâché project again, she tried to wash it down with a gulp of tea. The picture fell to the floor. Heat seared her mouth, and she rose to her feet, fanning her throat, wondering if the food would go down or come spewing out. After a few more moments struggling, she managed to swallow the unpleasant lump.

"Are you okay, dear?" Her hands knotting, Yana pounded Zita's back heartily, hard enough to bruise.

Zita cleared her throat, stepped away, and set down the dangerous cookie, eyeing it with more than a little suspicion. "Yes, I'm good. The tea was hot."

Yana slapped her hand to her forehead. "Oh, I'm sorry. I should've warned you. Do you like the cookies? Those used to be David's favorite! They're free of processed sugar, gluten, lactose, dyes, fiber, or eggs, and I devised the recipe myself for his special dietary needs. Do you think he could have some of those?"

"Pretty certain not." Zita tried to change the subject. Catching sight of the photograph on the floor, she picked it up and set it nearby.

With a glance downward, Yana clutched Zita's arm. "Can you give me some reassurance? David wanted to send my husband and me on a trip to Disney. I don't know if I can leave him alone though, in case he relapses and requires aid. Can you tell me how likely that is? Not like we can go until my husband is well enough, but it'd be a comfort."

Zita freed herself from the other woman's claws and tried to find a suitable answer. "I'm not a medical person, but I'm pretty sure your son won't go back to the way he was." *Death is normally permanent.*

Dmitri's mother smacked her hands together and beamed. "Good, he's a new man since he got better."

*Yes, he's a dead man.* Zita kept from saying it out loud, but she barely caught herself in time. A collection of pictures above an enormous fieldstone fireplace caught her eye. Unlike the multitude of photos in the room that were undoubtedly spawning with the doilies behind her back, these appeared to be a series of book covers. Thanks to her association with Wyn, Zita knew they were romance novels, given the array of shirtless, headless men. "You're a big reader?" *Hurry up, Dmitri. It's got to be easier to accuse you of setting me up to die than to make small talk.*

Dmitri's mother giggled girlishly. "Well, yes, but those aren't my books. Those are the first twelve books in David's top-selling series."

"His what?"

Raising her eyebrows, Dmitri's mother peered at her. "Didn't he mention he's a writer? He's got over a hundred books out. Releases a new one every two months or so. They're quite popular, especially the Lords of Imbroglio series. He's working on a spinoff, but you didn't hear it from me."

Zita nodded. "You can count on me to not tell anyone."

"Are you a fan?"

Thrilled she could be truthful, Zita said, "It's not my thing, but I got a friend who's probably read them."

Dmitri's mom wandered over to the wall and pulled the rope again. In the depths of the house, a foghorn echoed. "I'll just pull once more. He can be quite slow to get up during the day, and the poor boy was fretting over his father most of the night. My poor husband is in the hospital. He had a stroke yesterday, and we've been with him since then. Thank goodness his nice friend Victoria was willing to drop him off when I got through to her. It's a pity she was supposed to meet with someone else and couldn't stay to chat. She and David used to have the same gastroenterologist, and we would have lovely conversations in the waiting room."

Zita took a moment to wrap her mind around the alibi so casually handed her, and sympathy had her tone softening. "Ay, no. I hope your husband'll be okay?"

Inhaling deeply, Yana held a hand to her breast. "We can hope, and it's supposed to be one of the top hospitals in the country for strokes. I'm going to go back and stay with him. Maybe Victoria will drive Dmitri again tonight and chat this time. It's always nice to see her. We stayed at her vacation place two years ago. Did you know she had a helicopter pick up Dmitri so he wouldn't be subjected to the drive? Isn't that sweet? Such a pity she had to sell the place."

"I hate it when that happens," Zita managed. *I supposed it's like the rich version of taking your television to a pawn shop?*

Yana's barrage continued. "My ride should have been here by now, but I expect traffic slowed them. You haven't touched your food. Is there a problem with it?"

*And... back to lying.* "I'm not hungry," Zita said, praying her stomach would stay quiet.

A door flew open, and Dmitri staggered through, fangs bared and arms akimbo. His face seemed younger and more vulnerable without makeup, and his voice was all-American in intonation. "Mom? What's the emergency? Is Dad okay?" A t-shirt with a teddy bear with vampiric teeth and matching fuzzy pants featuring the same animal clung to his muscled frame. Once again, he moved with a grace that belied the uneven pace and placement of his steps.

Zita managed not to cheer at the interruption. *The difference between the picture and now, plus how he moves. His powers definitely cheated and gave him a sweet body that he's clueless on handling. He stinks like the hospital.*

Her pride in her son obvious in her face, Yana nonetheless began fussing over him. "Now, I know you need your sleep, but your friend is here."

The vampire shot Zita a puzzled look. "Arca?"

A horn honked outside.

"Ah, that's my ride, I must be going! If your new diet permits, a fresh batch of your favorite cookies are in the jar. You'll need your ID, so don't forget your wallet. See you at the hospital later." Yana kissed her son on both cheeks, gave him a quick hug, snatched up a Thermos, and headed out.

Dmitri returned the affection with a smile though he still blinked sleepily. "I'll be by after sunset."

"Bye, Yana!" Zita called, waving.

His eyes clearing, the vampire considered her abandoned food and tea. "You want me to pour those down the drain? Please say yes. The smell is making me nauseous."

Zita glanced toward the kitchen. "Won't they break the sink?"

"True. Trash can, then." A mirthless smile touched his lips as he picked up the picture Yana had shown her and set it among the others. "Ah, the hernia photo. Truly my best moment."

"She said the cookies were your favorite," Zita said.

His smile twisted, became self-deprecating, and he gestured toward the rows of images. "As you may have surmised from my proud parents' pictures, I was slowly dying before I became a vampire. So yes, I made my mother happy and told her that I loved her special cookies. They could be stomached without pain or horrible aftereffect, at least." He disappeared into the kitchen with the dishes.

Zita rubbed a hand over her hair and let herself pace. *This seemed simpler on the way here. How do I ask him if he's keeping Victoria as a midnight snack in the basement or if he set up the attack at the nightclub? This would be much easier if he'd been sleeping like I'd assumed when I decided to search his place.*

Unaware of her inner turmoil, Dmitri returned. "So, to what do I owe the pleasure of this visit?" He frowned. "And how did you find me?"

Zita weighed her answers, but decided on the truth, at least for the second question. "Incubus told me. He probably wouldn't have otherwise, but the cops have been lighting up his phone trying to reach you. While he gave the detective your cell phone, he didn't think they'd understand the whole vampiric lifestyle thing."

Dmitri disappeared downstairs for a second and returned with a phone in hand. "Of course. I had my phone off while we were in intensive care, then I crashed when the sun rose... I guess I'm so used to it being on all the time that I forgot to turn it back on." A second later, the device beeped imperiously. Glancing at it, his eyes widened. "I guess they have been trying to reach me. What's so urgent?" His body mirrored the confusion in his questions.

*If he's pretending not to know, he's good at it.* Zita tilted her head. "You didn't hear what happened at the club last night?"

"No, what? Did they run out of dry ice? Wait, the police were involved. Brawl? Did a bouncer hurt someone?" He pointed a finger at her. "That's it, isn't it? Sheriff bit someone."

Zita pursed her lips. "Tiger spiked the drinks of a bunch of patrons with meth that let him control them and then took the place hostage. He was defeated before the cops got inside, but a couple of people died." She remembered the scorch marks and the window Andy had broken. "Also, there might've been property damage."

He gasped and glanced down at his phone. "Seriously? I should call Victoria. She texted me asking me to come over last night. Since she's been pouring all her attention into the club the past few months, all that stress must've triggered her medical issues."

"That's part of the problem. Nobody's heard from her or seen her since she left with you—that Incubus knows of, though the cops were harassing him to find her last night and today."

The vampire looked so close to fainting that Zita took an involuntary step forward to catch him. "That can't be right. She sent me a text a couple hours after she dropped me at the hospital. I've got to get to her. Incubus is a fan and must've figured you'd be an ally. The authorities don't react well to those who dine on other people to survive." He rubbed his forehead.

Zita's sympathy lessened, and she stepped back.

Her face must've revealed her emotions because Dmitri waved his hand. "We spoke about this before. I take less than the blood donation vehicles. Why did you care enough to hunt me down during the day?"

She tried to think of a nice way to put it. "When Tiger attacked, he somehow knew I was there. Nobody knew I was going to be there who would've said anything other than you. Coincidentally, you left maybe fifteen minutes before he made his move. Now an old lady you've been chomping on is missing."

His eyes widened. "Maybe I would've been better off with the police! Are you saying that I would—Vic's my best friend. Yes, I did bite her recently for the first and only time. After I was attacked, she offered because I needed to heal. She can't afford to lose the blood, so I only took a token amount to avoid hurting her feelings. As far as telling anyone, I didn't know if you would show or not. Additionally, I don't get out much as being confined to after dark is limiting, and before that... well. We have already discussed that subject enough. I'll call Vic right now." His fingers raced over his phone, and he held it to his ear.

She folded her arms and waited.

The vampire's face fell, and he left a message for his friend to call him back. Pocketing the device again, he turned to Zita. "Vic has some chronic health issues. She's likely having a bad day and has turned off her phones, though normally she emails when that happens. I'll go to her place and roust her." He strode toward the door, then stopped, glancing at the covered windows.

"It's still daylight, yes. And you're in your teddy bear pants, if that matters," Zita said.

He paused and ran his hands down his sides as if surprised at his own apparel. "So I am. I'll change while you pull your car up."

She coughed into her fist. "I flew here as a bird."

"Fine, then, we'll take mine."

*Was there something in the cookies? The plan to break in and discreetly check if he's holding Victoria captive has spiraled out of control somehow.* Zita folded her arms across her chest and cocked her head to the side. In what she hoped was a quelling tone, she said, "We? We won't do anything, especially when you're wearing some toddler's pajamas."

Dmitri laughed, a humorless bark of sound. "The only way I can prove I didn't hurt my best friend is to show you. I'm not giving you her address unless I come with you. For all I know, you mean to harm her. The newspapers said you're accused of randomly beating up people, after all."

She shook her head and scowled at him. Her shoulders set and she tried to seem fierce. "You know the truth of that. Just give me her address, and I'll check on her." *I am a badass. You don't want to mess with me.*

The vampire patted her on the head and chuckled. "You're funny, and no. I'm going with you."

Zita slapped his hand away. "Hey!"

He narrowed his eyes, and his teasing demeanor fell aside. "Arca, you've made it perfectly clear who the bigger monster is here. You're a superhero who rescues people. I just eat people. You're a guest in my home, despite coming when you knew I'd be asleep. I'm going, or you're not getting her address." His fangs flashed as he spoke. He turned his back on her and headed down the stairs. "I'll be back up when I've got my big boy pants on, so your boring costume is less threatened by my fabulous sleepwear. Wait here."

Zita stared at his back and then plucked at her clothing. She ran a hand over her hair and stared around the home she'd meant to break into. Shame crept in. "Carajo."

***

After an interminable wait of at least ten minutes but not more than twenty, Dmitri returned upstairs. He had covered himself from head to toe in a long, military-style coat with a great many shiny buttons, a hat, sunglasses, and an immense scarf in an alternating pattern of scarlet and gold. Only the tip of his patrician nose emerged from the bundle. After a moment, he muttered to himself and loosened the scarf enough to allow her to see his face.

"What, did you rob a coat store? Vámonos, I've waited forever." Zita hopped to her feet, already ruing her rude greeting. She'd been trying not to think while doing pushups in a clear section of the floor where she stood no risk of knocking anything over or dislodging any of the pictures on the wall, all of which had seemed to smile accusingly at her.

Flinging one end of his scarf over his shoulder, Dmitri sniffed. "The cold is not my friend. My body temperature is significantly lower than yours, so frostbite comes quicker, unless I expend energy to stop it. If I do that, then I need to feed more often."

Zita followed him through the doily-draped house to the garage. Curiosity prompted her, and the question escaped without conscious thought. "What about the sun?"

Opening a door, he clicked a remote, and a car beeped. "Sunshine is fine if I don't mind being nearly blind, practically powerless, and feeling as if all exposed skin is on fire. Not to mention needing to eat again to repair the damage and the unavoidable narcolepsy if I'm not dying or actively doing something."

She shoved her hands into her sweatshirt pockets and followed him into the garage. Inwardly, she sent up a brief prayer of thanks that she wasn't undead. "That sounds fun, like malaria."

As he locked the door behind them, she checked out the garage. A minivan loomed. It was white and would've looked like any other vehicle at a soccer game were it not for the special door she associated with wheelchair lifts and the bright red racing stripe down the side. A purple stuffed bat hung from the rear-view mirror, grinning at her with fangs. The rest of the garage seemed to be the usual assortment of stuff people couldn't store elsewhere.

Trying to think of a way to apologize, she eyed the vehicle and offered a gruff compliment. "Nice bat."

"That's my mother's car. Mine is behind it. It has all-wheel drive." Dmitri waddled by the vehicle and stopped on the other side. He beamed and gestured at something she couldn't see. "This is my baby."

After skirting around the minivan, Zita spotted his car. A small, sporty sedan, it had two doors, sleek performance tires, and the spotless appearance of a car that'd never been driven. The darkened, reflective windows hid the color of the interior. "Blood red paint with black trim, seriously? Is that much window tint legal?"

Dmitri slid into the driver seat and pressed a button. The engine purred to life. "One can deride stereotypes or reclaim them for your own use. Besides, red goes well with my complexion, and I have a documented medical condition necessitating additional window tint." He put on a pair of black leather driving gloves.

"What complexion? Speaking of unnatural, what do your parents think of the whole undead thing?" She had to maneuver behind the vehicle as someone had wedged plastic trash cans between the nose of the sedan and the wall. Rather than squeeze in the narrow space between the garage door and the rear bumper, she vaulted over the trunk. A wave of new car smell washed over her as she slid into the passenger seat.

A crease appeared in his forehead. "My parents both know. Mom is just... in denial of certain aspects of my existence. How did your family take the shapeshifting vigilante thing?"

Zita buckled her seat belt as she eyed a pair of brand-new tennis rackets on the wall and stroked the smooth, supple leather seat. She didn't want to, but it was so soft that she couldn't help petting it, though she tried to hide the gesture. "They might not know."

He nodded and fiddled with the mirrors and the lights. "Enough said. Now, I trust you have a license, right?"

"Why?" She watched him.

The vampire shrugged and poked at a control. "Technically, I'm not supposed to drive without a licensed adult driver in the car."

She blinked. "What?"

Dmitri started to back up, then threw the vehicle into a sudden stop.

The seat belt bit into Zita as she was hurled against it with the cessation of movement.

"I only have my learner's permit. Prior to the vampirism, my illness made completion of a driver's course problematic."

Reaching up, he pressed a button on a little remote on the visor. He yawned and blinked sleepily.

The garage door moaned and squealed as it started to open.

Zita ran a hand back and forth over her hair. "Ni modo. You're about to doze off and don't know how to drive? Turn off the car and give me the keys," she said.

He protested. "It's my car!"

"You nearly hit the garage door already, and I don't want to choke on carbon monoxide while you figure out how a car works. I've been driving for years. I'm good at it. Just ask anyone." *Except for my friends or brothers or the coworker I gave a ride home to the one time. They're picky about silly things like traffic laws and what constitutes a road.*

"Fine, I could use a nap, but be careful. She's new. You'll need to hit me to wake me when we get there. Don't be afraid to punch my arm hard." He changed gears, and the car jolted forward, hitting the trash cans.

Zita snorted, reached over, and put the car in park. "Yeah. I'm driving."

After he managed to turn off the car, they switched places. His shoulders relaxed as he slid into his seat. "This will be fun," he said happily. "I've never been on a road trip before other than to a hospital. I'll put Vic's address in. Next time, I'll have supplies ready."

As the vampire hummed and set up the navigation system, Zita shook her head and forced herself to study the console and adjust the seat to accommodate the almost foot difference in their heights. The pedals alone seemed suited more to a space ship than anything she'd ever driven before. "We're just going to D.C. From another section of D.C. How does that qualify as a... no importa."

Dmitri fiddled with the GPS and his seatbelt and seemingly everything he could reach, finally finishing with a flourish. "Done!"

Zita turned on the vehicle and stared at the information projected on the windshield, before shaking her head. "Seriously? You got like a fancy movie screen in this too? Is there popcorn in the trunk? I could eat."

He beamed. "It's the latest in driver information systems, so you don't have to divert your eyes from the road to get essential information. It's great, isn't it? Oh, don't forget the butt heat!" Dmitri pressed a couple more buttons and failed to hide a yawn behind his hand.

"Órale, did some sales guy do a number on you or what?" Zita backed out, tires squealing, far faster than she had expected. When she shifted the sedan into drive, it pulled away smoothly... and quickly. Stabbing at the remote on the visor with a finger, she was gratified to see the garage doors lower. "This is going to be fun. My friends will be sorry they missed it."

"You did say you had your license, right?" he said, his words slurring.

Following the directions that the GPS' calm, cool computer voice gave her, Zita zoomed around a vehicle spreading salt. "You'll have to take my word for it."

"I should take... notes," he murmured.

Heat spread through her from the seat, and Zita purred as her muscles relaxed. She glanced over to see his eyes had closed and his body was limp in the seat. The only breathing she heard was her own. Reaching over, she checked his pulse. None. For all intents and purposes, she was driving around with a corpse in the car.

With a shudder, she tapped on the radio, flipping through the stations until she found a song upbeat enough to drown out her unease.

# Chapter Ten

**In Arca form,** Zita walked through the hall of Victoria's apartment building, reading door numbers until she came to a stop before the right one. She glanced over her shoulder and up at the black bubbles prominently located near the elevator. *Nice digs to have cameras inside. Good coverage and I think that model rotates enough to catch the whole hall, plus the lighting should allow a nice picture. Lot nicer than my place, that's for sure, but rent's got to be super high. However, even if they're charging for all the security, that sleepy guard in the lobby that Dmitri schmoozed isn't watching every second.*

She tapped her foot. While she'd happily run up the stairs, Dmitri had chosen to use the elevator. Glaring down the hall as if she could will him to move faster by force of will, she tried to be patient. *Victoria's his friend. I should wait for him to get here.*

After jogging up and down the short hallway a couple of times, her patience was done. "How long does it take an elevator to go eight floors?" Finally, she waved at the camera and then knocked. *I'll just start chit-chatting. He should be here any second.*

Her knuckles barely grazed it before the door slid open.

"Oye, that's never good." Raising her voice, she called into the apartment. "Victoria? We had questions for you. Me and Dmitri, if your slow-ass elevator ever gets him up here."

No one replied.

Trepidation stiffened her spine and made her hesitate. Swallowing hard, she knocked again, and the door opened the rest of the way in a wash of heat and rank odor.

Inside, white carpet and walls framed heavy, ornate furniture. Photographs lined a mantel above a lit gas fireplace. All that did, however, was showcase the trail of brownish-red drops leading down the hall from one of the chairs, an old wooden one with fancy curves that implied age, a high price tag, and very little comfort for anyone willing to sit in it. Brownish stains marred the end of a fireplace poker that lay askew under an overturned chair, the only items out of place in the room.

*An old lady, alone, and moving all stiff like that? Easy pickings for the wrong sort.* Acid bitter in her mouth, Zita paused in the doorway, then whirled and pounded on the neighbor's door.

Muttering and cursing from inside preceded the door easing open all of a half-inch. Whoever was inside did not remove the chain. "What? Who are you? Don't you know who I am?"

"So don't care. Call the police and an ambulance! Something's wrong in the apartment next door. I see blood, and I'm going in to see if somebody needs help," Zita shouted.

The door slammed shut, and the deadbolt clunked. "You can bet I'm calling the police!"

Swearing under her breath, Zita took a deep breath and squared her shoulders, already knowing what she would find. Her mind idly cataloged the smells: sage, cedar, fur, and a musty floral in an incense that made her nose itch, with the stink of blood and the even more unpleasant reek of death and bitter swamp water beneath it. She smoothed her hands on her pants and called out again. "Victoria?" *It may be a blessing that Dmitri's not here to see this.*

Entering, she glanced to the side—an office, with no sign of anyone other than a wall safe hanging open and a few bloody footprints on the carpet. White papers peeked out from the safe.

The empty desktop held only a pen and a paperweight, a chunk of crystal the size of her fist. Continuing on, she passed a kitchen gleaming with granite and stainless steel and entered a bedroom.

The fangless queen of the vampires lay upon the bed, her faded eyes open and sightless. Her mouth had cloth stuffed in it, likely from the dress that had been sliced open without marring the staid white underwear beneath. Slashes marred Victoria's thick body, though less blood showed than Zita expected. A thick spike of wood protruded from her chest. Her bare feet hung over the edge of the bed, barely recognizable beneath the gore. The position of her body spoke of agony, and her wrists and ankles bore raw red welts and gashes.

Skirting the gory trail, Zita walked over and touched the elderly woman's wrist. No pulse beat and the skin was cool to the touch. Two healing punctures marred the pale, waxy skin, and a purple mottling marred the skin by the sheets. This close, she noticed a line at Victoria's throat and leaned in to examine it. Closer, she could see a jagged tear, like a chunk had been ripped out, then muscle and bone and...

*Her head's been severed from her body. Dios be with her soul.*

Reeling back, Zita ran out of the apartment, a hand over her mouth. She bent over, hands on her knees, and inhaled, forcing herself to breathe evenly as if performing yoga. Nausea swirled, and she choked it back. After she sneezed three times, she brushed wetness from her eyes. *That poor woman and her stupid perfume.*

Dmitri exited the elevator, along with the security guard from the lobby. They both froze when they saw her doubled over.

The vampire's mouth opened and closed as his face tilted upward and his nose quivered. He licked his lips. "Arca? What's wrong?"

Raising his flashlight, the security guy stared at her.

Zita would have felt more threatened if the guard had held his light more like a club and less like a submarine sandwich, and if she hadn't just seen a beheaded body. She waved a hand toward Victoria's door. "The lady in there's dead. Don't let nobody in until the police come." Her accent dripped thickly in the words, and her voice was hoarse. The insides of her throat burned.

Dmitri had frozen in place. His smile was more of a rictus, and his voice cracked. "Not Vic..."

Hating every moment, Zita repeated herself. This time, she managed to add, "I'm sorry."

"Miz Timmons? Oh, no!" Gripping his flashlight, the guard ran to the doorway and stared into the living room. "Where? What if she needs help?"

*Carajo. Dmitri said she was his best friend. I can't let him see her.* "Bedroom," Zita said. "Some cabrón took her head off. She don't need no help no more. Leave her for the cops and their guys to do all their science stuff."

Flailing his arms and legs like he'd never learned how to run, Dmitri sped past the motionless security guy into the apartment.

She followed, grabbing his shoulder before he could get past the fireplace. "Dude, she's gone. You don't want to see her like that."

He threw off her hand and bared his fangs at her. His eyes burned with an unholy red glow. "Do not tell me what to do! You are mistaken! It's not her!"

Shifting to a gorilla, Zita seized his arm again as he started toward the bedroom and spun him to face the other direction. She hooted sadly.

"It can't be her," Dmitri whispered, voice breaking, all the anger seeping from his body and the light dying in his eyes. As she watched, his fangs retracted.

Unable to speak, Zita hooted again.

Dmitri's tensed muscles went limp, and he hung his head. "You're certain?"

She nodded, shifting back to Arca. "I'm sorry."

"Neither of you can be in here!" The security guy entered the apartment and gagged. He raised a hand to his mouth. "What's that smell?"

"Arca?" Dmitri broke the silence. "Victoria. Please tell me... did she suffer? I smell so much blood..."

The horrified face of the dead woman and the bloodbath in the room rose in Zita's memory. Combined with the rank smell she'd been trying to ignore, she felt her stomach flip again. She swallowed and lied. "No. Probably didn't feel a thing. He hit an artery." *And everything else in her neck.*

Dmitri suddenly wrapped his arms around Zita. Raw, animal sounds came from him, and his body shook. He lowered his head.

*If he thinks I'll let him snack on me...* Zita had slipped halfway out of his grasp and had almost reached a set of fireplace tools when she realized it wasn't an attack.

The security guard stared at the bedroom, then reversed course to the hallway. "You two, come out here until the police can talk to you."

"I can't hear her heartbeat. She was my best friend," Dmitri whispered. He lifted his head. Twin rose-tinted trails ran down his cheeks, and he hugged Zita again.

"Yes," Zita said lamely, patting his back with slightly more force than necessary. *At least his fangs are sheathed.* She stared at the pictures lining the fireplace to distract herself. One caught her eye, an aged photo hidden behind the others. A younger Victoria, sans the queen costume, stood with her arms linked with a male version of herself. Beside the man, a boy with similar features stared at the camera, somehow both expressionless and malevolent. They all stood in front of an oddly familiar mansion, the sort of rustic place with five bathrooms that wealthy people would call a cabin and only use for a week or two a year. She scanned the rest of the photos, picking out several, all older ones, that included the

Victoria and the man, but no others with the boy. Her mind kept turning back to the boy.

"Dmitri, who's the man in that picture?" Squirming free and grateful to have an excuse, Zita pointed to the image.

He straightened and wiped his eyes on his hand. Pale pink smears marred the pasty white of his hand. "What? Sorry. That's her brother. He died years ago."

"And the kid?" Zita asked.

Dmitri shook his head. "I don't know. Her brother's son, maybe? Victoria never said anything about him other than her brother's crazy ex moved away and had him start using another name."

Zita tried to keep her voice soft. "Focus, hombre. What did the kid's name change to?"

The vampire stared at the pictures and made as if to pick up one, aborting the gesture before he touched it. "I don't know. A girl's name and something real common. Johns?"

She kept her tone soft and level, despite her urge to shout. "Something like Tracy Jones?"

Confusion eroded the sorrow in his expression. "Yeah, that sounds right... Wait. Sobek?" Dmitri scowled, his fangs descending as anger darkened his expression.

*This explains why Wyn's location spell failed. I should tell her, so she knows the problem was that she used the wrong name.* Zita held up both hands. "Don't bite the messenger. Do you know what his original name was?"

The vampire hissed at her though he seemed more depressed than angry. "Now is not the time for your groundless paranoia. And no, I don't."

"You two need to wait in the hallway. Don't make me ask you again," the guard said. His hands, white from his tight grip on his flashlight, shook as he stared at the pair.

Her voice low, Zita said, "Are you staying or going?"

Dmitri glanced at the security guard and straightened. "I want in. You have to promise you'll keep me in the loop of your search and let me help. It can't be a coincidence that my best friend is murdered after you come around asking about her psycho possible-nephew. Promise me, or I'm charging into that bedroom right now."

Zita glanced toward the bedroom and shuddered. "You super don't want to do that."

His eyes narrowed, and crimson sparked in his irises. He leaned closer, towering over her and invading her space. "Don't I? Give me your word."

She had to resist the urge to shove him away. "Fine. You're in, you got my word. Can we leave now?"

With that, the lights extinguished, and Dmitri's body relaxed. He stepped back. "Why would we go?"

"I'm a masked vigilante. The cops will want petty details like my real name and address and other things I don't want to tell them," she reminded him, keeping her comment quiet.

The security guard seemed to vacillate between staring in horror at the entrance to the apartment and pacing the hall muttering.

She pressed Dmitri for an answer. "You don't have to come with me, but if you are, we got to go now before somebody arrives who knows what they're doing."

The vampire rubbed his forehead. He sailed into the hall, coat billowing around him like a cape. "Are things always this complicated around you?"

"Me?" She touched her chest and shook her head. "Don't blame me. I didn't kill her. So, you leaving or not?"

Dmitri stared at his friend's place and then closed his eyes, sighing. His nose twitched. "Let's go. If I stay here... I'll fall asleep again whether I want to or not and the police will think they have two corpses to handle."

Zita nodded and headed for the stairs.

The security guard said nothing until Zita reached out for the door handle. "Hey, you both need to stay so the police can question you."

Dmitri interposed himself between the guard and Zita, tilting his head toward the exit. He executed a little bow with a dramatic flourish. One hand waved at her to go. "I cannot stay now, but the police can reach me in the Intermediate Care Ward of Lowndes Memorial Hospital after eight in the evening. My name is David, and I will have my lawyer call them. You'll tell them for me, I hope."

Mechanically, the guard took the card. "Yes, I will tell them."

Zita fled down the stairs.

By the time Dmitri reached the bottom of the steps, she had his car purring in wait by the stairwell. Warmth flowed from the seats.

"Home, Jeeves. The day presses upon me," he said, settling into the leather with a sigh and looping his scarf to cover most of his face again. Despite the comment, his body was tight and trembling in a too-correct posture.

"Arca. And I'm not your chingado chauffeur," Zita growled. Her back was a mass of knotted tension as she kept the speed down and sedately drove by a police cruiser. The red and blue lights threw crazy colors into the car.

Her rebuke went unanswered, and she glanced over.

The vampire must've fallen asleep, for Dmitri's motionless corpse once again rode beside her.

She shuddered and gunned the engine.

# Chapter Eleven

**Loathing the necessity,** that night Zita showed up at the hospital Dmitri had mentioned. She slipped in through a side entrance wearing too-big scrubs she'd found at a local thrift store, catching the door behind a crowd of chattering staff. Detouring into the first supply closet she could find, she appropriated a janitorial cart, stuck Arca's long hair up under a plastic hair net and hung a surgical mask around her neck for good measure. She did her best to trudge slowly to the floor housing the Intermediate Care Ward. For the hundredth time, she checked to make certain her badge, borrowed from a locker, was turned so only the blank back of it showed. The antiseptic scent, mingled with paper and ailing humanity, made her nose twitch, and she tried hard not to think about her youthful stays in cancer units.

Her mind spun as she moved. *Funny how even how hospitals all smell the same. Rich D.C. ones like this have fancier machinery, a little extra paint, and a few decorations to distract from the same base misery, annoying fluorescents, and speckled floors. I wish I'd been able to get answers elsewhere, but I'm out of avenues. If nothing else, I need to find out how Tiger and DMS, or at least my brother, knew we'd be at the club. I wish they'd been prompt enough following up my tip about Victoria to have saved her.*

As she shoved open the door to the ward, a young nurse glanced at the cart and the badge. She took Zita by the arm. Shoes squeaking on the tile, the nurse hauled her along at a no-nonsense pace. "They sent someone? I can actually do my job instead of mopping for once! Room 222B, the second to last one on the left is the one that had the pipe leak. The patient's still in the room and in bad shape, so be quiet and keep your mask up."

Keeping her head down, Zita put her face mask on. "Okay. Should I get the trash?" The cheap paper mask made the lower half of her face feel overheated and crammed the loathsome reek of chemicals up her nose. She consoled herself that she could take it off soon.

Checking the clock, the nurse paused, then nodded. "Yes, no reason to wait until later. Shouldn't have much in it. Grab the trash in the room next to it if the family's out. They've been in there all day and most of last night..."

Elation rose. She could certainly mop a floor to give credence to her disguise, especially since handling those rooms would allow her to walk the length of the ward and find Dmitri. "Will do." Giving her cart a shove, Zita plodded into action.

Each room had a clear glass wall and a matching sliding door facing the hall, so checking for the vampire in each room was simple. In every room that held a patient, the door was shut, and she tried not to stare at any of them. To her delight, she glimpsed Dmitri in the room at the end of the hall, next to the one she had to mop. The bed near the vampire was empty.

One room over, a cop sat on a hard plastic chair, his eyes drooping. He stirred as she drew near.

*Of course, the room I need to mop to maintain my disguise is the only one with a guard.* Bringing her rattling cart to a stop, Zita tapped the mop and tried to seem unenthused as she pulled on too-large purple nitrile gloves. Just in case, she laid on her Mexican accent and prayed he wouldn't flip her hospital badge over. It'd be pretty obvious that she wasn't the man in the photograph. "A bathroom mess needs cleaning?"

He wrinkled his nose and waved her in. "Oh, yeah. Be quick, right?"

She bobbed her head and pushed the cart through, closing the glass door behind herself.

The lights were out, but the brightness of the hall outside gave the room a feeling of artificial twilight. In the hospital bed, a thin figure shivered beneath layers of blankets. With the endless shrieking alarms and hum of activity from the floor outside muted, the loudest sounds were the squeaking of her cart, the endless beeping and hissing of machinery, and harsh gasps from the patient, as if each breath was a struggle.

After skirting edges of the room, it took Zita only a couple minutes to clean the minuscule bathroom cubicle. When she finished, she ran the mop through the wringer and grabbed the trash can. She took a second to lower the mask, just to cool herself off and feel less trapped, though she kept her face away from the hallway. The scent of the patient's illness washed over her, infection and a nasty, sickly sweet odor. She gagged.

A scratchy voice complained, "I know you're there. Are you going to stare at me or give me something to help with the pain?" With a groan, the shape in the bed flopped over and rubbed bloodshot eyes. The pocked skin of his face, an odd yellow color, seemed to hang loosely from his skull and his remaining brown teeth flashed as he spoke. "Oh, it's you. You're a janitor?" He cackled until a series of wracking coughs cut him off.

Dumping the contents of the bin into the container on her cart, Zita grunted.

"I'd sue you since I can't walk again without surgery, but I'm dying soon anyway. At least I get the satisfaction of knowing that you clean blood and piss all day." His cracked lips tilted downward as if he'd bitten something bitter.

Zita blinked and pulled her face mask back up. *It's Goatee from the railroad tracks! I didn't recognize him all clean. Amazing how he looks even worse than before.* "Not like I got money."

Rubbing the scraggly hair clinging to his haggard face, he narrowed his eyes at her. "Clearly not. You know what? You should get me something to ease the pain since it's your fault I'm here."

She scoffed. "No mames, hombre. I barely touched you guys, and I only hurt your leg because you were so hopped up on drugs that you wouldn't stop."

He started to sit up but began coughing before he could get more than a syllable out. When he caught his breath again, he continued in a low tone. "The cops think I'm like you and all the other metafreaks and want to lock me up the same way they do things like you. I'm not. I'm a real person. Do you know what makes this all worse? If you'd left the vampire on the tracks, I wouldn't be dying. Or, at least I'd die happy after another dose. My friends would be alive, too."

Zita's eyebrows rose. "What did you tell them? That you and your friends were trying to murder someone, and I stopped you?" Unable to help herself, she picked up the cup with the straw by his bed and offered him the water.

He turned his head away and spat on the floor beside his bed. Blood and spit splattered. "Clean that, janitor. Earl fried and Phil went the way I'm going, organ failure. The fanged guy was already dead. All the train would've done was stop him from moving around, since nothing else we tried to do to him worked. I told everyone who would listen about how you attacked us out of nowhere and where you'd be at the Dance Mister. The cops and the man in the suit loved my helpfulness."

*Man in the suit? Could he mean Miguel? That clears Dmitri as the one who tipped DMS, but it's still possible he told Tiger.* Zita set the unwanted water back down and swiped the mop over the mess. "The cops and who? Wait, I attacked you?"

"Some DMS guy. If you didn't want the blame, you should've stuck around and talked to the police." He turned his back to her. "If you won't help me, I have nothing more to say. Get out and let me die in peace."

Torn, Zita paused and stared at his back. "I'm sorry your friends died." Finally, she opened the glass door and gave the cart a hard shove without looking.

Caught by the cart, a woman in a wet, puffy beige coat windmilled her arms, black boots slipping on the damp tile. A golden badge gleamed at her waist, visible against a thick blue sweater bared by the open jacket. An overstuffed brown leather bag hit the floor with a thud.

Before the woman could fall, Zita darted out and caught her arm, setting her upright. "Ay! So sorry," she said, her fake Mexican accent thick with nerves. *Gracias a Dios that my face is hidden even if it's Arca's. Please don't recognize me.*

"No problem, just watch where you're going," the woman muttered, and then eyed the cop guarding the door. "Not a word, Johnson."

He gestured zipping his lips shut though a smile tilted up the corners.

After smoothing her hair and straightening her coat, the female cop strode toward the nurse's station in short, powerful strides. Tapping on the counter to get the people behind the desk's attention, she pulled a badge from her belt. "Detective Faiza Haroon with the D.C. police. Can I speak to the shift supervisor?"

Behind the desk, a pretty young nurse, the same one who had greeted Zita, elbowed the heavyset man in scrubs beside her. With a sigh, he held up one finger, then returned to typing. Gray streaked his close-cropped hair, and he scowled at the computer screen. Once he'd finished hitting the last key with an audible click, he looked up. Wariness settled over his body as he took in the cop. "You got him. What do you need, officer?"

"I need to ask you some questions. Were you on duty last night?" the detective said.

Keeping her head lowered, Zita dug through her cart and got out a Wet Floors sign. Setting that up, she angled her cart closer to the cop and detective and busied herself mopping the detective's trail of water on the floor.

Rubbing stubby fingers across his forehead, the supervisor nodded. "I was."

"Right, can you tell me if this man came in?" The detective removed a picture from her bag and showed it to him.

He started to shake his head before he even glanced at it, then stopped. "You're in luck. Normally, I pay more attention to the patients and my staff than their visitors, but I remember him. He's in now, down at the end there. Last night he showed up not ten minutes into my shift with an old white lady. She was dressed up like Queen Victoria, even wearing one of those fancy black dresses and a veil on her head like a bride."

"This woman? How long were they here?" the detective said, showing him another picture.

He nodded. "That's her. The guy was here until a little after dawn. He's immediate family of one of our patients, but the queen left maybe ten minutes later. Guess she didn't want to sit in the comfy seats." The supervisor pointed down the hall toward a grouping of small ultramodern plastic chairs.

*Guess I don't need to verify Dmitri's whereabouts last night. I'll try to be quick and not upset the sick man by letting him know his son's lack of life bothers me.* Guilt lanced her. Realizing the detective's eyes were on her, Zita moved a few feet and cleaned there.

Apparently accepting her ruse, Detective Haroon turned her attention back to the supervisor. "Do you know how long they were here, if they spoke to anyone, and if they left at any time?"

A laugh escaped the supervisor. "Like I've got nothing to do but watch visitors, even weird ones? As I said before, the old lady left about ten minutes after I got here... maybe around eleven twenty last night, and the young guy stayed around until about the end of my shift, around six this morning. As far as I know, he didn't even use the bathrooms or get any coffee, but I also wasn't paying attention to him."

From her seat beside the supervisor, the young nurse glanced up from her computer. "The guy with the gorgeous purple eyes? His name's David. He was here all night with his parents. They used to be regulars here for reasons I can't disclose, but you'd remember him if you met him." She returned to her work, her lips smug.

Her supervisor raised his bushy eyebrows at his subordinate but directed his words to the cop. "You want to check with Enrique in security. I don't remember his last name, but he'll set you up with whatever videos you want. Main security office is in the basement, next to the morgue."

The nurse beside him patted her puff of ebony hair and flicked her fingers at the supervisor. "Enrique's last name is Matapang. Also hot and sends money home to his mama every month if you're curious."

Scribbling notes, the detective nodded. "My partner's already speaking to security, but I'll write down the name. Is there a room I can borrow while we're interviewing David?"

Shaking his head at his subordinate, the supervisor checked a screen. "David's father just got wheeled out for some tests. You could use his room if you do it within the next forty-five minutes. We don't keep conference rooms in this unit. Is he a danger to our patients?"

The detective blandly replied, "At this time, he's only a person of interest. I'll get my partner and be right back to speak to him."

After putting the mop away, Zita wheeled her cart to the elevator. She kept her pace sluggish though her mind raced. *I need to sneak in, warn Dmitri about the detectives if I can, and set up a meet for later. It'd look suspicious if I walked into that room now. Even if the whole undead thing makes my skin crawl, Dmitri doesn't deserve to be hounded for Sobek's crimes. Victoria's killing had a lot of Sobek's trademarks: the mangled feet, the cutting, and the surprise attack, even if he didn't have an unwilling audience as he prefers. Not to mention, we'll need Dmitri's help to get rid of Sobek's vampirism.*

Zita automatically pressed the door close button to encourage it to move faster. As she did, she saw the cop heading toward her.

"Hold the elevator!" Detective Haroon commanded.

Zita hit the button again and exhaled hard when the doors shut and she was still alone.

***

After returning her borrowed items to the closet where she'd found them, Zita scurried out of the hospital, keeping the mask over her face in case someone checked the hall cameras. Once outside, she tore off the face mask with a sigh of relief and stripped off her scrubs, leaving on only the Spandex-like sportswear. Changing shape to an owl, she flew up to the correct floor and counted windows until she found the right one. Landing on the sill, she shifted to a squirrel and peered inside.

The room was a mirror image of Goatee's, except that where his had seemed sterile, this one held personality. An empty bed took center stage, ringed by the same mysterious electronic equipment, but a colorful quilt covered in red and black embroidery hung at the end of the bed. At least one or two of the doilies from the house had migrated to the bedside table along with a few framed pictures. Dmitri sat in a low beige armchair, bent over a laptop, his back to the window. The document in front of him scrolled as his hands flew over the keyboard at superhuman speeds. A messy bag of something that resembled an incomplete doily sat neglected by the chair.

*Not many good hiding places and a glass wall. Awesome.* Zita took a deep breath and teleported inside behind the chair and well out of sight of the hall. Seeing motion outside the room, she dove beneath the chair and hid.

Had it not been for the constant sounds of typing, she would have thought Dmitri had slipped again into the corpse-like state he'd evinced during the day.

Someone knocked, and the glass door slid open. A man's voice asked, "Excuse me, are you David Derkach?"

Dmitri jumped to his feet, knocking over the tiny table he'd been using as a desk. Pens and papers scattered and rolled, while his laptop and phone hit the ground with more solid thuds. "Yes, is my father okay? Has something happened? Take me to him." Fear was thick in his voice and scent. His hammy accent was missing. One of his feet kicked his phone under the chair, nearly into the squirrel crouching there.

Zita edged back, trying to stay away. She swore mentally. *Not fast enough to warn him.*

Detective Haroon and a chubby older man walked in, badges clipped to their belts.

The male cop moved closer, hiding everything from his shoulders up from Zita. "It's all right, Mr. Derkach. This isn't about your father. We don't work at the hospital." He introduced himself as Detective Mack and then introduced Haroon. "I think you can guess why we're here."

Dmitri's feet moved closer, and he righted the table. "Ah, the detectives who've been calling me. Please, call me David. How can I help you?" His voice gentled from fear to caution.

Haroon spoke up, though she remained a step back from her partner, allowing Zita to see most of her face. "First, we need your permission to record this interview, both audio and video. It's not a big deal, just something to protect everyone's rights. Are you okay with that?"

"I guess so," he replied. He scooped up his laptop.

Detective Haroon tapped a black box clipped to the shoulder of her coat. After she stated their names and a file number, she had him agree to the recording again.

Once the formalities were done, her partner took over. "Now that's over, let's get started. In addition to getting your statement about the events of the nightclub, I understand you were familiar with Victoria Timmons?" His pen poised over a pad of paper.

A tremor ran through the vampire's melodious tones. "She was my best friend."

"I'm sorry for your loss. I'm sure you understand that we need to ask you some questions," the cop said, his voice gruff.

Dmitri continued to pick up his scattered belongings. "Phone, where is the phone? Yes, I understand."

"It fell under your chair. Do you want me to get it?" Haroon asked.

Dmitri got on his knees and swiped his arm under the chair. "I can do it."

Zita leapt out of the way, trying frantically not to emerge from underneath. *It won't help anyone if the cops think Dmitri and I are in cahoots.*

His fingers only inches from her squirrel body, Dmitri touched his phone and scrabbled at it with his fingertips.

Holding her breath, she shoved it a little closer.

He slapped his hand on it and withdrew it.

The detective cleared his throat. "Were you aware of the events at the Danz Mizer nightclub last night?"

"I heard Tiger, a former employee, took it hostage and there was fighting, but I left before anything started."

Haroon leaned forward. "Can you walk us through the events of that night?"

Dmitri's feet were silent as he picked up his belongings. "Even though I missed the action? I went to the club around ten or ten thirty. Vic—Victoria Timmons—told me that Muse and Arca had been asking for me, so I spoke to them in a booth in the VIP section."

"What did you discuss?" Mack's voice was brisk.

Zita felt a tremor run through the chair with the vampire's movement. "They asked me questions about a criminal named Tracy Jones, who also calls himself Sobek."

A pen scratched over paper as Mack wrote something. "Why did they ask you?"

Here Dmitri paused for a moment. "Sobek has been seen at the club in the past, and I'm a regular there. Since I'm usually in the manager's office, I introduced them to Vic. She asked me to take Arca and Muse around to the staff to see if they could find out more. While we were at the VIP bar, my mother reached Vic about my father's stroke, and we left immediately for here."

Her head tilting, Haroon inserted, "Why did your mother contact the victim and not you?" The detective scribbled notes.

Fabric rustled. "As you're aware, I'm not always good about leaving my phone on. Once Vic and I got here, I stayed here with my parents until sometime around dawn. My mother and I went home for some sleep. Mom woke me when Arca arrived with the news that Vic wasn't responding to anyone's calls. She has—" Dmitri's voice broke. When he began again, his tone held stress, though he had returned to his usual melodious baritone. "Vic had a chronic ailment, and I was concerned that she'd suffered an acute attack and required aid. She sent me a text asking me to go to her, but I didn't see it until Arca mentioned people had been trying to reach me."

Detective Mack's tone dripped with disapproval. "So, you went with a vigilante?"

The vampire grunted. "She wanted to ask Vic more questions about Sobek but needed my help to find her. I didn't want her to upset my possibly ill friend, so I went with. I hope you're looking into Sobek?"

The cop's feet shuffled a few steps. "Mr. Jones is a person of interest, but we have no concrete evidence of his involvement. Per DMS, none of the club witnesses could positively identify him, and Ms. Timmons' death did not match his pattern. Right now, this matter remains a D.C. police case. Would you continue? You went to Ms. Timmons' apartment?"

*As if DMS investigates anything that fast. They probably just ignored all the tips I called in.* Zita managed to keep herself from making a derisive noise aloud.

"But he—fine, yes, we went straight there. I took the slower elevator up with the security guard, and Arca reached the apartment first. Then she found..." His voice broke, and he cleared his throat. "Pardon. Arca wouldn't let me past the living room, so I don't know if I can be any more help."

If someone's voice could sharpen, Mack's did. "Why is that?"

"She said she verified Vic was beyond help and backed out right after, but that we needed to leave things as untouched as possible for forensics. We left after that," he said.

"Why did you leave before the police arrived?" Haroon asked.

Dmitri sighed. "I did tell the guard where you could find me. I have photodermatitis—it means I can't go in the sun without getting sick. It's the reason I sleep days, work nights, and have to depend on others to drive me places. Arca was disinclined to go to the police station, so she dropped me off at home. As soon as I woke up again, I left you a message and got a ride here."

*Got to give him credit for glossing over the undead bit,* Zita thought.

With the dubious tones of someone who's seen everything and given it a nuisance ticket, Mack said, "If you cannot be outside in the day, how did you get to Ms. Timmons' place?"

Dmitri cleared his throat. "Using many, many layers of clothing. Vic's building has a parking garage, so I knew I could get out there safely."

Mack's next words had Zita's tail wrapping around her.

"Can you offer contact information for either Arca or Muse?" Even if his tone was neutral, the detective's whole body tensed.

The vampire cleared his throat. "No. They came to me, and we did not exchange numbers. I'm told one of the bartenders gave Arca my home address."

Disappointment flashed on both cops' faces. Haroon asked, "Do you remember what shoes Arca was wearing?"

Dmitri paused. "Canvas tennis shoes in a dark purple. I remember thinking she had to be freezing in the purple Spandex with just a hoodie and the shoes that didn't quite match."

Clapping her paws over her mouth, Zita swallowed her outrage and avoided chittering at him in indignation. *They match! I dyed them real careful, so Wyn wouldn't get that pained expression she wears when she checks out my outfits. Why would the police care about my shoes, anyway?* She stared at her paws for a moment. *Ah, footprints.*

His voice bland, Mack dropped his bomb. "Were you aware that you are Ms. Timmons' primary heir and will receive the bulk of her estate, including her bank account and the nightclub?"

Shock lanced through Dmitri's voice. He must've dropped everything in his hands, as papers fluttered to the ground while pens hit with a clatter. "What? That's impossible. I mean, she mentioned her grandson wasn't getting the club because he's in Witness Protection, but I thought she was donating to charity..."

A big heavy pen rolled under the chair, right at her.

Zita stopped it and pushed it toward the front of the chair so it could be found more easily. *Don't look under here,* she willed the people above her. *At least this time it's not a phone. Maybe he won't notice.*

Dmitri grabbed stuff off the floor. "Give me just a moment," he said.

To her dismay, she saw him get to his knees. *Please don't give me away. Don't look.*

A second later, Dmitri's face appeared at the edge of the chair. His violet eyes widened at the sight of her.

She waved weakly and shoved his pen at him.

A faint tremor ran through his body, but Dmitri collected his pen and stood up. "I seem to have everything now."

"You're claiming you had no idea? The witnesses to the will both work at her club, which I understand you frequent enough to be allowed into employee-only areas." Detective Mack sounded impatient.

Haroon clucked her tongue. "Give him a chance, Mack. Perhaps he can explain it."

Dmitri's feet took a wider stance, and Zita suspected he'd put his hands on his hips. "I did not know and would have discouraged her from it if I had. We discussed wills from time to time, but only in the most general sense, as I wished to update mine with trust funds for my parents and knew she was familiar with the process. My health has been fragile most of my life, and Victoria knew that."

Both cops moved their feet, sliding into defensive positions. Mack scoffed, "Convenient. You don't appear ill now."

"I've worked hard at my recovery, and Vic was a big help."

*Is it really recovery if you die and become undead?* Zita wondered.

Detective Haroon dropped another bomb. "Did you ever have a sexual relationship with the victim?"

Something snapped, and the big pen fell in halves to the floor.

A man in a suit rapped on the glass door.

Dmitri's voice chilled immeasurably. "No. Vic had a chronic illness similar to my own, and we bonded over that, but it was more mentor and student than anything else. My lawyer is here now. If you have further questions, please feel free to speak with him."

"Thank you for your time. We'll be in touch," Mack threatened as he and his partner exited.

As soon as the detectives left, and he completed a brief verbal exchange with the man in the suit outside, Dmitri closed the big glass door. He swept across the room to the chair. "Did you need to accuse me of eating Vic again? I presume that's you, Arca."

Crawling out from beneath the chair, Zita shifted to Arca and hid behind the heavy beige armchair. "It is, and no." *I do not need anyone seeing me here. It wouldn't help Dmitri much either, but the only animal forms with speech tend to be loud and screechy.*

Sweeping up the remains of his pen, Dmitri tossed it into the trash with a clatter. "Not this time? Pity, it seems to be a trend today, and I do loathe being unfashionable. So, why were you spying on me?"

"That was accidental," Zita said. "I meant to warn you about the detectives and arrange a meet for the next step in the Sobek search, talking to that waitress Incubus mentioned. You know, like you had me promise to do. Once I saw the cops here, I didn't want to give them more ammo against you."

Dmitri came around the side of the chair, his arms folded over his chest. His expression was stony. "You couldn't call?"

"I don't have your number, and apparently you don't answer your phone anyway," she said dryly. Guilt still prickled at her. *I could have waited outside instead of sneaking in and eavesdropping.*

He had the grace to seem abashed and rubbed the back of his head. "Oh."

Someone knocked, and Zita shifted back to a squirrel.

Sighing, Dmitri pulled out his wallet and poked around in it. He tossed a business card to the floor. "Fine. Text, and I'll text back when I'm available so we can figure out something." Pocketing his things and turning away, the vampire strode to the door and pulled it open.

*Well, there's one more person I've pissed off. I need to call in backup on this before I screw it all up.* After checking to ensure no one could see her, Zita snatched up the card and teleported.

# Chapter Twelve

**Around lunchtime the next day,** Zita poked her head into Wyn's cramped office on the top floor of the graduate library. She glanced around. Little more than a closet, the room barely had space for the two small desks facing each other, both of which held piles of paper and an assortment of books that seemed to cry out with dusty dullness. Her friend sat at one desk, an elegant finger in a decrepit book and the other tapping delicately at her computer. The other office chair was empty; she had never actually seen anyone else there, though Wyn assured her that another librarian shared the space.

"Hey there! Sorry I'm late. Metro's running slow. What was with the super formal stuff earlier on the phone? Didn't I give you enough time for a couple cups of coffee before I called?"

Her friend set a bookmark in the book and pulled her magic purse from a desk drawer. Wyn kept her voice low, despite the walls shutting out the soft hum of activity outside the room. "I'm sorry about the runaround earlier. Go ahead and take a seat. We can eat here if we're careful not to spill on anything. The new dean of Alternative Religions was waiting for me when I got into my office and was sitting next to me when you called earlier. He's doing a rushed submission for a big, and admittedly interesting, project he wants my assistance on and the deadline's close. It'll require a lot of time to find all the information he wants. Since he's sort of my boss..." Her voice trailed off.

"Understood. We all have to make a living. No worries. You'll do fine. To know you is to love you and all that crap, so you'll be his favorite researcher in no time." Zita plopped into a hard plastic chair and got out the remaining half of her lunch. The rest had disappeared on the walk to the university from the Metro.

Annoyance warred with unhappiness in Wyn's expression as her friend fidgeted. "He likes me fine, and I'm already his favorite. That's the problem. A couple years ago, before we got our powers... I... we... well, we accidentally had sex at my coven's Winter Solstice party."

Zita's mouth ran away with her. "How do you accidentally have sex? Naked two-person luge sledding? Did either of you get frostbite?"

Reluctant laughter interrupted her musing. "Zita! No, we were both single and tipsy. A one-night fling with a visiting professor right before he returned to his own university seemed like a good idea at the time."

"So, more like a decision that turned out awkward than an accident. I totally get that." Zita opened a bag of vegetables, her body tensing as a thought occurred to her. "Is he harassing you? Do I need to hunt him down and kick his culo around? I totally will." She crunched into a carrot, scowling.

Her friend cleared her throat and delicately removed a yogurt and a spoon from her purse. "No, he made a couple of subtle advances, but he's kept it professional since then. I picked up that he's decided it would be unethical to ask me out as my almost-boss. So, he's waiting for me to make the first move, which isn't going to happen."

Zita paused. "That's good, right? He backed off?"

"He did. It's just awkward. Every now and again my control slips and I catch him wishing... Enough about that." Wyn sighed and peeled back the lid of her food. Her voice perked up. "What shenanigans were you contemplating today? Did you get the answers you needed when you were poking around last night? I scanned, and the closest rooms are all empty right now."

Knowing Wyn would be unhappy at the news of the murder, Zita took a deep breath. "Some, but they just raise more questions."

"Was Dmitri behind the attack? He seemed nice." As she tilted her head, light glinted from Wyn's glasses, an accessory worn to keep up appearances as she had not needed them once their powers manifested.

Unable to sit still any more, Zita got to her feet and paced the few steps in either direction that the space allowed. "Dmitri left the club because his dad had a stroke. That's for real. His mom said he was there all night, and they both had that hospital smell clinging to them. You know what I mean." She knew her friend would understand based on their shared time in the hospital as teens.

Wyn hummed in wordless agreement and spooned in a dainty mouthful of food.

An errant thought popped to mind. "Can your healing spell fix his dad?"

Her friend wrinkled her nose and stared morosely at her pitiful lunch, body hunching in on itself. "Maybe if I'd gotten to him right after the stroke, but honestly, I'd be afraid to try now. Brains are so complicated that I could do more harm than good. I can use the spell that keeps my aunt's Alzheimer's in check on him, which would promote healing and avoid infection or further degradation, but... I'm concerned his neural pathways need rebuilding via therapeutic measures."

"Wouldn't the spell put those right again?"

Rubbing her forehead, Wyn said, "Not necessarily. My healing spell puts things the way the body thinks they should be, which is why if I use it on someone with a hereditary disease, the illness won't go away, just any side effects. If his brain thinks there's no way to, say, walk again, then my healing might cut off his chances to learn to do so via physical therapy, though it would resolve any ruptures. I won't cut off a man's chance at a normal life if I can help it, and there's no ethical way to experiment to find out. Maybe if I had an in-depth discussion with a doctor who can access his files? With all the privacy laws, that isn't happening." Her face was still and placid, but her body tensed as if waiting for a blow.

Zita frowned. "That sucks, but yeah. We don't want to make things worse." As she paced by, she squeezed her friend's shoulder, knowing Wyn's inability to cure her aunt's Alzheimer's was a painful subject. She redirected to her original topic, hoping it would let Wyn recover. "So, as I was saying, hospital staff confirmed that Victoria dropped him off and ditched the place. While he was at the hospital, someone murdered the old lady in her apartment. Messily."

Her friend waited for her to continue, then realization struck. "Oh, Goddess. You two found the body."

Biting into another carrot, Zita tried to concentrate on the bright, earthy taste and not picture the scene. "Yeah. It was bad."

"Dmitri said she was his best friend. Did he see?" Wyn's eyes widened, and her expression was sympathetic.

Zita's voice was gruff. "No, I didn't let him. He didn't take it well." She forced herself to focus. "Anyway, Victoria's dead, and it turns out she was Sobek's aunt. Coincidentally, Sobek's mom had him using a different name from his birth one."

Wyn's eyes widened. "That's why my spell failed!"

After nodding at her friend, Zita continued, "We'll never find out what she knew now, so I figure our next step is to go question one of the waitresses, Domina."

Her friend's eyes went distant. "Ah, the one Incubus doesn't like."

Zita nodded. "She's practically my prime suspect. Not only is she a vamp who could be feeding Sobek, but she's also worked at the club for a while, so she could've guessed where Dmitri would've been sleeping the day he was attacked. When I texted him earlier, Dmitri swore up and down she wouldn't be in on anything like that but agreed we should chat with her. In any case, whether she's conspiring with him or an innocent, we need to warn her if someone's killing everyone who saw Sobek. So, yes, she's next on our list."

After another spoonful, Wyn inclined her head. "Logical. You want me there to ensure no duplicity on her part?"

"Honestly, Dmitri could do that. He's super-invested in helping us now Victoria's dead. I figure that if the vamp can convince strangers that sucking their blood is a great idea instead of a setup for a horror flick, he's got to be a people person. While he wanted to interview her today, his dad had some testing he preferred to be there for, plus he and his lawyer have to handle the cops. So, if you couldn't come, he would probably tell me if she's lying, but..." Zita inhaled and admitted, "I also want you there because I... I need you to help me be fair."

"Fair?" Wyn watched her thoughtfully, her forehead crinkling.

Zita paced, unable to sit still, her steps speeding up as her words tumbled out. "With the vampire. I've already insulted him a couple times without meaning to, and that's not right, especially with his dad being sick and his best friend murdered. I keep thinking Dmitri's a bad guy because all my senses tell me he's wrong, he eats people, and he's dead."

"Undead," her friend corrected. "And he said he just sips."

Waving a hand, Zita stopped for a second. "See? Just like that. I know he couldn't have killed the old lady. His reason for leaving the nightclub was legit. He's made a few cheesy jokes, but other than that hasn't been anything but polite. Even let me drive his new car."

"He clearly doesn't know you well," Wyn murmured.

Her defense shot out without thinking. "I'm an excellent driver." After a bite of broccoli, Zita resumed circling the room. "But I think I'm being a shitty person, and I don't want to be that way. I figured... I figured you could remind me, maybe give me a little mental slap if, no, when I start hassling him."

Wyn's eyes were soft. "I can help. I don't find him off-putting."

Zita cheered up. *With her as a buffer, I won't keep insulting him, and she can smooth over any remaining anger between us.* "Excellent. Between the two of us, we got this. Pan comido."

Her friend frowned at the computer as if it had offended her. "I'd like to be able to clear out as much of this project as possible before that snow hits next week. The last thing I want is to be stranded in the library with the new dean. Can the visit with Domina wait until after work?"

Zita nodded and checked the time. "Sure. We're planning to question her tomorrow night. Vampires apparently conk out from sunrise to sunset every day, so we can't ask questions until then anyway if Domina's out cold and I have to kick Dmitri awake every few minutes."

Hope lit Wyn's face. "Is Andy coming? He's been so busy lately."

"I called Andy, but he's doing discreet flyovers in Libya for the next few nights because Dragon was spotted earlier. Given he's the only person who can handle her other than the Tool..." Zita waved a hand.

"We hate her," Wyn murmured automatically.

"Right, so he doesn't have much choice, but he was hopeful his schedule would be back to normal next week, assuming next week's snowstorm doesn't derail him. Poor guy sounded so tired! We're going to climb rocks next weekend if he can get away. He's improved, hardly damages the mountains anymore. For now, though, I figure between you and me, we can handle one vampire."

Belatedly, she remembered the other person coming. "Oh, and Dmitri, too."

Wyn hummed. "Yes, that makes sense, but I still wish Andy could come."

Zita made a rude noise. "You and me both, amiga. We should get started driving before it gets too late, so how about we pick you up tomorrow at the Metro near here around nine? Have fun—but not too much fun! And if that dean turns into a problem, you can always reach me. I'll pop in and ensure he never has kids."

Her friend's eyes turned misty, and she sniffed. "Thank you."

"No hay bronca. What are friends for?" Zita shrugged and gave the other woman a light punch on the shoulder.

Wyn's tone was dry, but amusement ran through it. "The casual castration of our enemies, apparently."

***

The next night, Zita sat behind the wheel of Dmitri's sleek car again, the vampire in the soft leather passenger seat beside her. Wheels sliding only slightly on the worn, icy pavement of the turn, they pulled up at the Metro station's Kiss and Ride. She tapped her fingers as she waited behind a boxy white minivan that seemed to be picking up most of a men's soccer team. Her foot twitched with impatience, and the engine purred in response. *We're here. Are you?*

*Yes, but I don't see you,* Wyn sent.

Beside her, Dmitri stirred. On the way there, he'd broached the topic of Wyn healing his father, but had lapsed into an unhappy silence when Zita told him it wouldn't work and not to ask. His accent was back in force. "Is this a Metro station? You take me to the most interesting places. I had somehow thought we would go somewhere more exciting, like an abandoned plane hangar or an isolated mountain cabin."

"What, did you think I was going to drop by Muse's house?" Zita stared at him for a moment, wondering if he somehow knew of their usual meeting place at the airfield. She shrugged, clicking off her seat belt. After rolling down the window, she lifted herself on the windowsill and waved in the direction of the trains. *We're in the car most likely to be owned by a vampire, other than a hearse. Red with black trim.*

Dmitri didn't answer.

*I see you now.* A young man with the fine features of a model wafted their direction, his hips swinging in a very feminine way, mincing with each step.

Zita slid back inside and pressed the button to raise the window partway. "Found her. I'll have Muse get in on my side, so you don't have to risk the cold. Once we're all belted up, I'll drive us wherever we're going." She opened the door and stood outside, shivering.

Dmitri's voice emerged from the pile of fabrics hiding him as he poked at the GPS controls. "It's my car. I can drive it."

"Nope," she said.

As the male model reached the car, his image blurred into Wyn's usual Muse illusion. She tilted her head, a question on her face, apparently having overheard their exchange of words.

"He only has his learner's permit and doesn't know what he's doing," Zita explained, waving toward the open door. "So, I've got the wheel. Hop in the back!"

"Ah, no," Wyn said. "I'd like to live a bit longer. If he can't drive, I'm the only one left. Give me the keys." She held out an elegant hand.

"If it's any comfort, Arca, I find your driving exhilarating, especially when you manage to get one or more wheels off the ground. Your creative use of grassy medians is inspiring, even if you did refuse to ram the one barrier as I suggested," Dmitri called from inside.

Paling, Wyn said, "I'm definitely driving. No more arguments. Get in the back, Arca." She wiggled her empty hand at Zita as she considered Dmitri. "Gryffindor? I'm more into Ravenclaw, myself."

Dmitri fussed with his maroon and gold scarf. "Truly, it is hard to decide between the houses."

Zita started to protest being relegated to a rider but recognized her friend's obdurate expression. Wyn wasn't going to relent, so she dropped the keys into her hands with a grumble. After moving the driver's seat out of the way, she slipped into the back seat, cramped even for one of her petite stature. "At least turn on the butt heat back here."

"I know where that is. Can I press the buttons? I already put our destination in the computer," Dmitri said.

Wyn rubbed her eyes. "Fine."

"Oh! I almost forgot! I packed food! Every road trip needs food," Dmitri said, happily punching buttons.

After a moment, Zita shook her head. "I'm not drinking no blood, so there better be real food inside."

*Weren't you going to try being nicer?* Wyn reprimanded as she slid the seat way back and got into the car.

Dmitri sniffed. "Of course, it is food. I can only dine on the hoof, so to speak, but movies have taught me everything I need to know about road trips. Your snacks are in a cooler in the trunk."

As Wyn steered the car toward the main road, Zita had to ask. "What is it?"

"Four fried chickens, dry white toast, and a Coke." His voice held glee.

"Ay," Zita said, licking her lips. "Chicken sounds good." Guilt lanced through her. *Even Wyn and Andy don't usually think to bring something for me to eat, and they lived with me for months in quarantine. I have been unreasonable. Even if he's creepy and undead, he's just so... nice. Though he could use a few hints about what constitutes a meal. I mean, where're the vegetables?*

Wyn turned her head to stare at him. "You brought what?"

"Neither of you? I am disappointment." Dmitri laid a hand dramatically over his unbeating heart and sighed.

"I meant to ask, how is your poor father doing?" Wyn said.

The vampire glanced at Zita, his expression darkening. "He survives. The doctors want to keep him under observation given some anomalies. The reason we could come no earlier was because I wanted to wait until he slept before leaving. I am no stalker to stare at someone while they take their rest."

"It's hard to watch a loved one suffer like that," Wyn said. "May the Goddess bless him with good health soon."

"Thank you. My parents were my bastions when I was ill, and I can only aspire to repay them even a fraction." His gaze intense, Dmitri studied Wyn. "Do you know what I see when I look at you?"

Zita flicked her gaze to Wyn and then back to the vampire. Her hand crept to her seat belt in case she needed to move freely. "I do." *A helpless blood bag. Pues, not when I'm here.*

*Be nice,* Wyn sent.

Violet eyes met hers, his expression curious. "And what is that, little shapeshifter?"

"Scrawny arms. She needs a better workout regimen for them. I've tried to help her with them, but she's not interested even if she can't throw." Zita poked at one of Wyn's offending limbs.

Wyn pinched between her own brows for a moment before dropping her hand. "Did you actually just say that? Are you ever going to let me forget that? One bad toss..."

Dmitri threw his head back and laughed, the velvety peals of laughter musical. When he stopped, he dabbed at his eyes with a red handkerchief, tucking it back into a pocket beneath his voluminous coat. "No, Lady Arca, I fear you have mistaken me for a fitness trainer."

"I'm no lady," Zita said, her tension easing as the vampire leaned back into his seat, away from her friend. She bit her tongue to keep from saying more. *Despite all the muscles busy rippling under your clothing, you don't seem like the athletic sort, not with the way you walk as if the length of your stride surprises you. Look at me, all diplomatic and shit.*

*We're all proud of your self-restraint.* Wyn's tone was drier than burnt toast without butter. "Don't worry, no one has mistaken you for one, Arca."

Zita nodded at her friend. "Sí, that's right." She squinted at her friend when the other woman burst into giggles, and Dmitri once again unleashed his melodious laughter. "Wait..."

Sobering, Dmitri said, "What I see in the lovely Muse's eyes is courage and compassion and belief, not the desperation and covetousness of the other magic users who frequent Danz Mizer. She is Persephone in the endless night." The amusement lessened on his face until only his eyes held traces of it.

"Magic vamps?" Zita tried to throttle her next thought or at least keep it from leaking on the mental link with Wyn. *That sounded like the worst idea ever.*

Wyn glanced at him and then returned her attention to the road. "Your vampiric friends are witches?"

He cleared his throat. "Most of them, no, though no single strain of vampirism predominates, unfortunately. It would be easier if everyone shared the same strengths and weaknesses. A few might well use magic, but the VIP room is a haven for the monstrous and fair creatures of the night, including witches and shapeshifters and minor celebrities who wish to run through their fortunes quickly. We have rules for metas. They may not kill or addict those they drink from, all vampiric drinking is private and must be voluntary, and no sparkling vampires. No drinking from metahumans. No stalking, especially if they're possibly your soul mate. Also, no silver, stakes, or drinks on the VIP dance floor. Unpleasant stickiness, you understand."

Wyn giggled.

"Sparkling vampires? Like, you won't let them wear sequins or glitter? That's kind of sad and obviously not enforced much," Zita said, remembering some of the outfits from the club.

With an undignified snort, Dmitri said, "You are delightful. They may wear what they wish, but they may not sparkle in the sun. I may be a blood-drinking undead, but I have standards."

"As one does," Wyn said.

He grinned at her, showing off those lengthy, startlingly white canine teeth again. "So delightful to speak with someone who understands."

Zita decided to ask the question. "So why are you the prince?"

Dmitri sighed. "Prior to sleeping sickness that resulted in metahumans—the one last year, not the one in the Seventies—Victoria began a pleasant conceit. She took the title of queen and granted titles in her court to various and sundry. All staff and a few regulars, including myself, took pseudonyms." He gave a wry smile. "I became Count Dmitri Tepes, scion of Dracula. Once metahumans became known, Vic took a great many under her wing, incorporating them into the court. Danz Mizer serves as a minor sanctuary."

"And now you're Prince?" Zita said.

He nodded, and his too-white face took on a faint pink tinge. "Technically, I am the Crown Prince, heir to the imaginary throne. I seem to have taken an unplanned nap one afternoon..."

Zita and Wyn's eyes met in the rear-view mirror, remembering the comas that had ended with both of them in quarantine. Fortunately, neither of their powers had manifested immediately.

Wyn's voice was gentle. "You woke up in quarantine?"

With a shake of her head, Zita shuddered. "He woke up dead, possibly during his autopsy in the morgue."

Dmitri gagged, then gave Zita a careful look. "That would be a gruesome fate, one I strive to avoid. As it happens, I was not discovered before I awakened. Were I dead, this discussion would not be happening. I visited no morgue, nor did I suffer the indignity or torments of quarantine." He stared at his hands.

Zita waited for him to continue. She might have fidgeted, but she tried to suppress it.

When he resumed speaking, Dmitri's tone was sober. "I'm certain you understand gaining powers is one thing, but to awaken as a true monster? To those of us who found themselves more changed, with new needs, Vic offered a foundation, a shelter, and rules. While I've met only a few like myself, those who are..." He paused, as if searching for a word.

"Dead?" Zita offered.

*Diplomatic as usual, Zita. Ease up.* Wyn groaned across their mental connection.

A hint of a fang peeked out of his sharp-edged smile. "Ah, yes. And may I say that for someone who changes into animals, you've managed to avoid peeing on anything in the area for the past hour. It shows discipline on your part."

"I went before I left home, and yeah, I'm strict," Zita said.

A hand rose to Wyn's mouth, and she made a high-pitched sound as if trying to swallow a giggle.

Dmitri twisted in his seat to gawk at Zita, then snickered. "I shall treasure your unvarnished opinions for what they are. As I was saying before we got sidetracked, other vampires did wake in quarantine, where they were not the biggest leeches. I confess, I hope Vic's murderer and your Sobek are the same, for all DMS claims it doesn't fit his so-called pattern. I would hate to discover that we have multiple murderers lurking in a place I thought a haven for my kind."

"DMS hasn't proved good for much other than harassing quarantine survivors," Zita said.

"The voice of experience? Some confinements were worse than others, and New York City even managed to misplace a few patients. I confess I was dismayed to find that DMS missed Tiger when they swept through and arrested everyone else associated with the kidnapping ring last summer. When her grandson was whisked off to Witness Protection for his involvement, Vic was horrified, and that was when she began personally managing the club, instead of merely dropping in to hold court." Dmitri's voice saddened again as he mentioned his murdered friend, and he unselfconsciously dabbed at his eyes with the red handkerchief again.

Zita stuffed her mouth with a granola bar from her pocket and looked away.

A few wordless minutes later, the vampire perked up. "Very well, then. Shall we play a car game? I have downloaded a list of common travel games on my telephone."

Wyn rubbed her forehead and pressed the accelerator. "This is going to be a very long ride," she muttered.

# Chapter Thirteen

**An hour later,** they pulled up in front of the ostentatious colonnade of white pillars that sheltered a large brick house. A manicured lawn surrounded the building, dotted with trees tormented into formal, symmetrical shapes not found in nature. In the front seat of the car, Wyn and Dmitri exchanged brief comments about architecture and some mutual acquaintance named Mr. Darcy, while Zita fidgeted in the back.

Wyn took her time parking under the porte-cochere and exiting the car. She patted her hair, despite it seeming as perfect as always, then stepped to the side, away from the open car door.

Dying with impatience, Zita burst out of the back seat and onto the driveway. Her rapid exit necessitated an even faster stop to avoid careening into the dry three-tier fountain surrounded by bare, thorny bushes.

Still inside the car, Dmitri called out, "Just a moment!"

A young man hurried around the back of the vehicle. He had the wiry, muscular build and deep farmer's tan of someone who worked outside in the summer, all of which was very evident as he wore only tight pants and a poofy shirt, open to the waist. "Excellent. I am Bill and will be your valet today." He held out his hand to Wyn.

Beside the car, Wyn stared at Bill, keys dangling from her hand.

"I presume you are here for Domina's party? Drop off your keys with me, then follow the path around to the pool house."

"Yes, yes, we are. I require a minute as I am not ready," Dmitri called. Zipping and shuffling sounded from inside the car. "Perhaps I should have purchased a roomier model."

The women looked at each other.

Bill continued to stand with his hand out. He either ignored or didn't notice the goosebumps forming all over his very nice chest.

*I think Dmitri's touching up his makeup,* Wyn sent.

Zita made a face. *Why would he care?*

*Based on his discussion with Incubus at the nightclub, Domina might be an ex-girlfriend,* Wyn sent.

Real fear laced through Zita. *No wonder he didn't want to think she could be involved. You don't think he'll turn on us? Or worse, that we'll have to deal with their relationship drama?*

Amusement tinged Wyn's reply. *I think we're safe from him turning on us.*

*But not the drama?*

The valet wiggled his fingers. "I'm afraid valet service is mandatory to avoid blocking the drive. Terribly sorry," he said.

Wyn didn't reply to Zita but dropped the keys into Bill's hand.

He slid into the driver's seat and waited.

A minute later, Dmitri emerged. His practical and very warm coat was abandoned in the car, but he wore full makeup and a tuxedo, complete with a cape lined in red satin. Hand wipes peeked from one pocket, and a golden circle rested upon his brow. "Now, shall we? My humble preparations are complete."

Crossing her arms over her chest, Zita rolled her eyes. "Humble? Hombre, you're wearing a crown."

"True, but it's paper, and do you not see the smiley face on it?" Dmitri tapped the center decoration.

Zita raised her eyebrows. "The one with fangs and blood drops?"

Chin lifted and shoulders back, Dmitri laced his fingers together over his chest. "Yes. True power has the luxury of laughing at itself," he proclaimed, voice booming. An impish grin ruined the imperious expression, and he laughed. "It should drive Domina quite mad. She's a big believer in maintaining appearances and despises this emoji."

The valet pulled away in the car, driving it over to a nearby building with four separate garage doors. Getting out of the car, he opened the garage and scurried back to the driver's seat.

Wyn hid a laugh behind her hand.

Despite herself, Zita felt a smile tug at the corners of her lips. "Ah, now that I understand. At least we know where your car will be." She nodded to where the valet was backing the vehicle into the garage. "Órale, let's get going before Domina has time to run out the back when she finds out we're here."

"Wait, was I not supposed to tell her we were coming?" Dmitri sounded puzzled.

She spun around to face the vampire. "You told her?"

He blinked at her. "It was polite. Also, how do you think I got the address?"

"I thought you knew it or got it from a computer!" Zita said. She rubbed her hands on the sides of her pants. "Fine, then, hopefully, she doesn't know *why* we're coming?"

Dmitri glared at her. "If it was supposed to be a secret, you could have said. I told her you wanted to ask her about Sobek. Do you need to read our texts?" His voice flattened, and his smile was gone. His muscles tensed.

Her hands curling, Zita opened her mouth to speak.

"No, that's fine. You didn't know," Wyn said. She bumped Zita with her shoulder. "Isn't it?" *Agree with me. If he were anyone else, you'd let it go.*

Zita inhaled and forced her fingers to unclench. "You're right. I should have said. Sorry. At least she's here," she said grudgingly.

He relaxed. "Good."

"Shall we?" Wyn glided over to a crushed marble path lined with larger stones and strolled to the back of the house.

*** 

After walking around the outside of the mansion, Zita spotted a single-story building, built like a huge solarium with floor-to-ceiling glass windows and a roof liberally studded with skylights. The crushed white marble path crunched and shifted underfoot, reflecting the gentle lights of tiny solar lamps that lined the edges, along with fist-sized chunks of larger rocks.

Remembering Dmitri's comments about sunlight and vampires, Zita snickered. "Bet she doesn't hang out there much in the daytime."

Wyn shushed her with a glance toward their vampire companion.

Dmitri's face could have been carved from ice. "Likely not. Domina is far more photosensitive than I. Any exposed skin will burst into flames after a few minutes in sunlight or even under a UV lamp."

Zita's amusement died, and she saw Wyn blanch beside her. "Oh. That's awful."

He nodded.

When the now-subdued trio reached the door, Wyn tapped it.

A blast of heat and chlorine-scented air washed over them when a heavy-set woman answered the door, clad in sensible shoes, a black dress with a white apron, and a tiny white hat. Sweat glistened on her forehead, and strands of hair curled out around her face from where they escaped a low bun. "Yes?" Her voice was whispery and cracking.

*Sedentary life, though she's got the strong arms of a busy housekeeper,* Zita assessed absently. She frowned, noting the columns of dual puncture wounds winding their way up the inside of one arm, some scabbing and bruised, and one so new it still bled.

Wyn flashed a friendly, charming smile. "We're here to see Domina? Muse, Arca, and Dmitri?"

The maid stared at them. While most of her face was blank, her eyes held a horrified expression. "One moment. Please wait out here." She closed the door.

"Domina does love her theatrics. Now she'll make us wait." Dmitri rolled his eyes.

With a teasing smile, Wyn declared, "That's Arca's favorite thing!"

Zita wrinkled her nose at her friend and began jogging in place. "Sí, I'm known for my patience, especially this late at night."

Dmitri's eyebrows rose. "Late? It's only ten."

"Morning person." Wyn made a moue of disgust.

He shuddered. "You grow more frightening each time we meet, Arca."

"Funny, nobody else seems to be intimidated by me. We need to be ready for trouble. Did either of you see the bite marks all up her arm?" Pressing her face against the glass, Zita tried to peer through the steamed-up windows.

From the view offered, an Olympic-length swimming pool took up two-thirds of the space inside. A single form did laps in it. The rest of the building formed a loose rectangle around the pool. A bar with a grill sat empty along one wall. At the far end of the room, a dark brown contraption held a dark-haired person with pale skin in front of an ornate folding screen. Other people, mostly males from the general shapes, sat or lay in varying positions around her on giant pillows and couches. The sturdy form of the maid approached the cluster of people. A doorway led off into another room.

Wyn shook her head. "I was watching her face, not her arms. You do know peeping through the windows is rude, right?"

"No, I had not noticed, though she did smell of blood. How far up her arm?" Dmitri said, his voice tight.

Ignoring Wyn's mild rebuke, Zita gestured at her own arm to illustrate. "Wrist to elbow on the inside, some new, some old."

He straightened his paper crown absently, his lips turning down. "No one should be biting the same person that often. It's not healthy for the blood donor."

"Just telling you what I saw." She rubbed at the window and continued trying to see inside. Squinting, she watched the maid stop by a plump brunette clad in what appeared to be a black corset and a matching long loincloth that left most of her legs bared. Atop her head, she wore a shiny, silver pointy thing, as if she'd attempted to mold the Statue of Liberty's crown from tin foil. The brunette made a gesture, and the swimmer got out of the water.

"What is on her head? She looks like someone plucked one of those fancy Polish chickens except for the crest. It's sad when a chicken wears something better." Zita shook her head and tried to see more.

Beside her, Wyn and Dmitri stepped up to the window.

"Bless her heart, it's like a tiny Vegas showgirl headdress on a budget," Wyn breathed, shaking her head.

Dmitri cleared his throat. "I believe it's a poor interpretation of Akasha's headdress from a movie."

The door opened, and the honey badger bouncer from the nightclub scowled at the trio hovering near the glass. She held the door open. "She'll see Arca and Muse now." Water dripped from one muscled arm and ran down her plain black swimsuit.

"Excellent," Wyn said. Tilting her chin up, she sailed inside, though the cheeks and the tips of her illusion's ears had pinkened.

Zita stepped through, and Dmitri made to follow her.

The honey badger shifter barred his progress. "Not you. She says you're specifically not invited inside."

Dmitri drew back from the doorway as if burned. "Really, Sheriff? I thought we were friends?"

Sheriff shrugged though she seemed uncomfortable. "Her place, her rules. You can always wait in the car where it's warmer."

Comprehension dawned on Dmitri's face. "The car's locked in one of the garages here. I have no choice but to stand in the cold."

A muscular shoulder twitched, and Sheriff bit her lip before her face shuttered. "Guess you're out of luck then."

"We'll try to hurry," Wyn assured him. *I don't like this.*

*Me either. Be ready to run or fight,* Zita sent back as she fell in behind Wyn. She flexed her shoulders and unzipped her sweatshirt, the stifling, humid heat making the garment uncomfortable.

Strings of tiny lights adorned the floor-to-ceiling windows, and indirect illumination lit the pool and everything else with a soft, warm glow. The rough pebbled surface of the ground closest to the pool penetrated the thin soles of her sneakers, and she automatically put herself between Wyn and the water. Spiky potted palms decorated the corners of the room, and elegant wicker sofas and chairs were dispersed throughout.

Sheriff slammed the door shut behind them and shuffled ahead to wait closer to the others. Her steps had a bounce, that combined with the muscular build, made Zita suspect the other woman boxed regularly.

The brunette waitress they'd seen at the club reclined in a carved chair, a strange wooden contraption that dwarfed her and seemed to surround her with hundreds of polished cherry blades. By her feet, large pillows were scattered on the ground. Two shirtless men in matching Speedos and bow ties reclined on two of the pillows. Another pair of men—wearing poofy shirts and tight pants—reclined on nearby sofas, their lips very red and smug. The maid stood partially behind the chair, eyes downcast. As Zita watched, three more men in the same shirts entered the room and began setting up a large metal dog crate. Their faces were averted, but she recognized Bill the Valet's body and movement.

Domina slanted her gaze at Wyn, then Zita, lingering on the shapeshifter. Like Dmitri, she sat preternaturally still and only breathed before speaking. Unlike him, however, her stance was not a boneless relaxation so much as a taut, tension-filled pose. "You sought an audience. What brings you here?" White fangs flashed as she spoke.

Her attention returned to the bizarre chair, and Zita's mouth opened of its own accord even as she sidled into a position that would allow her to see all of them. "What kind of vampire sits on a chair made of stakes? I mean, trip once and boom. Dead. That's how it works, right?" She scanned the others surrounding the waitress and subtly nudged Wyn away from where Sheriff lurked. *Domina's the only one of this set who's dead—undead—though the two guys on the sofa both have fangs. They're less creepy though since they're sweating and breathing as normally as possible in this sauna.*

The waitress' mouth opened and closed without speaking, and her eyes bored into Zita.

Sheriff gave a cough that sounded suspiciously like a laugh.

"It's a copy of a chair from a popular television show," Wyn said softly. *Everyone here except Sheriff glows with magic, either innate like Domina and the vampires on the sofa, or externally applied, like two guys on the pillows and the housemaid. If it comes to a fight, my shield might keep them out or break the spell. I haven't quite figured out what magic she's using on them, but I'm guessing it's nothing good.*

Domina glared at the honey badger shifter before returning her attention to Wyn and Zita.

*Please let me handle this. We need information from her. We should do this the smart way.* Wyn tucked a strand of pale hair behind her ear. "I apologize. My friend may or may not be serious, but we came to ask if you could tell us anything about Tracy Jones.

He patronized the Danz Miser club at times and naturally gravitated toward you, we heard."

Settling back into her chair, Domina nodded. "Very well. Keep your poorly dressed pet leashed."

Zita pointed two fingers at her eyes, and then at the vampiress, but kept her attention on all the people arrayed against them. "Why is everyone such a hater about my clothes? I can wear this, or I can walk around naked everywhere, which just makes people act weird." She paused and glanced back at the door.

Outside, Dmitri's white face pressed against the glass, squishing his features in an unflattering way.

Zita continued, "Weirder. And I'm nobody's pet."

"True, then you might have manners," Domina snapped. "Be silent until you are spoken to."

*Did she really just tell me to shut up?* Her hands in fists, Zita set them on her hips. "Not my thing. And it's a legit question about that collection of stakes."

"It's a throne," Domina bit out. She settled back into her seat. "I don't know why I'm wasting my time speaking to you two morons."

Wyn's mouth tightened. "We'd appreciate any information you can give us." *She doesn't seem particularly interested in helping, so I'll drop party line and scan her. Try to ask questions about Sobek to get her thinking about him.*

*Sweet! I thought being all diplomatic was going to kill me, and now I get to play to one of my strengths: annoying stuck-up pendejos.* Scanning the chair up and down, Zita grinned and needled the vampire more. "Oh, a fancy toilet. Glad it's got a practical use. Maybe having all that junk in your trunk helps cushion it, cause it looks hella uncomfortable. Did Sobek buy that for you?"

The comfort of the telepathic connection cut out as Wyn's eyes grew distant.

"I have a memory foam..." Domina cut herself off. Rage crept across her face. Her hands gripped the edges of her chair so hard that the knuckles turned an even paler shade of white. The men at her feet stirred restlessly, and the two on the sofas rose to their feet. "What is your interest in Sobek? He's merely a retired businessman, and no, he did not. He doesn't have the money."

Sheriff shuffled in to loom behind Zita, so close that the odor of wet fur and chlorine drowned out everything else nearby.

Angling her body to keep the other shifter in her peripheral vision, Zita bumped Wyn so furniture stood between her friend and any direct attacks. "It's not enough that the man's a psycho killer and drug dealer? Where's he at?"

Domina waved a hand. "Sorry, I can't tell you anything about Sobek."

Wyn glanced around, her brow furrowing. Warmth touched Zita's mind as her friend forged the telepathic connection again. *Sobek sold the meth business in exchange for a relic and some cash. He whined a lot about his legal bills and plans for petty vengeance, but she ignored that. She has as little to do with him as possible and is planning to refuse to feed him any more of her blood. His last feeding was a few days ago, and then he left to go back to his hideout.*

Zita flicked a glance at her friend. *Does she know where he is or what he's planning?*

Her outward serenity unwavering, Wyn pursed her lips and considered the men at Domina's feet. *No. Whoever took over his meth business has been helping Sobek and paying her. He's kept them as separate as possible. Domina thinks he'll buy us if she can capture us... and plans an attempt, though she's never met him in person. She's hoping Dmitri will freeze enough outside to be weakened so he can be taken too. Also, she's furious neither of us will meet her eyes.*

"Are you going to lie to our faces like that? You knew both his names and apparently what's in his bank account. Quit posing and just answer the questions," Zita said. *Like I'll waste time staring into her eyes when they outnumber us and include at least two with sweet abs?*

Domina rose from her erstwhile throne. "How dare you challenge me and accuse me of lying?"

The guys in the silly shirts hissed and bared fangs, both scuttling to stand near the throne. At the vampiress' curt gesture, both of the Speedo guys rose and posed near the silly chair as well. The maid hid behind the others.

"Why do people keep asking me that? And seriously, when did a challenge become a bad thing?" Zita rolled her eyes. "If you act like a pendejo, you're going to get smacked down. Duh." Now that she'd seen them all move, she could guess at their skills. *With that foot placement and movement, the Speedo guys are dancers, and they don't have fangs. The frilly shirt brothers don't move like anything in particular, so weekend sports only, but they're not dead even if they're vamps. Domina doesn't appear to do anything or have any particular toning. So, Sheriff's the real physical threat in both forms since she likely boxes.*

Domina snapped her fingers. "That's it. I'm done. Arca, you can put yourself in the crate, or my men will hurt your friend."

Wyn gestured, and a shimmering sphere appeared around her, transparent, but glimmering with rainbow reflections like a giant soap bubble. Ice dripped from her voice. "I won't be used like that."

Zita relaxed a little, recognizing her friend's protection against magic. A wordless protest left her when one of the male vampires lunged for Wyn.

Her friend held up a finger toward Zita.

The vampire rebounded off the glistening bubble, hitting it hard and caroming away. He landed on his rear with a howl.

"Sorry," Wyn said, peering at him.

With a sniff, Domina waved him to the side. "Enough, Titus. I didn't mean the witch. You with the cage! Turn around. My ugly pet, take off your mask, and let the shapeshifter see you."

The last portion of the cage snapped into place, and the three men putting it together turned around. One was Bill, as Zita had guessed. Another wore a mask, and he removed the fabric covering his face...

Zita gaped. "Ben?"

He stared mutely at her, his face oddly blank.

*Bad enough when I thought she'd bitten him, but she's done something to him.* Something about him made Zita's skin creep. "What did you do to the poor guy?" she demanded, turning to glare at Domina.

The waitress smirked. "At last, I have your attention. Now get into the cage and shift into something cute. And fuzzy." Her eyes met Zita's, red igniting within them.

Crimson washed over Zita, stealing all vision from her. When it cleared, she found herself standing beside the dog cage, touching it. Revulsion ran through her. She shook her head and yanked her hand away.

As if from a distance, she heard Wyn say, "Arca? What are you doing?"

Beside her, Ben remained motionless, sour sweat and iron tainting his scent.

Domina's voice was smug. "She's mine now and doing anything I want her to do. Now into the cage with you, shapeshifter."

"No and no. I don't do girls or cages," Zita said, facing the vampiress and raising both middle fingers at her.

Domina lifted her head to stare down her nose at her. "You're not worth the trouble of all this."

Zita grabbed Ben's arm and shoved him in the direction where Wyn waited in her glowing bubble of magic. "Run to Muse! She'll keep you safe!"

He staggered a few steps, collided with the bubble, and hurtled to the side. Ben hissed, showing fangs.

"Ni modo, dude," Zita said. She scowled at Domina. "He loved his powers."

"Now he loves being a vampire and taking my place as a blood donor. He's going to make me a lot of money, and he couldn't be happier. Kill her and throw the healer in the cage!" Domina screamed. Red lit her eyes, and she glared at Wyn.

Wyn sniffed. Her bubble didn't waver. "As if. That tells me what the spell is on the others, so that's handy to know. Don't meet her eyes, Arca, she's got mind-control magic or a touch of it, anyway."

Feeling movement behind herself and smelling wet fur and chlorine, Zita dropped low and swung her leg out in a low sweeping kick.

Sheriff squawked and fell.

Ben sat where he had fallen, staring around with a blank expression.

Hemmed in by the pool on the one side and the need to keep the honey badger from Wyn, Zita backed up toward the door.

Sheriff and two of the male vampires attacked simultaneously, but the preternaturally fast men reached her first.

Stepping aside to dodge, Zita seized the arm and shoulder of one vamp and used his momentum to slam him into the other vamp. Her skin prickled, and she started to dodge, but it was too late.

The honey badger shifter jumped on top of her, knocking her down.

While Zita managed to break her fall enough to avoid banging her head, the heavy weight of the other woman held her in place, and her back ached from the impact with the textured concrete.

Sheriff raised her arm to strike.

Zita shifted into a kangaroo, the smaller head of the animal allowing her to dodge Sheriff's punch. Her shoes shredded.

Plowing her fist into the floor with a crack, Sheriff howled, yanking back her injured appendage and shaking it.

After drawing back her powerful hind legs, Zita kicked the other shifter in the stomach, releasing her arms at the same time. She tried not to slash with the claws on her toes, not wanting to disembowel the other woman.

Sheriff flew backward into the pool with a splash. When she surfaced, sputtering and coughing, she glared Zita's direction. Hair sprouted and her hands deformed as she took her first stroke back to land. She sank under the water with a gargling sound.

Remembering how long it'd taken the other woman to change shape at the club, Zita swore. *I can't let her drown.*

As she leapt into the water, she changed shape to a walrus. Waves crashed into each other and out of the pool when her bulk hit the surface. Shoving Sheriff's mutating mass with her broad head, Zita paddled to the edge of the pool and tossed the other shifter out on the side farthest from Wyn. Returning to her Arca form, she levered herself out and checked the room.

Wyn had retreated to stand near a wall, the delicate soap bubble of her spell still visible. The vampire Titus sat next to it, shaking his head as if stunned.

*Slow learner. You're good here if I lure Sheriff away?* Zita thought. Stepping carefully, she moved away from the pool edges, slippery with water and hurried toward the door.

*Peachy,* Wyn sent.

Two of the vamps, one with a bloody nose and the other with a rapidly swelling black eye, launched themselves at her again with superhuman speed.

She did a bandeira, flipping out of the way.

They hit the badger shifter, who was just uncurling.

Her body still bulging and shaking in transformation, Sheriff screamed and slashed at the vampires, who limped away. Her stomach bore a thin red line, but no serious damage.

Zita threw open the door and waited, adrenaline singing in her veins. Her legs tensed to flee. *Can't let Sheriff tear apart anyone inside, especially since Wyn isn't immune to her.* She glanced over at the curious man peering into the building. "Dmitri, get away from the door. Don't want to get you hurt," she said, sotto voce.

Dmitri worried his paper crown in his hands. "I thought we were going to ask questions politely?"

"We tried diplomatic. Given that Domina's guards jumped us with no provocation—"

He coughed, lifting both eyebrows. "I'm undead, not deaf."

Zita amended her words. "Okay, little provocation. Domina was planning to capture me and Muse anyway so I think that anything she may have taken the wrong way is on her."

The vampires closest edged away from the enraged badger.

As she uncurled, Sheriff's beady eyes searched for a target.

"Come on, Sheriff, you gonna let me toss you around like that?" Zita bellowed.

The human-sized honey badger squealed and rounded the pool toward her.

"Boys, back to me! Sheriff, get her!" Domina called out. Uneasiness sang in her voice.

Zita focused on the other shifter and darted out the door. After the overheated pool area, ice seemed to stab her lungs with every breath, and her feet stung from the cold and the sharp rocks. Regardless, she forced her legs to move down the marble path. *I need to lure the badger out and keep her there until she shifts back or sees reason. She didn't seem to stay in badger form long at the club. Wyn, you going to be okay in there?*

"Get someone to invite me inside. I can help," Dmitri said.

"Sí, when I can. Step back from the door, so Sheriff doesn't mow you down," Zita said.

*I'm fine,* Wyn sent. *You stay safe and don't let her hurt you. I can't cast anything while I've got my bubble up, and Domina's told her vamps to stay away from the doors for some reason, but to get you if you come back inside. If anyone manages to get close, I'll let you know and call Andy, but if he's fighting Dragon...*

Sheriff poked her snout out, lips curling away from sharp teeth. Her attention turned toward the vampire who still stood near the door, shivering.

Dmitri smiled and wiggled his eyebrows at the hairy shifter. "Ah, my friend, come, we can chat while I gaze into your lovely eyes. Remember how we used to—"

*He's going to get himself killed.* Hurling a small rock at the badger, Zita watched with satisfaction as it bounced off the other shifter's oversized nose.

Sheriff snarled at her.

"What, you lose me already? You're not even trying!" Zita backpedaled, her mind split between her friend's comments and determining her next move. *If Andy's fighting Dragon, a city could be at stake. Domina wants you as a captive. I've apparently talked her out of wanting me alive.*

*Yes, you do have an ineffable flare for diplomacy. Keep safe. I'm good here, and I somehow doubt she or her companions have any idea how hard it would be for them to capture me when they can't touch me or mind control me.*

Her mind spinning, Zita said, *Yes, but all they have to do is break your concentration and then they can grab you. They could start chucking stuff at you, squirt you with a hose, or shoot you.* Leaping off the path onto the crunchy but less painful withered grass, she shifted to a Tibetan wild ass, figuring the kiang's speed and adaptation to its cold homeland would be useful.

Wyn's wince somehow translated over their mental connection. *Please stop. It's disturbing that you're planning ways others could more effectively attack me.*

"I will tear you apart! Stand still!" Sheriff howled, racing after Zita. Despite her size, she still moved as fast or faster than an actual honey badger.

The night no longer seemed as cold. Her hooves, though tender from her earlier barefoot run over the rocks, handled zigzagging across the stony path well as Zita trotted a convoluted path around the pool house. Moonlight revealed dark blotches on the white marble pathway. Unable to speak, Zita turned her head toward the badger, braying a laugh. *Just keeping it real. I'll be inside again as soon as I can. By the way, Dmitri wants an invite inside so he can do something.*

*That's classic,* Wyn sent, but her tone was abstracted.

Spotting a thick tree to one side, Zita angled toward it. A glance at her pursuer proved that the badger cornered better than the dragon had and tricking her into crashing against the tree wouldn't work. Instead, she galloped behind a corner of the house and stopped. She lowered her head and prepared.

Sheriff barreled around the corner, panting and bristling with anger.

Zita kicked her, feeling bone break beneath her hoof, and took off running again. She'd led the growling badger on one more lap before her pursuer finally dropped and began her painful-looking transformation.

*Finally.* She scurried to Sheriff and waited for the other to finish shifting.

Dmitri drifted over to stand beside her.

Zita returned to her Arca shape and glanced toward the building, concern for Wyn nagging at her. "Can you bring her inside when she's done?"

The vampire pursed his lips and shook his head. "I may bring her to the doorstep but not a millimeter farther. Get me an invitation, and then I may assist you."

"Weird, but okay. Can you at least knock when you get Sheriff there, and I'll haul her inside? Don't want to have her get frostbite or nothing, after all." As soon as the vampire nodded, Zita sprinted, limping slightly, back into the building.

Letting the door fall shut quietly behind her, Zita slipped into a ginga and scanned for enemies as she advanced.

Most of the vampires clustered near Domina, all showing signs of small injuries save for the vampiress. One of the poofy shirt guys stood with his back to the door—Ben, she thought, recognizing the bald head and the scar. Wyn, still encased in her protective bubble, stood a few feet away. Within the protective confines of the shield, the maid cowered behind Zita's friend, her expression somewhere between confused and angry.

"Is Sheriff down?" Wyn asked. *Domina tried to have the human maid strike me. It seems passing through my bubble removed Domina's control of her mind.*

Ben started to turn toward Zita, fists lifting to strike. One of his eyes was swollen nearly shut.

Pivoting, Zita threw herself into a quick armada, kicking him in the face and sending him to the ground. "Yes. Sorry, Ben." She jerked her head toward the door, hoping her friend would get the message.

"When we reach the door, run for it! Go!" Wyn barreled past her, dragging the maid along.

Zita followed them, keeping her body between the women and the vampires.

A knock sounded.

Her motions mechanical, the maid opened the door.

Dmitri stood there, carrying a naked and drowsy Sheriff. "May I please enter?"

The maid froze at the sight of the vampire.

Rising to her feet, Domina shrieked, "Don't let him in! Close it!"

The maid shot a vengeful glare at Domina. "You'll be hearing from my lawyer and the cops!" She paused, facing Dmitri. "Come on in. Make yourself at home."

With an evil grin, Dmitri bowed and gently set Sheriff just inside the door. He stepped back outside and out of the way of the maid with a bow.

The maid scurried past, slamming the door in her wake.

Dmitri threw open the door again. As the warm air rushed out, his cape swirled dramatically around him, and he stalked inside. He veered to avoid Zita. "I am Dmitri, Prince of the—"

Ben surged to his feet, charging at Zita.

She danced aside.

Slipping on the wet edge, Ben crashed into Dmitri.

Dmitri squawked, and both men toppled into the pool.

Keeping half her attention on the vampires remaining above water, Zita inched over to check on the swimmers.

Flailing and twisting, Ben and Dmitri thrashed their arms and legs in a tangle at the bottom of the pool. After a few more seconds, they managed to separate, and Ben swam to the top. He inhaled loudly as he broke the surface, then paddled to the side of the pool.

Just as Zita was about to shift and rescue Dmitri, he stilled and stood up. He began stomping through the water toward the closest ladder, his cloak a brilliant swirl of red and black around him. His crown was gone.

Domina pointed toward Zita and Wyn. "Kill them! Meet up at the house!" As her vampiric minions, including Ben, leaped to obey, she scrambled to her feet. The dancers helped her stand. Darting around them, she teetered on the high spike heels of her sandals, which wrapped around her feet and scaled her legs to the knee like silvery vinyl kudzu.

"Block the door with your bubble," Zita said, angling her body defensively. She edged away from the pool and began backing up toward her friend. *There's too many! How can I take them all at once without killing anyone?*

# Chapter Fourteen

**As Zita eyed the vampires** and tried to figure out how to escape without permanently hurting anyone, Wyn nodded and backed up to the doorway. Her shield filled the opening.

Stopping halfway between her chair and the door, Domina scowled. In the pool, Ben paced Zita's movements and clung to the edge nearby. Streaming around the vampiress, the rest of Domina's vampires rushed at Zita fast en masse. Too fast. They were on her before she could finish retreating to Wyn's bubble.

*Can't let them circle me. If I shift too small, they might be fast enough to stomp me. The floor's cement, so I can't risk throwing them there. Guess they all want to go swimming.* Zita shifted to a gorilla and dodged to the side, closer to the water. She grabbed the one with the black eye and shoved him into the pool. She stomped on Titus' foot.

He bent over.

Vaulting over his back and knocking him down with her weight, she used the momentum to seize Bill the Valet by his arm and hurl him toward his friends.

The vampire with the bloody nose dodged Bill, darted around him, and clawed at her.

Seizing his arm, she pulled him partially past her and used his body as a shield as she tried to get to the far side of the pool, where she could force them to move single file and grant herself enough time to get away.

Titus hit his buddy, unable to pull his punch in time.

*I didn't think they'd hurt each other. So much for that.* Zita growled, showing her own canines, and tossed the poor guy with the bloody nose into the water.

Titus hesitated, but Ben and the vamp with the black eye launched themselves from the water, grabbing at her leg.

"Enough! Stop!" Dmitri's voice echoed in the pool room, and the vampires froze.

Zita danced backward, panting.

Ben and the two injured vampires fell back into the pool and sank.

Dmitri sighed and finished climbing out of the pool. He threw the sodden mass of his cape over his shoulder and flipped his soggy hair out of his face. Smoothing his tuxedo, he raised his chin. Red glinted in his eyes. Lifting a hand above his head, he flicked his fingers imperiously upward.

Ben and the swimming vamps resurfaced. They swam to the edge of the pool and held onto it, gazes glued to Dmitri.

Domina crossed her arms under her chest, lowered her eyes, and all but purred at him. She fingered a strand of her hair. "Dmitri. We do not need to play these games, you and I."

Zita hooted derisively and realized she was still a gorilla. After cautiously moving away from everyone fanged, she switched back to her Arca form and repeated what she'd originally meant to say. "Why does she suddenly sound like she's trying to phone sex him? I'm no prude, but I'm not into voyeurism or nothing."

To be safe, she avoiding directly walking by the vampires, passing the two dancers instead. She paused, an idea sparking, and changed direction to take their arms.

*Hush,* Wyn sent. *Maybe he can talk her into surrendering if no one—I mean you—continues to antagonize her.*

"Games should not result in injuries or imprisonment." Dmitri flicked his disapproving gaze at the cage and Domina's vampires.

Dragging a lock of hair slowly across her cleavage, Domina continued her flirtation. "Step aside and have your pets kneel. I am a dark empress of darkness. For all we meant to each other, I will allow you a place of honored servitude at my side." She sauntered a few steps toward the door, hips swaying, and her back arching.

Zita rolled her eyes. Pity welled in her when she noted the tidy lines of bite marks up the dancers' arms, similar to what the maid had evinced. To keep them safer, she interposed herself between the men and Domina as she herded them toward Wyn. *Think your bubble will free them too?*

Rather than seeming enthralled by the vampiress, Dmitri's face lost all softness, growing cold and haughty. "You think stealing a few lines from one of my books will make me overlook what you've done to these men? I thought you hid a softer inner side, but the truth is that you only hid the extent of your crimes."

Domina sneered, her flirtatiousness falling away. "You always were a naïve, romantic fool."

"I know that book. I love that book," Wyn whispered, her eyes wide. Her protective bubble still shimmered around her, and she nodded at Zita. *Good idea. The magic on them is all domination. I know what I'm looking at now.*

Absently, without taking his eyes from Domina, Dmitri said, "Thank you. I'm always happy to meet a fan."

Zita assessed the room and shook her head. Everyone else was staring as if glued to an episode of a telenovela. "What is wrong with you people? So weird." She shook her head and shoved a dancer into Wyn's shield.

Hands on her hips, Domina abandoned all pretense of civility. "Step down, Dmitri. It doesn't matter what title a dead woman decided to grant her boytoy. You have no power, only a fondness for setting ridiculous rules for others to follow. I have a court. I have the start of an army and allies with money. You have, what? A badly dressed shapeshifter who can't heal herself, an airheaded healer, and a wet, off-the-rack tuxedo?"

The dancer stumbled through, his blank expression giving way to confusion, followed by shame and anger.

Sympathy on her face, Wyn murmured something softly to him.

Dmitri straightened his shoulders and marched toward Domina. Red burned in his cheeks and his eyes. Water dripped off him as he strode toward her. "You know Victoria and I were platonic, and you overestimate your power. Free these men now or I will. Prove you still have some shred of decency within you. Perhaps the police will be gentler with you if you make the right decision for once."

The other vampires made way for him.

Domina screeched. "No. You're a hack with no real power! I'm sorry I ever let you slobber on me. If I could, I'd give you your virginity back, you loser!"

"I so didn't need to know that. Great! Now I sound like Wingspan." Zita winced and went back to ignoring the conversation as much as possible. Encouraged by her success with the first guy in a Speedo, she shoved the second dancer into Wyn's shield as well.

He shed the blank look for a shattered expression, but his friend put an arm around him.

Zita hissed at Wyn. "You said no relationship drama! Give the dancers blankets from your purse."

"How'd she know what we do?" one dancer asked. His eyes were haunted.

Wyn shushed her again. "I never promised, and I only brought one." She reached into her bag and withdrew a faded blanket, offering it to the closer dancer. After a second, she dug out a business card and offered that too. "This hotline might help if you need to talk to someone later about... all this."

"Maybe she came to one of our shows to get ideas. You know I heard Arca pole dances," his friend whispered back. He took the card.

Gritting her teeth to keep from arguing that she wasn't a stripper, Zita waved toward the blanket. "Share this. Follow the lights out the front of the estate, and you'll hit the neighbor's house. Call the police. Sorry about the cold."

One of the men snatched the blanket and wrapped it around both their shoulders. He nodded.

Wyn stepped aside, and the two men ran past her, huddled together under the dubious warmth of the blanket.

Domina took a few rapid steps forward, but she halted when Wyn's magic once again blocked the door. "Curse you all! Why did those drug-addled fools waste their time at the tracks? I should've told Tiger to kill you at the club too, not just the shifter."

Blinking her eyes sleepily, Sheriff stirred. She spoke, her voice slow and groggy, "You knew Tiger would do that? Why? I understood why you were mad at Dmitri for breaking your heart and Arca for beating up homeless by the Metro, but people died at the club. Innocent people. I could've died, and I'm your friend. What happened to just giving them a good scare?"

Dmitri's expression was thoughtful. "She would need a heart for it to break. I see that now. She left me, Sheriff, when a wealthier target came along. Now, Domina, you might've innocently heard Victoria was dead... but the only way you'd know the details of the railroad tracks—which the police are as yet unaware—is if you were involved in the murder attempt on me. I never meant anything to you other than as a tool, did I?"

Domina started to protest, but he waved a hand, and she stopped speaking as if her vocal cords had failed her.

"You forget that I am no Renfield. I am a king among the undead. Now, all of you will take seats and wait for the police to arrive." Dmitri gestured toward the furniture.

All the other vampires rushed to sit, including Domina, who seemed ready to kill him. She tried one last appeal to the badger shifter. "Don't believe them, Sheriff. You know I'm your friend."

Dmitri frowned. "Enough of that. Think for yourselves, children." His voice cracked out like a whip. "Domina, tell Sheriff the truth."

"What, that she's a gullible idiot I used for muscle? Give her a mental nudge, and she's the perfect mindless beast to unleash on enemies," the vampiress said. She clapped a hand over her mouth. "Curse you, Dmitri."

While the most battered of the vampires showed no response, Ben and Bill both blinked. Rising from his seat, Ben hastened to put as much distance between himself and Domina as possible, turning his back to her. After a second, Bill went to stand beside him.

"Don't meet her eyes," Wyn said softly to Sheriff. "She controls people if they meet her eyes."

Sheriff's broad shoulders slumped. "Is that why I shifted? I wouldn't have... I can't keep from hurting people in that shape." She rose and stomped past them all to the bar. Reaching under the counter, she took out a mug and poured herself a beer. She yawned. "I'm out, Domi. Don't think I won't tell the cops everything I know too."

The vampiress glared at Ben, and he stiffened.

"Domina..." Dmitri said warningly.

Air escaped Ben's throat in a cough, and he spun back, his face blank. "Forgive me, my empress," he said.

"Apparently, eye contact is not required for her control over vampires." Wyn pursed her lips and made a few smooth gestures. Pink fog rose around Domina and the men still beside her.

"Just vampires of her own line," Dmitri said absently.

Domina sniffed. "You may continue to grovel, as well you should. These idiots may have temporarily caught me, but I am too valuable for my employer to allow me to rot in jail. They will have me out again soon."

"You keep telling yourself that. Leave Ben alone. Isn't it enough that you'll cost him a job he loved?" Zita placed herself between Ben and Domina, careful to stay out of the magical mist. Her skin prickled with nerves to have him at her back, and she angled herself to catch him in her peripheral vision.

A slight smile touched Domina's lips. "His previous life is of no concern. Now, he lives to serve, as do all of my children. That one is too unattractive to attend me in person, so he was created to ease my burdens. It's a pity you had to come before he could be delivered. What is this pink mist?" She gave a dainty yawn.

Zita made a face. "He's a person, not a pair of socks to be handed around."

"You share socks? That seems unhygienic," Dmitri said.

"Ignorant fools. I made him the vampire he is today, and he'll make me so much money...the perfect blend of strength and weakness...just right..." As she spoke, the vampiress' words began to slur together, and her eyes lowered. She slumped as she slipped into the same corpselike repose Dmitri had shown in the car. Her two remaining vampires already slept.

Zita shuddered.

One of the sleeping vampires let out a horrendous snore. Somehow, that helped.

Dmitri set a hand on Ben's shoulder. "Be who you are, not what she commands."

The other man's face cleared.

His voice gentle, Dmitri said, "Do you wish to remain a vampire? Or to do whatever she had in mind for you?"

Confusion on his face, Ben shook his head. "No. I hate being a vampire. She said I was just going to be a walking blood bag for some drug."

Zita frowned. *Blood for a drug?*

*The pink meth! Remember, Sobek's chemist used the blood of metas in it?* Wyn sent.

"Then, come with me if you want to live," Dmitri said, taking the other man's wrist and leading him to the only unoccupied couch. His face was expectant.

"What?" Zita said.

"Heathens! They recognize neither classic literature nor movies," the vampire grumbled as he strolled over to the folding screen. Lifting it as if it were weightless, he carried it to Ben's sofa and set it up in front of it.

Ben sat. "Terminator," he said.

After giving Ben an approving nod, Dmitri turned back to the others. "This," he said, "is what makes me a king. Not Vic. Not because I could make other vampires. Not because I could force their adoration, and certainly not because I was tacky enough to declare myself a ruler. I cannot undo his memories, but I can remove his vampirism if it is what he truly wants. If any of the other vampires wish to be changed back, I will attend to them later."

"I do want that," Ben said.

Dmitri said, "Then give me your wrist."

Ben held out his arm, shoving the sleeve out of the way.

After pulling the folding screen in front of Ben, Dmitri paused and glanced back at the others. "Mind the others for me. I will be distracted." He stepped behind the screen.

Zita turned her back and tried not to listen.

Sheriff poured herself another drink. "Anyone else thirsty?"

Sucking sounds came from behind the screen.

"No, we're good," Zita said, exchanging a glance with Wyn. "You know, I'm just going to move the car so we can leave when we're ready."

***

Unlike at the railroad tracks, this time Zita stayed long enough for the police to arrive and take preliminary statements. The now-docile vampires had been split into two groups: Domina's enthusiastic supporters, and those, like Ben, who had been turned or otherwise forced to obey against their will. The luxurious house was swarming with every possible type of law enforcement. Zita, Wyn, and Dmitri gave their initial statements, went meekly where they were told to stand, and then kept walking. Between the chaos and the dark, no one stopped them. By mutual agreement, they remained silent until they left Domina's land.

Well, mostly silent. Dmitri had the hiccups.

He removed a wipe from the packet he'd carried in his pocket and dabbed at his mouth. He turned to the others and said, "Did I get it all? Good. It is distasteful to have someone stuck between your teeth." He grinned, his eyes alight with red, showing his gleaming white fangs.

Wyn said softly, "You're good. Ben seemed happier."

The vampire's cheerfulness dissipated. "He did. I wouldn't have unmade him otherwise."

"You were surprisingly helpful, Dmitri. Good job," Zita said as they marched to where she'd parked the car while waiting for the police to arrive.

Dmitri, his face pink and rosy, bounded along near her, but his tone was cranky. "Why, did you think I would simply throw up my hands and cry out to be rescued? Or perhaps I would run around biting people the way I supposedly ate Victoria?"

Wyn's eyebrows rose. She alone picked her way down the street, preferring the asphalt to the grass. "No one's accused you of that."

He looked at Zita.

Her face burning, Zita hoped her dark skin would hide her guilt. "I didn't accuse you of eating Domina," she tried.

*I can see why you asked for my aid.* Wyn pinched her forehead between her brows. "Arca," she sighed. "I apologize for my friend's... for my friend. Her opinions are not shared in this."

Dmitri considered Wyn for a silent moment. "Your sympathy is appreciated, but I'm familiar with it. Arca is hardly the first to voice their issues with me."

Shame welled in her, and Zita flushed. Her eyes on the ground, she mumbled, "It's nothing against you, but your body gives off conflicting information. You seem alive, but only if nobody looks too close. Dead's not generally a good thing when it applies to people, and undead is weird to me."

Wyn protested. "He looks fine!"

Everything she'd noticed crystallized and Zita tried again to explain the problem. "He only breathes right before he talks, and he doesn't have a heartbeat. His body's too cold, and he smells not-alive. Not decaying or nothing, but dead, with no sweat or anything else you'd scent from a living being. His body doesn't move. Everybody moves just a little, breathing, tiny muscle shifts, but he's got nothing until he actually does something. When he's asleep during the day, his face loses all animation and locks on one expression. It's a visceral reaction like you're not real, but you are, you know?"

"You're more coherent than Sheriff, who had similar problems with me. Domina worked tirelessly to win her over. It was one of the reasons I thought she hid a heart beneath her facade, but I know the truth now," Dmitri murmured. "It doesn't matter what I do, that uncanny valley will always separate me." He glanced back toward the house with its cluster of police vehicles, his shoulders tight and set.

*Screwed up again.* Zita made another attempt. "That may be how you are and all, but my problem with your state is my bad. It's on me for not dealing, not you. I'm sorry. You've been nice and helpful and sort of funny, and I've been riding you about something you can't help. That's not right, and I would call out anybody who did that to someone else. I'll do better." She licked her lips and took a deep breath.

The vampire paused, and his voice was quiet. "I had not expected an apology, but it's accepted."

Zita grunted. "Good. We cool enough? For now?"

"An apology is poor recompense for accusing me of murder and refusing to allow your friend to heal my dad. We'll see if you can actually live up to those words. Also, I find it offensive that you find me only mildly amusing when I am hilarious." He paused and ran his tongue over the tip of one of his canines as he glanced back at lights behind them.

Wyn held up a pale hand. "Wait, what did she say about your father?"

"She said not to ask you to heal him because you wouldn't do it," he said.

Zita protested, "That's not exactly what I said."

Her friend cleared her throat, her pretty face twisting with unhappiness. "I can't heal him, not without an in-depth consultation with his doctor. My spell works best on traumatic injuries, and my concern was that it might make any neurological damage permanent and prevent recovery of any lost abilities. It's an upsetting limitation I've run up against before, and Arca knows the topic bothers me. If you can get me in, however, I can cast something that would prevent it from worsening. Perhaps it will speed up his healing. She already asked if I'd do that."

The vampire glanced at Zita. "That is a more cogent explanation than the one Arca gave. Perhaps I misjudged the depths of her animosity. I will speak to the police about the railroad tracks, so it is clear that you were not abusing the homeless so much as defending me. While I had hoped to avoid letting them know about my status, any others Domina turned against their will must be unmade. I can only hope that the detective and the DMS agent handling the case will agree to keep that information on a need-to-know basis."

Weariness and awareness of various minor aches ran through Zita as the last of her adrenaline faded. "Thanks. It'll help if the police don't think I've got a kink on for randomly bullying people. I feel bad enough that two of the guys from the tracks didn't survive the fight. The one that touched the rail died right off, of course. Turns out the meth killed one of the others, and the last one is on life support." Spotting the car, she headed toward it.

While Wyn made appalled noises, her mental voice was quiet and warm. *Good job, Zita. Not an insult in there.*

*Fair's fair. If I'm going to give others crap for being pendejos, I got to avoid being one myself, neta?* Zita shrugged.

After a pause to duck down so a prisoner transport cargo van could squeeze past, they got into the car, with Zita sliding into the back seat with no complaints this time. The cooler of chicken that she'd moved to there helped. Once everyone was buckled, Wyn started the car.

"So, Domina didn't know where Sobek was, at least not that we got her to mention. What's our next step?" Wyn asked.

The drumstick she'd unearthed from the cooler turned to sawdust in her mouth at the reminder of the missing murderer. Zita managed to swallow and said, "We keep working with what we got. Maybe find out which lawyer handled the contract between Victoria and Sobek. He's got to bill Sobek, right? That means a mailing address or at least a phone number."

Wyn spoke first. "That's one avenue. We also know from our first entanglement with Sobek that the pink meth is made using meta blood, so if we find a location where metahumans have disappeared, we may also find him."

His tone thoughtful, Dmitri offered, "That requirement would explain why Domina claimed to be valuable to them beyond mere arrogance. She can scent a meta if they bleed around her though she'd have no idea of power. The woman always did lack subtlety."

Fear crept over Zita, and her eyes met Wyn's in the rear-view mirror. "Can all vampires do that?" *What if DMS builds an army of meta-sniffing undead and hunts us all down?*

*Try to be optimistic. Don't jump right away to the DMS apocalypse scenario even if you've probably got a carefully labeled bag somewhere to handle it,* Wyn urged.

Silently, Zita admitted, *Proper preparation for emergencies is just smart. My general human-caused apocalypse bag should be fine.* She made a mental note to pick up more paper for her label-maker.

Laughter came over their mental link.

Dmitri snorted. "Most can't. All the ones who can make progeny can, and a handful of others. I can, of course. If there's no injury, I just get the general sense of meta or not, and one or two metas might slip by if they have the right kind of power. Vampires, of course, I know the full extent of their power just being near them."

Zita took a huge bite of the drumstick before anything could slip out. *See? Chewing. Not saying anything. He's fine. I'm fine. Heal me up when we stop again though, my feet got scraped up, and my back is a huge bruise.*

Hair flew in a pale halo around her face as Wyn shivered. "Domina has mind control powers. If their manufacturing process mirrors blood magic enchantment theory, they could have used her to make the mind control version of the drug."

"Mental control of others is her biggest strength," Dmitri admitted. "That does make sense, though I am surprised you'd dabble in blood magic."

Wyn wrinkled her nose. "I don't. My ways are a path of Wicca. We've fought a witch who is basically a blood alchemist, so I read up on it."

After another bite, Zita thought things through to their natural and horrifying conclusion. She tucked away the remains of the chicken leg, her stomach souring at her own thoughts. "Domina's converted share her weaknesses and strengths, right? So, they'd have her sun allergy and daytime sleepies, making them easier to corral for the price of a few sunlamps. The meth dealers wouldn't have to risk being mind-controlled if they just go in during the day to collect blood and stuff. They could even store the vamps tied up in morgue drawers with their feet facing out and poke them in the leg when they need to draw blood. Leave a disposable, normal human in the vamp cage whenever they have to feed."

"People are not disposable," Dmitri said, his body tense.

She held up her hands to forestall any more protests. "Oye, I agree with you. So, if the narcos have a bunch of vamps, they've got captive blood banks. That might be what she meant about Ben being a cash cow. He had a pretty sweet power set. Maybe it was enough to make him a source of the mind control blood and would allow him to create more vamps for them."

"Between that and the vivisection scenario... Your mind is a practical but frightening place, Arca." Dmitri said. His voice sounded appalled.

Wyn laughed, but tension sang in the bell-like tones. "You have no idea how true that is."

Zita said, "What? I'm just saying what it would make sense for them to do. I didn't say it's right, because it's awful and wrong." She glanced at Dmitri. "Because vampires are people too."

Dmitri leaned toward Wyn and tilted his head to eye Zita as well. "I grow even more eager to unmake Sobek and any other of Domina's victims after Arca's terrifying discourse on the subject of vampiric slavery. If nothing else, Sobek's meth operation should be hindered by Domina's arrest. The ability to create vampires is rare. Combined with mind control, it's practically unique. It's limited to her—and me, of course, but I could not be induced to do so."

Zita groaned. "Which is why she was so certain she wouldn't stay in jail."

"You will let me know if you find out more?" Dmitri said.

Although her attention seemed to be on the road, Wyn inclined her head. "Yes, we will endeavor to include you."

Zita wrinkled her nose, seeing no alternatives. "I won't leave you out of that if I have a choice. Our next step has to be to tip off DMS that someone might be planning to break Domina out. We don't want another bloodbath like the one that freed Sobek in October—"

Dmitri laughed. "Oh, sorry, you weren't making a pun on purpose? Please continue."

With a sidelong glance at him, she did so. "We don't want that or to have Domina mind-controlling her way loose. Once we do that, we can go back to researching the lawyer and missing metas." *DMS hasn't acted on any of my previous tips on this case, either to Parzarri direct or the general line, but I'll have to risk calling again. I could have Wyn, as Muse, give the same tip to both Miguel and Parzarri. My brother's been on TV after the nightclub attack to justify her calling him, and he'd do something about it. If Muse makes the call, he's got less chance to guess my secret.*

Wyn made a minute adjustment to the rear-view mirror. "I had heard that DMS has a site they've repurposed to a meta prison, and that bill passed Congress to have all metas attend court via video conferencing instead of physically being present. While unfortunately necessary, I hope that will prevent Domina from escaping custody. That said, we have a more immediate issue to consider."

The vampire sat up straight. "Ah, a fun topic at last. Are we being pursued again? Will we be engaging in additional evasive maneuvers? Can I film it this time?"

Wyn tensed. "Do I want to know what he's talking about, Arca?"

"Probably not," Zita said. "We're good." She willed Dmitri not to say more.

The vampire sniffed. "We were followed when we came to get you. She would not allow me to video it, nor would she ram anything as I suggested, though I appreciated her creativity in escaping them."

Zita leaned forward. "That's because I'm a safe and responsible driver who should be allowed to drive more."

Without taking her eyes from the road, Wyn shuddered. "Or not. We're clear as far as I can tell. The real problem is I don't know where we're going. Can someone give me an address?"

Dmitri's shoulders slumped. "Ah, how prosaic."

# Chapter Fifteen

**Five days later and an hour past her usual bedtime,** Zita stood on the darker half of the hospital helipad, avoiding the lights. The streetlights from the wealthy neighborhood below glowed like a lace pattern where it filtered through the barren tree branches. An icy wind cut across the roof, bringing up goosebumps on the unprotected part of her legs.

In the brighter section of the helipad, a hand clawed at the edge, and then Dmitri crawled onto the roof like a human cockroach, his insectoid and disjointed four-limbed gait unnatural. He stood up and walked normally over to the helipad, the brilliant light making his too-white features even paler. His eyes glowed crimson.

*It's like he's trying to let the cameras get a clear view while he's as creepy as possible. Not making it easy to be better about the undead thing.* Zita couldn't resist a shiver that had little to do with the temperature. She hissed, "Over here, in the dark!"

The vampire scurried to her side.

"What's up?" She leaned against a vent. If that widened the gap between them, she consoled herself that at least she looked casual about it.

He snapped, "Where have you been? You have no call to criticize my phone answering or lack thereof. I called you at sunset." Without the accent, his voice sounded younger, vibrating with stress.

"I'm here now, and you said we needed to talk." Zita folded her arms over her chest, wary. *Something is definitely upsetting him and given how well he took his ex-girlfriend's sick harem...*

Running a hand over his hair, Dmitri took a deep, unnecessary breath and closed his eyes. When his eyes reopened, they were his usual violet, but filled with fear. "My mom is missing. She took me home this morning, but she came back to be with Dad. Her van's in the garage here, but she never made it to his room. I filed a police report, but the cops said another agency claimed the case. They haven't contacted me yet at all."

*Unless she had some of those cookies with her, she's in trouble. She could take down an army with enough of those rocks.* Even she had called him back as soon as she'd gotten his message, Zita remembered the bright, bubbly woman and felt guilty. "Dude, I don't have her. If you asked me here to help you search, I will. If necessary, I'll call in sick tomorrow."

Dmitri wrung his hands, his fangs out. "Who could have taken her? Where could she be? She was going to stay here in case the snow storm tonight and tomorrow makes it too dangerous to journey back and forth between here and home. What if something happens to Dad? He's defenseless." He glanced toward the closed hospital roof door and grimaced.

She held up a hand to stop any further comments. "I can't look for your mom and guard your dad at the same time. Also, the hospital won't let a vigilante or even an adorable animal hang out unattended. Plus, I got to sleep sometime too."

Although he seemed as if he was considering arguing with her for a moment, he sighed and agreed. "Yes, but you likely know a great many sketchy people. Surely one of your dubious acquaintances can be a bodyguard or something?"

Given the circumstances, she decided to let the shot about her acquaintances go, especially since he wasn't necessarily wrong. Zita frowned. "You have strange expectations of the amount of socializing masked vigilantes do. A detective is the best shot at finding your mom, and the only ones I know are all out of town on other cases. If you insist, I might know a group that'd guard your dad, but they'll charge for it, and I don't think they do detecting. I think they outsource that part."

Dmitri jolted forward, his hands curling into claws as if he fought the urge to grab her. "Are they any good?" His canines glinted as he spoke.

She shifted her weight to balance the balls of her feet in case she needed to fight. *I can't blame him for being wound super-tight.* "They're crazy skilled and lucky, but they've also worked for some real losers. We've had to fight them a few times."

"Can they keep my dad safe? Will they find my mother?" he asked, snarling. His fingers flexed, and his eyes glowed red.

Holding up her hands in surrender, Zita said, "Put the teeth away and chill. As far as I can tell, they stick to the terms of their contracts, and they do whatever the papers say. Again, I don't know if they can find your mom, but I know they do rescues. At a minimum, if they're working for you, they won't be working against you. I'll contact them if you want."

Dmitri glanced at the sky. "Get them, immediately. We'll meet here."

She shook her head. "No, let's meet in the closed-off section of the garage instead. It's too cold up here, and I have a feeling you'll need to pay them or something. I'll text when I hear back from them, but I don't know how often they check the only number I have for them or where they're based."

"Fine. It's better that way. They locked the door to the helipad here, anyway. I'll be here until sunrise," he said. "I want to protect my dad as long as possible."

"Got it." Saluting him with two fingers, Zita ran to the edge of the building and leapt off the edge, shifting back into a snowy owl.

***

A couple hours before dawn, a tired Zita flew into the murky top corner of the hospital parking garage. She landed in a clear patch and shifted to Arca, then did a partial shift to gain cat attributes for the improved vision. Walking carefully to avoid slipping on iced-over puddles, unexpected gaps in the pavement, or little heaps of loose pebbles, she prowled the confines of the closed section. Lit only by diffuse, indirect light escaping the rest of the garage and the nearest stairwell, it was dim and shadowy. The cameras mounted on the ceiling would catch blurry shapes at best—perfect for a clandestine meeting between a vigilante, a vampire, and a mercenary team. The cement floor held rust stains and cracks, with a large rectangular chunk missing, but the walls seemed sturdy enough and blocked out the worst of the wind. Yellow construction ribbon flapped gently as it fenced off the area. Cigarette smoke stung her nose by the flimsy barrier. Feet sounded on the stairs and then light spilled from the closest exit as two distinctive people strolled into the area.

Walking with a relaxed, muscular stride, the burly bear shifter came to a stop not far away. "Dark. Hey, Arca," Kodiak said.

"The better for the cameras not to see us, my dear." Trixie cackled and came closer in her usual long-legged pseudo-military stride. For once, she wore a subdued business outfit, all dark colors, if old-fashioned, with a...

Zita paused. She had to ask. "Is that an accordion? Do you have a monkey in a hat too?" Retrieving the flip phone she reserved for her Arca activities from a pocket, she snapped the battery back into it.

"Ooh, can I? By the way, it's a vintage barrel organ, not an accordion." Trixie clapped her hands and rocked on her feet, mischief gleaming on her face as she gazed at Kodiak.

Mournfully, the big hairy man snorted and said, "No monkeys. Don't give her ideas, Arca." He stood with his considerable weight balanced, his feet apart and arms at his side in a pose that screamed military experience. Like Trixie, he wore no mask.

Zita grinned. After she'd sent a text to Dmitri about their arrival, she returned her attention to the pair. "Do you guys need more light? Freelance is still scoping things out, I assume."

Kodiak grinned. "I'm good, yeah?"

Trixie said, "I enjoy stumbling around blind for the boss' amusement. Who can resist his happy little giggles?"

Rubbing her forehead as she tried to picture the taciturn sniper giggling, Zita decided to just nod.

Digging into her pocket, Trixie pulled out something and tossed it at Zita.

Zita snatched it from the air before it could hit her nose. Wyn's purple rock and cord lay in her hand.

"It's broken. Doesn't work anymore," Trixie said, pouting.

Zita smothered a smile. "I'll let Muse know." She crammed it into a pocket.

The vampire whipped through the stairwell doors before Zita had managed more than three additional revolutions of the area. "Finally! What took so long?" Dmitri strode over, the bottom of his black military-style trench coat slapping at his legs as he walked.

"I texted to let you know what was up," Zita said. "They had to get here from wherever they were. You should be grateful they're even here tonight. The roads suck, and I don't know how far they had to come. Speaking of which, the big guy is Kodiak, and the woman with the organ grinder but no monkey is Vaudeville." Awareness ran through her, and she turned in time to see Freelance's dark form slip over the wall and into the garage. As usual, she appreciated the tight, toned form blurred under layers of cloth and bulletproof padding. She waved toward him and licked her lips. "And this is their boss... Freelance." A part of her wondered if he would say his real name tonight or keep using the nickname she'd coined for him.

Dmitri grunted and eyed the mercenaries. While Trixie's barrel organ earned a dubious frown, some of his tension dissipated as he eyed Kodiak's huge form and Freelance's six feet of predatory stillness wrapped in dark combat gear. He pointed at the sniper. "Arca said you guard people. Do you also rescue them? Does that include people who've been kidnapped?"

The mercenary inclined his head.

"It's one of the things we're known for," Vaudeville said. She opened her mouth to say more but closed it after a glance at her companions.

The vampire gave a brusque nod. "While you were gone, Arca, I got a call. Mom's kidnappers want me to wait at Danz Mizer for further instructions, but I don't want to leave Dad unprotected here any longer than necessary. Also, I can't answer phones during the day."

Setting down his bag, Freelance withdrew a large sheaf of papers. He shuffled through them, made a note on one page, and then held it out to Dmitri.

The vampire bolted to him with inhuman speed, holding his wallet and a pen. "How much for a down payment? Bring my mom back. I'll pay anything."

"Dude, at least pretend to negotiate. It's not like mercenaries have price stickers," Zita said.

Freelance's goggles studied Zita for a moment before his attention returned to Dmitri. His hand, which had hovered over his weapon at the sudden movement, retreated from the holster.

Trixie moaned dramatically. "Aw, Mama Vaudeville wanted that pair of diamond-encrusted stilettos. You know Kodiak will get the fun bodyguard duty, and I'll end up on the phones again because of my winning personality." She bit her lip and turned pleading eyes to Freelance.

He shook his head. "Kodiak on bodyguard nights."

After making a rude noise, Trixie said, "Fine, I've got bodyguard days then. I'm telling you, boss man, all work, and no play makes you a very dull boy and a terrible spoilsport." After a moment, she adopted a more businesslike tone and waved a hand at the papers Freelance still held. "That's our standard terms and price schedule. Sign or initial the flagged lines. A down payment is required, and we encourage tipping."

"Seriously?" Zita said.

Trixie gave an insouciant shrug. "It could happen. We wouldn't object."

Zita peered at the paperwork. "Do you for real carry around contracts all the time?" Colorful tags waved to her from some of the pages. "Tagged with little arrows? Órale, if you're going to go all out, why not use little gun labels instead?"

Freelance paused, then glanced at Kodiak. A nearly inaudible mechanical murmur escaped him.

The bear shifter groaned and tapped his ear. "All right, I'll check for them while I'm sitting around, but food's going on the expense report too."

Dmitri growled, showing long white canines as he snatched the papers and walked over to a building support. "I don't care about haggling or the... Yes, fine." He removed a rectangular piece of paper from his wallet. After he pressed it against the cement, he waved the pen above it. "Who do I make the down payment out to? I want no delays."

"Oye, Dmitri, there are so many things wrong with just carrying around a blank check with you everywhere. Seriously. What happens if your wallet gets stolen? How do you know you can even trust these people?" Zita said.

Dmitri glared at her, and his purple eyes shifted red. "You recommended them. Why would you recommend people you don't trust?"

She held up her hands, palms out. "Just keeping it real. I'll shut up now."

"I knew you cared, Arca, behind that oblivious and sporty exterior." Trixie set a hand over her heart and grinned. She turned toward the irate vampire. "Your father will have a bodyguard and regular checks with a charming and brilliant doctor, while other operatives will evaluate the situation and see what we can find. We'll call in subcontractors as necessary, but we usually operate with as small of a team as possible. The final page has a summary."

Dmitri flipped to the last page and scribbled his name, his eyes fading back to their normal shade. "Sold." He squinted at the page, shook his head, and wrote out the check.

Restless, Zita tapped her fingers on her leg. She said, "Now we know it's a kidnapping, and she didn't slip on ice and end up in the ER or something—I checked every hospital and morgue in a decent radius earlier tonight—Muse can do a tracking spell to find her. It'd be good to know what we're walking into this time, so it doesn't end up like the pool party."

Raising his head from the money, the vampire glared at her. "Or like Victoria? The detectives mentioned the details you left out."

Zita winced. She tried to change the subject and remembered what Wyn had said about the tracking spell. "Can you get me something of your mom's that has DNA on it? Like a dirty old shoe or something?"

Dmitri wrinkled his forehead. "Toothbrush? I could stop home for something." He held the check out.

"Yeah, I can see dental hygiene being a big thing in your family, so that would work." Zita paused a moment, but he didn't seem to appreciate or get the joke, so she continued. "I think she'd also want your mom's full name. I'm guessing these guys will need her picture and more info too since they haven't met her."

Vaudeville bounced over to Dmitri and pointed at orange tags in his contract. His check disappeared into her pocket. "There's a list of things we like to know about missing persons and bodyguard clients here. The most important bits are the medical info, so if you fib about anything, don't do it there. If your dad is a patient here, we'll need a waiver to let us see his medical records so we can safely move him if necessary."

Since they seemed to be handling the rest, Zita poked her thumb toward the main parking area. "I'll see if I can sniff anything out at your mom's car. Did you want to try too, Kodiak?"

Kodiak gave a half-laugh. "No, I need to start guarding his dad, and I saw you tracking in Brazil, so I know your nose is good. Security wouldn't be thrilled with a bear sniffing around the garage, and I don't want to panic any sick folks."

Dmitri frowned at the papers and began filling them out.

The bear shifter clapped Dmitri on the shoulder. "How about you show Vaudeville and me to your dad? We'll meet up with the others at the club after you've had a chance to complete the paperwork and get that toothbrush for Arca."

The vampire nodded, skimming the page. "I'll need to check some information at home as well. Since you took an eternity to get here, I arranged for Incubus to sit at the club until I could arrive. I'll have him hang out there to handle the phones until you come to pick up the information, in case I'm asleep by the time you're done."

Trixie nodded. "One of us will show up to man the phones once we determine if your dad can be moved to a more discreet location or not, so if your friend can stay until then, that'd be good."

Wringing his hands, Dmitri said, "Will do. Mom's van is in level 3-C if you want to go there, Arca, but I don't know what you'll find."

"Hopefully, something useful. If I have to track her scent inside, I'll need the hospital staff not to stop me from roaming around as a dog. Muse might be able to pretend to be my handler, but it'll take her a few hours to gather tracking spell stuff and get here." Zita tapped her fingers on her thigh, hoping the mercenaries would take the hint and offer to help.

Freelance inclined his head.

Taking that as agreement, Zita shifted to a bloodhound and grinned. Her long tongue tumbled out of her mouth as she loped off toward the ramp to the next level.

"Arca! Work with these people! You lied to me about Victoria, and I won't have you holding back information again!" Dmitri called after her.

Behind her, a wheeze of discordant sound came from the organ Trixie held. "Betrayal already? The plot thickens. This will be so much fun!" Trixie exclaimed.

***

The open section of the big garage under the hospital was chilly but relatively well lit. It still contained more than enough dark corners for Zita to sneak through, even in a bloodhound's oversized frame. Despite the early hour, many parking spots were full, and people seemed to migrate in and out every few minutes. Yana's minivan was one among many, but none of the others had a silly grinning bat hanging from the rear-view mirror, a racing stripe, and a wheelchair lift.

She inhaled deeply, taking in the scent of individuals, worry, and car exhaust among the hospital smells. After shifting back to Arca, she shielded her actions from the cameras as she unlocked the van. Returning to a bloodhound form, she snuffled around the interior. Her tail wagged as the canine part of her brain reveled in the work. After isolating the base scents of the three people who regularly rode in the van, she figured out who was who. Dmitri's scent was obvious. By process of elimination, the female scent was his mother and the other male his father. *Dad likes his booze. Bet the doctor will tell him to stop after this stroke.*

Her fur prickled along her spine in a not-unpleasant tingle of awareness, and she could guess who watched. Zita lifted her head from the seat and turned to see Freelance near the wall, all but invisible in the shadows of the vehicle. She smacked her lips and groaned. *Yes, smearing drool all over a seat will definitely encourage him to treat me like an equal. Fine. They might have a clue. May as well finish what I was doing before I talk to him again.*

Dropping back down to the pavement, Zita trailed Yana's scent to the stairwell. Retracing her steps, she returned to the minivan and changed to Arca. *I'd wake Wyn and Andy to help, but he couldn't do much and Wyn... well, saying she's not a morning person is an understatement. By the time she got here, this place would be hopping.*

Zita ran a hand through her hair. "Yana—Dmitri's mom—left the car about a day ago and went toward the stairs over there. Her trail stops right in front of them, with no scent on the door, so I'm guessing someone pulled up, stuffed her into a van, and took off. Alternately, someone could've held the door for her. I need to sniff the steps to be certain, but someone's got to handle security if they show up while I do so."

He nodded. Turning away, the mercenary set down his backpack and dug through it.

"Am I waiting for something?" she asked when no explanation was forthcoming. After a few minutes of pacing and eying her companion, she got a plastic bag of fruit and nut bars out of her pocket and opened it. "You want? Blueberry honey nut protein bars. Made them myself."

The mercenary shook his head.

Once she'd finished her snack, she tried waiting for a few minutes before she got bored and rifled through the vehicle for any additional information. Nothing useful surfaced, and it was a relief when her concentration was interrupted by a few sharp knocks on a window.

A SWAT officer stood outside.

Her heart almost stopped, and then she realized Freelance had added a hard tactical helmet to his usual uniform, under which his goggles protruded, and patches to the shoulders that resembled police insignia. From a distance or to a distracted observer, he would resemble a member of the police. *Excellent.*

He held out a harness with the K-9 SQUAD emblazoned on the black fabric. A real one, not like the cheap costume one she occasionally used with her friends and had modified to allow her to break it with little effort.

"Do I want to know how you got those? Or why you're carrying them around?" Zita asked as she hopped out of the minivan.

To her surprise, Freelance answered, his raspy mechanical tones whispering. "Vaudeville. Best not to ask."

Zita locked the vehicle. "No luck in the car. Yana was the last person in it before me, and everything matches Dmitri's timeline." She rubbed her forehead. "You might want to have Vaudeville ask people if they remember her, assuming she can rein in the wacky. When I met Yana, she was real friendly and chatty, the sort of person people remember."

Freelance's head tilted. "Met?"

A short laugh escaped Zita, and she automatically went on the defensive. "His mom. That's her first name. We met when I went to check his house for a different missing person, not for like a date thing. He's a decent guy, but I like guys who are more active and less... dead." She remembered Domina's overshare, and said, "I think he likes drama with his chicks, too, based on his ex."

The mercenary gazed at her.

Realizing her mistake, she colored. "Oh, you weren't asking if we had a relationship. What did you want?" *I'm too used to my family jumping all over any interactions with single men.*

"Description?" Freelance said.

For a second, Zita was confused. "His ex-girlfriend? Evil with a side of slutty gold digger and no decent muscle tone? She's in jail."

His goggles regarded her silently.

She slapped herself in the forehead. "Ay, I am full of win today. You meant his mom. Yana's around a hundred and fifty-eight centimeters—I mean five foot six inches—and does a combination of manual labor and aerobics. Nice biceps, good flexibility for somebody near sixty. She has an American accent and short curly hair, black and silver. Dmitri's got her eyes, though she blinks at a normal rate. She smelled like the hospital, Irish Spring soap, and wool. Don't eat her cookies."

He inclined his head. "Clothes?"

Zita had to think about it. "Couple days ago, she had the beige support sneakers they sell to old people and a matching button-up sweater. Clothes aren't my thing. You should ask Dmitri. I'd do it, but he's not thrilled with me right now."

Glancing around, he said, "What happened with Victoria?"

She huffed out a breath. "He didn't tell you? She was the owner of Danz Mizer and the person I was searching for when I met his mom. When we went to check on her a week ago, I found her cut up in her apartment. I didn't let Dmitri see the body and told him she didn't suffer. The cops must've told him more. It was... bad, very bad. Turns out she was maybe Sobek's auntie, so she might've been murdered just to keep her quiet."

After a pause, he nodded and held out the harness.

*Right, we need to verify Yana didn't take the stairs and convince any security that we have a legit reason for being there.* Zita returned to bloodhound shape.

She inhaled, trying to concentrate on the barrage of olfactory information, including the enticing and subtle male scent of her silent companion, instead of the thought of voluntarily allowing herself to be tied up. *It's to save Dmitri's mom. It's not real. I'm not helpless, and I can always change shape and escape.*

As the harness slipped over her head, she shivered and blew out a huff of air, even though his gloved hands were gentle.

# Chapter Sixteen

**Later that day,** snow crunched under Zita's feet as she jogged in place, wearing her Arca form. While the streets had been cleared, the sidewalks were a mishmash, as individual businesses were responsible for their own strips. Some had attended to the duty with more enthusiasm than others. In front of the closed Danz Mizer, no shoveling had been done at all. Yellow police tape still lined the doors of the club, snapping and snarling in the biting wind on the one side where it had been pulled away from the door frame.

Zita glanced at the collection of boot treads by the entry, shoving a long lock of hair from her face as she waited for Wyn to catch up.

Wearing her Muse guise, Wyn daintily picked her way through the snow, carefully placing each foot after a near-fall on the icy pavement earlier. She'd updated her illusion spell to allow it to switch between two versions of the same woman: one wearing a short, glittery dress and heels, and the other in a form-fitting parka, short skirt, and knee-high boots.

Zita kept jogging to keep herself warm. Even with the too-big rubber boots and thrift shop coat she'd thrown over her hooded sweatshirt and Spandex-like costume, she was freezing. Seeing her friend's tiny illusory costume only made the chill cut deeper. *It doesn't help that I feel like we're being watched.*

Behind her, Wyn grumbled. "Remind me again why we're reveling in arctic temperatures? The snow storm's not over yet, just pausing, the weathermen said. Nobody else is stupid enough to be out." She waved her hand around them.

They were the only pedestrians. Few vehicles lined the street, with the closest being a white extended cab pickup truck that bore more rust than snow.

Zita rolled her eyes. Despite knowing her friend wasn't actually upset about helping, she answered anyway. "Because a woman's missing? With everything shut down by the weather, neither of us have work anyway. We'll pick up the stuff for the tracking spell and exchange information with the mercenaries. Did you want to do the spell here?"

Her friend lifted her gaze from the ground and speared Zita with it. "Perhaps, but I'd want to call in Wingspan first so he can take us where we need to go faster. We have a meeting set up?" She glanced around, her tone indicating displeasure. *It's not with that creepy mercenary leader, is it?*

*Only if I'm lucky, but I doubt he'd say much even if he shows.* As a shiver of awareness ran through her, Zita answered the rest out loud and discreetly scanned the street for the source of her disquiet. "Dmitri hired them and asked us to play nice together. When we had to call it quits earlier this morning, we agreed to meet up here in an hour, pool our findings, and pick up some stuff."

Huffing and puffing, Wyn paused and eyed Zita. "Did he tell you all to work together or did he tell you to behave yourself? And why are we here now if the meeting's not for an hour?"

"You got so little faith in me. We're here early to scout," Zita said, choosing to ignore the fact that her friend's intuition was right about the vampire's words. She waved at the ground. "From the footprints, Kodiak and Dmitri are here. Since the vamp said Incubus would help out, he's likely here too, plus two others, one of which is a woman or a dude with girly shoes. They're probably people cleaning or handling that delivery in the docking bay."

"Who delivers in several feet of snow? The door's shut, so how could you tell?" Wyn struggled not to slip as she walked the last few feet.

After steadying her friend, Zita shrugged, still uneasy. She rapped on the door hard with her knuckles. "People with bills to pay? They got lights on in there, and I hear shouting. If nobody answers here, we can tromp around to that entrance to get in." A subtle whir caught her attention, and she unzipped her coat, preparing to rip it and her boots off if necessary. A second later, her brain caught up and recognized the sound. *Oh, you're not going to like this.*

*Like what?* Wyn sent.

Freelance landed beside them and hooked his grapple gun onto his belt.

With a surprised squeal, Wyn slipped.

Zita reached out and grabbed her flustered friend before she could hit the ground. "Hey, Freelance. Scouting?"

All he said was "Trouble inside."

With a quick curse, Zita checked the door. *Locked.* "Hide me from the cameras, okay?"

Wyn and Freelance stood on either side of her.

After a precious minute, mentally wishing for her full locksmith kit, Zita got the door unlocked. A series of gunshots rang out from farther inside.

Freelance pushed past her, handgun out, immediately stepping out of the hall into a cloakroom.

Trepidation grew as Zita followed. Voices murmured in another room. Holding a finger to her lips to ask her friend for silence, she dragged Wyn into the cloakroom opposite the mercenary. *I smell blood and guns. Hide and stay put until I tell you it's okay. This level is shaped like a frying pan, and we came in the wrong end, the handle part that'll make us easy targets if someone's here.*

Wyn nodded and crouched behind a small podium.

Zita stripped off her coat and the massive rubber boots she'd been wearing. Shifting to a panther with the hope that the black fur would hide her in the shadows, she sidled down the wall and peeked out into the club proper, checking for danger.

Freelance joined her two seconds later, hovering close to the other wall with a handgun out and down at his side.

Wyn dropped Zita's outerwear into her purse, biting her lip.

The main room of the dance club had changed little since she'd last seen it, a room of toppled tables and chairs that converged on a bar. An acrid chemical scent overlay the sweat, fear, and spilled alcohol that had permeated it before. Multiple surfaces bore a thin coat of gray powder. On the stairs leading up to the VIP area, a massive furry form slumped against the railing, which had been half-torn from its supports.

Freelance jerked his chin toward the bar, the more exposed route through the room—had she been in human form.

With a nod, Zita darted forward, beneath tables, scanning for enemies. So many people had passed through here that her feline nose could not differentiate between them.

Behind her, Freelance advanced forward along the walls toward the steps.

By the dark, polished wood of the bar, Incubus and Detective Mack lay in a puddle of blood. The bartender coughed weakly, while the cop held his stomach in a fetal curl. A third man lay face down in the kitchen doorway. The missing section of his head told her she didn't need to check for a pulse.

She gulped.

As she crept to the injured men, a foul odor rose from the cop. Zita had hunted and butchered animals to eat enough to recognize it. She gave the room one last scan to ensure it was safe for her friend before shifting to Arca and then again partially back to panther for the enhanced senses. Sights and scents sharpened, but her hearing did not improve. She called out, "Gut wound, Muse, cop first. Hug the walls in case someone's upstairs in a sniping position."

Wyn gasped and rushed past Zita, falling to her knees by the men. The verdant tendrils of her healing spell rose as she chanted.

When the magic touched Mack, his body relaxed.

Freelance was nowhere to be found. Zita started to head up the stairs, then hesitated, not wanting to leave her friend unprotected.

Wyn continued healing. *Go.*

An animalistic growl came from upstairs, and Zita ran that direction.

Freelance was already there, pressing a neatly folded napkin to Kodiak's shoulder.

In bear form, Kodiak lay at the top of the steps. One of his legs was a bloody mess clearly incapable of supporting his bulk, and more blood oozed from his shoulder. With a whine, he dug into his own leg and pulled out a small red-smeared bead. He dropped it to the side with an exhausted sigh and waved a paw toward the Employee Only door. "Group. Big guy bit me with fangs, and somebody's payload was silver. Not healing right. They went after Dmitri. In the office."

His gun raised, Freelance began to clear the room, checking each booth and table. Catching Zita's gaze, he pointed to her, and then the Employee Only door, then to himself and the main stairs.

She nodded to Freelance and sprinted to the door. *Muse, Kodiak's hit and can't heal naturally. He needs magic stat before he bleeds out. By the top of the main stairs.*

*I'm on it once I'm done with these two. They're in bad shape,* Wyn sent.

After verifying that neither man was in the line of fire from the doorway, Zita shoved a swinging door all the way open and took in the hallway in a glance: supply cubby, utilitarian stairs leading down, and an open office. She caught the door, stepped inside, and then shut it behind herself silently. Keeping her back by the wall, she focused on the office. A cautious check revealed the long narrow room was empty of people. Chairs and blankets were scattered across the floor, and a wallet and toothbrush sat on the end of the desk. She picked it up and flipped it open. Dmitri's learner's permit grinned saucily up at her. Her nose twitched as she sorted through scents. The most recent were old blood, sour sweat, and stagnant swamp... *Sobek!*

Downstairs, voices rose again, a gun barked three times, and then a woman cried out. The rumble and protesting squeal of a garage door opening reached her sensitive ears.

*That wasn't Wyn. Nobody's out front, and the most logical place for the loading dock is next to the kitchen in the rear of the club.* After an extended sniff of the wallet to ensure she had Dmitri's scent, Zita dropped it back on the desk and ran for the docks. She vaulted over the first set of steps in the employee stairwell, landing on the railing of the second, and then somersaulted to the floor. Emerging in the back hallway, she dashed through the only unmarked doors between a storeroom and the kitchen and found the loading dock.

It was little more than a single-truck garage, the sort that could hold a local delivery van but not a full-sized semi. Puddles tinted red gathered where a vehicle had been parked on the plain cement floor, stained and scarred with years of use. The corrugated steel door was up, letting in the cold and enough sun to highlight the time-grayed walls and bare, flickering fluorescents in the ceiling.

By the doorway, Detective Haroon lay unconscious, blood seeping from her head and lesser injuries on her arm. Her gun was several feet away, closer to a massive black SUV. A man leaned out the window with pistol. The vehicle's engine rumbled.

Zita retreated to the dubious cover of a pile of boxes before he could shoot her. *Cop with a head wound and shot arm near the loading dock, but alive. Bad guys with guns here, so handle the injured you're already with first. Dmitri's wallet is on his desk if you need it for a tracking spell later.*

Wyn sent a preoccupied mental mumble back.

Freelance raced up, avoiding the direct line of sight of the doorway.

Without being asked, Zita hissed, "SUV with guns. Cop down."

The mercenary lifted his handgun and gave a brusque nod.

Red brake lights shone as the SUV backed out and sped away, heavy-duty winter tires spraying slush behind it.

Zita darted forward and checked the cop's pulse. It still beat, and Haroon seemed to be breathing easily, each breath visible in the chill air of the open garage. After a second of hesitation, she ripped the little square box of the camera off the cop's shoulder and stuffed it into her pocket. *If I have to fight Sobek later, maybe I can film it, so they have proof I'm not running around beating up the homeless.*

As she prepared to launch herself after the departing vehicle, Freelance ripped open a pouch at his waist, ejected a cartridge from his long gun, and loaded a new one. He ran to the street.

She chased behind him. "Don't blow up the SUV! They've got Dmitri!" Zita shouted.

Lifting his gun, Freelance fired a single shot at it.

The SUV sped up and around the corner.

"You missed?" she said. Exhaust and sweat and Dmitri's blood all bombarded her nose with information, and chill seeped up through the cement into the bottoms of her feet.

He glanced at her and then sprinted in the opposite direction of the SUV, still carrying his weapon.

*I'm following the bad guys. They kidnapped Dmitri.* Shifting to a peregrine falcon, she lifted off the ground and took flight into the wintry sky.

In clearer weather, finding a single black SUV in D.C. would've been impossible. In the lull of a snowstorm, however, the only matching vehicle moved away from the club so quickly that even the heavy snow tires slipped on a particularly icy turn. Another car, one that had failed the same turn, sat at an angle on the sidewalk by the intersection, and the SUV careened by, narrowly missing it.

Despite the thick window tint that prevented her from seeing more than multiple forms inside, Zita followed it. When a battered white pickup accelerated down the road two blocks behind and following the same path, she kept a wary eye on it. *Friend or foe? The last thing I need is to be outnumbered even more when I'm trying to rescue people.*

The truck accelerated around the same icy corner without sliding at all and avoided the crashed car with apparent ease.

She circled to check the driver of the second car. When she spotted the glint of light on goggles and a face hidden behind a black mask, she cawed a laugh. *Ah. Mercenary. Maybe he didn't miss.*

Ahead of them, the SUV slowed and signaled to get onto an on-ramp for the Beltway.

*Keeping pace with them on the highway is hard, and I've been up most of the night.* Noting the pickup at a stoplight, she dove toward it, using the speed to get there before the light could change. Zita shifted to Arca outside it and tapped on the window. She danced in place, trying to keep her bare feet from freezing in the slushy, icy mess on the road.

The window opened with a smooth automation belied by the apparent age of the vehicle. Freelance surveyed her.

"Bueno. Hang on, I don't want frostbite!" Taking a couple steps back, Zita ran and jumped, grabbing the window and sliding her body inside. She grinned at him and settled into the passenger seat, belting herself in. "What, you think you get all the fun? They just hit the highway going west, but you knew that, right?"

While he said nothing, he rolled up the window and accelerated when the light changed. For a car that seemed decrepit, it had a hearty, steady growl that suggested a powerful engine.

"Thanks for the lift. This definitely beats risking losing them and pulling a muscle trying to keep up. I'm guessing you attached some kind of tracker to their car when you shot them, right?"

Freelance inclined his head.

Zita grinned and maneuvered her feet directly below the heat vents near the floor. *Gracias a Dios for working heaters.* "Sorry about asking if you missed earlier. Is that custom ammo you guys modified or can anyone buy it?"

He didn't respond to that, instead neatly letting his truck fall back so the SUV was well ahead, but not out of sight.

She didn't let that stop her. "Ah, custom then. So, what's the plan? The rest of your team will catch up once Muse heals Kodiak, and the cops let them leave?"

After a moment, his raspy mechanical voice broke the silence. "Scout. Call in location. Limited range tracking device. Get hostages out."

"Still a pretty sweet trick, though, turning it into a bullet." Her mind raced, considering possibilities. Zita tapped her fingers on her thigh and eyed the brake lights flaring ahead. "That's the same plan I had, down to sneaking the hostages out and waiting for the cops to arrest Sobek's sorry ass. They better throw him in jail for good this time. I have a contingency to step in and interfere before my friends and yours arrive if he starts in on the torture. I've seen the results of that last time I took too long, and I don't want to see it again." Remembering poor Jennifer Stone and her brother, Zita winced.

To her surprise, he spoke, "Stone was schizophrenic before."

"Neta, but being tortured didn't help her none, did it? Or the guy captured with her. I figure we have to move if it gets too close to nightfall to get Dmitri and his mom out."

"Why nightfall?" Freelance drove like he walked, without a trace of aggression or anything to deter from the smooth economy and speed of forward motion.

She stared out the window. "Sobek's a sadist. He won't start on Yana until Dmitri can watch, and the vampire's impossible to keep awake in the daytime. Probably didn't even stir when they carried him out of there. Not to mention, I smelled Dmitri's blood in the garage, so he's hurt already and will need blood when he wakes up." Zita managed to keep from saying her next thought. *The last thing we need is to fight both Sobek and Dmitri.*

The mercenary glanced at her, and his chin tilted in a small nod. He switched lanes, allowing greater distance to come between their vehicle and the SUV.

As she considered possible approaches and plans, Zita let the conversation lapse into a comfortable silence.

Wyn broke it mentally several minutes later. *Zita? Everyone's stable here now, and the detectives have additional police coming soon. Where are you? I found your clothing.*

*We're westbound on I-66. Sobek's SUV is sitting in the left lane so this might be a long ride,* Zita sent.

*We? You didn't sneak into the back of Sobek's vehicle, did you?* Now dismay ran through their connection from her friend.

*How stupid do you think I am? We is Freelance and me. He's driving a seriously loaded pickup truck, and we're following using some tracking thingy he shot onto Sobek's SUV. It's too cold to risk freezing what little culo I have off and exhausting myself before we even get to wherever we're going.* Zita decided not to mention that hiding in Sobek's SUV had been a possibility she'd considered before noticing the mercenary's vehicle.

Her friend did not seem as soothed as she should've been. *Freelance? Are you okay? Do you need to be rescued?*

Zita glanced over at the silent driver and grinned. She thought his goggles slanted her direction a moment. *No, we good. We're practically bonding.*

*I'll call Andy.*

*No hay bronca, though I'd love his help when we start rescuing people. If you keep the mental link up, I'll let you know when the bad guys stop. Freelance will probably call his team in then too, if you want to hang near them. I don't know how many vehicles they have, but none of them will be as fast as Wingspan. Oh, and you should find out the address for Victoria's mountain cabin. The bad guys seem to be heading west, but I'm hoping they're not going all the way to the mountains.*

Wyn gave a murmur of assent. *Incoming police. Talk soon.* The connection went quiet, but she could still feel the warm link in the back of her mind.

Zita's mind sped through scenarios. She remembered how quickly Freelance had neutralized Jennifer Stone and absconded with the sick woman before. "Vaudeville said you guys did lots of rescues..."

That won her a sidelong glance.

She voiced her thoughts. "Órale, how's this for a preliminary plan? We track them and scout it out. Call it in to our respective friends and have them alert the cops. I'll slash the tires on their cars or rip out battery wires to keep them from being able to leave in a vehicle. When our backup's in position, we sneak out Dmitri and his mom while the cops are prepping to go in. If we need to take action before our friends show up, I'll run distraction duty. You concentrate on getting the prisoners out."

"Me?" While emotion was hard to tell with the voice changing tool he used, she thought it sounded more curious than not.

"You've more experience sneaking out of places with people, and I'm good at being loud. And not killing people. Because nobody needs to die today, right?" She eyed her companion.

When he didn't speak, Zita continued. "Glad you agree. We'll work out meet points and specifics once we have a clue where we're going and what we're up against. While I wouldn't place no bets on it, if we're lucky, it'll be four or five disorganized thugs in a broken-down old house and Sobek."

Freelance drove another mile or two before he said, "Agreed. The U.S. investigates deaths too closely."

"Chido." Zita settled into a more comfortable position and frowned at the snowflakes starting to come in rapid succession again. *Guess the snowstorm's waking up. Awesome.* Another thought hit her. A delightful and decadent one. "Hey, does your tricked-out ride have butt heat?"

# Chapter Seventeen

**The decrease in speed and the complaints of her stomach** woke Zita. As she sat up, she glanced outside, and the dashboard clock told her that morning had turned to afternoon during her nap. Beside her, Freelance continued to drive. Surreptitiously, she wiped drool from the side of her mouth as she checked their surroundings.

From the occasional stop sign, they had left all highways behind. The truck crawled up a partially plowed road that wound around and through a thickly wooded area. The SUV was nowhere to be seen, and she surmised that they had been forced to drop back out of visible distance. A snow plow, followed by a Mercedes was the only traffic. By the time they passed a billboard advertising a nearby luxury ski resort, the road seemed to be empty of anything other than snowy forest, mailboxes in various states of disrepair, the occasional fancy estate gate, and sudden, phenomenal views down a mountain.

"Sorry about that. I was up most of the night. Where are we? Pennsylvania, Virginia, or West Virginia?" Zita's stomach rumbled, and she dug in her pockets for the last of her snacks. Plastic rustled as she hauled out a bag of trail mix and offered it to her silent companion. *Wish I'd had time to eat more earlier when I went to get Wyn.*

With a brusque shake of his head, Freelance refused the food. "West Virginia."

As she ate trail mix, Zita thought of Dmitri's road trip supplies wistfully. The chicken had kept her fed most of the week, distributed throughout a number of meals. She licked her lips. *Would be nice to have some of that now, but I can only fit so much in my pockets. They're already bulging with just a couple basic lock picks, my vigilante phone, and the cop's camera thing. I should see how that works.*

As she munched, Zita withdrew the cop's body camera and poked at it until she thought she had a grasp of the simple controls. Feeling the weight of Freelance's attention, she said, "It's hard to testify in court as a masked vigilante. Not certain how low of a profile you keep, but I'm guessing you don't like to do so either. If we're running off with the prisoners, we need proof of his wrongdoing so the cops can throw Sobek in jail forever. I've learned the hard way that I need to leave the cops proof that anyone I tie up is actually a criminal. If I don't, they can claim anything they want, and I'm suddenly a psycho with a Spandex kink."

When he didn't reply, she decided he agreed and tucked the device away in her pocket. She finished her snack and sent a quick mental message to her friends about their location. *If Wyn hadn't left the party line up all this time, I'd have to wait for her to check on me or use my phone to update them.*

Fifteen minutes later, Freelance slowed more. "They're stopping." He nodded to a closing set of gates, stone with iron or aluminum fencing that locked off a driveway from the road.

Zita practically shouted with glee at the thought of moving faster than a crawl. Despite the promise of action, she noted the boxes near the landscaping lights. "Drive was plowed earlier today, and they've got cameras on the gate. I can disable that and any alarms so you can walk up the drive instead of fighting through feet of snow. Between the weather and me, their gate security's about to have a bad day. We're not parking right here?"

He shook his head.

She grinned. "Por supuesto, wouldn't want to get boxed in. Nearby, then." She grinned and stretched as much as the seat belt would allow. "I'll be in animal form as much as possible since bare feet suck in the snow. How about we agree to stick together until the place is visible, and then I'll scout in and out as an animal? You can get into a good firing position or something in case they try to run in their cars before I disable them." *Plus the time it takes me to scout should allow him time to slog somewhere with visibility. Head-to-toe black won't help him hide in all this snow.*

He nodded.

***

Unlike the last two places where he'd done business, Sobek's mountain hideaway was definitely not a decrepit row house staffed with a few incompetent gang members or a warehouse with only a single guard.

Zita surveyed the grounds from above as a golden eagle, grateful the snow of earlier had eased off enough to allow her to fly. Although the piney woods remained wild, the area around the cluster of buildings had been cleared for at least a half an acre in every direction. Her primary focus was on the structures and the occasional people she could see. Somewhere at the edge of the trees, Freelance was or would be choosing his observation post.

The closest edifice was a not-quite mansion with a split personality; the bottom floor was log and stone construction, while the upper story seemed to be floor-to-ceiling windows.

After a second, Zita recognized it. *Oh, hey, I was right! Wyn, they're stopping at Victoria's place. Did you tell the cops?*

Assent hummed through the mental link.

A driveway looped between the house and a multi-car garage to the northwest before straggling off to the south. Tire tracks led to one of the doors in the inches of snow that had fallen since whenever the asphalt had been plowed. A tidy yellow and white barn sat to the north of the garage, with fenced grazing area stretching out on two sides of it. A lonely shed, roof buckling under snow, sat at the pasture's farthest boundary. Two hundred feet away from the barn, two large, low metal buildings huddled together, obviously newer and cheaper than any of the other buildings. Between all the buildings, long poles held two netless basketball backboards.

Zita tsked mentally. *It's like a farm got a weird makeover on the cheap. What did they need all that for? It's pointless unless they're all gyms of some kind. That would be cool, but unlikely.*

As she looped by the woods, searching for the mercenary, she did a quick pass through the cow shed to verify it was what it seemed from above: abandoned and empty, undisturbed by anything other than small animals.

Once she managed to find him, mostly by figuring out what tree had the best view of the area and sufficient size to hide a fully-grown man, Zita landed near the mercenary. She shifted to Arca and tried not to wince at the frigid bite of the branch on her feet. "Shed's clear. I'll hit the garage and work my way clockwise until I end at the house. It'll be the hardest one since it's got all those windows on the upper floor. If Dmitri and his mom are in an outbuilding, we might be able to sneak them out without having to fight. Wingspan can land in the pasture or the basketball court and pick them up, so they'd be exposed as little time as possible, though all subtlety's gone once he's close."

No response.

After waiting an entire second, she said, "Right then. It's a plan. We sneak the prisoners out when the cops are ready to come in or sunset, whichever comes first, and get them to safety. Muse will fly on Wingspan so if they're hurt or we're hurt, she can heal us. Then the authority types can negotiate with or mop up Sobek or whoever's left. When my friends last checked in, the cops were using the resort nearby as a staging ground and trying to get a SWAT team or something up here discreetly. Kodiak was with them on the ground there for now, and Vaudeville stayed back in D.C. with Dmitri's dad."

He remained silent though she thought she caught a flicker of movement beneath the winter camouflage poncho that concealed him.

"I'll take that as approval and awe of my amateurish but undeniably sweet skills," she said, grinning at him.

"Sub-aural com frequency?" he said.

*Sub-aural com? Oh, he means party line.* She shook her head and hauled out the lie her friends told everyone to keep Wyn's telepathy secret. "No, sorry. It's a magic thing. Muse casts it whenever we need it, and I don't know if she can include others when she's not present. Did you have any luck with your satellite phone?" Not surprisingly, her cell didn't work in the mountains, but his satellite phone had patchy reception by the truck.

Freelance shook his head. After a rapid scan of the area, he touched her arm and held out a small object to her.

Taking the proffered item, she studied it. At first, it resembled a necklace made of a strand of dark brown strangely synthetic yarn, with a hard object sewn inside it. After a second, she realized what it was. "Oh, it's an earpiece. This will shift with me?"

He nodded.

After putting it over her head and looping most of it behind her ears and under the thick, heavy mass of Arca's long hair, she paused. "You do realize I can't speak as an animal, right? I'll only be able to hear you, not respond."

His head inclined.

Zita huffed and grumbled. "I know most shapeshifters can talk as animals, but I can't. I don't know how they do it. Animals don't have the same kind of vocal cords and mouth structures as humans. It should be impossible for them to... never mind. I'm off to see what we're up against. Worst comes to worst, I'll tell you where the prisoners are and signal my friends for a pickup. You get the prisoners out on Wingspan while I can run a distraction. You just go with my friends. I can fly home from here if necessary." *Or teleport.*

Freelance tilted his head at her and said, "Foolhardy."

"What are our options? You've got the most experience freeing people from situations like this," she said. *And hopefully, we can keep the body count down if I'm leading off as many of the bad guys as possible.* She ran a hand over her hair, forward and back, preparing to shift.

He nodded. "Be careful, amateur."

That startled a smile out of her. "You too."

***

A short time later, Zita squeezed through a gap in the garage's soffit as a raccoon, and clung to the wall, high above the cement floor. No one else was there, and she didn't see any cameras. Basic tools and hardware were scattered in and around a toolbox on a steel workbench. Two snowmobiles and a riding lawnmower sat separate from four identical black SUVs, one of which still had water dripping from it. A fifth vehicle, a dusty and salt-spattered pickup truck, had a snow plow attached to the front. A wooden rack tacked up by the garage doors held a tidy row of keys. She rubbed her tiny black paws together, gleefully. *Time to have some fun. I'll hide the keys, then hit the batteries.*

Twenty minutes later, she brushed off a short length of black battery wire from her sweatshirt and tapped her earpiece. "Done.

Confirmed first building's a garage. Exiting now. What's our status?" Shifting back to a raccoon, she exited through the same hole she'd come in through.

Freelance's voice whispered back. "Movement. Your four o'clock."

Changing shape again to a turkey vulture, she flew to the barn, keeping a wary eye on three men until they plodded into the house. The familiar predatory strides of one stocky form identified him as Sobek. Her feathers ruffled across her back, and she forced herself to return to scouting.

Once she'd snuck inside, again adopting a raccoon form, she scurried through the barn. It had been remodeled to serve as a basic barracks, with beds upstairs and all other rooms downstairs. She raced through it as quickly as stealth and the desire to hide several boxes of gun cartridges allowed. Finishing up, she moved to the northernmost of the metal buildings to the east.

The stench of rotten eggs and garbage leaking around the cheap window seals convinced her to stay outside. After a quick shift to Arca to retrieve the cop's camera, she took a minute to video the setup, moving methodically around the perimeter. "Found a drug lab and what looks like storage. Domina must've been wrong about Sobek handing his meth business over to someone else," she whispered, both for the recording and the mercenary.

"Patrol approaching lab," Freelance rasped over the com.

Zita hurried to get a shot of the storage area, tucked away the camera, and then shifted to an Arctic fox. She darted under the propane tank between the two metal buildings. As she crouched there and waited for the guards to pass, she scrunched her nose up at a tang in the air. While the fetid lab and the tank's contents still stunk, another scent nipped at her nose, a sharp plastic one with a chemical edge to it. Wary, she followed her nose to the corner closest to the meth lab and discovered an unobtrusive square package taped to the interior of the leg where it would be invisible... unless someone was less than two feet high. She eyed the curious box and realized the tiny black antenna, the only part that protruded from the leg, was part of a receiver.

*Bomb? On a propane tank next to a meth lab? No mames.*

Shifting to a raccoon, she pried it off the tank, praying it wouldn't explode. After a quick check to ensure that she couldn't be seen by either the patrol or her mercenary ally, she teleported to the empty cow shed. After burying it under a pile of snow, she teleported back to the propane tank. Switching to a bird, she assessed her next target.

The last metal building stymied her at first. While it had windows, curtains hid the interior. Most were dark, but the one end had white translucent ones just thick enough to prevent her from seeing what was inside.

Finding a gap near the foundation, she squeezed inside as a mouse. A squeak of dismay escaped her as she scurried under a rusty metal cart and climbed it to peek over the lip at the top.

Most of the building was one big room with three rows of unconscious men chained to cots, each with an arm outstretched and an IV inserted. It reeked with a miasma of blood and sweat from multiple unwashed bodies. Among the other olfactory information, she caught Dmitri's scent, but he was not on any of the cots. The closest row of prisoners had the sunken cheeks and unnatural gauntness of forced inactivity and little food, but the others seemed as if a healthy soccer team had chosen to nap at the same time, save for their paleness and the heavy shackles on each one. Wheeled metal carts, including the one she hid in, sat snug against the walls at the end of each aisle of cots. Dark curtains drowned out the sunlight, save for where it leaked in around the edges. Fluorescents gave everything a wan tone. A bathroom door hung open along the back wall, while the only other interior door seemed to be a reinforced steel one, studded with thick bolts and barred.

Two bored guards played cards nearby as cameras brooded overhead, keeping her from exploring more.

*If that bomb had exploded, it might've taken out all these people and the meth lab,* she realized with horror.

A buzzer went off, and one guard groaned. "Time to check the veggies." He stood up and set the Uzi on his seat. Retrieving the cart from the first aisle of cots, he set a cattle prod atop it and shuffled down the row, giving each prisoner a perfunctory check of basic vital functions. As he went, he marked off something on a list. The other guard tapped his cards on his leg.

After returning the cart, the ambulatory guard moved to the next row and repeated his actions with the second cart.

Zita glanced at the barred door. *Dmitri and Yana must be in there, but the guard will take my hiding place in a few seconds. I'll try to get into that back room from the outside after I go through the main house. This room lacks places to hide, even small ones, and shifting would alert them that I'm not a rodent. Once they know I'm here, they might kill all their captives and move on. Someone is clearly prepared to do that, or they wouldn't be setting bombs so close. I can't risk the prisoners' lives.* Regretfully, she slipped out while she could.

*** 

After taking a quick minute to update Freelance and get him moving closer to the building with the prisoners—this time to an agreed upon spot so she wouldn't have to search for him—the main house proved easier to infiltrate. While it had alarms on the doors and windows, it lacked cameras and guards. Following a quick assessment, she entered as a rat through a loose roof joint. Once she'd gotten down to the human areas, she switched to a sleek dark gray tabby. The first bedroom yielded little, other than a sleeping Sobek and the stench of old blood. She left that one quickly. The second, oddly locked from the outside, was an empty guest bedroom that showed signs of use.

Zita pried open the door to the third bedroom and slunk through the suite, ears perked. Like the other bedrooms, it had floor-to-ceiling windows muffled and veiled in heavy brocade drapes. Massive rustic wooden furniture loomed, throwing shadows everywhere. An open closet held slick men's suits that reeked of cologne, enough sour tobacco, wood, and spice scent to choke on. Or in her case, sneeze repeatedly.

Loud footsteps approached.

# Chapter Eighteen

**Zita squeezed under an oversized wardrobe** in the bedroom right before the doors burst open. Light streamed in as two pairs of boots entered and circled the room. They opened the closets and rifled through them, ran through the bathroom, and one man even got down on his knees and glanced under the high bed.

She offered a silent prayer of thanks that she'd chosen a different hiding place.

From the doorway, Sobek spoke, his voice groggy and his gesture slow as he rubbed his eyes. "What's going on?" His broad form threw shadows over the room as he blocked the hallway light.

Unable to resist, Zita inched forward until she could see more.

As he shifted from foot to foot, one guard glanced at his companion and answered. "Sensor went off on the door, sir, and we heard something when we came to check it."

Zita cursed mentally at the stupidly strong cologne, her eyes watering.

Sobek growled and yawned. "He put alarms on his doors? Figures. Untrusting bastard. Is it clear?"

"Seems so." The guards stared steadfastly at the ground.

The psychopath sniffed. "Probably forgot to close it completely, and it popped open when the house was settling. It's an old house. You're done here. Go back to the security room downstairs."

"We're not done with our search—" one began.

His hand dropped to the large knife belted at his waist. Sobek crooned, "My playthings are unavailable until dark. Did I hear you volunteer to amuse me?"

Both guards paled. "No, sir, we'll go now."

"I'll lock up here." Arms folded over his chest, Sobek watched them go. Once the others were gone, he snorted and strolled around the room, poking into drawers. He picked up a watch, put it on, and admired the glinting gold on his wrist.

To her dismay, Zita realized his mouth was too red, and his skin an unhealthy white. While his body still drew breath, each one was too far apart. She wrapped her tail around herself. *He must be close to turning vampire.*

As if echoing her thoughts, Sobek smiled at himself in the mirror, turning his head to admire the extended, wicked canines that now protruded far more than his other jagged teeth. "Not long now. Soon I'll be immortal." His phone shrilled. With an annoyed grunt, he swiped the phone and held it close. "What's wrong? I'm checking your precious room and don't see anything out of place. And what is that noise?"

Even with feline ears, Zita couldn't make out the words or voice on the other end of the call, thanks to a loud rhythmic roar like a plane or train.

Sobek could clearly understand whoever it was. Distaste grew on his face, and he spat his words. "What do you mean you're almost here? You visited this weekend. What happened to keeping you unknown from the little people? Yeah, I'll have them clear it for you." He waited.

Whatever answer he received made his face contort further. "What? How did they find us?"

*Please don't mean what I think you mean,* Zita thought.

The psychopath snarled. "That stupid vigilante again? Don't blame my men. We extracted the vampire and got away, despite far more people being there than expected."

Zita forced her breathing to stay quiet and shallow. *They know. Well, that's why I disabled all the cars. We can still do this.*

As he paced back and forth in the room, Sobek rubbed the hilt of the knife strapped at his hip. "What? How did they convince the police to get a force to assault this place? Aren't you supposed to stop that kind of thing from happening?"

The person on the phone was angry enough that a few phrases were audible. "You shot law enforcement and didn't kill them! On camera!" The rest of their words were lost in the background noise.

Sobek snarled. "We left everyone mostly alive once we saw the first badge per your rant about attracting attention last time. Don't tell me what to do! I'll grab the chemist and the best of the blood bags. The men can ready product crates for shipment and load up the more pliant donors in the cars. We'll just kill any leftovers. No big loss. I took enough of the vampire's blood that we can just turn more later, and he won't be our problem. His blood's got a nice bite, better than the stuck-up bitch, so it might even take less to make more vamps. I'll just have one of the boys open the windows on his room. You'll owe me for losing my house, though."

After stifling her urge to punch the psychopath for his callous dismissal of the lives of the prisoners, Zita concentrated. *Wyn? Andy? Sobek's definitely here. They know you're coming with the police. Freelance and I have to move in because they're planning to kill the prisoners.*

A grim smile broke through on Sobek's face, and his voice dripped with obsequiousness. "Yeah, warmer climates suit me fine. I'll get someone to do that. You see if those federal connections buy us any delays before the officials move in."

After a dismayed exclamation, Wyn sent, *I'll alert the authorities here once I verify they're not part of the conspiracy.*

Andy added, *We'll get into the air so we can pick you and the prisoners up when she's done. Did you ever get a final head count? Not that it matters to me, but it might help the cops.*

After lowering his phone, Sobek scooped up the watch and hurled it against the wall hard enough to make it shatter and dent the wall. He pulled out his knife and petted it as if it were a toy dog, his shoulders heaving as he brought himself under control. "No. Patience. We'll get where the U.S. can't touch me, and then we'll have another talk about who really owns the business. No more bowing to a human." With a growl, he stormed from the room, the door closing behind him with a click, followed by a louder one.

Zita poked her head out, verifying everyone had gone. Her mind whirled as she tried to calculate how many people were on the estate. *Freelance and me. About seventeen prisoners, counting Dmitri and his mom. Sobek, some guy in a lab coat, and at least eight guards, though they've got an unknown person with federal ties coming in somehow. Have the cops blocked off the roads yet? I knew I shouldn't have trusted the Man.* While she waited for Wyn's response, she crept toward the closet and the closest window to exit and get the mercenary going on the rescue.

*They're working on it,* Andy sent.

Rather than risking the exposure of crossing the wide, empty center of the room or revealing her teleportation to any hidden cameras, she darted to the giant dresser closest to the windows. She squeezed under the bottom and crawled on her stomach toward the windows. As she reached the end nearest the bed, her nose twitched at a faint, unexpected scent, discernible beneath the overwhelming itch of the cologne only because of the olfactory dissonance and her proximity. Disbelief raging in her, she turned her head. Nestled flush with the bottom of the dresser, a second featureless square, identical to the one on the propane tank, greeted her.

*No mames. Another bomb?* Refraining from swearing aloud on the chance someone would hear, she switched to a raccoon. She pried it loose as gently as possible.

Extricating herself from under the dresser, she pulled the bomb out and ran the remaining five feet to the curtains on her hind legs. Once she was safely hidden, she checked the window.

*Of course, it has an alarm on it.* She huffed and squinted, trying to avoid jiggling the explosive too much. From her current vantage point, she couldn't see the shed where she'd buried the other one, and she ran the risk of getting high enough for Freelance to see her if she moved to another window. Finally, she teleported as far to the west as she could and did a series of quick teleports to arrive at the shed in about fifteen seconds, avoiding any route that would've been visible to her ally. *Hot or not, he doesn't need to know my secrets.*

She buried the second bomb on the opposite side of the cow shed from the first one.

Interrupting her brief but fervent prayer that no more explosives laced the property, Andy sent, *The cops have the roads cut off now. What are you and the mercenary doing?*

In the form of a white ermine, Zita kicked the last bit of snow over the top of the explosive and stuck a twig in at the top with her mouth. *Keep them away from the cow shed. I moved a couple of bombs there and marked the spots with sticks.*

Andy groaned. *Will do, but I can tell you they'll probably refuse to move in without a bomb squad at hand if you're finding those. Other than risking death by TNT and playing in the snow, what's happening? Is there a plan?*

*Por supuesto, I have a plan. Do you need to ask?* Zita huffed and ran her tongue over her teeth a few times, trying to get the piney taste of the branch out of her mouth.

*I hate you doing this alone.* Wyn fretted over the link.

Zita scampered back toward the barn. *I'm not alone. Freelance is here, and he's experienced or something. Once I fill him in, we'll make our move to get the prisoners out. I'll let you know when we exit the building, and you can swoop in and carry them off. Just not by the cow shed.*

*Cow shed bad. We got that,* Andy sent.

Wyn's disapproval transmitted clearly. *Freelance's extensive experience murdering everyone in his way is what we're worrying about.*

*First, you don't know that that's exactly how they rescue people, and second, have faith in me. I got this. Pan comido.* Behind a bush, Zita shifted to a turkey vulture and tried to smother her own concerns. She launched herself into the air. As she flew over, movement caught her eye. Men—most of the guards on the estate, she guessed—had shovels and were busily scraping the basketball court clean.

*For once, it's not your plan we're worried about,* Wyn sent.

Ever truthful, Andy amended her statement. *Not just your plan, anyway.*

*Haters. My friends are all hating haters.* Zita flapped her wings and soared higher, searching for the mercenary's latest hiding spot.

***

"We need to move now."

Between his white poncho and snowshoes, Freelance had been surprisingly difficult to find. As soon as Zita had located him in the woods closest to the prisoner building, she shifted back to Arca and began whispering.

"They got an inside guy, so Sobek knows the cops are coming and is going to try to run off before they arrive. He gave orders to kill any prisoners they can't move, so we need to stop them. Right now, they're busy packing and plowing, but they've still got a couple guys on duty. Here, wear this." She pulled the camera from her pocket and shoved it at him.

He glanced at it and then at her.

Zita sighed and shifted her weight on the branch where she stood. "I recorded the meth lab, but I couldn't use it in the captives' room because of the guards and cameras. Our best bet to not get arrested is proving they're doing bad stuff, and our actions were necessary to save lives."

Freelance inclined his head but made no move to take the device.

She growled. "While I can stuff it in my pocket, I can't shift with it in a position to record anything. When I'm human, it'd stick out on my clothes like a sore thumb or a target. Plus, if I'm trying not to break it, I can't shift and fight as well. You, on the other hand, are already in black and wearing so many little pockets and pouches and other crap, they might not notice it. Even with that poncho on, you can still record sounds."

The mercenary studied her.

"Also, if you wear it, you won't be on camera. It does audio too, but I'm not real worried about you getting caught on that," she added, unable to resist a tight grin.

Freelance took it. After a moment of examining the camera, he affixed it to his belt.

She beamed. "Try not to record me doing illegal stuff if you can help it."

A mechanical rasp escaped him.

"The building with all the prisoners is the metal one south of the propane tank." She gestured to it. "I didn't see Dmitri or his mom, but it's the only place I smelled him, and I didn't get to at least one room of it. Dmitri's definitely injured. Additionally, fifteen others that we have to save are chained to beds in the same building. It had two armed guards inside. They move like thugs, but they're comfortable with their firearms. A bunch of other guards are right in front of the building, shoveling snow. I counted four cameras inside, and I'm guessing Sobek has another camera on Dmitri and his mom given he filmed his captives last time too."

Freelance said, "Weapons?"

"The guards had cattle prods and an Uzi each in the prison. In the lab building, the guard had a stun gun and a pistol, but it was in a holster so I couldn't tell what kind. House guards had pistols. The barn they're using as a barracks had mostly 9mm pistols, and I hid most of their cartridges. If they don't go on a bathroom cleaning spree, they should be limited to whatever they've got on them for ammo. I found two bombs and hid those too by the cow shed." She grinned.

When that failed to get a response, Zita continued, "Once we've got the prisoners free, I'll summon Wingspan so he can land in the meadow. If he can't find us, do you have a flare, or do I need to steal one from their garage?"

Freelance tapped a flare-shaped item on his belt.

Zita bit back the urge to ask what else he was packing. *So not the time.* "I'll set off an alarm in the main house and keep running distractions until you can get across the cleared ground to the building. Should I figure about ten minutes for that, even with your snowshoes?"

His gaze on her, he withdrew the grapple gun from his belt and fired it.

She blinked and followed the rope to where the grappling hook anchored in the prisoner building roof.

With a faint whir, Freelance bent low, bringing his feet off the ground, and arrived seconds later. He unsnapped the snowshoes from his feet and hooked them on his backpack as he collected his things. With a practiced parkour move, he descended to the ground and turned his head to her.

"Right, then. What was I thinking?" Zita shifted to an Arctic fox and darted across, counting on her white coat to hide her progress across the snow. *The biggest drawback to working with the man is he keeps distracting me with all that sexy competence.*

Once she stood beside him, the mercenary attached the grapple gun to his belt and stole to the corner of the building. He did not turn to see if she followed.

*He doesn't leave footprints in snow. Of course not. That explains why he was so hard to find.* Bemused, Zita padded after.

# Chapter Nineteen

**At the corner of the prison building,** Zita came to a halt by Freelance. He had flattened himself against the building and held up a warning hand she didn't need. She peeked around the edge to see the men she could already hear and smell.

Two guards waited by the only official entrance to the big, metal building, one pounding the snow flat with his feet as he paced and the other shuffling around, his hands hidden under his armpits. Both had shovels, handguns at their waists, and surly expressions.

The door opened, and a prison guard stomped out. Accepting a shovel, he and the other men walked toward the basketball court. Despite the roar of snowblowers, his complaint was audible. "We have to shovel by hand? Are you kidding me? We're not even due for a shipment, and it's freezing!"

*Guess they didn't check inside the bag of fertilizer for the keys. We'll have to move fast and pray they're focused on the snow since the basketball court is right there.* Zita's tongue lolled, and her tail wagged once, but she remained in place until they were out of sight. She darted to the door and paused to check on her companion. Even with vulpine ears, Freelance's passage was little more than the rustle of stiff fabric.

The men working nearby seemed focused on their duties and didn't seem to see her.

After shifting to a white gorilla, she stepped to flank one side of the door.

Freelance withdrew a heavy flashlight and nodded, positioning himself where he would not easily be seen through her white body.

She knocked.

A man's voice rose in a query inside.

She waited and then knocked again when the entrance remained shut.

Cursing, a man yanked the door open, an Uzi held loosely in his hands.

Zita shoved his gun upward, twisting to pluck it from his hands.

At the same time, Freelance stepped forward and jammed the flashlight into the back of the man's neck, slapping a hand over the guard's mouth. The light emitted the distinctive crackle and snap of a stun gun.

With a muffled shriek, the guard collapsed writhing.

Moving fast, Zita hauled him inside and laid him by the door. She stripped off his cattle prod.

Freelance secured the guard's hands and feet with plastic cuffs, then slapped black duct tape over the man's mouth in quick, practiced moves.

After emptying the guard's gun of all cartridges, including the one in the chamber, Zita set the firearm down on a table. She ran to the closest camera, using the cattle prod to hit it upward so it would record only ceiling.

The rows of prisoners lay silent, but the atmosphere was charged as if something ineffable had changed. Other than an empty bed, everything seemed similar, not that she took more than a second to look before racing to the next camera.

A buzzer sounded, and Sobek's voice came over an intercom. "Why, is that my old friend Arca? And you brought a friend. It's very rude to break into another person's home, you know. Is this the same man who burst into fire?"

His motions economical, Freelance frisked the tied-up guard.

*Aideen would be so pissed that Sobek thinks she's a dude, but at least he remembers her.* Zita hit the camera and moved to the next.

Sobek gave a harsh laugh, sounding far too gleeful. "I'm guessing not. Well, how are things going? Aren't you going to say anything? Oh, and now you're cutting off my view? Tsk, that's terribly rude."

Her back prickling, Zita glanced over at Freelance as she finished the third camera and scurried to the last one.

The mercenary held up a set of keys.

"Did you know someone stole all the car keys? I'm guessing it's the kind of petty trick you'd play. A few of my men have checkered pasts, though, so they should be able to get past that minor obstacle." Sobek's voice seemed conversational. An unseen man made an unintelligible comment behind him, and he snarled, the façade dropping.

Zita whacked the final camera, perhaps a bit harder than she should have, as it fell off its bracket and hung limply. The cattle prod casing cracked. *I'm not giving that psychopath anything he'd enjoy.*

Sobek's pout was audible in his voice. "Since you don't want to talk, I'll just listen to you die. Wake up, minions."

All around the room, the prisoners sat up in eerie unison. Unfastened restraints fell away, and red glinted in their eyes.

"I apologize for not handling you and your friend myself, but we're relocating, and I don't have the time. Of course, depending on which friend you've brought with you, you might be able to kill them all, but only the guard's here of his own free will. I suspect you have issues with murder, but those are the breaks. Minions, kill Arca and her friend. Block the door to stop them from getting out. When they're dead, kill each other." Sobek laughed over the speaker and then cut out suddenly.

Still moving as if synchronized, the controlled people staggered to their feet. While a few were clearly weak, all of them had been healthy young men before their imprisonment and remained larger than her. A handful of the better nourished bared their teeth, showing fangs. As she watched, others hissed, and their eyes shone red above their elongated canines.

*Most are vampires, the breathing, sweaty kind.* She glanced at Freelance and shifted to Arca, then partially changed to a bear for the added strength. "We can't hurt them. They're not in control of themselves. I don't suppose you have enough stun gun charges or those shotgun cartridges you used on me when we first met?"

Freelance shook his head and hefted a cart, holding it between himself and the oncoming prisoners like a lion tamer's stool. He glanced toward the outside door—blocked—and then stepped toward her.

The prisoners lunged en masse.

As she backed up, a doorknob bumped into Zita's back. *Dmitri and Yana's room? If we go in there, we can get away and maybe escape through the window. We can figure out what to do with these people once they're safe ... assuming Freelance doesn't abscond with Dmitri and his mom, leaving me to face everything else on my own, which is a possibility.*

"Toss me the key. We'll get cover in the other room," she shouted, ducking under a poorly aimed haymaker. She tried the cattle prod on her attacker, but it didn't even buzz. Desperate, she settled for using it as a staff, striking with it hard enough to drive a pair of attackers staggering back. In the brief interval before they returned, she undid the bar.

Dropping his cart, the mercenary lithely vaulted an empty cot to stand beside her. He slid the key into the lock and entered the room.

Zita darted in after him and went to shove the door shut. Two of the healthier men tried to push their way in, but she battered them with the cattle prod until it broke and then pushed with her enhanced strength.

They fell back into the people behind them.

"Sorry!" She slammed the door closed and locked it as soon as their grasping hands were clear. "Lock's crap on this side. It won't hold long even if they're screwed up from being held prisoner. We need to get Dmitri and Yana out, stat."

Freelance's rasp interrupted her. "Problem."

"Seriously? More?" Mentally swearing, Zita turned to see what he meant. From outside, the rattling blast and steady rhythm of a helicopter approached. *It won't matter if the roads are closed if Sobek escapes via helicopter!*

Dmitri lay under layers of chains, crisscrossing back and forth across his body in a patch of sunlight allowed in by the translucent white curtains. As at the railroad tracks, he seemed more dead than not, though this time his appearance was even more gruesome, as if he were now almost completely desiccated. His face had sunken into a skull-like mask. Dmitri's long hair was white, and an actual wooden landscaping stake protruded from his torso. His eyes were closed, but his mouth gaped open, fangs showing in a soundless scream. One arm was stretched out, bound into position, with his sleeve pushed up and an IV extruding from the deathly pale and withered arm, even though no tubing connected it to anything. An empty IV stand lay toppled beside his table. Scalpels and other sharp implements glinted from a nearby cart.

Freelance stood near the door, holding Yana in a position that was half restraint, half carry. Keys dangled from one finger. His head turned toward the windows.

Dirty and disheveled, Dmitri's mom did not seem to notice anything other than her son and the fact she could not go to him. She held out her arms toward the bound vampire and sobbed. Her slurred words were barely coherent, and shivers shook her every few seconds. Angry marks—blue and black and weeping red—

encircled her ankles and wrists where she'd struggled against the manacles now abandoned at her feet. "My baby isn't dead! He needs my help! Can't you hear him calling me? Let me go to him!"

The mercenary's mechanical whisper came over her ear unit. "Calm her."

*Me? Use my mad diplomatic skills to get a hysterical mom to settle down? We'd end up with her nuking the world or something.* Zita shook her head. "Yana, stop screaming before you make things worse. You're right, he's alive, and we're going to help him."

Freelance's skepticism was almost palpable, but the older woman lowered her volume to moans, rubbing at her forehead.

"Keep holding her. We've got to hurry before they bust down those doors. If we wake Dmitri up, he might be able to neutralize the prisoners since some of them are vamps." Taking a shaky breath, Zita rushed to the vampire.

The door boomed and shuddered as something or someone on the other side slammed into it.

With an internal prayer of thanks for her temporarily enhanced strength, Zita dragged the whole table to the side, out of the sunlight.

The contorted pose of the vampire relaxed into a more natural position.

His new stance allowed her to more easily free him, so she did so as quickly as possible, grateful that Sobek or whoever had put on the restraints had used strong chains, but simple locks. When they were half off, exposing the wooden stake, she braced herself and pulled the wood out. "Dmitri, wake up. You got to call off a bunch of vampires before they eat us."

Dmitri's eyes flew open, and his chest heaved... once... twice. The burning orbs of his eyes held nothing human, only hunger as they skimmed over the Zita and Freelance, fastening on his mom and her bleeding wrists. He lunged that direction with an animalistic snarl, but stopped, the last layer of restraints holding him back.

*Maybe freeing him wasn't my best idea,* Zita thought.

Freelance shoved Yana behind himself and drew his gun.

The vampire ripped off the final chains and rose to his feet.

"No! No shooting!" Wincing, Zita grabbed a scalpel and slashed the back of her forearm, opening an inch-long cut. She stepped between Dmitri and the others. *So stupid. So unsanitary. I am washing this arm eight million times later in holy water. I wonder if the Pope would mind blessing it if I break into the Vatican? Is that a sin? Dios, don't let me turn into a vampire.*

Dmitri stopped and turned as if drawn back by an invisible cord, and then he was upon her.

Pain streaked up her arm as he pulled it up in a rough grip and buried his cold fangs in the open wound. Zita bit her lip as she tried to ignore that and the vile sucking sounds. Her other hand curled with the instinctive need to pull him off her. "Keep Yana back."

An ominous cracking sound came from the door.

"On second thought, get her ready to go through the window. Gotta save somebody after all this," Zita said through gritted teeth. A wave of dizziness rushed through her.

Dmitri's face was hidden, but his hair darkened to its usual shining ebony perfection.

"Hombre, let up!" Zita slapped the side of Dmitri's head.

After a second, Freelance hauled Yana over to stand under the windows.

"David?" His mom frowned, confusion on her face and her earlier obsessive focus fading.

Another thud and the door bowed visibly.

Zita smacked the vampire again and shouted, "Dude! Enough! You need to save your mom!"

Dmitri detached himself, staggering away and wiping his mouth. He slid toward the ground and yawned.

Unable to stop herself, Zita cradled her injured arm close to her body. "Don't go to sleep now. Get up. You got to stop a bunch of vamps and controlled folks from hurting us... from hurting your mom!"

The vampire's eyes, no longer red, flew open. "Mom? Mom!"

The door blew open, shattering under the combined forces of three men. They fell into the room in a tangle of bodies, and more people surged in behind them.

"Carajo," Zita said, backing toward the window. She seized a length of discarded chain and wrapped it around her fist.

Freelance was already perched on the windowsill. A surprised Yana was unceremoniously stuffed halfway out.

From his position on the floor, Dmitri wiggled a finger. "Nuh-uh. Stop. None of that now."

As one, the crowd stopped and turned to stare at him.

The vampire wiggled his finger at the crowd and bopped himself in the nose. He giggled. "Oops. Now, no more violence. Why don't you all go get comfortable in the other room? Arca, could you assist me up and have Tall, Dark, and Ominous over there help my mother out of the window? It's a good thing she isn't heavier, or she'd look like Pooh stuck in the rabbit hole."

Once the controlled people filed out, Zita dropped the chains and walked to Dmitri, eying him cautiously. She offered him her hand. "Freelance is his own man, but I'm assuming since you're paying the bills, he's fine with that."

Dmitri jolted as if he'd just remembered. "So I am! Please help my mom down." He grasped Zita's hand with his smooth, cold one and got to his feet. He swayed.

After removing Yana from the window, Freelance dropped soundlessly, then held out his hand and helped the older woman down.

Zita released Dmitri's hand after he appeared relatively stable on his feet. "You okay?"

"Never felt a rush like this before. I feel great," Dmitri said. He peered at her arm. "Did I bite you? I am so sorry. I don't even have cookies and juice for you."

His mother rushed over and hugged him. "David!" She burst into tears.

"Hi, Mom! Don't cry. Let's go see how my other friends are doing. I shouldn't get too far from them," Dmitri said, taking his mother's arm and steering her into the main room. "Ah, the decor in here is still an early medical horror movie, but better than the cut-rate dungeon vibe in my cell. Here, Mom, get off your feet. Have I ever told you how much I appreciate you? Because I do."

With a glance at the mercenary, Zita followed and looked around. She helped herself to some gauze from a cart and tried wrapping her arm, hoping to stop the seeping blood. The controlled people sat, sometimes two on a bed, as if watching an intriguing show. "Why do they keep saying 'Brains'?"

Freelance took the gauze and wrapped her cut, then took up a position closer to the door.

Dmitri giggled and steered his mother to a bed. "It's daytime, so my powers are reduced. I must maintain my power over the non-vampires to keep the drug from reasserting itself by periodically sending them a command. Having them utter homage to classic horror cinema, even if you failed to recognize it, seemed to impinge on their free will the least. The vampires I can simply tell what to do, so I've ordered them to be calm. Really, Arca, how do you survive with so little true culture? Should we have a makeover and movie night sometime?"

"I do fine. No makeovers." Her voice sounded defensive. She hated it when that happened.

The vampire strode to her though his steps lacked balance more than usual and his approach meandered. He hugged her.

Zita choked in surprise and patted his back.

As he released her, Dmitri beamed. "You do well enough for an uncouth barbarian, but fear not, I love you. A platonic love—for I sometimes wonder if you would stake me in my sleep—but a deep love. Deep. In here. Where my heart no longer beats. And it has nothing to do with your delightful, delicious blood." He thumped his chest and giggled, his accent back in place.

Speechless, Zita stared at him.

"You know, your friend Muse is so pretty. Erato made flesh. She should come to movie night. Do you think—hey, is that my scariest employee? You have great taste in mercenaries, Arca! I love him too, especially the way he's terrifying. He's getting a huge tip." Dmitri crossed to the silent man, his arms wide as if to hug him, then stopped.

Freelance... twitched.

The vampire chortled but perhaps driven by a hitherto unseen survival instinct, did not embrace the mercenary. "You would've killed me to protect my mother! You're the best! I love you too! Hugs for everyone?" He held out his arms to the room.

Yana rubbed her forehead. "Son, perhaps you should sit down for a bit and have some coffee," she tried.

With a hasty glance around, Zita removed herself from arm's reach.

Dmitri gave an exaggerated pout. "What, no one? Aw, come give me a hug! I love hugs, especially the warm ones because I'm usually so cold. But not right now! Team Hug! Everyone who needs a hug, come hug me!"

Most of the drugged patients staggered to him and flopped their arms around him.

Zita exchanged a glance with Freelance. "I guess we know now why he doesn't drink meta blood," she said.

The mercenary gave a brusque nod.

"It's always something. You want to see what they're up to outside?" A loud thrum came from that direction, changing pitch and then cutting off. Zita's feet had moved to the door before she even realized it. *The helicopter! I can't let Sobek get away!*

Freelance nodded twice and flowed around all the others to join her, shrugging his white poncho on again.

From somewhere beneath all the people, Dmitri's muffled but cheerful voice announced, "Team Hugs for the win!"

"Keep an eye on these guys, Dmitri! Cops will be here soon!" Zita called, speeding up so she could get outside without being hugged again.

Freelance was on her heels.

# Chapter Twenty

**Zita and Freelance peered** out the doorway of the prison building. Huge piles of snow surrounded the hastily cleared basketball court, in the center of which a large helicopter reigned over an assembly of guards carrying shovels and snowblowers. The vehicle's dual-passenger doors hung half open, giving a glimpse of dark shapes moving inside, though the rotors were still. One man placed a big cooler into the cargo compartment of the helicopter, slammed it shut, and banged on the metal side. No one seemed to have noticed the pair in the doorway.

"Dmitri? Can you control these guys, too?" Zita called over her shoulder, keeping her voice low. *If the drunk vamp can control all these guys, I can get to Sobek without a problem. If not, seven's going to be a lot to fight, especially if they're hopped up on drugs or if any more come out of the helicopter. Andy, Wyn, you guys incoming?*

*We've been trying to cooperate with law enforcement, but there have been some not-unexpected delays. In addition to the difficulties in travel currently, the various agencies are arguing. Oh, and DMS really wants to arrest us. Nonetheless, an offensive team of some sort has reached the property and are working their way through the woods,* Wyn sent.

After disentangling himself from the group hug, the vampire staggered to the door and looped an arm around her shoulders. "I'll try."

Zita shrugged him off.

Dmitri squinted and grimaced. "Too cold and bright. Stings. Nope, no vamp blood in any of the visible miscreants. Wait, I have an idea." He raised his voice, and it rang out. "Hey, you, brutish thug! Come, look into my eyes so that I may command you!" The vampire held out his arms to the closest thug, almost falling out the door into the snow.

The guards turned.

Freelance twitched.

Zita swore inwardly and grabbed the back of Dmitri's shirt, shoving him back inside. "Defend your people if you need to. Remember, Freelance... happy nonlethal damage." *Guess we're on our own for a few more minutes.*

"What? It's daytime. Ask me again at night, and I'll have them dancing!" the vampire called out from somewhere behind her.

Wearing a black face mask and huge sunglasses that hid his eyes, a stocky man leaned out of the helicopter and gestured to Zita and Freelance. "Kill them, then get away to wait for further instructions." The voice identified him as Sobek. He banged the passenger door shut.

As the helicopter's engine roared to life, and the blades began to spin overhead, the guards circled around the vehicle and closed in on the prison building.

Zita eyed the approaching enemies and sprang out of the doorway, advancing a couple steps toward them. Her feet protested the immersion in the snow, but she ignored it as much as possible, adrenaline still singing in her veins. "You know, your boss is leaving. He'll never know if you just surrender like smart people."

They lifted their weapons.

"You do realize the problem if you try to shoot me when you're all standing in a semicircle like that, right?" she tried, moving more toward the center.

One barked a short, surprised burst of laughter, and those on either side of her holstered their weapons. Then all of them charged her. Or tried to. The attackers on the shoveled court rushed forward while the men in the deep snow staggered in slow motion her direction. Two still aimed their guns at her.

"If you're determined to play rough, I gave you a chance." Zita shifted to a woolly mammoth and charged, the snow no obstacle for her great weight and size. As she swung her long trunk, she grabbed the only man who had an Uzi and lifted him from the ground.

Pistols roared as the two men shot, but she didn't feel more than a sting on a knee.

The other guards fell back as the captive man screamed.

In her peripheral vision, the mercenary was a pale blur. Another guard fell.

She shook her prisoner until he dropped his firearm and then tossed him into a snowbank. With another quick, if ponderous, step forward, she seized someone else, throwing him as well.

The thrum of the helicopter's engines deepened. Most of the remaining men pulled their handguns. One backed up.

Her trunk coiled, and she reached for a third.

Freelance stepped up beside the retreating guard and seized his elbow. He wrenched it backward and followed up with a pair of rapid strikes and a sweep that brought the man to the ground. Pulling out plastic cuffs, he had the man's arms and legs immobilized behind his back before the guard had a chance to resist. With more cuffs in hand, he advanced on the last guy she'd tossed into the snow.

Guns boomed.

Zita lurched away, but a sharp line of pain streaked along her side, and another bloomed above one of her ears. While a portion of her instincts urged her to trample them, she instead smacked the gun out of the hand of the one who'd shot at her head. Grabbing him, she waved him in front of her face as she turned toward the others, hoping to deter further shots.

The remaining two men paused and aimed.

A chorus of male voices spoke in her mind, revealing that Andy wore his Wingspan shape. *We come.*

*Good.* Despite her small injuries, Zita grinned inwardly and swept out her trunk in an arc, hitting both men with the guy she was holding and the curving side of a tusk. She tossed her latest prisoner in Freelance's direction or the area where she thought he'd last been.

Sitting up, one of the other guards grabbed the fallen Uzi and aimed it at her.

As her fur prickled, she shifted to an Arctic fox and darted into the soft snow, burrowing fast.

He fired a short barrage.

Untouched, she exploded out of the snow, shifting into a bull moose as she emerged. "Surprise!" It came out as a bellow, but she felt he got the gist of it as she hooked him in her massive antlers and threw him. Zita looked around for more. Her breath steamed in the cold, and she stomped a hoof seeing them all cuffed or otherwise being restrained by the mercenary. She snorted.

The screaming whine of engines changed pitch as the helicopter lifted off the ground, shooting forward a few feet and hovering unsteadily.

Zita galloped toward the helicopter, pushing herself faster. Her mind cycled through forms. *Not a peregrine, I'm not diving anywhere near those blades. Jumping on is too stupid dangerous, even for me, but I'm not letting Sobek get away. If I don't stop them now, they'll just set up again at another location.*

Bound guards struggled in the surrounding snow, with Freelance handling the last free two as she passed.

She charged after the helicopter, getting close enough to have to fight the downwash of wind from the rotors. *I have to jump. At least Dmitri, his mom, and Freelance will all be safe. The mercenary gets hurt like a regular human.*

The helicopter rose quickly, too quickly, leaving the ground and any chance of catching it on foot. It shot forward, then lifted up, narrowly missing a backboard.

After shifting to a gyrfalcon, she fought to get her speed up. Once the downwash became too much for the small form, she flew a bit higher, then did a backflip to fly inverted just long enough to snag the strut with her claws. Returning to her Arca shape, she hauled her body right-side up and twined both arms and legs around it. "Help Dmitri," she shouted into her com and eyed the door locks.

The helicopter was well above the tops of the buildings and forest, but still below the gray clouds. It began to travel horizontally faster. A second later, the vehicle shuddered.

She glanced down. A grappling hook hung off the strut, and a dark shape rapidly approached at the end of a rope.

Freelance appeared and grabbed onto the strut. His voice spoke over the com. "Can you fly helicopters?"

Even with the earpiece in, she could barely make out his words. "No." Changing into an orangutan, she switched her grip and reached down to haul him up to the strut beside her, with the body of the helicopter providing some minor aid against the pull of the wind.

"I can." The mercenary wrapped himself around the strut despite it forcing him into close proximity with her. He stared up at the closed doors.

Despite the pressure of the rushing, freezing winds, she grinned at him and switched back to Arca, giving them both more room, though he was still close. "Fine. You take the pilot and turn this around. I'll handle the others, maybe get them talking. Sometimes they'll pause everything just to tell you their plans. It's bizarre, but they don't usually shoot you at the same time, so I'll take it. I've never understood that. Do you?"

After she crawled up to the pilot door, careful to stay below the windows, Zita grabbed a lock pick from her pocket and switched to an orangutan again. She reached up and jammed the pick into the lock, trying to reassure herself. *It's just like unlocking a car, which you've done hundreds of times. Just not at high speed and rising altitude while freezing to death and using hands that are less dexterous than your usual ones. Go faster before the two of you fall off.*

Just as it clicked open, the helicopter shook under a particularly icy gust of wind.

Zita's numb fingers fumbled, and she dropped her pick. She keened at the loss and changed back to Arca. She flattened herself and inched backward, stopping near the mercenary. "Pilot's open."

Somehow keeping the bulk of his weight off her, Freelance crawled over her and past, a fleeting moment of blessed warmth and insulation.

Once he reached the pilot door, Zita reached in her pocket for another pick, careful of her dwindling supply. "Why are you even up here instead of running off with your clients? Are you having fun too? I hate to say it, but I kind of am. Underneath the terror and the adrenaline, of course."

He looked back at her.

The door slid open, bringing welcome heat and a mishmash of scents: cologne, sickness, chemicals, old blood, and stagnant swamp. A stocky form—clad in a business suit and a ski mask with sunglasses—stood in the doorway, one gloved hand gripping an interior handle. A Colt M1911 glinted evilly in his other meaty hand. Even if his voice hadn't identified him earlier, Zita recognized the belligerent stance and shape as Sobek.

"Timing, dude, we were having a moment!" Zita shifted to an orangutan and grasped the strut with her feet. She swung one hairy arm up and smacked his hand hard enough to make him exclaim and drop the weapon.

The gun tumbled and disappeared.

Leaning down, Sobek swiped at her, hampered by the need to hold a grab bar.

With no little enjoyment, Zita slapped him hard enough to knock off his sunglasses and send him stepping back. She grabbed the floor and pulled herself up, switching mid-move into a fluffy black cat. Since he still blocked her path, she sank her claws into his leg and swarmed up him, leaping off his back into the sanctuary of the interior. Reaching the opposite side of the helicopter, she spun around.

Her fur fluffed up, and she glanced around, taking in the tight quarters with a displeased hiss. A wide bench seat lined the back wall, with only a single man in a surgical mask staring at her from it. Glimpses of cargo boxes showed behind the big seat. Above her head, a stretcher took up most of the center area with one end fastened to the far wall. She could see an emaciated man's hand hanging limply from it, a thick manacle encircling the fragile wrist. Toward the front, two lounger-style seats were divided by a low console table, and a carpeted wall separated everything from the cockpit. A small window, currently open only a finger's width, allowed limited access to the pilot, perhaps large enough only to pass a drink or allow conversation. A Thermos sat on the table, smelling strongly of Domina and blood. DMS Special Agent Carter Parzarri sat strapped into the other lounge chair, hands poised over the laptop and an irritated expression on his face.

Zita couldn't bring herself to be surprised though her suspicions had not crystallized before. *I knew I recognized that nasty cologne from somewhere. This explains why DMS has been so full of suck catching Sobek. Victoria was murdered within hours of me tipping them that she might know more about where he was. My first instincts were right, I shouldn't have trusted anyone in the government I don't know.* Anger and guilt burned.

Pulling the door mostly shut as he turned, Sobek's voice held sadistic glee. "You again? There's no room for a hippo here, and I don't see your fiery friend anywhere nearby." He drew a knife from his belt, his grip the easy one of long familiarity. Without the glasses, his beady eyes glowed red behind his mask.

She flicked the end of her tail at him, keeping a wary eye on all of them. *How close to vampire is he?*

Sobek moved too fast, stabbing at her.

Zita jumped, landing on the bench seat, and ran across the lap of the guy in the surgical mask, who batted ineffectually at her, and into the empty seat. Faint movement behind Parzarri gave her hope that Freelance had taken out the pilot.

The knife impaled the wall by where she'd been, and Sobek whirled to face her.

"Try to get rid of her without destroying our transportation. We're in a bit of a hurry if we're going to reach our next flight, plus I need to finish setting up that idiot Garcia as a scapegoat. Do I need to shoot her for you?" Parzarri asked conversationally, pulling his weapon, a Glock 22.

*Does he mean my brother Miguel?* Zita's eyes narrowed, her ears laid flat, and her back arched, fur lifting along it. A low growl escaped.

Sobek caressed the knife handle with his thumb, his red eyes dreamy as he watched her. "You keep your gun. I'll get rid of her my way."

Parzarri shrugged and put his firearm back into an underarm holster. "Do it, and get rid of her before her friend Wingspan locates us. Based on DMS records, she's usually the delaying tactic before the heavy shows up and ends fights for her."

Irritation at his (accurate) assessment had her claws emerging without conscious thought and pricking into the leather of the seat.

She noticed Parzarri did not fasten the thumb break on his holster, no doubt planning to shoot her as soon as she stopped paying attention. With a hiss, she raced toward the agent.

Sobek followed.

After shifting to a chimpanzee, Zita snatched Parzarri's laptop. Smashing the traitorous agent's face with it, she batted Sobek's attempt at a stab away and brought it down on Sobek's head.

The computer broke in half, and Sobek staggered.

The helicopter tilted, and she hoped that meant they were headed back to the mountain property. *Well, it's a good time to turn around, given that all eyes are on me.*

Zita threw the pieces at Parzarri's head and stole his gun when he reflexively lifted his arm to shield his face, exposing the weapon. Scrambling over the table and into the other seat, she threw open the window to the pilot's compartment and dropped the Glock in. *You'd better be driving this thing, Freelance,* she thought.

Parzarri swore.

She grinned. *Yeah, you should've shot me earlier.*

Her moment of inattention was sufficient to allow Sobek to grab her left arm in a crushing grip and yank her toward him. He lifted the knife in his other hand.

She howled, clawing at his face before he could do more than clip her side with the blade. Still, the wound burned—of course, the same area that still bore a gash from the shots earlier—and the scent of blood filled the air.

His mask caught in her fingers and slid upward, covering his eyes. Fangs descended in his mouth.

After changing to a snake, she dropped to the floor and slithered rapidly toward the bench seat.

Sobek staggered, bringing up his free hand to shove the mask up. "I will slice you to pieces and drink your blood from your still-beating heart as you scream," he snarled.

The guy in the surgical mask shrieked as she came close and undid his seat belt, bolting to the chairs opposite.

Parzarri sighed.

Zita hid under the seats near the cargo. *Are you guys close yet?*

*We're circling the property, about to let off the agents. Where are you?* Wyn replied.

Focusing, Zita sent, *We're in a helicopter. DMS Agent Parzarri was the boss all along, and he's here with Sobek. Freelance is piloting so we should be land back there soon. Basketball court should have a bunch of guys tied up in the snow.*

A meaty hand swiped under the seat with the knife.

She recoiled. Taking a deep breath, she waited for another sweep to get close enough. *Pues, it's not fatal, and he's still breathing so it might work. I hate going that small though.*

When Sobek's hand came back her direction, Zita shifted to a bullet ant. Rapidly, she jumped on his hand and stung him multiple times.

He yanked his hand out so fast that she tumbled off though not without one last sting. "She bit me!"

Crawling to the cargo boxes, Zita switched back to her cat form.

A heavy thud preceded bloodcurdling, incoherent shrieks. Sobek writhed on the floor, clutching an empty, shaking, and rapidly swelling hand.

Her loathing for the psychopath warred with her guilt at inflicting that much pain on anyone. *He kills people for fun, enough for the FBI to note his pattern. He hurt my brother, Jen Stone, and Miss Gloria.*

Someone squeaked in the main seating area.

Parzarri spoke a moment later. "To be honest, I didn't think you had it in you to poison him, but perhaps you were angry? No matter. Sobek is aggravating, if useful. Nonetheless, I believe I hold the upper hand. Come out and turn into Arca. No shapeshifting or clever tricks after that or I'll slit this man's throat."

Squeezing under the seat, Zita peered out.

Sobek took up half the floor, his big body in a fetal curl around his hand as he alternately tried to curse and weep the pain out.

Parzarri stood by the discarded remains of the laptop, using the smaller mask-clad man as a shield. With a flick of his fingers, he pressed Sobek's knife close to his hostage's throat. The bottom edge of the surgical mask slowly turned red from a nick. "Oops, he wiggled." His eyes lit on her. "Ah, there you are. Come on out now, slowly."

Reluctantly, Zita crept out, never taking her eyes off the agent. Once she was clear and out of arm's reach, she changed into Arca.

Freelance's quiet rasp came over the com. "Bank which direction? When?"

"Sí, that's a good idea. You don't want to hurt your own guy, do you?" she tried. Her head tilted, letting her long, dark hair veil her expression.

"He's a good chemist who works cheap, but I'm sure I can find another. I only need enough cash to retire and live on a nice island somewhere with all the amenities. Now, enough of your delays. You're going to jump out of this helicopter." Hauling his hostage with him, Parzarri edged toward the helicopter door. When his attention turned to stepping over Sobek, his blade moved away from the chemist's throat for a moment.

"If you didn't have a hostage, I could take you with my LEFT hand tied behind my BANK," she said. She braced herself, automatically moving into a more balanced stance.

The agent scoffed. "That's not how the expression g—"

The helicopter cut a hard left.

Thrown off balance, Parzarri grabbed at the walls for balance. His hostage staggered and fell. The pieces of the laptop slid over and slapped against Sobek's face.

Zita rushed forward, switching to a gorilla, and seized Parzarri's wrist. She twisted it until he dropped the knife, then kicked the blade under the bench seat.

Parzarri jabbed her injured side with a punch and bent to his ankle, fingers scrabbling under his pant leg.

Air rushed out of her as pain radiated everywhere, but Zita grabbed his questing hand. She yanked it upward and back, forcing him to drop or dislocate his own shoulder.

His back arched and Parzarri bent backward.

The man in the surgical mask crawled on his hands and knees to hide under the stretcher. He curled up there, hands over his head.

Without releasing Parzarri from the hold, Zita used her other hand to check his ankle. Unsurprised, her fingers found a full holster. Clumsy with their larger size, she ripped the weapon out of it with more force than she had intended.

Parzarri fell with a yelp.

She released his arm before it broke and grabbed the back of his shirt with her free hand. Her foot ran into Sobek's bulk, and she retreated, not wanting to entice him into joining the fight. Her side ached, and she raised Parzarri's backup weapon, a cute little Ruger revolver.

Glove-clad fingers slid open the window to the pilot area.

A trickle of amusement ran through her, and she spun Parzarri around and marched him to his chair, dropping the revolver through the window.

It closed behind the weapon, again staying open only a notch.

Movement behind her had her turning without releasing Parzarri, and a wave of cold slapped her as the wind's noise increased.

Sobek no longer convulsed on the floor of the helicopter. The door gaped open. His voice, however, trailed behind him. "I am a vampire! I am immortal! You will never be free..."

Dragging Parzarri with her, she ran to that side of the helicopter and looked down. *Carajo.*

Falling feetfirst, Sobek was far below them, legs bent as if he intended to land from an ordinary leap. He shouted more, high and wild and insane, the volume fading and the words unintelligible as the distance between them increased.

The helicopter tilted, forcing her to seize the grab bar to keep from sliding out with her prisoner.

From under the stretcher, the chemist under shrieked, tumbling toward her, but he grabbed a dangling strap and held on.

Parzarri struggled. "Don't you dare! Don't you dare!" he cried, leaning away from the open door. Terror showed on his face.

*Sobek can't jump from this height, can he? After all this, is he getting away?* Zita inhaled sharply.

Before she could do anything, Sobek hit the snow-covered ground... and splattered. Red blood stained the snow beneath his broken form.

Zita released the grab bar and crossed herself. *Dios have mercy. Guess he wasn't as immortal and vampire as all that.*

Then the body burst into flames as the sun came out from behind the clouds.

Her mouth dropped.

The helicopter evened out and continued steadily toward the mountain property.

Parzarri made an abortive attempt to get free of her.

She growled in his ear and shoved him back into his seat. After pulling the door shut, she shifted to Arca. Her fake Mexican accent dripped from each word. "Sit. Don't talk. Don't try nothing else."

The guy still hiding under the stretcher nodded rapidly, his eyes wide.

In the distance, a giant bird flew toward them, thunder rumbling with each flap of his enormous wings. *We're coming. We're bringing Kodiak and the police detectives,* Wyn sent.

*Ah, the fighting's over, but we need to ensure Parzarri doesn't weasel out of punishment. Sobek killed himself. Freelance is flying the helicopter back to the house. Mansion. Snooty ski farm? Whatever you call that place. I'll need a heal but nothing major.*

Her mental voice timid, Wyn said, *He survived being shot and losing a lot of blood before. Are you certain Sobek's dead?*

Zita glanced out the window and shuddered. *Oh, sí, he real dead. Don't land by the cow shed.*

An avian screech of laughter echoed like thunder.

Out loud, she called out, "Inbound Wingspan. So, don't try anything or I will have my friend the heavy finish the fight for me."

*It couldn't have happened to a nicer fellow. Oh, we also have a fine sampling of law enforcement officials. Try to be discreet when you drool over the SWAT men,* Wyn sent.

"The cops will be meeting us with my team at the property, so get ready for jail." She sent a brief reply to her friend over the mental link. *I am appreciative of Dios' fine creations.*

Wyn sent, *Is that what the kids call it these days?*

A black-gloved hand lifted in acknowledgment in the window.

Parzarri leaned back against his seat, straightening his suit with a smarmy smile. Sometime while she'd stared at Sobek's remains, he'd managed to get his phone out. "Excellent. What a pity there's no evidence of any wrongdoing on my part left after the tragic explosions." He pressed a button and looked out the window expectantly at the house and property, barely visible.

The area around the cow shed exploded, with dark chunks of dirt and withered grass decorating the pristine white.

The agent gaped at the destroyed meadow. "What? Who moved my bombs?"

"What? Oh, they seemed unsafe where they were, so I relocated them for you. You can thank me now. I don't mind." Zita grinned.

Parzarri scowled, but his face evened out. "I was coerced. Sobek preyed upon me with his vampiric powers. I can't wait to tell the police about my ordeal, kidnapped by that awful creature. The mind control is just now wearing off."

She tsked and put her hands on her hips, letting them drop when her wounds protested the movement. Weariness made every motion an effort, and she was far too aware of each injury. "You were the one giving orders and in control of the whole operation, Parzarri."

He sneered at her. "Yes, and I did it far better and far more profitably than that deranged psychopath. I even found a use for metas that benefited society, or at least me, but who's going to tell them that? You? I think an experienced agent with decades in law enforcement will be believed over a vigilante or two, assuming you even make it to court to testify. I can lie about being mind-controlled or say anything else I want."

After a second of panic, Zita remembered her insurance policy. "Hey, up front. Did you get all that?

A fist with a thumb pointing upward appeared in the window. The helicopter began a controlled descent.

It was Zita's turn to smirk.

# Epilogue

**A week later,** Zita, as Arca, stretched her arms over her head and strode into the VIP area of the still-closed Danz Mizer. She surveyed the empty club, which stank of cleansers. In their respective superhero disguises, Wyn and Andy sat in one of the larger booths of the VIP area with Dmitri, who wore a tuxedo and full makeup. A stack of paperback books sat beside the vampire, and one was open in front of him. Only a few lights were on, and someone had set up a screen with a DVD player. "Guys!"

They waved.

Zita headed over and plopped down next to Andy. "Sorry I'm late. A neighbor stopped by, and I got tied up."

Andy grimaced and passed her a bottled water. "I'm afraid to ask if you mean that literally."

Zita snickered, her smile widening as she remembered the reason for Gloria's late-night visit. "No, of course not. She was just happy about some news I gave her a few days ago and brought me a cake and pictures of her grandniece's baby. Real nice of her."

With his false accent in place, Dmitri murmured, "I would have written that to have more sexy bondage and less prosaic pictures, but such is life." He dashed a signature across a page of the book, and then closed it, shoving it toward the stack of others.

"Speaking of writing, are you going to give up being an author and be a big-time club owner now, Dmitri? I hear there's money in it," Zita said.

"Please say no," Wyn said. She had a glass of something pink and bubbly in front of her. As she smiled, she carefully deposited all the books into her purse.

The vampire laughed and tucked away a fat, ornate pen. "No."

"So, you're selling the place?" Andy asked. Like Zita, he toyed with a bottle of water.

After striking a thoughtful pose, Dmitri said, "No. My dear friend entrusted it to me with her dying breath, and D.C.'s monsters still need a place to go. I thought I would continue the tradition of the club as a haven in her honor. Unfortunately, I believe I must also police the other vampires, given Domina's example. I despise the thought of enforcing the rules, but someone must do it. Incubus will take the manager job as he actually knows how to run such a place. Should any of you wish for a low-paying job assisting me with the club or the other vampires once it reopens, let me know."

"Low paying?" Wyn asked. "I can do better than minimum wage."

The vampire shrugged. "While I was granted permission to continue maintenance on the place while it remains closed and repair the broken window—"

"Sorry about that," Andy said.

Dmitri dismissed his concerns with a flick of his hand. "Do not concern yourself. It was justified. The authorities will not release Victoria's funds or authorize operating the club until they conclude their investigation into Sobek's entanglement in Victoria's fiscal affairs. My income and financial planning did not include the possibility of having to support an unrelated business, and thus pay raises will have to wait until the club brings in a profit. Not to mention, mercenaries do not accept payment plans."

Andy and Wyn both winced.

Zita raised her hands. "Sorry, buey. I told you to read before signing."

He waved a hand. "The price was not unreasonable, and I found it well worth it for the services rendered. Speaking of such, I did talk to the police about the railroad tracks, so the assault charges have been dropped against Arca. Have you heard anything on Parzarri's trial?"

Zita grinned. "Thanks."

Wyn took a long drink from her glass and smiled. "Besides being crucified in the news? To avoid culpability, every agency he's ever worked for is reviewing his cases for a reason to add to charges against him. He's now in solitary confinement in the jail. Apparently, other inmates heard he'd been a federal agent before and beat him up before the guards pulled them off."

Dmitri smiled. "Excellent. I can only hope he enjoys his time alone for the next several decades. Some of the vampires used as blood donors will also testify, as Parzarri observed the turning process a few times and spoke openly in their presence. Per the victims' requests, I'll be unmaking them for the next few months, as I've told the government that it is a tiring process that only allows me to do one at a time, spaced days apart."

"Is it?" Wyn asked.

He shrugged, a sly grin slipping across his face. "As far as the government knows."

After sipping her water, Zita sat up straight. "I meant to ask, how are your parents?"

Real happiness showed on the vampire's face. "They're doing great. Mom found a craft therapy group and is learning to knit while she deals with the trauma from the kidnapping. She'll be taking a month-long vacation with my dad to recuperate and relax. It seems my father has made remarkable progress healing and his doctors feel a vacation would be perfect following the successful conclusion of his current course of physical therapy.”

Wyn beamed.

“Cool,” Zita said.

“Speaking of happier subjects, Wingspan and Muse, would you perhaps grab the food? I ordered one of those giant subs from a local shop for you as well as some appealing red cookies they also had.” Dmitri smiled again.

At the mention of food, Zita jumped to her feet. “Where? I can get it.”

Dmitri licked his lips. “Actually, Arca, I wanted a quick word with you? Perhaps in private?”

She waved her hands at Wyn and Andy. “We don’t keep a lot of secrets from each other.”

“Sadly,” Andy murmured.

Wyn elbowed him.

He cleared his throat. “I... wanted to thank you for your actions when I was a prisoner and reassure you that you are not going to be a vampire. For me, I must repeatedly feed my blood to someone to turn them, and we have not done so. Additionally, I doubt you could be turned even if we had.”

Wyn made a surprised noise. On their mental link, she sent, *You let him bite you?*

Her voice gruff, Zita shrugged. “You’re welcome.” *He needed it to heal and was going after his mom. That’s not right. I had to do something.*

A wave of pride and affection came through their link from Wyn.

*Yeah, whatever. Not a big deal.* Zita’s face grew warm, and she looked away.

Curiosity ran through Andy’s voice though he shot the women a sidelong glance. “So why couldn’t you turn Arca? Because she wouldn’t want it?”

The vampire steepled his fingers and pursed his lips. "As Domina showed, people can be changed against their will if the vampire is strong enough. No, the issue is your blood. It is..."

"Fun and interesting like me?" Zita said.

Dmitri laughed. "Fine, yes, you are a nummy treat." For some reason, he affected a British accent for the words.

Andy snickered. "Classic."

Zita's eyes narrowed, sensing sarcasm, but she decided not to make an issue of it.

With an amused glance at the other man, Dmitri continued, "At last, someone who recognizes quality television. Everyone likes music, yes? Most metas are an amateur soloist or quartet. My power could convince them to eschew classical music forever in favor of rap. It is possible. Arca's blood is like a professional symphony orchestra. I might convince a portion to play a few songs, but the entire group? No. If I exhausted my power trying too hard, I could die of the effort, and that portion I changed would be playing classical again as if nothing had happened. I have not met a vampire stronger than myself, so the odds are good no vampire could change you."

"That might just be Arca," Wyn said, amusement in her voice. "She can be obsessive about her interests."

Tossing a lock of long hair over her shoulder, Zita said, "She means to say I'm focused and disciplined, and she is incredibly jealous. Also, she has wimpy arms."

Wyn slapped Zita's shoulder lightly.

Dmitri chuckled. "It's more than mental focus or any innate recalcitrance. I suspect if I am right—and like most, I do love being right, even when I'm wrong—that the three of you and the lovely Carolyn Gyllen are all too strong. I'd have to scent everyone's blood to be certain. That was not a creepy preface to asking anyone to harm themselves to check, by the way. It's the reason we do not allow vampires to feed from metas, no matter how delectable their blood might be." His eyes glinted with a hint of red.

"So, you getting plastered after drinking my blood has nothing to do with it?" Zita prompted.

Dmitri straightened the collar on his shirt. "That might be a factor."

"Yeah, well, thanks for letting me know. You mentioned a giant sandwich and cookies?" Zita said.

The vampire eyed her. "The sub is in the refrigerator in the kitchen, and the cookies are in a bag next to it. Didn't you say you had cake with your neighbor?"

Zita nodded. "Sí, but that was earlier. This is now."

Wyn and Andy laughed.

***

Weeks later, Zita clung to the side of a skyscraper in her Arca form. She was happily sore from a tough climb done at top speed at an hour when she'd normally be sleeping. Between the moon and the lights of New York, she had enough light to see, and the unseasonably warm March weather meant that the exertion of the climb was enough to keep her comfortable without wearing more than her costume. Her small, light backpack was a sweaty spot of heat on her back. Police sirens sounded, and lights flashed in the streets below.

With a glance to assess Freelance's position—he had just achieved the roof on his section of the building—Zita grinned and hurried, climbing the last few feet in a glorious rush. She flung a foot over the ledge and hauled herself up. Sliding the rest of her body onto the rooftop, she rolled into a crouch to be less visible from the street but wasn't able to stifle an exhilarated laugh.

Freelance lay flat several feet away, watching the street.

"Sounds like the cops are close. Think someone saw us?" she whispered, peeking down.

His goggles turned to the nearly full moon overhead and then returned to her.

Zita checked below. Nothing to show anyone had noticed them. "Neta, definitely possible, but it looks like the cars are stopping a few buildings away. We should split soon, but I think we got a few minutes. You're good getting down and away, right?" she said, getting to her feet and retreating from the edge of the large building.

No answer.

Digging in her small backpack, she pulled out a packet of wipes, a plastic bag, and her bottle of water. She cleaned her hands with the wipes, then offered those and the bag to him. "You want a snack before you go? I made some protein bars. It's dates and cashews and stuff, but it's supposed to taste like cinnamon rolls."

He shook his head once and then tilted it at her.

"High caloric needs, and, dude, look at what we just did, sans powers or fancy gear." Zita grinned at him and withdrew a bar.

Freelance's goggles turned toward the city. He stepped backward and removed the framework for his glider from his backpack. "Blossoming Vale Quarry?"

She snorted, bit off a chunk of the bar, and chewed it. Zita tapped her fingers on the wide cement ledge, setting the bag down beside her. "That's the new one in Pennsylvania, right? Is it open now? Sweet. Rematch there?"

Her companion nodded, and then tapped his goggles, giving his glider a quick but methodical examination.

Glancing over, she smiled. "You're taking off?"

He packed up his belongings.

"Cool. Good climb. Congrats on a clean win. I'll get you next time. Text the details when you know them." After chugging more water, she munched, gazing over New York.

Beside her, fabric rustled as Freelance stepped onto the ledge.

She waved. "Don't get yourself shot before I can beat you climbing at the quarry."

He adjusted a strap and saluted her. Without further conversation, he leapt off and glided away.

Zita watched him go, absently admiring his lean form and sweet parasail until the darkness hid him. When she reached for another protein bar, she noted one was missing. Leaping to her feet, she shouted in the direction Freelance had gone, "See you at the rematch! Bring protein bars for the prize!"

Life was good.

# Spanish and Portuguese Glossary

These are definitions of the words as Zita uses them in the book, and may not include all possible variations. The Spanish is primarily Mexican in usage and slang. Needless to say, anything marked with "Vulgar" should not be used in polite company.

**arca**: Spanish. A chest or ark. Zita originally used it referring to Noah's ark in *Super*.

**armada**: Portuguese. The capoeira version of a reverse roundhouse kick.

**ay**: Spanish. An interjection, similar to "Oh."

**bandeira**: Portuguese. Capoeira move where a fast cartwheel is immediately followed by a side flip.

**basta**: Spanish. Enough.

**borrachos**: Spanish. Drunks.

**buey**: Spanish. Dude.

**cabrón**: Spanish. Bastard or asshole. Has other meanings, but that's how it's used in this book. Vulgar.

**capoeira**: Portuguese. A fast, fluid Brazilian martial art known for its acrobatic and dance-like kicks, spins, and other techniques.

**carajo**: Spanish. Shit. Vulgar.

**caramba**: Spanish. A mild interjection of surprise or dismay.

**chido**: Spanish. Cool.

**chingado/chingada**: Spanish. Fucked or fucking. This has other meanings as well, but this is how Zita generally uses it. Vulgar.

**culo**: Spanish. Butt. Vulgar.

**Dios**: Spanish. God.

**esquiva diagonal**: Portuguese. A capoeira low dodge where one hand covers the face and the body is turned diagonally to the attacker.

**gancho**: Portuguese. A capoeira hook kick that strikes with the heel or sole of the foot.

**ginga**: Portuguese. The most basic capoeira footwork, a moving fight stance.

**gracias a Dios**: Spanish. Thank God or Thanks be to God.

**hombre**: Spanish. Man.

**horchata**: Spanish. A chilled, sweetened drink made with grains or nuts. The version Zita makes is a rice milk with cinnamon and vanilla.

**loco/loca**: Spanish. Crazy man or woman.

**mano**: Spanish. Bro. Abbreviated form of "hermano" as Zita uses it.

**narcos**: Spanish. Drug dealers.

**neta**: Spanish. Really, for real, you know.

**ni modo**: Spanish. Interjection. No way.

**no hay bronca**: Spanish. No problem.

**no importa**: Spanish. Never mind or not important.

**no mames**: Spanish. No fucking way or you're kidding me. Vulgar.

**novelas**: Spanish. Short for telenovelas. Spanish-language soap operas/television dramas.

**obvio**: Spanish. Obviously.

**órale**: Spanish. An interjection. Can be used like heck yeah, right on, listen, hey, or hurry up.

**oye**: Spanish. An interjection that can be used as hey, listen, or yo.

**pendejo/pendeja**: Spanish. A jerk or asshole. Vulgar.

**pinche**: Spanish. An insult intensifier word. Can be used for "freaking," "sucky," or "fucking" dependent on context. Vulgar.

**por favor**. Spanish. Please.

**por supuesto**. Spanish. Of course.

**pues**: Spanish. An interjection, equivalent of well, then, or since.

**semita pacha**: Spanish. A flat yellow cake with a jam filling and sugar topping

**señora**: Spanish. Courtesy title for a married woman. Similar to Ma'am.

**sí**: Spanish. Yes.

**sopa de pollo salvadoreña**: Spanish. A hearty Salvadoran chicken soup.

**telenovelas**: Spanish. Spanish-language soap operas/television dramas.

**vámonos**: Spanish. Let's go.

# From the Author

**Thank you for reading!**

Please consider leaving reviews for any books you've enjoyed. Reviews assist other readers in finding books and let authors know what they've done right (or wrong).

The Lords of Imbroglio series written by Dmitri is entirely fictional and not meant to represent or claim any other author's work. Sorry, romance readers.

For the latest on past and future releases, monthly chatter, free short stories, and the occasional other freebie, subscribe to the newsletter on my website, www.karendiem.com. You can also use the website to contact me, browse free content, or find me on social media sites (Twitter, Facebook, etc.). Since I'd hate to read the same stuff everywhere, I do try to post different information in each place. New release notices are the exception and go everywhere.

# Arca Chronology

See my website for the most up-to-date list.

*Super*

*Washout* (Short Story)

*Octopus* (Short Story)

*Human*

*Tourists* (Short Story)

*Power*

*Pie* (Short Story)

*Roses in December* (Short Story)

*Monster*

*Toga* (Upcoming)